The Summer of the Swans

Illustrated by Ted CoConis

The Summer of the Swans

Sara Godfrey was lying on the bed tying a kerchief on the dog, Boysie. "Hold your chin up, Boysie, will you?" she said as she braced herself on one elbow. The dog was old, slept all the time, and he was lying on his side with his eyes closed while she lifted his head and tied the scarf.

Her sister Wanda was sitting at the dressing table combing her hair. Wanda said, "Why don't you leave Boysie alone?"

"There's nothing else to do," Sara answered without looking up. "You want to see a show?"

"Not particularly."

"It's called 'The Many Faces of Boysie.' "

"Now I know I don't want to see it."

Sara held up the dog with the kerchief neatly tied beneath his chin and said, "The first face of Boysie, proudly presented for your entertainment and amusement, is the Russian Peasant Woman. Taaaaaa-daaaaaa!"

"Leave the dog alone."

"He likes to be in shows, don't you, Boysie?" She untied the scarf, refolded it and set it carefully on top of the dog's head. "And now for the second face of Boysie, we travel halfway around the world to the mysterious East, where we see Boysie the Inscrutable Hindu. Taaaaaaa-daaaaaa!"

With a sigh Wanda turned and looked at the dog. "That's pathetic. In people's age that dog is eighty-four years old." She shook a can of hair spray and sprayed her hair. "And besides, that's my good scarf."

"Oh, all right." Sara fell back heavily against the pillow. "I can't do anything around here."

"Well, if it's going to make you that miserable, I'll watch the show."

"I don't want to do it any more. It's no fun now. This place smells like a perfume factory." She put the scarf over her face and stared up through the thin blue material. Beside her, Boysie lay back down and curled himself into a ball. They lay without moving for a moment and then Sara sat up on the bed and looked down at her long, lanky legs. She said, "I have the biggest feet in my school."

"Honestly, Sara, I hope you are not going to start listing all the millions of things wrong with you because I just don't want to hear it again."

"Well, it's the truth about my feet. One time in Phys Ed the boys started throwing the girls' sneakers around and Bull Durham got my sneakers and put them on and they fit perfectly! How do you think it feels to wear the same size shoe as Bull Durham?"

"People don't notice things like that."

"Huh!"

"No, they don't. I have perfectly terrible hands—look at my fingers—only I don't go around all the time saying, 'Everybody, look at my stubby fingers, I have stubby fingers, everybody,' to *make* people notice. You should just ignore things that are wrong with you. The truth is everyone else is so worried about what's wrong with *them* that—"

"It is very difficult to ignore the fact that you have huge feet when Bull Durham is dancing all over the gym in your shoes. They were not stretched the tiniest little bit when he took them off either."

"You wear the same size shoe as Jackie Kennedy Onassis if that makes you feel any better."

"How do you know?"

"Because one time when she was going into an Indian temple she had to leave her shoes outside and some reporter looked in them to see what size they were." She leaned close to the mirror and looked at her teeth.

"Her feet *look* littler."

"That's because she doesn't wear orange sneakers."

"I like my orange sneakers." Sara sat on the edge of the bed, slipped her feet into the shoes, and held them up. "What's wrong with them?"

"Nothing, except that when you want to hide something, you don't go painting it orange. I've got to go. Frank's coming."

She went out the door and Sara could hear her crossing into the kitchen. Sara lay back on the bed, her head next to Boysie. She looked at the sleeping dog, then covered her face with her hands and began to cry noisily.

"Oh, Boysie, Boysie, I'm crying," she wailed. Years ago, when Boysie was a young dog, he could not bear to hear anyone cry. Sara had only to pretend she was crying and Boysie would come running. He would whine and dig at her with his paws and lick her hands until she stopped. Now he lay with his eyes closed.

"Boysie, I'm crying," she said again. "I'm really crying this time. Boysie doesn't love me."

The dog shifted uneasily without opening his eyes.

"Boysie, Boysie, I'm crying, I'm so sad, Boysie," she wailed, then stopped and sat up abruptly. "You don't care about anybody, do you, Boysie? A person could cry herself to death these days and you wouldn't care."

She got up and left the room. In the hall she heard the tapping noise of Boysie's feet behind her and she said without looking at him, "I don't want you now, Boysie. Go on back in the bedroom. Go on." She went a few steps farther and, when he continued to follow her, turned and looked at him. "In case you are confused, Boysie, a dog is supposed to comfort people and run up and nuzzle them and make them feel better. All you want to do is lie on soft things and hide bones in the house because you are too lazy to go outside. Just go on back in the bedroom."

She started into the kitchen, still followed by Boysie,

who could not bear to be left alone, then heard her aunt and Wanda arguing, changed her mind, and went out onto the porch.

Behind her, Boysie scratched at the door and she let him out. "Now quit following me."

Her brother Charlie was sitting on the top step and Sara sat down beside him. She held out her feet, looked at them, and said, "I like my orange sneakers, don't you, Charlie?"

He did not answer. He had been eating a lollipop and the stick had come off and now he was trying to put it back into the red candy. He had been trying for so long that the stick was bent.

"Here," she said, "I'll do it for you." She put the stick in and handed it to him. "Now be careful with it."

She sat without speaking for a moment, then she looked down at her feet and said, "I hate these orange sneakers. I just *hate* them." She leaned back against the porch railing so she wouldn't have to see them and said, "Charlie, I'll tell you something. This has been the worst summer of my life."

She did not know exactly why this was true. She was doing the same things she had done last summer—walk to the Dairy Queen with her friend Mary, baby-sit for Mrs. Hodges, watch television—and yet everything was different. It was as if her life was a huge kaleidoscope, and the kaleidoscope had been turned and now everything was changed. The same stones, shaken, no longer made the same design.

But it was not only one different design, one change; it was a hundred. She could never be really sure of anything this summer. One moment she was happy, and the next, for no reason, she was miserable. An hour ago she had loved her sneakers; now she detested them.

"Charlie, I'll tell you what this awful summer's been like. You remember when that finky Jim Wilson got you on the seesaw, remember that? And he kept bouncing you up and down and then he'd keep you up in the air for a real long time and then he'd drop you down real sudden, and you couldn't get off and you thought you never would? Up and down, up and down, for the rest of your life? Well, that's what this summer's been like for me."

He held out the candy and the stick to her.

"Not again!" She took it from him. "This piece of candy is so gross that I don't even want to touch it, if you want to know the truth." She put the stick back in and handed it to him. "Now if it comes off again—and I mean this, Charlie Godfrey—I'm throwing the candy away."

Charlie looked at the empty sucker stick, reached into his mouth, took out the candy, and held them together in his hand. Sara had said she would throw the candy away if this happened again and so he closed his fist tightly and looked away from her.

Slowly he began to shuffle his feet back and forth on the step. He had done this so many times over the years that two grooves had been worn into the boards. It was a nervous habit that showed he was concerned about something, and Sara recognized it at once.

"All right, Charlie," she said wearily. "Where's your sucker?"

He began to shake his head slowly from side to side. His eyes were squeezed shut.

"I'm not going to take it away from you. I'm going to fix it one more time."

He was unwilling to trust her and continued to shake his

head. The movement was steady and mechanical, as if it would continue forever, and she watched him for a moment.

Then, with a sigh, she lifted his hand and attempted to pry his fingers loose. "Honestly, Charlie, you're holding onto this grubby piece of candy like it was a crown jewel or something. Now, let go." He opened his eyes and watched while she took the candy from him and put the stick in. The stick was now bent almost double, and she held it out to him carefully.

"There."

He took the sucker and held it without putting it into his mouth, still troubled by the unsteadiness of the bent stick. Sara looked down at her hands and began to pull at a broken fingernail. There was something similar about them in that moment, the same oval face, round brown eyes, brown hair hanging over the forehead, freckles on the nose. Then Charlie glanced up and the illusion was broken.

Still holding his sucker, he looked across the yard and saw the tent he had made over the clothesline that morning. He had taken an old white blanket out into the yard, hung it over the low clothesline, and then got under it. He had sat there with the blanket blowing against him until Sara came out and said, "Charlie, you have to fasten the ends down, like this. It isn't a tent if it's just hanging in the wind."

He had thought there was something wrong. He waited beneath the blanket until she came back with some clothespins and hammered them into the hard earth, fastening the edges of the blanket to the ground. "Now, *that's* a tent."

The tent had pleased him. The warmth of the sun coming through the thin cotton blanket, the shadows of the trees moving overhead had made him drowsy and comfortable and now he wanted to be back in the tent.

Sara had started talking about the summer again, but he did not listen. He could tell from the tone of her voice that she was not really talking to him at all. He got up slowly and began to walk across the yard toward the tent.

Sara watched him as he walked, a small figure for his ten years, wearing faded blue jeans and a striped knit shirt that was stretched out of shape. He was holding the sucker in front of him as if it were a candle that might go out at any moment.

Sara said, "Don't drop that candy in the grass now or it's really going to be lost."

She watched while he bent, crawled into the tent, and sat down. The sun was behind the tent now and she could see his silhouette. Carefully he put the sucker back into his mouth.

Then Sara lay back on the hard boards of the porch and looked up at the ceiling.

*I*n the house Wanda and Aunt Willie were still arguing. Sara could hear every word even out on the porch. Aunt Willie, who had been taking care of them since the death of their mother six years ago, was saying loudly, "No, not on a motorcycle. No motorcycle!"

Sara grimaced. It was not only the loudness of Aunt Willie's voice that she disliked. It was everything—the way she bossed them, the way she never really listened, the way she never cared what she said. She had once announced loud enough for everyone in Carter's Drugstore to hear that Sara needed a good dose of magnesia.

"It isn't a motorcycle, it's a motor *scooter*." Wanda was speaking patiently, as if to a small child. "They're practically like bicycles."

"No."

"All I want to do is to ride one half mile on this perfectly safe motor scooter—"

"No. It's absolutely and positively no. No!"

"Frank is very careful. He has never had even the tiniest accident."

No answer.

"Aunt Willie, it is perfectly safe. He takes his mother to the grocery store on it. Anyway, I am old enough to go without permission and I wish you'd realize it. I am nineteen years old."

No answer. Sara knew that Aunt Willie would be standing by the sink shaking her head emphatically from side to side.

"Aunt Willie, he's going to be here any minute. He's coming all the way over here just to drive me to the lake to see the swans."

"You don't care *that* for seeing those swans."

"I do too. I love birds."

"All right then, those swans have been on the lake three days, and not once have you gone over to see them. Now all of a sudden you *have* to go, can't wait one minute to get on this devil motorcycle and see those swans."

"For your information, I have been dying to see them, only this is my first chance." She went out of the kitchen and pulled the swinging door shut behind her. "And I'm going," she said over her shoulder.

Wanda came out of the house, slammed the screen door, stepped over Boysie, and sat by Sara on the top step. "She never wants anyone to have any fun."

"I know."

"She makes me so mad. All I want to do is just ride down to see the swans on Frank's motor scooter." She looked at Sara, then broke off and said, "Where did Charlie go?"

"He's over there in his tent."

"I see him now. I wish Frank would hurry up and get here before Aunt Willie comes out." She stood, looked down the street, and sat back on the steps. "Did I tell you what that boy in my psychology class last year said about Charlie?"

Sara straightened. "What boy?"

"This boy Arnold Hampton, in my psychology class. We were discussing children who—"

"You mean you talk about Charlie to perfect strangers? To your class? I think that's awful." She put her feet into the two grooves worn in the steps by Charlie. "What do you say? 'Let me tell you all about my retarded brother—it's so interesting'?" It was the first time in her life that she had used the term "retarded" in connection with her brother, and she looked quickly away from the figure in the white tent. Her face felt suddenly hot and she snapped a leaf from the rhododendron bush by the steps and held it against her forehead.

"No, I don't say that. Honestly, Sara, you—"

"And then do you say, 'And while I'm telling you about my retarded brother, I'll also tell you about my real hung-up sister'?" She moved the leaf to her lips and blew against it angrily.

"No, I don't say that because you're not all that fascinating, if you want to know the truth. Anyway, Arnold Hampton's father happens to be a pediatrician and Arnold is sincerely interested in working with boys like Charlie. He is even helping start a camp which Charlie may get to go to next summer, and all because I talked to him in my psychology class." She sighed. "You're impossible, you know that? I can't imagine why I even try to tell you anything."

"Well, Charlie's our problem."

"He's everybody's. There is no— Oh, here comes Frank." She broke off and got to her feet. "Tell Aunt Willie I'll be home later."

She started quickly down the walk, waving to the boy who was making his way slowly up the street on a green motor scooter.

Wait, wait, you wait." Aunt Willie came onto the porch drying her hands on a dish towel. She stood at the top of the steps until Frank, a thin boy with red hair, brought the motor scooter to a stop. As he kicked down the stand she called out, "Frank, listen, save yourself some steps. Wanda's not going anywhere on that motorcycle."

"Aw, Aunt Willie," Frank said. He opened the gate and came slowly up the walk. "All we're going to do is go down to the lake. We don't even have to get on the highway for that."

"No motorcycles," she said. "You go break your neck if you want to. That's not my business. Wanda, left in my care, is not going to break her neck on any motorcycle."

"Nobody's going to break his neck. We're just going to have a very uneventful ride down the road to the lake. Then we're going to turn around and have a very uneventful ride back."

"No."

"I tell you what," Frank said. "I'll make a deal with you."

"What deal?"

"Have you ever been on a motor scooter?"

"Me? I never even rode on a bicycle."

"Try it. Come on. I'll ride you down to the Tennents' house and back. Then if you think it's not safe, you say to me, 'Frank, it's not safe,' and I'll take my motor scooter and ride off into the sunset."

She hesitated. There was something about a ride that appealed to her.

Sara said against the rhododendron leaf, "I don't think you ought to. You're too old to be riding up and down the street on a motor scooter."

She knew instantly she had said the wrong thing, for at once Aunt Willie turned to her angrily. "Too old!" She faced Sara with indignation. "I am barely forty years old. May I grow a beard if I'm not." She stepped closer, her voice rising. "Who says I'm so old?" She held the dish towel in front of her, like a matador taunting a bull. The dish towel flicked the air once.

"Nobody said anything," Sara said wearily. She threw the leaf down and brushed it off the steps with her foot.

"Then where did all this talk about my age come from, I'd like to know?"

"Anyway," Frank interrupted, "you're not too old to ride a motor scooter."

"I'll do it." She threw the dish towel across the chair and went down the steps. "I may break my neck but I'll do it."

"Hold on tight, Aunt Willie," Wanda called.

"Hold on! Listen, my hands never held on to anything the way I'm going to hold on to this motorcycle." She laughed, then said to Frank, "I never rode on one of these before, believe me."

"It's just like a motorized baby carriage, Aunt Willie."

"Huh!"

"This ought to be good," Wanda said. She called, "Hey, Charlie," waited until he looked out from the tent, and then said, "Watch Aunt Willie. She's going to ride the motor scooter."

Charlie watched Aunt Willie settle herself sidesaddle on the back of the scooter.

"Ready?" Frank asked.

"I'm as ready as I'll ever be, believe me, go on, go on."

Her words rose into a piercing scream as Frank moved the scooter forward, turned, and then started down the hill. Her scream, shrill as a bird's cry, hung in the still air. "Frank, Frank, Frank, Frankeeeeee!"

At the first cry Charlie staggered to his feet, staring in alarm at Aunt Willie disappearing down the hill. He pulled on one side of the tent as he got to his feet, causing the other to snap loose at the ground and hang limp from the line. He stumbled, then regained his balance.

Wanda saw him and said, "It's all right, Charlie, she's having a good time. She *likes* it. It's all right." She crossed the yard, took him by the hand, and led him to the steps. "What have you got all over yourself?"

"It's a gross red sucker," Sara said. "It's all over me too."

"Come on over to the spigot and let me wash your hands. See, Aunt Willie's coming back now."

In front of the Tennents' house Frank was swinging the scooter around, pivoting on one foot, and Aunt Willie stopped screaming long enough to call to the Tennents, "Bernie, Midge, look who's on a motorcycle!" Then she began screaming again as Frank started the uphill climb. As they came to a stop Aunt Willie's cries changed to laughter. "Huh, old woman, am I! Old woman!" Still laughing, she stepped off the scooter.

"You're all right, Aunt Willie," Frank said.

Sensing a moment of advantage, Wanda moved down the walk. She was shaking the water from her hands. "So can I go, Aunt Willie?"

"Oh, go on, go on," she said, half laughing, half scolding. "It's your own neck. Go on, break your own neck if you want to."

"It's not her neck you have to worry about, it's my arms," Frank said. "Honest, Aunt Willie, there's not a drop of blood circulating in them."

"Oh, go on, go on with you."

"Come on, Little One," Frank said to Wanda.

Aunt Willie came and stood by Sara, and they watched Wanda climb on the back of the motor scooter. As Wanda and Frank drove off, Aunt Willie laughed again and said, "Next thing, *you'll* be going off with some boy on a motorcycle."

Sara had been smiling, but at once she stopped and looked down at her hands. "I don't think you have to worry about that."

"Huh! It will happen, you'll see. You'll be just like Wanda. You'll be—"

"Don't you see that I'm nothing like Wanda at all?" She sat down abruptly and put her lips against her knees. "We are so different. Wanda is a hundred times prettier than I am."

"You are just alike, you two. Sometimes in the kitchen I hear you and I think I'm hearing Wanda. That's how alike you are. May my ears fall off if I can hear the difference."

"Maybe our *voices* are alike, but that's all. I can make my voice sound like a hundred different people. Listen to this and guess who it is. 'N–B–C! Beautiful downtown Burbank.' "

"I'm not in the mood for a guessing game. I'm in the mood to get back to our original conversation. It's not how you look that's important, let me tell you. I had a sister so beautiful you wouldn't believe it."

"Who?"

"Frances, that's who."

"She wasn't all that beautiful. I've seen her and—"

"When she was young she was. So beautiful you wouldn't believe it, but such a devil, and—"

"It is *too* important how you look. Parents are always saying it's not how you look that counts. I've heard that all my life. It doesn't matter how you look. It doesn't matter how you look. Huh! If you want to find out how much it matters, just let your hair get too long or put on too much eye makeup and listen to the screams." She got up abruptly and said, "I think I'll walk over and see the swans myself."

"Well, I have not finished with this conversation yet, young lady."

Sara turned and looked at Aunt Willie, waited with her hands jammed into her back pockets.

"Oh, never mind," Aunt Willie said, picking up her dish towel and shaking it. "I might as well hold a conversation with this towel as with you when you get that look on your face. Go on and see the swans." She broke off. "Hey, Charlie, you want to go with Sara to see the swans?"

"He'll get too tired," Sara said.

"So walk slow."

"I never get to do anything by myself. I have to take him everywhere. I have him all day and Wanda all night. In all this whole house I have one drawer to myself. *One drawer*."

"Get up, Charlie. Sara's going to take you to see the swans."

Sara looked down into his eyes and said, "Oh, come on," and drew him to his feet.

"Wait, there's some bread from supper." Aunt Willie ran into the house and came back with four rolls. "Take them. Here. Let Charlie feed the swans."

"Well, come on, Charlie, or it's going to be dark before we get there."

"Don't you rush him along, hear me, Sara?"

"I won't."

Holding Sara's hand, Charlie went slowly down the walk. He hesitated at the gate and then moved with her onto the sidewalk. As they walked down the hill, his feet made a continuous scratching sound on the concrete.

When they were out of earshot Sara said, "Aunt Willie thinks she knows everything. I get so sick of hearing how I am exactly like Wanda when Wanda is beautiful. I think she's just beautiful. If I could look like anyone in the world, I would want to look like her." She kicked at some high grass by the sidewalk. "And it does too matter how you look, I can tell you that." She walked ahead angrily for a few steps, then waited for Charlie and took his hand again.

"I think how you look is the most important thing in the world. If you *look* cute, you *are* cute; if you *look* smart, you *are* smart, and if you don't look like anything, then you aren't anything.

"I wrote a theme on that one time in school, about looks being the most important thing in the world, and I got a D—a *D*! Which is a terrible grade.

"After class the teacher called me up and told me the same old business about looks not being important, and how some of the ugliest people in the world were the smartest and kindest and cleverest."

They walked past the Tennents' house just as someone inside turned on the television, and they heard Eddie Albert singing, "Greeeeeeen acres is—" before it was turned down. Charlie paused a moment, recognizing the beginning of one of his favorite programs, looked up at Sara, and waited.

"Come on," Sara said. "And then there was this girl in my English class named Thelma Louise and she wrote a paper entitled 'Making People Happy' and she got an A. An *A*! Which is as good as you can get. It was sickening. Thelma Louise is a beautiful girl with blond hair and naturally curly eyelashes, so what does she know? Anyway, one time Hazel went over to Thelma Louise's, and she said the rug was worn thin in front of the mirror in Thelma Louise's room because Thelma Louise stood there all the time watching herself."

She sighed and continued to walk. Most of the houses were set close together as if huddled for safety, and on either side of the houses the West Virginia hills rose, black now in the early evening shadows. The hills were as they had been for hundreds of years, rugged forest land, except that strip mining had begun on the hills to the north, and the trees and earth had been hacked away, leaving unnatural cliffs of pale washed earth.

Sara paused. They were now in front of Mary Weicek's house and she said, "Stop a minute. I've got to speak to Mary." She could hear Mary's record player, and she longed to be up in Mary's room, leaning back against the pink dotted bedspread listening to Mary's endless collection of records. "Mary!" she called. "You want to walk to the pond with me and Charlie and see the swans?"

Mary came to the window. "Wait, I'm coming out."

Sara waited on the sidewalk until Mary came out into the yard. "I can't go because my cousin's here and she's going to cut my hair," Mary said, "but did you get your dress yesterday?"

"No."

"Why not? I thought your aunt said you could."

"She did, but when we got in the store and she saw how much it cost she said it was foolish to pay so much for a dress when she could make me one just like it."

"Disappointment."

"Yes, because unfortunately she can't make one *just* like it, she can only make one *kind of* like it. You remember how the stripes came together diagonally in the front of that dress? Well, she already has mine cut out and I can see that not one stripe meets."

"Oh, Sara."

"I could see when she was cutting it that the stripes weren't going to meet and I kept saying, 'It's not right, Aunt Willie, the stripes aren't going to meet,' and all the while I'm screaming, the scissors are flashing and she is muttering, 'The stripes will meet, the stripes will meet,' and then she holds it up in great triumph and not one stripe meets."

"That's awful, because I remember thinking when you

showed me the dress that it was the way the stripes met that looked so good."

"I am aware of that. It now makes me look like one half of my body is about two inches lower than the other half."

"Listen, come on in and watch my cousin cut my hair, can you?"

"I better not. I promised Aunt Willie I'd take Charlie to see the swans."

"Well, just come in and see how she's going to cut it. She has a whole book of hair styles."

"Oh, all right, for a minute. Charlie, you sit down right there." She pointed to the steps. "Right there now and don't move, hear me? Don't move off that step. Don't even stand up." Then she went in the house with Mary, saying, "I really can't stay but a minute because I've got to take Charlie down to see the swans and then I've got to get home in time to dye my tennis shoes—"

"Which ones?"

"These, these awful orange things. They make me look like Donald Duck or something."

Charlie sat in the sudden stillness, hunched over his knees, on the bottom step. The whole world seemed to have been turned off when Sara went into the Weiceks' house, and he did not move for a long time. The only sound was the ticking of his watch.

The watch was a great pleasure to him. He had no knowledge of hours or minutes, but he liked to listen to it and to watch the small red hand moving around the dial, counting off the seconds, and it was he who remembered every morning after breakfast to have Aunt Willie wind it for him. Now he rested his arm across his legs and looked at the watch.

He had a lonely feeling. He got this whenever he was by himself in a strange place, and he turned quickly when he heard the screen door open to see if it was Sara. When he saw Mrs. Weicek and another woman he turned back

and looked at his watch. As he bent over, a pale half circle of flesh showed between the back of his shirt and his pants.

"Who's the little boy, Allie?"

Mrs. Weicek said, "That's Sara's brother, Charlie. You remember me telling you about him. He's the one that can't talk. Hasn't spoken a word since he was three years old."

"Doesn't talk at all?"

"If he does, no one's ever heard him, not since his illness. He can understand what you say to him, and he goes to school, and they say he can write the alphabet, but he can't talk."

Charlie did not hear them. He put his ear against his watch and listened to the sound. There was something about the rhythmic ticking that never failed to soothe him. The watch was a magic charm whose tiny noise and movements could block out the whole clamoring world.

Mrs. Weicek said, "Ask him what time it is, Ernestine. He is so proud of that watch. Everyone always asks him what time it is." Then without waiting, she herself said, "What time is it, Charlie? What time is it?"

He turned and obediently held out the arm with the watch on it.

"My goodness, it's after eight o'clock," Mrs. Weicek said. "Thank you, Charlie. Charlie keeps everyone informed of the time. We just couldn't get along without him."

The two women sat in the rocking chairs on the porch, moving slowly back and forth. The noise of the chairs and the creaking floor boards made Charlie forget the watch for a moment. He got slowly to his feet and stood looking up the street.

"Sit down, Charlie, and wait for Sara," Mrs. Weicek said.

Without looking at her, he began to walk toward the street.

"Charlie, Sara wants you to wait for her."

"Maybe he doesn't hear you, Allie."

"He hears me all right. Charlie, wait for Sara. Wait now." Then she called, "Sara, your brother's leaving."

Sara looked out the upstairs window and said, "All right, Charlie, I'm coming. Will you wait for a minute? Mary, I've got to go."

She ran out of the house and caught Charlie by the arm. "What are you going home for? Don't you want to see the swans?"

He stood without looking at her.

"Honestly, I leave you alone for one second and off you go. Now come on." She tugged his arm impatiently.

As they started down the hill together she waved to Mary, who was at the window, and said to Charlie, "I hope the swans are worth all this trouble I'm going to."

"We'll probably get there and they'll be gone," she added. They walked in silence. Then Sara said, "Here's where we cut across the field." She waited while he stepped carefully over the narrow ditch, and then the two of them walked across the field side by side, Sara kicking her feet restlessly in the deep grass.

$\mathcal{T}$here was something painfully beautiful about the swans. The whiteness, the elegance of them on this dark lake, the incredible ease of their movements made Sara catch her breath as she and Charlie rounded the clump of pines.

"There they are, Charlie."

She could tell the exact moment he saw them because his hand tightened; he really held her hand for the first time since they had left Mary's. Then he stopped.

"There are the swans."

The six swans seemed motionless on the water, their necks all arched at the same angle, so that it seemed there was only one swan mirrored five times.

"There are the swans," she said again. She felt she would like to stand there pointing out the swans to Charlie for the rest of the summer. She watched as they drifted slowly across the water.

"Hey, Sara!"

She looked across the lake and saw Wanda and Frank,

who had come by the road. "Sara, listen, tell Aunt Willie that Frank and I are going over to his sister's to see her new baby."

"All right."

"I'll be home at eleven."

She watched as Wanda and Frank got back on the motor scooter. At the roar of the scooter, the startled swans changed direction and moved toward Sara. She and Charlie walked closer to the lake.

"The swans are coming over here, Charlie. They see you, I believe."

They watched in silence for a moment as the sound of the scooter faded. Then Sara sat down on the grass, crossed her legs yoga style, and picked out a stick which was wedged inside one of the orange tennis shoes.

"Sit down, Charlie. Don't just stand there."

Awkwardly, with his legs angled out in front of him, he sat on the grass. Sara pulled off a piece of a roll and tossed it to the swans. "Now they'll come over here," she said. "They love bread."

She paused, put a piece of roll into her own mouth, and sat chewing for a moment.

"I saw the swans when they flew here, did you know that, Charlie? I was out on our porch last Friday and I looked up, and they were coming over the house and they looked so funny, like frying pans with their necks stretched out." She handed him a roll. "Here. Give the swans something to eat. Look, watch me. Like that."

She watched him, then said, "No, Charlie, small pieces, because swans get things caught in their throats easily. No, that's *too* little. That's just a crumb. Like *that*."

She watched while he threw the bread into the pond, then said, "You know where the swans live most of the time? At the university, which is a big school, and right in the middle of this university is a lake and that's where the swans live. Only sometimes, for no reason, the swans decide to fly away, and off they go to another pond or another lake. This one isn't half as pretty as the lake at the university, but here they are."

She handed Charlie another roll. "Anyway, that's what Wanda thinks, because the swans at the university are gone."

Charlie turned, motioned that he wanted another roll for the swans, and she gave him the last one. He threw it into the water in four large pieces and put out his hand for another.

"No more. That's all." She showed him her empty hands.

One of the swans dived under the water and rose to shake its feathers. Then it moved across the water. Slowly the other swans followed, dipping their long necks far into the water to catch any remaining pieces of bread.

Sara leaned forward and put her hands on Charlie's shoulders. His body felt soft, as if the muscles had never been used. "The swans are exactly alike," she said. "Exactly. No one can tell them apart."

She began to rub Charlie's back slowly, carefully. Then she stopped abruptly and clapped him on the shoulders. "Well, let's go home."

He sat without moving, still looking at the swans on the other side of the lake.

"Come on, Charlie." She knew he had heard her, yet he still did not move. "Come *on*." She got to her feet and stood looking down at him. She held out her hand to help him up, but he did not even glance at her. He continued to watch the swans.

"Come on, Charlie. Mary may come up later and help me dye my shoes." She looked at him, then snatched a leaf from the limb overhead and threw it at the water. She waited, stuck her hands in her back pockets, and said tiredly, "Come on, Charlie."

He began to shake his head slowly back and forth without looking at her.

"Mary's coming up to help me dye my shoes and if you don't come on we won't have time to do them and I'll end up wearing these same awful Donald Duck shoes all year. Come *on*."

He continued to shake his head back and forth.

"This is why I never want to bring you anywhere, because you won't go home when I'm ready."

With his fingers he began to hold the long grass on either side of him as if this would help him if she tried to pull him to his feet.

"You are really irritating, you know that?" He did not

look at her and she sighed and said, "All right, if I stay five more minutes, will you go?" She bent down and showed him on his watch. "That's to right there. When the big hand gets *there*, we go home, all right?"

He nodded.

"Promise?"

He nodded again.

"All right." There was a tree that hung over the water and she went and leaned against it. "All right, Charlie, four more minutes now," she called.

Already he had started shaking his head again, all the while watching the swans gliding across the dark water.

Squinting up at the sky, Sara began to kick her foot back and forth in the deep grass. "In just a month, Charlie, the summer will be over," she said without looking at him, "and I will be so glad."

Up until this year, it seemed, her life had flowed along with rhythmic evenness. The first fourteen years of her life all seemed the same. She had loved her sister without envy, her aunt without finding her coarse, her brother without pity. Now all that was changed. She was filled with a discontent, an anger about herself, her life, her family, that made her think she would never be content again.

She turned and looked at the swans. The sudden, unexpected tears in her eyes blurred the images of the swans into white circles, and she blinked. Then she said aloud, "Three minutes, Charlie."

Sara was lying in bed with the lights out when Wanda came into the bedroom that night. Sara was wearing an old pair of her father's pajamas with the sleeves cut out and the legs rolled up. She watched as Wanda moved quietly across the room and then stumbled over the dressing-table stool. Hobbling on one foot, Wanda opened the closet door and turned on the light.

"You can put on the big light if you want. I'm awake," Sara said.

"*Now* you tell me."

"Did you have a good time, Wanda?"

"Yes."

"Did you get to see the baby?"

"He was so cute. He looked exactly like Frank. You wouldn't have believed it."

"Poor baby."

"No, he was darling, really he was, with little red curls

all over his head." She undressed quickly, turned off the closet light, and then got into bed beside Sara. She smoothed her pillow and looked up at the ceiling. "Frank is so nice, don't you think?"

"He's all right."

"Don't you like him?" She rose up on one elbow and looked down at Sara in the big striped pajamas.

"I said he was all right."

"Well, what don't you like?"

"I didn't say I didn't like him."

"I know, but I can tell. What don't you like?"

"For one thing, he never pays any attention to Charlie. When he came up the walk tonight he didn't even speak to him."

"He probably didn't see him in the tent. Anyway, he likes Charlie—he told me so. What else?"

"Oh, nothing, it's just that he's always so affected, the way he calls you Little One and gives you those real meaningful movie-star looks."

"I love it when he calls me Little One. Just wait till someone calls *you* Little One."

"I'd like to know who could call me Little One except the Jolly Green Giant."

"Oh, Sara."

"Well, I'm bigger than everyone I know."

"You'll find someone."

"Yes, maybe if I'm lucky I'll meet somebody from some weird foreign country where men value tall skinny girls

48

with big feet and crooked noses. Every time I see a movie, though, even if it takes place in the weirdest, foreignest country in the world, like where women dance in gauze bloomers and tin bras, the women are still little and beautiful." Then she said, "Anyway, I hate boys. They're all just one big nothing."

"Sara, what's wrong with you?"

"Nothing."

"No, I mean it. What's really wrong?"

"I don't know. I just feel awful."

"Physically awful?"

"Now don't start being the nurse."

"Well, I want to know."

"No, not physically awful, just plain awful. I feel like I want to start screaming and kicking and I want to jump up and tear down the curtains and rip up the sheets and hammer holes in the walls. I want to yank my clothes out of the closet and burn them and—"

"Well, why don't you try it if it would make you feel better?"

"Because it wouldn't." She lifted the top sheet and watched as it billowed in the air and then lowered on her body. She could feel the cloth as it settled on the bare part of her legs. "I just feel like nothing."

"Oh, everybody does at times, Sara."

"Not like me. I'm not anything. I'm not cute, and I'm not pretty, and I'm not a good dancer, and I'm not smart, and I'm not popular. I'm not anything."

"You're a good dishwasher."

"Shut up, Wanda. I don't think that's funny."

"Welllll—"

"You act like you want to talk to me and then you start being funny. You do that to me all the time."

"I'm through being funny, so go on."

"Well, if you could see some of the girls in my school you'd know what I mean. They look like models. Their clothes are so tuff and they're invited to every party, every dance, by about ten boys and when they walk down the hall everybody turns and looks at them."

"Oh, those girls. They hit the peak of their whole lives in junior high school. They look like grown women in eighth grade with the big teased hair and the eye liner and by the time they're in high school they have a used look."

"Well, I certainly don't have to worry about getting a used look."

"I think it is really sad to hit the peak of your whole life in junior high school."

"Girls, quit that arguing," Aunt Willie called from her room. "I can hear you all the way in here."

"We're not arguing," Wanda called back. "We are having a peaceful little discussion."

"I know an argument when I hear one, believe me. That's one thing I've heard plenty of and I'm hearing one right now. Be quiet and go to sleep."

"All right."

They lay in silence. Sara said, "The peak of my whole

life so far was in third grade when I got to be milk monitor."

Wanda laughed. "Just give yourself a little time." She reached over, turned on the radio, and waited till it warmed up. "Frank's going to dedicate a song to me on the Diamond Jim show," she said. "Will the radio bother you?"

"No."

"Well, it bothers me," Aunt Willie called from her room. "Maybe you two can sleep with the radio blaring and people arguing, but I can't."

"I have just barely got the radio turned on, Aunt Willie. I have to put my head practically on the table to even hear it." She broke off abruptly. "What was that dedication, did you hear?"

"It was to all the girls on the second floor of Arnold Hall."

"Oh."

"I mean what I say now," Aunt Willie called. "You two get to sleep. Wanda, you've got to be up early to get to your job at the hospital on time, even if Sara can spend the whole day in bed."

"I'd like to know how I can spend the whole day in bed when she gets me up at eight o'clock," Sara grumbled.

"Aunt Willie, I just want to hear my dedication and then I'll go to sleep."

Silence.

Sara turned over on her side with the sheet wrapped

tightly around her body and closed her eyes. She was not sleepy now. She could hear the music from the radio, and the sound from the next room of Charlie turning over in his bed, trying to get settled, then turning over again. She pulled the pillow over her head, but she could not block out the noises. Oddly, it was the restless sounds from Charlie's room which seemed loudest.

Charlie was not a good sleeper. When he was three, he had had two illnesses, one following the other, terrible high-fevered illnesses, which had almost taken his life and had damaged his brain. Afterward, he had lain silent and still in his bed, and it had been strange to Sara to see the pale baby that had replaced the hot, flushed, tormented one. The once-bright eyes were slow to follow what was before them, and the hands never reached out, even when Sara held her brother's favorite stuffed dog, Buh-Buh, above him. He rarely cried, never laughed. Now it was as if Charlie wanted to make up for those listless years in bed by never sleeping again.

Sara heard his foot thump against the wall. It was a thing that could continue for hours, a faint sound that no one seemed to hear but Sara, who slept against the wall. With a sigh she put the pillow back beneath her head and looked up at the ceiling.

"That was my dedication. Did you hear it?" Wanda whispered. "To Little One from Frank."

"Vomit."

"Well, I think it was sweet."

The thumping against the wall stopped, then began again. It was a sound that Sara had become used to, but tonight it seemed unusually loud. She found herself thinking how this had been Charlie's first movement after his long illness, a restless kicking out of one foot, a weak movement then that could hardly be noticed beneath the covers, but now, tonight, one that seemed to make the whole house tremble.

"Don't tell me you don't hear that," she said to Wanda. "I don't see how you can all persist in saying that you don't hear Charlie kicking the wall."

Silence.

"Wanda, are you asleep?"

Silence.

"Honestly, I don't see how people can just fall asleep any time they want to. Wanda, are you really asleep?"

She waited, then drew the sheet close about her neck and turned to the wall.

*I*n his room Charlie lay in bed still kicking his foot against the wall. He was not asleep but was staring up at the ceiling where the shadows were moving. He never went to sleep easily, but tonight he had been concerned because a button was missing from his pajamas, and sleep was impossible. He had shown the place where the button was missing to Aunt Willie when he was ready for bed, but she had patted his shoulder and said, "I'll fix it tomorrow," and gone back to watching a game show on television.

"Look at that," Aunt Willie was saying to herself. "They're never going to guess the name. How can famous celebrities be so stupid?" She had leaned forward and shouted at the panelists, "It's Clark Gable!" Then, "Have they never heard of a person who works in a store? A person who works in a stork is a *clerk*—Clerk Gable—the name is *Clerk Gable!*"

Charlie had touched her on the shoulder and tried again to show her the pajamas.

"I'll fix it tomorrow, Charlie." She had waved him away with one hand.

He had gone back into the kitchen, where Sara was dyeing her tennis shoes in the sink.

"Don't show it to me," she said. "I can't look at anything right now. And Mary, quit laughing at my tennis shoes."

"I can't help it. They're so gross."

Sara lifted them out of the sink with two spoons. "I know they're gross, only you should have told me that orange tennis shoes could not be dyed baby blue. Look at that. That is the worst color you have ever seen in your life. Admit it."

"I admit it."

"Well, you don't have to admit it so quickly. They ought to put on the dye wrapper that orange cannot be dyed baby blue. A warning."

"They do."

"Well, they ought to put it in big letters. Look at those shoes. There must be a terrible name for that color."

"There is," Mary said. "Puce."

"What?"

"Puce."

"Mary Weicek, you made that up."

"I did not. It really is a color."

"I have never heard a word that describes anything better. Puce. These just look like puce shoes, don't they?" She set them on newspapers. "They're—Charlie, get out of the way, please, or I'm going to get dye all over you."

He stepped back, still holding his pajama jacket out in front of him. There were times when he could not get anyone's attention no matter what he did. He took Sara's arm and she shrugged free.

"Charlie, there's not a button on anything I own, either, so go on to bed."

Slowly, filled with dissatisfaction, he had gone to his room and got into bed. There he had begun to pull worriedly at the empty buttonhole until the cloth had started to tear, and then he had continued to pull until the whole front of his pajama top was torn and hung open. He was now holding the jacket partly closed with his hands and looking up at the ceiling.

It was one o'clock and Charlie had been lying there for three hours.

He heard a noise outside, and for the first time he forgot about his pajamas. He stopped kicking his foot against the wall, sat up, and looked out the window. There was something white in the bushes; he could see it moving.

He released his pajamas and held onto the window sill tightly, because he thought that he had just seen one of the swans outside his window, gliding slowly through the leaves. The memory of their soft smoothness in the water came to him and warmed him.

He got out of bed and stood by the other window. He heard a cat miaowing and saw the Hutchinsons' white cat from next door, but he paid no attention to it. The swans

were fixed with such certainty in his mind that he could not even imagine that what he had seen was only the cat.

Still looking for the swans, he pressed his face against the screen. The beauty of them, the whiteness, the softness, the silent splendor had impressed him greatly, and he felt a longing to be once again by the lake, sitting in the deep grass, throwing bread to the waiting swans.

It occurred to him suddenly that the swan outside the window had come to find him, and with a small pleased smile he went around the bed, sat, and slowly began to put on his bedroom slippers. Then he walked out into the hall. His feet made a quiet shuffling sound as he passed through the linoleumed hall and into the living room, but no one heard him.

The front door had been left open for coolness and only the screen door was latched. Charlie lifted the hook, pushed open the door, and stepped out onto the porch. Boysie, who slept in the kitchen, heard the door shut and came to the living room. He whined softly when he saw Charlie outside on the porch and scratched at the door. He waited, then after a moment went back to the kitchen and curled up on his rug in front of the sink.

Charlie walked across the front porch and sat on the steps. He waited. He was patient at first, for he thought that the swans would come to the steps, but as time passed and they did not come, he began to shuffle his feet impatiently back and forth on the third step.

Suddenly he saw something white in the bushes. He got up and, holding the banister, went down the steps and crossed the yard. He looked into the bushes, but the swans were not there. It was only the cat, crouched down behind the leaves and looking up at him with slitted eyes.

He stood there, looking at the cat, unable to understand what had happened to the swans. He rubbed his hands up and down his pajama tops, pulling at the torn material.

The cat darted farther back into the bushes and disappeared.

After a moment Charlie turned and began to walk slowly across the yard. He went to the gate and paused. He had been told again and again that he must never go out of the yard, but those instructions, given in daylight with noisy traffic on the street, seemed to have nothing to do with the present situation.

In the soft darkness all the things that usually confused him—speeding bicycles, loud noises, lawn mowers, barking dogs, shouting children—were gone, replaced by silence and a silvery moonlit darkness. He seemed to belong to this silent world far more than he belonged to the daytime world of feverish activity.

Slowly he opened the gate and went out. He moved past the Hutchinsons' house, past the Tennents', past the Weiceks'. There was a breeze now, and the smell of the Weiceks' flowers filled the air. He walked past the next house and hesitated, suddenly confused. Then he started through the vacant lot by the Akers' house. In the darkness it looked to him like the field he and Sara had crossed earlier in the evening on their way to see the swans.

He crossed the vacant lot, entered the wooded area, and walked slowly through the trees. He was certain that in just a moment he would come into the clearing and see the lake and the white swans gliding on the dark water. He continued walking, looking ahead so that he would see the lake as soon as possible.

The ground was getting rougher. There were stones to stumble over now and rain gullies and unexpected piles of trash. Still the thought of the swans persisted in his mind and he kept walking.

Charlie was getting tired and he knew something was wrong. The lake was gone. He paused and scanned the field, but he could not see anything familiar.

He turned to the right and began to walk up the hill. Suddenly a dog barked behind him. The sound, unexpected and loud, startled him, and he fell back a step and then started to run. Then another dog was barking, and another, and he had no idea where the dogs were. He was terribly frightened and he ran with increasing awkwardness, thrashing at the weeds with his hands, pulling at the air, so that everything about him seemed to be running except his slow feet.

The sound of the dogs seemed to him to be everywhere, all around him, so that he ran first in one direction, then in another, like a wild animal caught in a maze. He ran into a bush and the briers stung his face and arms, and he thought this was somehow connected with the dogs and thrashed his arms out wildly, not even feeling the cuts in his skin.

He turned around and around, trying to free himself, and then staggered on, running and pulling at the air. The dogs' barking had grown fainter now, but in his terror he did not notice. He ran blindly, stumbling over bushes and against trees, catching his clothing on twigs, kicking at unseen rocks. Then he came into a clearing and was able to gain speed for the first time.

He ran for a long way, and then suddenly he came up against a wire fence that cut him sharply across the chest. The surprise of it threw him back on the ground, and he sat holding his hands across his bare chest, gasping for breath.

Far down the hill someone had spoken to the dogs; they had grown quiet, and now there was only the rasping sound of Charlie's own breathing. He sat hunched over until his breathing grew quieter, and then he straightened and noticed his torn pajamas for the first time since he had left the house. He wrapped the frayed edges of the jacket carefully over his chest as if that would soothe the stinging cut.

After a while he got slowly to his feet, paused, and then began walking up the hill beside the fence. He was limping now because when he had fallen he had lost one of his bedroom slippers.

The fence ended abruptly. It was an old one, built long ago, and now only parts remained. Seeing it gone, Charlie

felt relieved. It was as if the fence had kept him from his goal, and he stepped over a trailing piece of wire and walked toward the forest beyond.

Being in the trees gave him a good feeling for a while. The moonlight coming through the leaves and the soft sound of the wind in the branches were soothing, but as he went deeper into the forest he became worried. There was something here he didn't know, an unfamiliar smell, noises he had never heard before. He stopped.

He stood beneath the trees without moving and looked around him. He did not know where he was. He did not even know how he had come to be there. The whole night seemed one long struggle, but he could not remember why he had been struggling. He had wanted something, he could not remember what.

His face and arms stung from the brier scratches; his bare foot, tender and unused to walking on the rough ground, was already cut and sore, but most of all he was gripped by hopelessness. He wanted to be back in his room, in his bed, but home seemed lost forever, a place so disconnected from the forest that there was no way to get from one to the other.

He put his wrist to his ear and listened to his watch. Even its steady ticking could not help him tonight and he wrapped the torn pajamas tighter over his chest and began to walk slowly up the hill through the trees. As he walked, he began to cry without noise.

*I*n the morning Sara arose slowly, letting her feet hang over the edge of the bed for a moment before she stepped onto the floor. Then she walked across the room, and as she passed the dressing table she paused to look at herself in the mirror. She smoothed her hair behind her ears.

One of her greatest mistakes, she thought, looking at herself critically, was cutting her hair. She had gone to the beauty school in Bentley, taking with her a picture from a magazine, and had asked the girl to cut her hair exactly like that.

"And look what she did to me!" she had screamed when she got home. "Look! Ruined!"

"It's not that bad," Wanda had said.

"Tell the truth. Now look at that picture. Look! Tell the truth—do I look anything, anything at *all*, even the tiniest little bit, like that model?"

Wanda and Aunt Willie had had to admit that Sara looked nothing like the blond model.

"I'm ruined, just ruined. Why someone cannot take a perfectly good magazine picture and cut someone's hair the same way without ruining them is something I cannot understand. I hope that girl fails beauty school."

"Actually, your *hair* does sort of look like the picture. It's your face and body that don't."

"Shut up, Wanda. Quit trying to be funny."

"I'm not being funny. It's a fact."

"I didn't make smart remarks the time they gave you that awful permanent."

"You did too. You called me Gentle Ben."

"Well, I meant that as a compliment."

"All right, girls, stop this now. No more arguing. Believe me, I mean it."

Sara now looked at herself, weighing the mistake of the hair, and she thought suddenly: I look exactly like that cartoon cat who is always chasing Tweetie Bird and who has just been run over by a steam roller and made absolutely flat. This hair and my flat face have combined to make me look exactly like—

"Sara!" Aunt Willie called from the kitchen.

"What?"

"Come on and get your breakfast, you and Charlie. I'm not going to be in here fixing one breakfast after another until lunch time."

"All right."

She went into the hall and looked into Charlie's room. "Charlie!"

He was not in his bed. She walked into the living room. Lately, since he had learned to turn on the television, he would get up early, come in, and watch it by himself, but he was not there either.

"Charlie's already up, Aunt Willie."

In the kitchen Aunt Willie was spooning oatmeal into two bowls.

"Oatmeal again," Sara groaned. "I believe I'll just have some Kool-Aid and toast."

"Don't talk nonsense. Now, where's Charlie?"

"He wasn't in his room."

She sighed. "Well, find him."

"First I've got to see my shoes." She went over to the sink and looked at the sneakers. "Oh, they look awful. Look at them, Aunt Willie. They're gross."

"Well, you should have left them alone. I've learned my lesson about dyeing clothes, let me tell you. You saw me, I hope, when I had to wear that purple dress to your Uncle Bert's funeral."

"What color would you say these were?"

"I haven't got time for that now. Go get your brother."

"No, there's a name for this color. I just want to see if you know it."

"I don't know it, so go get your brother."

"I'll give you three choices. It's either, let me see—it's either pomegranate, Pomeranian, or puce."

"Puce. Now go get your brother."

"How did you know?"

"Because my aunt had twin Pomeranian dogs that rode in a baby carriage and because I once ate a piece of pomegranate. Go get your brother!"

Sara put down the shoes and went back into the hall. "Charlie!" She looked into his room again. "Oh, Charlie!" She went out onto the front porch and looked at Charlie's tent. It had blown down during the night and she could see that he wasn't there.

Slowly she walked back through the hall, looking into every room, and then into the kitchen.

"I can't find him, Aunt Willie."

"What do you mean, you can't find him?" Aunt Willie, prepared to chide the two children for being late to breakfast, now set the pan of oatmeal down heavily on the table.

"He's not in his room, he's not in the yard, he's not anywhere."

"If this is some kind of a joke—" Aunt Willie began. She brushed past Sara and went into the living room. "Charlie! Where are you, Charlie?" Her voice had begun to rise with the sudden alarm she often felt in connection with Charlie. "Where could he have gone?" She turned and looked at Sara. "If this is a joke . . . "

"It's not a joke."

"Well, I'm remembering last April Fool's Day, that's all."

"He's probably around the neighborhood somewhere, like the time Wanda took him to the store without saying anything."

"Well, Wanda didn't take him this morning." Aunt Willie walked into the hall and stood looking in Charlie's room. She stared at the empty bed. She did not move for a moment as she tried to think of some logical explanation for his absence. "If anything's happened to that boy—"

"Nothing's happened to him."

"All right, where is he?"

Sara did not answer. Charlie had never left the house alone, and Sara could not think of any place he could be either.

"Go outside, Sara. Look! If he's not in the neighborhood, I'm calling the police."

"Don't call until we're sure, Aunt Willie, please."

"I'm calling. Something's wrong here."

Sara was out of her pajamas and into her pants and shirt in a minute. Leaving her pajamas on the floor, she ran barefoot into the yard.

"Charlie! Charlie!" She ran around the house and then stopped. Suddenly she remembered the swans and ran back into the house.

"Aunt Willie, I bet you anything Charlie went down to the lake to see the swans."

Aunt Willie was talking on the telephone and she put one hand over the receiver and said, "Run and see."

"You aren't talking to the police already?" Sara asked in the doorway.

"I'm not talking to the police, but that's what I'm going to do when you get back. Now quit wasting time."

"Just let me get my shoes."

She ran back into the kitchen and put on the sneakers, which were still wet. Then she ran out of the house and down the street. As she passed the Weiceks', Mary came out on the porch.

"What's the hurry?" she called.

"Charlie's missing. I'm going to see if he's down at the lake."

"I'll go with you." She came down the steps, calling over her shoulder, "Mom, I'm going to help Sara look for Charlie."

"Not in those curlers you're not."

"Mom, I've got on a scarf. Nobody can even tell it's rolled."

"Yeah, everyone will just think you have real bumpy hair," Sara said.

"Oh, hush. Now what's all this about Charlie?"

"We couldn't find him this morning and I think he might have got up during the night and gone to see the swans. He acted awful when we had to leave."

"I know. I saw you dragging him up the street last night."

"I had to. It was the only way I could get him home. It was black dark. You couldn't even see the swans and he still wouldn't come home."

"I hope he's all right."

"He's probably sitting down there looking at the swans, holding onto the grass, and I'm going to have to drag him up the hill screaming all over again. He's strong when he wants to be, you know that?"

"Hey, you've got your shoes on."

"Yeah, but they're still wet."

"You'll probably have puce feet before the day's over."

"That's all I need."

They turned and crossed the field at the bottom of the hill.

"Let's hurry because Aunt Willie is at this moment getting ready to call the police."

"Really?"

"She's sitting by the phone now. She's got her little card out with all her emergency numbers on it and her finger is pointing right to *POLICE*."

"Remember that time the old man got lost in the woods? What was his name?"

"Uncle somebody."

"And they organized a posse of college boys and the Red Cross brought coffee and everything, and then they found the old man asleep in his house the next morning. He was on a picnic and had got bored and just went home."

"Don't remind me. Probably as soon as Aunt Willie calls the police we'll find Charlie in the bathroom or somewhere."

They came through the trees and into the clearing around the lake. Neither spoke.

"Yesterday he was sitting right here," Sara said finally. "Charlie! Charlie!"

There was no answer, but the swans turned abruptly and began to glide to the other side of the lake. Sara felt her shoulders sag and she rammed her hands into her back pockets.

"Something really has happened to him," she said. "I know it now."

"Probably not, Sara."

"I *know* it now. Sometimes you just know terrible things. I get a feeling in my neck, like my shoulders have come unhinged or something, when an awful thing happens."

Mary put one hand on her arm. "Maybe he's hiding somewhere."

"He can't even do that right. If he's playing hide-and-seek, as soon as he's hidden he starts looking out to see how the game's going. He just can't—"

"Maybe he's at the store or up at the Dairy Queen. I could run up to the drugstore."

"No, something's happened to him."

They stood at the edge of the water. Sara looked at the swans without seeing them.

Mary called, "Charlie! Charlie!" Her kerchief slipped off and she retied it over her rollers. "Charlie!"

"I was so sure he'd be here," Sara said. "I wasn't even worried because I knew he would be sitting right here. Now I don't know what to do."

"Let's go back to the house. Maybe he's there now."

"I know he won't be."

"Well, don't get discouraged until we see." She took Sara by the arm and started walking through the trees. "You know who you sound like? Remember when Mary Louise was up for class president and she kept saying, 'I know I won't get it. I know I won't get it.' For three days that was all she said."

"And she didn't get it."

"Well, I just meant you sounded like her, your voice or something," Mary explained quickly. "Now, come on."

When Sara entered the house with Mary, Aunt Willie was still sitting at the telephone. She was saying, "And there's not a trace of him." She paused in her conversation to ask, "Did you find him?" and when Sara shook her head, she said into the telephone, "I'm hanging up now, Midge, so I can call the police. Sara just came in and he wasn't at the lake."

She hung up, took her card of emergency phone numbers and began to dial.

There was something final about calling the police and Sara said, "Aunt Willie, don't call yet. Maybe—"

"I'm calling. A hundred elephants couldn't stop me."

"Maybe he's at somebody's house," Mary said. "One time my brother went in the Hutchinsons' to watch TV and we—"

"Hello, is this the police department? I want to report a missing child."

She looked up at Sara, started to say something, then turned back to her telephone conversation. "Yes, a missing child, a boy, ten, Charlie Godfrey. G-o-d-f-r-e-y." Pause. "Eighteen-oh-eight Cass Street. This is Willamina Godfrey, his aunt. I'm in charge." She paused, then said, "Yes, since last night." She listened again. "No, I don't know what time. We woke up this morning, he was gone. That's all." She listened and as she answered again her voice began to rise with concern and anger. "No, I could not ask his friends about him because he doesn't have any friends. His brain was injured when he was three years old and that is why I am so concerned. This is not a ten-year-old boy who can go out and come home when he feels like it. This is not a boy who's going to run out and break street lights and spend the night in some garage, if that's what you're thinking. This is a boy, I'm telling you, who can be lost and afraid three blocks from home and cannot speak one word to ask for help. Now are you going to come out here or aren't you?"

She paused, said, "Yes, yes," then grudgingly, "And thank you." She hung up the receiver and looked at Sara. "They're coming."

"What did they say?"

"They said they're coming. That's all." She rose in agitation and began to walk into the living room. "Oh, why don't they hurry!"

"Aunt Willie, they just hung up the telephone."

"I know." She went to the front door and then came

back, nervously slapping her hands together. "Where can he *be*?"

"My brother was always getting lost when he was little," Mary said.

"I stood right in this house, in that room," Aunt Willie interrupted. She pointed toward the front bedroom. "And I promised your mother, Sara, that I would look after Charlie all my life. I promised your mother nothing would ever happen to Charlie as long as there was breath in my body, and now look. Look! Where is this boy I'm taking such good care of?" She threw her hands into the air. "Vanished without a trace, that's where."

"Aunt Willie, you can't watch him every minute."

"Why not? Why can't I? What have I got more important in my life than looking after that boy? Only one thing more important than Charlie. Only one thing—that devil television there."

"Aunt Willie—"

"Oh, yes, that devil television. I was sitting right in that chair last night and he wanted me to sew on one button for him but I was too busy with the television. I'll tell you what I should have told your mother six years ago. I should have told her, 'Sure, I'll be glad to look after Charlie except when there's something good on television. I'll be glad to watch him in my spare time.' My tongue should fall out on the floor for promising to look after your brother and not doing it."

She went back to the doorway. "There are a hundred

things that could have happened to him. He could have fallen into one of those ravines in the woods. He could be lost up at the old mine. He could be at the bottom of the lake. He could be kidnaped." Sara and Mary stood in silence as she named the tragedies that could have befallen Charlie.

Sara said, "Well, he could not have been kidnaped, because anybody would know we don't have any money for ransom."

"That wouldn't stop some people. Where are those policemen?"

Sara looked down at the table beside the television and saw a picture Charlie had drawn of himself on tablet paper. The head and body were circles of the same size, the ears and eyes overlapping smaller circles, the arms and legs were elongated balloons. He had started printing his name below the picture, but had completed only two letters before he had gone out to make the tent. The *C* was backward.

Wanda had bought him the tablet and crayons two days ago and he had done this one picture with the brown crayon. It gave Sara a sick feeling to see it because something about the picture, the smallness, the unfinished quality, made it look somehow very much like Charlie.

Aunt Willie said, "When you want the police they are always a hundred miles away bothering criminals."

"They're on their way. They said so," Mary said.

"All right then, where are they?"

Mary blinked her eyes at this question to which she had no answer, and settled the rollers beneath her scarf.

"I still can't get it out of my head that Charlie went back to see the swans," Sara said.

"He really was upset about having to go home. I can testify to that," Mary said.

Aunt Willie left the room abruptly. When she came back she was holding a picture of Charlie in one hand. It was a snapshot of him taken in March, sitting on the steps with Boysie in front of the house.

"The police always want a photograph," she said. She held it out so Mary and Sara could see it. "Mrs. Hutchinson took that with her Polaroid."

"It's a real good picture of him," Mary said.

Sara looked at the picture without speaking. Somehow the awkward, unfinished crayon drawing on the table looked more like Charlie than the snapshot.

"It was his birthday," Aunt Willie said mournfully, "and look how proud he was of that watch Wanda bought him, holding his little arm straight out in the picture so everyone would notice it. I fussed so much about Wanda getting him a watch because he couldn't tell time, and then he was so proud just to be wearing it. Everyone would ask him on the street, 'What time is it, Charlie? Have you got the time, Charlie?' just to see how proud he was to show them."

"And then those boys stole it. I think that was the meanest thing," Mary said.

"The watch was lost," Aunt Willie said. "The watch just got lost."

"Stolen," Sara snapped, "by that crook Joe Melby."

"I am the quickest person to accuse somebody, you know that. You saw me, I hope, when I noticed those boys making off with the Hutchinsons' porch chairs last Halloween; but that watch just got lost. Then Joe Melby found it and, to his credit, brought it back."

"Huh!"

"There was no stealing involved."

Mary said, giggling, "Aunt Willie, did Sara ever tell you what she did to Joe?"

"Hush, Mary," Sara said.

"What did she do?"

"She made a little sign that said *FINK* and stuck it on Joe's back in the hall at school and he went around for two periods without knowing it was there."

"It doesn't matter what I did. Nobody's going to pick on my brother and I mean it. That fink stole Charlie's watch and then got scared and told that big lie about finding it on the floor of the school bus."

"You want revenge too much."

"When somebody *deserves* revenge, then—"

"I take my revenge same as anybody," Aunt Willie said, "only I never was one to keep after somebody and keep after somebody the way you do. You take after your Uncle Bert in that."

"I hope I always do."

"No, your Uncle Bert was no good in that way. He would never let a grudge leave him. When he lay dying in the hospital, he was telling us who we weren't to speak to and who we weren't to do business with. His dying words were against Jeep Johnson at the used-car lot."

"Good for Uncle Bert."

"And that nice little Gretchen Wyant who you turned the hose on, and her wearing a silk dress her brother had sent her from Taiwan!"

"That nice little Gretchen Wyant was lucky all she got was water on her silk dress."

"Sara!"

"Well, do you know what that nice little Gretchen Wyant did? I was standing in the bushes by the spigot, turning off the hose, and this nice little Gretchen Wyant didn't see me—all she saw was Charlie at the fence—and she said, 'How's the *retard* today?' only she made it sound even uglier, 'How's the *reeeeetard*,' like that. Nothing ever made me so mad. The best sight of my whole life was nice little Gretchen Wyant standing there in her wet Taiwan silk dress with her mouth hanging open."

"Here come the police," Mary said quickly. "But they're stopping next door."

"Signal to them," Aunt Willie said.

Before Mary could move to the door, Aunt Willie was past her and out on the porch. "Here we are. This is the house." She turned and said over her shoulder to Sara, "Now, God willing, we'll get some action."

Sara sat in the living room wearing her cut-off blue jeans, an old shirt with *Property of State Prison* stamped on the back which Wanda had brought her from the beach, and her puce tennis shoes. She was sitting in the doorway, leaning back against the door with her arms wrapped around her knees, listening to Aunt Willie, who was making a telephone call in the hall.

"It's no use calling," Sara said against her knees. This was the first summer her knees had not been skinned a dozen times, but she could still see the white scars from other summers. Since Aunt Willie did not answer, she said again, "It's no use calling. He won't come."

"You don't know your father," Aunt Willie said.

"That is the truth."

"Not like I do. When he hears that Charlie is missing, he will . . ." Her voice trailed off as she prepared to dial the telephone.

Sara had a strange feeling when she thought of her father. It was the way she felt about people she didn't know well, like the time Miss Marshall, her English teacher, had given her a ride home from school, and Sara had felt uneasy the whole way home, even though she saw Miss Marshall every day.

Her father's remoteness had begun, she thought, with Charlie's illness. There was a picture in the family photograph album of her father laughing and throwing Sara into the air and a picture of her father holding her on his shoulders and a picture of her father sitting on the front steps with Wanda on one knee and Sara on the other. All these pictures of a happy father and his adoring daughters had been taken before Charlie's illness and Sara's mother's death. Afterward there weren't any family pictures at all, happy or sad.

When Sara looked at those early pictures, she remembered a laughing man with black curly hair and a broken tooth who had lived with them for a few short golden years and then had gone away. There was no connection at all between this laughing man in the photograph album and the gray sober man who worked in Ohio and came home to West Virginia on occasional weekends, who sat in the living room and watched baseball or football on television and never started a conversation on his own.

Sara listened while Aunt Willie explained to the operator that the call she was making was an emergency. "That's why I'm not direct dialing," she said, "because I'm so upset I'll get the wrong numbers."

"He won't come," Sara whispered against her knee.

As the operator put through the call and Aunt Willie waited, she turned to Sara, nodded emphatically, and said, "He'll come, you'll see."

Sara got up, walked across the living room and into the kitchen, where the breakfast dishes were still on the table. She looked down at the two bowls of hard, cold oatmeal, and then made herself three pieces of toast and poured herself a cup of cherry Kool-Aid. When she came back eating the toast Aunt Willie was still waiting.

"Didn't the operator tell them it was an emergency, I wonder," Aunt Willie said impatiently.

"Probably."

"Well, if somebody told me I had an emergency call, I would run, let me tell you, to find out what that emergency was. That's no breakfast, Sara."

"It's my lunch."

"Kool-Aid and toast will not sustain you five minutes." She broke off quickly and said in a louder voice, "Sam, is that you?" She nodded to Sara, then turned back to the telephone, bent forward in her concern. "First of all, Sammy, promise me you won't get upset—no, promise me first."

"He won't get upset. Even *I* can promise you that," Sara said with her mouth full of toast.

"Sam, Charlie's missing," Aunt Willie said abruptly.

Unable to listen to any more of the conversation, Sara took her toast and went out onto the front porch. She sat on the front steps and put her feet into the worn grooves that Charlie's feet had made on the third step. Then she ate the last piece of toast and licked the butter off her fingers.

In the corner of the yard, beneath the elm tree, she could see the hole Charlie had dug with a spoon; all one morning he had dug that hole and now Boysie was lying in it for coolness. She walked to the tree and sat in the old rope swing and swung over Boysie. She stretched out her feet and touched Boysie, and he lifted his head and looked around to see who had poked him, then lay back in his hole.

"Boysie, here I am, look, Boysie, look."

He was already asleep again.

"Boysie—" She looked up as Aunt Willie came out on the porch and stood for a minute drying her hands on her apron. For the occasion of Charlie's disappearance she was wearing her best dress, a bright green bonded jersey, which was so hot her face above it was red and shiny. Around her forehead she had tied a handkerchief to absorb the sweat.

Sara swung higher. "Well," she asked, "is he coming?" She paused to pump herself higher. "Or not?"

"He's going to call back tonight."

"Oh," Sara said.

"Don't say 'Oh' to me like that."

"It's what I figured."

"Listen to me, Miss Know-it-all. There is no need in the world for your father to come this exact minute. If he started driving right this second he still wouldn't get here till after dark and he couldn't do anything then, so he just might as well wait till after work and then drive."

"Might as well do the sensible thing." Sara stood up and really began to swing. She had grown so much taller since she had last stood in this swing that her head came almost to the limb from which the swing hung. She caught hold of the limb with her hands, kicked her feet free, and let the swing jerk wildly on its own.

"Anyway," Aunt Willie said, "this is no time to be playing on a swing. What will the neighbors think, with Charlie missing and you having a wonderful time on a swing?"

"I knew he wouldn't come."

"He is going to come," Aunt Willie said in a louder voice. "He is just going to wait till dark, which is reasonable, since by dark Charlie will probably be home anyway."

"It is so reasonable that it makes me sick."

"I won't listen to you being disrespectful to your father, I mean that," she said. "I know what it is to lose a father, let me tell you, and so will you when all you have left of him is an envelope."

Aunt Willie, Sara knew, was speaking of the envelope in her dresser drawer containing all the things her father had had in his pockets when he died. Sara knew them all— the watch, the twenty-seven cents in change, the folded dollar bill, the brown plaid handkerchief, the three-cent stamp, the two bent pipe cleaners, the half pack of stomach mints.

"Yes, wait till you lose your father. Then you'll appreciate him."

"I've already lost him."

"Don't you talk like that. Your father's had to raise two families and all by himself. When Poppa died, Sammy had to go to work and support all of us before he was even out of high school, and now he's got this family to support too. It's not easy, I'm telling you that. *You* raise two families and then I'll listen to what you've got to say against your father."

Sara let herself drop to the ground and said, "I better go. Mary and I are going to look for Charlie."

"Where?"

"Up the hill."

"Well, don't *you* get lost," Aunt Willie called after her.

From the Hutchinsons' yard some children called, "Have you found Charlie yet, Sara?" They were making a garden in the dust, carefully planting flowers without roots in neat rows. Already the first flowers were beginning to wilt in the hot sun.

"I'm going to look for him now."

"Sawa?" It was the youngest Hutchinson boy, who was three and sometimes came over to play with Charlie.

"What?"

"Sawa?"

"What?"

"Sawa?"

"*What?*"

"Sawa, I got gwass." He held up two fists of grass he had just pulled from one of the few remaining clumps in the yard.

"Yes, that's fine. I'll tell Charlie when I see him."

Sara and Mary had decided that they would go to the lake and walk up behind the houses toward the woods. Sara was now on her way to Mary's, passing the vacant lot where a baseball game was in progress. She glanced up and watched as she walked down the sidewalk.

The baseball game had been going on for an hour with the score still zero to zero and the players, dusty and tired, were playing silently, without hope.

She was almost past the field when she heard someone call, "Hey, have you found your brother yet, Sara?"

She recognized the voice of Joe Melby and said, "No," without looking at him.

"What?"

She turned, looked directly at him, and said, "You will be pleased and delighted to learn that we have not." She continued walking down the street. The blood began to pound in her head. Joe Melby was the one person she did not want to see on this particular day. There was something disturbing about him. She did not know him, really, had hardly even spoken to him, and yet she hated him so much the sight of him made her sick.

"Is there anything I can do?"

"No."

"If he's up in the woods, I could help look. I know about as much about those hills as anybody." He left the game and started walking behind her with his hands in his pockets.

"No, thank you."

"I *want* to help."

She swirled around and faced him, her eyes blazing. "I do not want your help." They looked at each other. Something twisted inside her and she felt suddenly ill. She thought she would never drink cherry Kool-Aid again as long as she lived.

Joe Melby did not say anything but moved one foot back and forth on the sidewalk, shuffling at some sand. "Do you—"

"Anybody who would steal a little boy's watch," she said, cutting off his words, and it was a relief to make this accusation to his face at last, "is somebody whose help I can very well do without." Her head was pounding so loudly she could hardly hear her own words. For months, ever since the incident of the stolen watch, she had waited for this moment, had planned exactly what she would say. Now that it was said, she did not feel the triumph she had imagined at all.

"Is that what's wrong with you?" He looked at her. "You think I stole your brother's watch?"

"I know you did."

"How?"

"Because I asked Charlie who stole his watch and I kept asking him and one day on the school bus when I asked him he pointed right straight at you."

"He was confused—"

"He wasn't that confused. You probably thought he wouldn't be able to tell on you because he couldn't talk, but he pointed right—"

"He *was* confused. I gave the watch *back* to him. I didn't take it."

"I don't believe you."

"You believe what you want then, but I didn't take that watch. I thought that matter had been settled."

"Huh!"

She turned and started walking with great speed down the hill. For some reason she was not as sure about Joe Melby as she had been before, and this was even more disturbing. He did take the watch, she said to herself. She could not bear to think that she had been mistaken in this, that she had taken revenge on the wrong person.

Behind her there were sudden cheers as someone hit a home run. The ball went into the street. Joe ran, picked it up, and tossed it to a boy in the field. Sara did not look around.

"Hey, wait a minute," she heard Joe call. "I'm coming."

She did not turn around. She had fallen into that trap before. Once when she had been walking down the street, she had heard a car behind her and the horn sounding and a boy's voice shouting, "Hey, beautiful!" And she had turned around. She! Then, too late, she had seen that the girl they were honking and shouting at was Rosey Camdon on the opposite side of the street, Rosey Camdon who was Miss Batelle District Fair and Miss Buckwheat Queen and a hundred other things. Sara had looked down quickly, not knowing whether anyone had seen her or not, and her face had burned so fiercely she had thought it would be red forever. Now she kept walking quickly with her head down.

"Wait, Sara."

Still she did not turn around or show that she had heard him.

"Wait." He ran, caught up with her, and started walking beside her. "All the boys say they want to help."

She hesitated but kept walking. She could not think of anything to say. She knew how circus men on stilts felt when they walked, because her legs seemed to be moving in the same awkward way, great exaggerated steps that got her nowhere.

She thought she might start crying so she said quickly, "Oh, all right." Then tears did come to her eyes, sudden and hot, and she looked down at her feet.

He said, "Where should we start? Have you got any ideas?"

"I think he's up in the woods. I took him to see the swans yesterday and I think he was looking for them when he got lost."

"Probably up that way."

She nodded.

He paused, then added, "We'll find him."

She did not answer, could not, because tears were spilling down her cheeks, so she turned quickly and walked alone to Mary's house and waited on the sidewalk until Mary came out to join her.

She and Mary were almost across the open field before Sara spoke. Then she said, "Guess who just stopped me and gave me the big sympathy talk about Charlie."

"I don't know. Who?"

"Joe Melby."

"Really? What did he say?"

"He wants to help look for Charlie. He makes me sick."

"I think it's nice that he wants to help."

"Well, maybe if he'd stolen your brother's watch you wouldn't think it was so nice."

Mary was silent for a moment. Then she said, "I probably shouldn't tell you this, but he didn't steal that watch, Sara."

"Huh!"

"No, he really didn't."

Sara looked at her and said, "How do you know?"

"I can't tell you how I know because I promised I wouldn't, but I *know* he didn't."

"How?"

"I can't tell. I promised."

"That never stopped you before. Now, Mary Weicek, you tell me what you know this minute."

"I promised."

"Mary, tell me."

"Mom would kill me if she knew I told you."

"She won't know."

"Well, your aunt went to see Joe Melby's mother."

"What?"

"Aunt Willie went over to see Joe Melby's mother."

"She didn't!"

"Yes, she did too, because my mother was right there when it happened. It was about two weeks after Charlie had gotten the watch back."

"I don't believe you."

"Well, it's the truth. You told Aunt Willie that Joe had stolen the watch—remember, you told everybody—and so Aunt Willie went over to see Joe's mother."

"She wouldn't do such a terrible thing."

"Well, she did."

"And what did Mrs. Melby say?"

"She called Joe into the room and she said, 'Joe, did you steal the little Godfrey boy's watch?' And he said, 'No.'"

"What did you expect him to say in front of his mother? 'Yes, I stole the watch'? Huh! That doesn't prove anything."

"So then she said, 'I want the truth now. Do you know who did take the watch?' and he said that nobody had *stolen* the watch."

"So where did it disappear to for a week, I'd like to know."

"I'm coming to that. He said some of the fellows were out in front of the drugstore and Charlie was standing there waiting for the school bus—you were in the drugstore. Remember it was the day we were getting the stamps for letters to those pen pals who never answered? Remember the stamps wouldn't come out of the machine? Well, anyway, these boys outside the store started teasing Charlie with some candy, and while Charlie was trying to get the candy, one of the boys took off Charlie's watch without Charlie noticing it. Then they were going to ask Charlie what time it was and when he looked down at his watch, he would get upset because the watch would be gone. They were just going to tease him."

"Finks! *Finks!*"

"Only you came out of the drugstore right then and saw what they were doing with the candy and told them off and the bus came and you hustled Charlie on the bus before anybody had a chance to give back the watch. Then they got scared to give it back and that's the whole story. Joe didn't steal the watch at all. He wasn't even in on it. He came up right when you did and didn't even know what had happened. Later, when he found out, he got the watch back and gave it to Charlie, that's all."

"Why didn't you tell me before this?"

"Because I just found out about it at lunch. For four months my mother has known all about this thing and never mentioned it because she said it was one of those things best forgotten."

"Why did she tell you now?"

"That's the way my mom is. We were talking about Charlie at the dinner table, and suddenly she comes up with this. Like one time she casually mentioned that she had had a long talk with Mr. Homer about me. Mr. Homer, the principal! She went over there and they had a long discussion and she never mentioned it for a year."

"That is the worst thing Aunt Willie has ever done."

"Well, don't let on that you know or I'll be in real trouble."

"I won't, but honestly, I could just—"

"You promised."

"I know. You don't have to keep reminding me. It makes me feel terrible though, I can tell you that." She walked with her head bent forward. "Terrible! You know what I just did when I saw him?"

"What?"

"Accused him of stealing the watch."

"Sara, you didn't."

"I did too. I can't help myself. When I think somebody has done something mean to Charlie I can't forgive them. I want to keep after them and keep after them just like Aunt Willie said. I even sort of suspected Joe Melby hadn't really taken that watch and I still kept on—"

"Shh! Be quiet a minute." Mary was carrying her transistor radio and she held it up between them. "Listen."

The announcer was saying: "We have a report of a missing child in the Cass section—ten-year-old Charlie Godfrey, who has been missing from his home since sometime last night. He is wearing blue pajamas and brown felt slippers, has a watch on one wrist and an identification bracelet with his name and address on the other. He is a mentally handicapped child who cannot speak and may become alarmed when approached by a stranger. Please notify the police immediately if you have seen this youngster."

The two girls looked at each other, then continued walking across the field in silence.

Mary and Sara were up in the field by the woods. They had been searching for Charlie for an hour without finding a trace of him.

Mary said, "I don't care how I look. I am taking off this scarf. It must be a hundred degrees out here."

"Charlie!" Sara called as she had been doing from time to time. Her voice had begun to sound strained, she had called so often. "Charlie!"

"Sara, do you know where we are?" Mary asked after a moment.

"Of course. The lake's down there and the old shack's over there and you can see them as soon as we get up a little higher."

"*If* we get up a little higher," Mary said in a tired voice.

"You didn't have to come, you know."

"I wanted to come, only I just want to make sure we don't get lost. I have to go to Bennie Hoffman's party tonight."

"I know. You told me ten times."

"So I don't want to get lost." Mary walked a few steps without speaking. "I still can't figure out why I was invited, because Bennie Hoffman hardly knows me. I've just seen him two times this whole summer at the pool. Why do you think he—"

"Come on, will you?"

"It seems useless, if you ask me, to just keep walking when we don't really know which way he went. Aunt Willie thinks he went in the old coal mine."

"I know, but she only thinks that because she associates the mine with tragedy because her uncle and brother were killed in that coal mine. But Charlie wouldn't go in there. Remember that time we went into the Bryants' cellar after they moved out, and he wouldn't even come in there because it was cold and dark and sort of scary."

"Yes, I do remember because I sprained my ankle jumping down from the window and had to wait two hours while you looked through old *Life* magazines."

"I was not looking through old magazines."

"I could hear you. I was down there in that dark cellar with the rats and you were upstairs and I was yelling for help and you kept saying, 'I'm going for help right now,' and I could hear the pages turning and turning and turning."

"Well, I got you out, didn't I?"

"Finally."

Sara paused again. "Charlie! Charlie!" The girls waited

in the high grass for an answer, then began to walk again. Mary said, "Maybe we should have waited for the others before we started looking. They're going to have a regular organized posse with everybody walking along together. There may be a helicopter."

"The longer we wait, the harder it will be to find him."

"Well, I've got to get home in time to bathe and take my hair down."

"I know. I *know*. You're going to Bennie Hoffman's party."

"You don't have to sound so mad about it. I didn't *ask* to be invited."

"I am not mad because you were invited to Bennie Hoffman's party. I couldn't care less about Bennie Hoffman's party. I'm just mad because you're slowing me up on this search."

"Well, if I'm slowing you up so much, then maybe I'll just go on home."

"That suits me fine."

They looked at each other without speaking. Between them the radio began announcing: "Volunteers are needed in the Cass area in the search for young Charlie Godfrey, who disappeared from his home sometime during the night. A search of the Cheat woods will begin at three o'clock this afternoon."

Mary said, "Oh, I'll keep looking. I'll try to walk faster."

Sara shrugged, turned, and started walking up the hill, followed by Mary. They came to the old fence that once separated the pasture from the woods. Sara walked slowly beside the fence. "Charlie!" she called.

"Would he come if he heard you, do you think?"

Sara nodded. "But if they get a hundred people out here clomping through the woods and hollering, he's not going to come. He'll be too scared. I know him."

"I don't see how you can be so sure he came up this way."

"I just know. There's something about me that makes me understand Charlie. It's like I know how he feels about things. Like sometimes I'll be walking down the street and I'll pass the jeweler's and I'll think that if Charlie were here he would want to stand right there and look at those watches all afternoon and I know right where he'd stand and how he'd put his hands up on the glass and how his face would look. And yesterday I knew he was going to love the swans so much that he wasn't ever going to want to leave. I know how he feels."

"You just think you do."

"No, I *know*. I was thinking about the sky one night and I was looking up at the stars and I was thinking about how the sky goes on and on forever, and I couldn't understand it no matter how long I thought, and finally I got kind of nauseated and right then I started thinking, Well, this is how Charlie feels about some things. You know how it makes him sick sometimes to try to print letters for a long time and—"

"Look who's coming," Mary interrupted.

"Where?"

"In the trees, walking toward us. Joe Melby."

"You're lying. You're just trying to make me—"

"It is him. Look." She quickly began to tie her scarf over her rollers again. "And you talk about *me* needing eyeglasses."

"Cut across the field, quick!" Sara said. "No, wait, go under the fence. Move, will you, Mary, and leave that scarf alone. Get under the fence. I am not going to face him. I mean it."

"I am not going under any fence. Anyway, it would look worse for us to run away than to just walk by casually."

"I cannot walk by casually after what I said."

"Well, you're going to have to face him sometime, and it might as well be now when everyone feels sorry for you about your brother." She called out, "Hi, Joe, having any luck?"

He came up to them and held out a brown felt slipper and looked at Sara. "Is this Charlie's?"

Sara looked at the familiar object and forgot the incident of the watch for a moment. "Where did you find it?"

"Right up there by the fence. I had just picked it up when I saw you."

She took the slipper and, holding it against her, said, "Oh, I *knew* he came up this way, but it's a relief to have some proof of it."

"I was just talking to Mr. Aker," Joe continued, "and he said he heard his dogs barking up here last night. He had them tied out by the shack and he thought maybe someone was prowling around."

"Probably Charlie," Mary said.

"That's what I figured. Somebody ought to go down to the gas station and tell the people. They're organizing a big search now and half of the men are planning to go up to the mine."

There was a pause and Mary said, "Well, I guess I could go, only I don't know whether I'll have time to get back up here." She looked at Joe. "I promised Bennie Hoffman I'd come to his party tonight. That's why my hair's in rollers."

"Tell them I found the slipper about a half mile behind the Akers' at the old fence," Joe said.

"Sure. Are you coming to Bennie's tonight?"

"Maybe."

"Come. It's going to be fun."

Sara cleared her throat and said, "Well, I think I'll get on with my search if you two will excuse me." She turned and started walking up the hill again. There seemed to be a long silence in which even the sound of the cicadas in the grass was absent. She thrashed at the high weeds with her tennis shoes and hugged Charlie's slipper to her.

"Wait a minute, Sara, I'll come with you," Joe Melby said.

He joined her and she nodded, still looking down at the slipper. There was a picture of an Indian chief stamped on the top of the shoe and there was a loneliness to the Indian's profile, even stamped crudely on the felt, that she had never noticed before.

She cleared her throat again. "There is just one thing I

want to say." Her voice did not even sound familiar, a tape-recorded voice.

He waited, then said, "Go ahead."

She did not speak for a moment but continued walking noisily through the weeds.

"Go ahead."

"If you'll just wait a minute, I'm trying to think how to say this." The words she wanted to say—I'm sorry— would not come out at all.

They continued walking in silence and then Joe said, "You know, I was just reading an article about a guru over in India and he hasn't spoken a word in twenty-eight

years. *Twenty-eight years* and he hasn't said one word in all that time. And everyone has been waiting all those years to hear what he's going to say when he finally does speak because it's supposed to be some great wise word, and I thought about this poor guy sitting there and for twenty-eight years he's been trying to think of something to say that would be the least bit great and he can't think of anything and he must be getting really desperate now. And every day it gets worse and worse."

"Is there supposed to be some sort of message in that story?"

"Maybe."

She smiled. "Well, I just wanted to say that I'm sorry." She thought again that she was going to start crying and she said to herself, You are nothing but a big soft snail. Snail!

"That's all right."

"I just found out about Aunt Willie going to see your mother."

He shrugged. "She didn't mean anything by it."

"But it was a terrible thing."

"It wasn't all that bad. At least it was different to be accused of something I *didn't* do for a change."

"But to be called in like that in front of Aunt Willie and Mary's mother. No, it was terrible." She turned and walked into the woods.

"Don't worry about it. I'm tough. I'm indestructible. I'm like that coyote in 'Road Runner' who is always getting flattened and dynamited and crushed and in the next scene is strolling along, completely normal again."

"I just acted too hastily. That's one of my main faults."

"I do that too."

"Not like me."

"Worse probably. Do you remember when we used to get grammar-school report cards, and the grades would be on one part of the card, and on the other side would be personality things the teacher would check, like 'Does not accept criticism constructively'?"

Sara smiled. "I always used to get a check on that one," she said.

"Who didn't? And then they had one, 'Acts impetuously and without consideration for others,' or something like that, and one year I got a double check on that one."

"You didn't."

"Yes, I did. Second grade. Miss McLeod. I remember she told the whole class that this was the first year she had ever had to give double checks to any student, and everyone in the room was scared to open his report card to see if he had got the double checks. And when I opened mine, there they were, two sets of double checks, on acting impetuously and on not accepting criticism, and single checks on everything else."

"Were you crushed?"

"Naturally."

"I thought you were so tough and indestructible."

"Well, I am"—he paused—"I think." He pointed to the left. "Let's go up this way."

She agreed with a nod and went ahead of him between the trees.

There was a ravine in the forest, a deep cut in the earth, and Charlie had made his way into it through an early morning fog. By chance, blindly stepping through the fog with his arms outstretched, he had managed to pick the one path that led into the ravine, and when the sun came out and the fog burned away, he could not find the way out.

All the ravine looked the same in the daylight, the high walls, the masses of weeds and wild berry bushes, the trees. He had wandered around for a while, following the little paths made by dirt washed down from the hillside, but finally he sat down on a log and stared straight ahead without seeing.

After a while he roused enough to wipe his hands over his cheeks where the tears and dirt had dried together and to rub his puffed eyelids. Then he looked down, saw his bare foot, put it on top of his slipper, and sat with his feet overlapped.

There was a dullness about him now. He had had so

many scares, heard so many frightening noises, started at so many shadows, been hurt so often that all his senses were worn to a flat hopelessness. He would just sit here forever.

It was not the first time Charlie had been lost, but never before had there been this finality. He had become separated from Aunt Willie once at the county fair and had not even known he was lost until she had come bursting out of the crowd screaming, "Charlie, Charlie," and enveloped him. He had been lost in school once in the hall and could not find his way back to his room, and he had walked up and down the halls, frightened by all the strange children looking out of every door, until one of the boys was sent out to lead him to his room. But in all his life there had never been an experience like this one.

He bent over and looked down at his watch, his eyes on the tiny red hand. For the first time he noticed it was no longer moving. Holding his breath in his concern, he brought the watch closer to his face. The hand was still. For a moment he could not believe it. He watched it closely, waiting. Still the hand did not move. He shook his hand back and forth, as if he were trying to shake the watch off his wrist. He had seen Sara do this to her watch.

Then he held the watch to his ear. It was silent. He had had the watch for five months and never before had it failed him. He had not even known it could fail. And now it was silent and still.

He put his hand over the watch, covering it completely. He waited. His breathing had begun to quicken again. His hand on the watch was almost clammy. He waited, then

slowly, cautiously, he removed his hand and looked at the tiny red hand on the dial. It was motionless. The trick had not worked.

Bending over the watch, he looked closely at the stem. Aunt Willie always wound the watch for him every morning after breakfast, but he did not know how she did this. He took the stem in his fingers, pulled at it clumsily, then harder, and it came off. He looked at it. Then, as he attempted to put it back on the watch, it fell to the ground and was lost in the leaves.

A chipmunk ran in front of him and scurried up the bank. Distracted for a moment, Charlie got up and walked toward it. The chipmunk paused and then darted into a hole, leaving Charlie standing in the shadows trying to see where it had gone. He went closer to the bank and pulled at the leaves, but he could not even find the place among the roots where the chipmunk had disappeared.

Suddenly something seemed to explode within Charlie, and he began to cry noisily. He threw himself on the bank and began kicking, flailing at the ground, at the invisible chipmunk, at the silent watch. He wailed, yielding in helplessness to his anguish, and his piercing screams, uttered again and again, seemed to hang in the air so that they overlapped. His fingers tore at the tree roots and dug beneath the leaves and scratched, animal-like, at the dark earth.

His body sagged and he rolled down the bank and was silent. He looked up at the trees, his chest still heaving with sobs, his face strangely still. After a moment, his eyelids drooped and he fell asleep.

Charlie! Charlie!"

The only answer was the call of a bird in the branches overhead, one long tremulous whistle.

"He's not even within hearing distance," Sara said.

For the past hour she and Joe Melby had been walking deeper and deeper into the forest without pause, and now the trees were so thick that only small spots of sunlight found their way through the heavy foliage.

"Charlie, oh, Charlie!"

She waited, looking down at the ground.

Joe said, "You want to rest for a while?"

Sara shook her head. She suddenly wanted to see her brother so badly that her throat began to close. It was a tight feeling she got sometimes when she wanted something, like the time she had had the measles and had wanted to see her father so much she couldn't even swallow. Now she thought that if she had a whole glass of ice water—and she was thirsty—she probably would not be able to drink a single drop.

"If you can make it a little farther, there's a place at the top of the hill where the strip mining is, and you can see the whole valley from there."

"I can make it."

"Well, we can rest first if—"

"I can make it."

She suddenly felt a little better. She thought that if she could stand up there on top of the hill and look down and see, somewhere in that huge green valley, a small plump figure in blue pajamas, she would ask for nothing more in life. She thought of the valley as a relief map where everything would be shiny and smooth, and her brother would be right where she could spot him at once. Her cry, "There he is!" would ring like a bell over the valley and everyone would hear her and know that Charlie had been found.

She paused, leaned against a tree for a moment, and then continued. Her legs had begun to tremble.

It was the time of afternoon when she usually sat down in front of the television and watched game shows, the shows where the married couples tried to guess things about each other and where girls had to pick out dates they couldn't see. She would sit in the doorway to the hall where she always sat and Charlie would come in and watch with her, and the living room would be dark and smell of the pine-scented cleaner Aunt Willie used.

Then "The Early Show" would come on, and she would

sit through the old movie, leaning forward in the doorway, making fun, saying things like, "Now, Charlie, we'll have the old Convict Turning Honest scene," and Charlie, sitting on the stool closer to the television, would nod without understanding.

She was good, too, at joining in the dialogue with the actors. When the cowboy would say something like, "Things are quiet around here tonight," she would join in with, "Yeah, *too* quiet," right on cue. It seemed strange to be out here in the woods with Joe Melby instead of in the living room with Charlie, watching *Flame of Araby*, which was the early movie for that afternoon.

Her progress up the hill seemed slower and slower. It was like the time she had won the slow bicycle race, a race in which she had to go as slow as possible without letting a foot touch the ground, and she had gone slower and slower, all the while feeling a strong compulsion to speed ahead and cross the finish line first. At the end of the race it had been she and T.R. Peters, and they had paused just before the finish line, balancing motionless on their bicycles. The time had seemed endless, and then T.R. lost his balance and his foot touched the ground and Sara was the winner.

She slipped on some dry leaves, went down on her knees, straightened, and paused to catch her breath.

"Are you all right?"

"Yes, I just slipped."

She waited for a moment, bent over her knees, then she called, "Charlie! Charlie," without lifting her head.

"Oh, Charleeeeee," Joe shouted above her.

Sara knew Charlie would shout back if he heard her, the long wailing cry he gave sometimes when he was frightened during the night. It was such a familiar cry that for a moment she thought she heard it.

She waited, still touching the ground with one hand, until she was sure there was no answer.

"Come on," Joe said, holding out his hand.

He pulled her to her feet and she stood looking up at the top of the hill. Machines had cut away the earth there to get at the veins of coal, and the earth had been pushed down the hill to form a huge bank.

"I'll never get up that," she said. She leaned against a tree whose leaves were covered with the pale fine dirt which had filtered down when the machines had cut away the hill.

"Sure you will. I've been up it a dozen times."

He took her hand and she started after him, moving sideways up the steep bank. The dirt crumbled beneath her feet and she slid, skinned one knee, and then slipped again. When she had regained her balance she laughed wryly and said, "What's going to happen is that I'll end up pulling you all the way down the hill."

"No, I've got you. Keep coming."

She started again, putting one foot carefully above the other, picking her way over the stones. When she paused, he said, "Keep coming. We're almost there."

"I think it's a trick, like at the dentist's when he says,

'I'm almost through drilling.' Then he drills for another hour and says, 'Now, I'm really almost through drilling,' and he keeps on and then says, 'There's just one more spot and then I'll be practically really through.' "

"We must go to the same dentist."

"I don't think I can make it. There's no skin at all left on the sides of my legs."

"Well, we're really almost practically there now, in the words of your dentist."

She fell across the top of the dirt bank on her stomach, rested for a moment, and then turned and looked down the valley.

She could not speak for a moment. There lay the whole valley in a way she had never imagined it, a tiny finger of civilization set in a sweeping expanse of dark forest. The black treetops seemed to crowd against the yards, the houses, the roads, giving the impression that at any moment the trees would close over the houses like waves and leave nothing but an unbroken line of black-green leaves waving in the sunlight.

Up the valley she could see the intersection where they shopped, the drugstore, the gas station where her mother had once won a set of twenty-four stemmed glasses which Aunt Willie would not allow them to use, the grocery store, the lot where the yellow school buses were parked for the summer. She could look over the valley and see another hill where white cows were all grouped together by a fence and beyond that another hill and then another.

She looked back at the valley and she saw the lake and

for the first time since she had stood up on the hill she remembered Charlie.

Raising her hand to her mouth, she called, "Charlie! Charlie! Charlie!" There was a faint echo that seemed to waver in her ears.

"Charlie, oh, Charlie!" Her voice was so loud it seemed to ram into the valley.

Sara waited. She looked down at the forest, and everything was so quiet it seemed to her that the whole valley, the whole world was waiting with her.

"Charlie, hey, Charlie!" Joe shouted.

"Charleeeeee!" She made the sound of it last a long time. "Can you hear meeeeee?"

With her eyes she followed the trail she knew he must have taken—the house, the Akers' vacant lot, the old pasture, the forest. The forest that seemed powerful enough to engulf a whole valley, she thought with a sinking feeling, could certainly swallow up a young boy.

"Charlie! Charlie! Charlie!" There was a waver in the last syllable that betrayed how near she was to tears. She looked down at the Indian slipper she was still holding.

"Charlie, oh, Charlie." She waited. There was not a sound anywhere. "Charlie, where are you?"

"Hey, Charlie!" Joe shouted.

They waited in the same dense silence. A cloud passed in front of the sun and a breeze began to blow through the trees. Then there was silence again.

"Charlie, Charlie, Charlie, Charlie, Charlie."

She paused, listened, then bent abruptly and put

Charlie's slipper to her eyes. She waited for the hot tears that had come so often this summer, the tears that had seemed so close only a moment before. Now her eyes remained dry.

I have cried over myself a hundred times this summer, she thought, I have wept over my big feet and my skinny legs and my nose, I have even cried over my stupid shoes, and now when I have a true sadness there are no tears left.

She held the felt side of the slipper against her eyes like a blindfold and stood there, feeling the hot sun on her head and the wind wrapping around her legs, conscious of the height and the valley sweeping down from her feet.

"Listen, just because you can't hear him doesn't mean anything. He could be—"

"Wait a minute." She lowered the slipper and looked down the valley. A sudden wind blew dust into her face and she lifted her hand to shield her eyes.

"I thought I heard something. Charlie! Answer me right this minute."

She waited with the slipper held against her breasts, one hand to her eyes, her whole body motionless, concentrating on her brother. Then she stiffened. She thought again she had heard something—Charlie's long high wail. Charlie could sound sadder than anyone when he cried.

In her anxiety she took the slipper and twisted it again and again as if she were wringing water out. She called, then stopped abruptly and listened. She looked at Joe and he shook his head slowly.

She looked away. A bird rose from the trees below and

flew toward the hills in the distance. She waited until she could see it no longer and then slowly, still listening for the call that didn't come, she sank to the ground and sat with her head bent over her knees.

Beside her, Joe scuffed his foot in the dust and sent a cascade of rocks and dirt down the bank. When the sound of it faded, he began to call, "Charlie, hey, Charlie," again and again.

Charlie awoke, but he lay for a moment without opening his eyes. He did not remember where he was, but he had a certain dread of seeing it.

There were great parts of his life that were lost to Charlie, blank spaces that he could never fill in. He would find himself in a strange place and not know how he had got there. Like the time Sara had been hit in the nose with a baseball at the Dairy Queen, and the blood and the sight of Sara kneeling on the ground in helpless pain had frightened him so much that he had turned and run without direction, in a frenzy, dashing headlong up the street, blind to cars and people.

By chance Mr. Weicek had seen him, put him in the car, and driven him home, and Aunt Willie had put him to bed, but later he remembered none of this. He had only awakened in bed and looked at the crumpled bit of ice-cream cone still clenched in his hand and wondered about it.

His whole life had been built on a strict routine, and as long as this routine was kept up, he felt safe and well. The same foods, the same bed, the same furniture in the same place, the same seat on the school bus, the same class procedure were all important to him. But always there could be the unexpected, the dreadful surprise that would topple his carefully constructed life in an instant.

The first thing he became aware of was the twigs pressing into his face, and he put his hand under his cheek. Still he did not open his eyes. Pictures began to drift into his mind; he saw Aunt Willie's cigar box which was filled with old jewelry and buttons and knickknacks, and he found that he could remember every item in that box—the string of white beads without a clasp, the old earrings, the tiny book with souvenir fold-out pictures of New York, the plastic decorations from cakes, the turtle made of sea shells. Every item was so real that he opened his eyes and was surprised to see, instead of the glittering contents of the box, the dull and unfamiliar forest.

He raised his head and immediately felt the aching of his body. Slowly he sat up and looked down at his hands. His fingernails were black with earth, two of them broken below the quick, and he got up slowly and sat on the log behind him and inspected his fingers more closely.

Then he sat up straight. His hands dropped to his lap. His head cocked to the side like a bird listening. Slowly he straightened until he was standing. At his side his fingers twitched at the empty air as if to grasp something.

He took a step forward, still with his head to the side. He remained absolutely still.

Then he began to cry out in a hoarse excited voice, again and again, screaming now, because he had just heard someone far away calling his name.

At the top of the hill Sara got slowly to her feet and stood looking down at the forest. She pushed the hair back from her forehead and moistened her lips. The wind dried them as she waited.

Joe started to say something but she reached out one hand and took his arm to stop him. Scarcely daring to believe her ears, she stepped closer to the edge of the bank. Now she heard it unmistakably—the sharp repeated cry— and she knew it was Charlie.

"Charlie!" she shouted with all her might.

She paused and listened, and his cries were louder and she knew he was not far away after all, just down the slope, in the direction of the ravine.

"It's Charlie, it's Charlie!"

A wild joy overtook her and she jumped up and down on the bare earth and she felt that she could crush the whole hill just by jumping if she wanted.

She sat and scooted down the bank, sending earth and pebbles in a cascade before her. She landed on the soft ground, ran a few steps, lost her balance, caught hold of the first tree trunk she could find, and swung around till she stopped.

She let out another whoop of pure joy, turned and ran down the hill in great strides, the puce tennis shoes slapping the ground like rubber paddles, the wind in her face, her hands grabbing one tree trunk after another for support. She felt like a wild creature who had traveled through the forest this way for a lifetime. Nothing could stop her now.

At the edge of the ravine she paused and stood gasping for breath. Her heart was beating so fast it pounded in her ears, and her throat was dry. She leaned against a tree, resting her cheek against the rough bark.

She thought for a minute she was going to faint, a thing she had never done before, not even when she broke her nose. She hadn't even believed people really did faint until this minute when she clung to the tree because her legs were as useless as rubber bands.

There was a ringing in her ears and another sound, a wailing siren-like cry that was painfully familiar.

"Charlie?"

Charlie's crying, like the sound of a cricket, seemed everywhere and nowhere.

She walked along the edge of the ravine, circling the large boulders and trees. Then she looked down into the ravine where the shadows lay, and she felt as if something had turned over inside her because she saw Charlie.

He was standing in his torn pajamas, face turned upward, hands raised, shouting with all his might. His eyes were shut tight. His face was streaked with dirt and tears. His pajama jacket hung in shreds about his scratched chest.

He opened his eyes and as he saw Sara a strange expression came over his face, an expression of wonder and joy and disbelief, and Sara knew that if she lived to be a hundred no one would ever look at her quite that way again.

She paused, looked down at him, and then, sliding on the seat of her pants, went down the bank and took him in her arms.

"Oh, Charlie."

His arms gripped her like steel.

"Oh, Charlie."

She could feel his fingers digging into her back as he clutched her shirt. "It's all right now, Charlie, I'm here and we're going home." His face was buried in her shirt and she patted his head, said again, "It's all right now. Everything's fine."

She held him against her for a moment and now the hot tears were in her eyes and on her cheeks and she didn't even notice.

"I know how you feel," she said. "I know. One time when I had the measles and my fever was real high, I got lost on my way back from the bathroom, right in our

house, and it was a terrible feeling, terrible, because I wanted to get back to my bed and I couldn't find it, and finally Aunt Willie heard me and came and you know where I was? In the kitchen. In our kitchen and I couldn't have been more lost if I'd been out in the middle of the wilderness."

She patted the back of his head again and said, "Look, I even brought your bedroom slipper. Isn't that service, huh?"

She tried to show it to him, but he was still clutching her, and she held him against her, patting him. After a moment she said again, "Look, here's your slipper. Let's put it on." She knelt, put his foot into the shoe, and said, "Now, isn't that better?"

He nodded slowly, his chest still heaving with unspent sobs.

"Can you walk home?"

He nodded. She took her shirttail and wiped his tears and smiled at him. "Come on, we'll find a way out of here and go home."

"Hey, over this way," Joe called from the bank of the ravine. Sara had forgotten about him in the excitement of finding Charlie, and she looked up at him for a moment.

"Over this way, around the big tree," Joe called. "That's probably how he got in. The rest of the ravine is a mass of brier bushes."

She put one arm around Charlie and led him around the tree. "Everybody in town's looking for you, you know that?" she said. "Everybody. The police came and all the neighbors are out—there must be a hundred people looking for you. You were on the radio. It's like you were the President of the United States or something. Everybody was saying, 'Where's Charlie?' and 'We got to find Charlie.'"

Suddenly Charlie stopped and held up his hand and Sara looked down. "What is it?"

He pointed to the silent watch.

She smiled. "Charlie, you are something, you know that? Here we are racing down the hill to tell everyone in great triumph that you are found, *found*, and we have to stop and wind your watch first."

She looked at the watch, saw that the stem was missing, and shook her head. "It's broken, Charlie, see, the stem's gone. It's broken."

He held it out again.

"It's *broken*, Charlie. We'll have to take it to the jeweler and have it fixed."

He continued to hold out his arm.

"Hey, Charlie, you want to wear my watch till you get yours fixed?" Joe asked. He slid down the bank and put his watch on Charlie's arm. "There."

Charlie bent his face close and listened.

"Now can we go home?" Sara asked, jamming her hands into her back pockets.

Charlie nodded.

They walked through the woods for a long time, Joe in the lead, picking the best path, with Charlie and Sara following. From time to time Sara turned and hugged Charlie and he smelled of trees and dark earth and tears and she said, "Everybody's going to be so glad to see you it's going to be just like New Year's Eve."

Sara could not understand why she suddenly felt so good. It was a puzzle. The day before she had been miserable. She had wanted to fly away from everything, like the swans to a new lake, and now she didn't want that any more.

Down the hill Mr. Rhodes, one of the searchers, was coming toward them and Joe called out, "Mr. Rhodes, Sara found him!"

"Is he all right?" Mr. Rhodes called back.

"Fine, he's fine."

"Sara found him and he's all right. He's all right."

The phrase passed down the hill from Dusty Rhodes, who painted cars at the garage, to Mr. Aker to someone Sara couldn't recognize.

Then all the searchers were joining them, reaching out to pat Charlie and to say to Sara, "Oh, your aunt is going to be so happy," or "Where *was* he?" or "Well, now we can all sleep in peace tonight."

They came through the woods in a big noisy group and out into the late sunlight in the old pasture, Sara and Charlie in the middle, surrounded by all the searchers.

Suddenly Sara sensed a movement above her. She looked up and then grabbed Charlie's arm.

The swans were directly overhead, flying with out-stretched necks, their long wings beating the air, an awkward blind sort of flight. They were so low that she thought they might hit the trees, but at the last moment they pulled up and skimmed the air just above the treetops.

"Look, Charlie, look. Those are the swans. Remember? They're going home."

He looked blankly at the sky, unable to associate the heavy awkward birds with the graceful swans he had seen on the water. He squinted at the sky, then looked at Sara, puzzled.

"Charlie, those are the swans. Remember? At the lake?" she said, looking right at him. "They're going home now. Don't you remember? They were—"

"Hey, there's your aunt, Charlie. There's Aunt Willie coming."

Sara was still pulling at Charlie's arm, directing his attention to the sky. It seemed urgent somehow that Charlie see the swans once again. She said, "Charlie, those are—"

He looked instead across the field and he broke away from Sara and started running. She took two steps after him and then stopped. Aunt Willie in her bright green dress seemed to shine like a beacon, and he hurried toward her, an awkward figure in torn blue pajamas, shuffling through the high grass.

There was a joyous yell that was so shrill Sara thought it had come from the swans, but then she knew that it had come from Charlie, for the swans were mute.

"Here he is, Willie," Mrs. Aker called, running behind Charlie to have some part in the reunion.

Aunt Willie was coming as fast as she could on her bad legs. "I never thought to see him again," she was telling everyone and no one. "I thought he was up in that mine.

I tell you, I never thought to see him again. Charlie, come here to your Aunt Willie."

Charlie ran like a ball rolling downhill, bouncing with the slope of the land.

"I tell you this has been the blackest day of my life"— Aunt Willie was gasping—"and I include every day I have been on earth. Charlie, my Charlie, let me look at you. Oh, you are a sight."

He fell into Aunt Willie's arms. Over his head Aunt Willie said through her tears to Mrs. Aker, "May you never lose your Bobby, that's all I got to say. May you never lose your Bobby, may none of you ever lose anybody in the woods or in the mine or anywhere."

Sara stood in the pasture by the old gray shack and watched the swans disappear over the hill, and then she watched Charlie and Aunt Willie disappear in the crowd of people, and she felt good and loose and she thought that if she started walking down the hill at that moment, she would walk with the light movements of a puppet and never touch the ground at all.

She thought she would sit down for a moment now that everyone was gone, but when she looked around she saw Joe Melby still standing behind her. "I thought you went with the others."

"Nope."

"It's been a very strange day for me." She looked at the horizon where the swans had disappeared.

"It's been one of my stranger days too."

"Well, I'd better go home."

Joe walked a few steps with her, cleared his throat, and then said, "Do you want to go to Bennie Hoffman's party with me?"

She thought she hadn't heard him right for a moment, or if she had, that it was a mistake, like the boy who shouted, "Hey, beautiful," at Rosey Camdon.

"What?"

"I asked if you wanted to go with me to the party."

"I wasn't invited." She made herself think of the swans. By this time they could probably see the lake at the university and were about to settle down on the water with a great beating of wings and ruffling of feathers. She could almost see the long perfect glide that would bring them to the water.

"I'm inviting you. Bennie said I could bring somebody if I wanted to. He begged me to bring someone, as a matter of fact. He and Sammy and John and Pete have formed this musical group and they're going to make everybody listen to them."

"Well, I don't know."

"Why not? Other than the fact that you're going to have to listen to some terrible guitar playing. Bennie Hoffman has had about one and a half lessons."

"Well . . ."

"It's not any big deal, just sitting in Bennie Hoffman's back yard and watching him louse up with a two-hundred-dollar guitar and amplifier."

"I guess I could go."

"I'll walk over and pick you up in half an hour. It won't matter if we're late. The last fifty songs will sound about the same as the first fifty."

"I'll be ready."

When Sara came up the walk Wanda was standing on the porch. "What is going on around here, will you tell me that? Where is Charlie?"

"We found him. He's with Aunt Willie, wherever that is."

"Do you know how I heard he was lost? I heard it on the car radio when I was coming home. How do you think that made me feel—to hear from some disc jockey that my own brother was missing? I could hardly get here because there are a hundred cars full of people jamming the street down there."

"Well, he's fine."

"So Mr. Aker told me, only I would like to see him and find out what happened."

"He got up during the night sometime—this is what I think happened—to go see the swans and ended up in a ravine crying his heart out."

Wanda stepped off the porch and looked across the street, leaning to see around the foliage by the fence. She said, "Is that them over there on the Carsons' porch?"

Sara looked and nodded.

"Honestly, Charlie still in his pajamas, and Aunt Willie in her good green dress with a handkerchief tied around her forehead to keep her from sweating, and both of them eating watermelon. That beats all."

"At least he's all right."

Wanda started down the walk, then paused. "You want to come?"

"No, I'm going to a party."

"Whose?"

"Bennie Hoffman's."

"I didn't think you were invited."

"Joe Melby's taking me."

"Joe Melby? Your great and terrible enemy?"

"He is not my enemy, Wanda. He is one of the nicest people I know."

"For three months I've been hearing about the evils of Joe Melby. Joe Melby, the thief; Joe Melby, the fink; Joe Melby, the—"

"A person," Sara said coldly, "can occasionally be mistaken." She turned and went into the living room, saw Boysie sleeping by the door and said, "Boysie, we found Charlie." She bent and rubbed him behind the ears. Then she went into the kitchen, made a sandwich, and was starting into the bedroom when the phone rang.

"Hello," she said, her mouth full of food.

"Hello, I have a long-distance call for Miss Willamina Godfrey," the operator said.

"Oh, she's across the street. If you'll wait a minute I'll go get her."

"Operator, I'll just talk to whoever's there," Sara heard her father say.

She said quickly, "No, I'll go get her. Just wait one minute. It won't take any time. She's right across the street."

"Sara? Is this Sara?"

"Yes, this is me." The strange feeling came over her again. "If you wait a minute I'll go get Aunt Willie."

"Sara, did you find Charlie?"

"Yes, we found him, but I don't mind going to get Aunt Willie. They're over on the Carsons' porch."

"Is Charlie all right?"

"He's fine. He's eating watermelon right now."

"Where was he?"

"Well, he went up into the woods and got lost. We found him in a ravine and he was dirty and tired and hungry but he's all right."

"That's good. I was going to come home tonight if he hadn't been found."

"Oh."

"But since everything's all right, I guess I'll just wait until the weekend."

"Sure."

"So I'll probably see you Saturday, then, if nothing turns up."

"Fine."

"Be sure to tell Willie I called."

"I will."

A picture came into her mind of the laughing, curly-headed man with the broken tooth in the photograph album, and she suddenly saw life as a series of huge, uneven steps, and she saw herself on the steps, standing motionless in her prison shirt, and she had just taken an enormous step up out of the shadows, and she was standing, waiting, and there were other steps in front of her, so that she could go as high as the sky, and she saw Charlie on a flight of small difficult steps, and her father down at the bottom of some steps, just sitting and not trying to go further. She saw everyone she knew on those blinding white steps and for a moment everything was clearer than it had ever been.

"Sara?"

"I'm still here."

"Well, that was all I wanted, just to hear that Charlie was all right."

"He's fine."

"And I'll see you on Saturday if nothing happens."

"Sure."

"Good-by."

She sat for a minute still holding the receiver and then

she set it back on the telephone and finished her sandwich. Slowly she slipped off her tennis shoes and looked down at her feet, which were dyed blue. Then she got up quickly and went to get ready for the party.

Grace Livingston Hill is one of the most popular authors of all time because of her unique style of combining elements of the Christian faith with tasteful and exciting romance.

Find out why generations of readers of all ages have been entertained and inspired by the fiction of Grace Livingston Hill.

Grace Livingston Hill ... fiction that fills the heart as well as the spirit!

GRACE LIVINGSTON HILL

According to the Pattern
An Unwilling Guest

Two complete and unabridged novels in one volume

Barbour Books
164 Mill Street
Westwood, New Jersey 07675

According to the Pattern

Chapter 1
A Fallen Idol

Mrs. Claude Winthrop sat in her pretty sitting room alone under the lamp-light making buttonholes. Her eyes were swimming in stinging tears that she would not for the world let fall. She felt as if a new law of attraction held them there to blind and torture her. She could not let them fall, for no more were left; they were burned up by the emotions that were raging in her soul, and if these tears were gone her eyeballs would surely scorch the lids. She was exercising strong control over her lips that longed to open in a groan that should increase until it reached a shriek that all the world could hear.

Her fingers flew with nervous haste, setting the needle in dainty stiches in the soft white dress for her baby girl. She had not supposed when she fashioned the little garment the day before and laid it aside ready for the finishing that she would think of its wearer to-night in so much agony. Ah, her baby girl, and her boy, and the older sister!

Almost the tears fell as another dart pierced her heart, but she opened her eyes the wider to hold them back and sat and sewed unwinkingly. She must not, must not cry. There was momentous thinking to be done to-night. She had not had time to consider this awful thing since it had come upon her. Was she really sure beyond a doubt that it was so? How long ago was it that she took little Celia, happy and laughing, in the trolley to the park? How little she thought what she was going out to meet as she lifted the child from the car and smilingly humored her fancy to follow a by-path through the woods. How the little feet had danced and the pretty prattle had babbled on like a tinkling brook that needed no response, but was content with its own music.

And then they had come to the edge of the park drive where they could look down upon the world of fashion as it swept along, all rubber-tired and silver-mounted, in its best array. She had sighed a happy little sigh as she surveyed a costly carriage surmounted by two servants in white and dark-green livery and saw the discontented faces of the over-dressed man and woman who sat as far apart as the width of the seat would allow, and appeared to endure their drive as two dumb animals might if this were a part of their daily round. What if she rode in state like that with a husband such as he? She had shuddered and been conscious of thankfulness over her home and her husband. What if Claude did stay away from home a good deal evenings! It was in the way of his business, he said, and she must be more patient. There would come a time by and by when he would have enough, so that they could live at their ease, and he need not go to the city ever any more. And into the midst of the bright dream she had conjured came little Celia's prattle:

"Mamma, see! Papa tumming'! Pitty lady!" She had looked down curiously to see who it was that reminded the child of her father, and her whole being froze within her. Her breath seemed not to come at all, and she had turned so ghastly white that the baby put up her hand and touched her cheek, saying, "Mamma, pitty mamma! Poor mamma!"

For there on the seat of a high, stylish cart drawn by shining black horses with arched necks, and just below a tall elegant woman, who was driving, sat her husband. Claude! Yes, little Celia's papa! Oh, that moment!

She forced herself to remember his face with its varying expressions as she had watched it till it was out of sight. There was no trouble in recalling it; it was burned into her soul with a red-hot iron. He had been talking to that beautiful woman as he used to talk to her when they were first engaged. That tender, adoring gaze; his eyes love-lighted. It was unmistakable! A heart-breaking revelation! There was no use trying to blind herself. There was not the slightest hope that he could come home and explain this away as a business transaction, or a plot between him and that other woman to draw her out into the world, or any of those pretty fallacies that might happen in books. It was all true, and she had known it instantly. It had been revealed to her as in a flash, the meaning of long months of neglect, supposed business trips, luncheons, and dinners at the club instead of the homecoming. She knew it. She ought to have seen it before. If she had not been so engrosed in her little world of the household she would have done so. Indeed, now that she knew it, she recognized also that she had been given warnings of it. Her husband had done his best to get her out. He had suggested and begged, but she had not been well during the first years of the two elder children, and the coming of the third had again filled her heart and mind. Her home was enough for her, always provided he was in it. It was not enough for him. She had tried to make it a happy one; but perhaps she had been fretful and exacting sometimes, and it may be she had been in fault to allow the children to be noisy when their father was at home.

He had always been fond of society, and had been brought up to do exactly as he pleased. It was hard for him to be shut in as she was, but that was a woman's lot. At least it was the lot of the true mother who did not trust her little ones to servants. Ah, was she excusing him? That must not be. He was her husband. She loved him deeply, tenderly, bitterly; but she would not excuse him. He was at fault, of course. He should not have been riding with a wealthy woman of fashion while his own wife came to the park on the trolley and took care of her baby as he passed by. He was not a man of wealth yet, though they had hoped he would one day be; but how did he get into this set? How came he to be sitting beside that lovely lady with the haughty air who had smiled so graciously down upon him. Her soul recoiled even now as she remembered that her husband should be looking up in that way to any woman — that is, any woman but herself — oh, no! Not even that! She wanted her husband to be a man above, far above herself. She must respect him. She could not live if she could not do that. What should she do? Was there anything to do? She would die. Perhaps that was the way out of it — she would die. It would be an easy affair. No heart could bear many such mighty grips of horror as had come upon hers that afternoon. It would not take long. But the children — her three little children! Could she leave them to the world — to another woman, perhaps, who would not love them? No, not that. Not even to save them from the shame of a father who had learned to love another woman than his wife. She reasoned this out. It seemed to her that her brain had never seen things so clearly before in all her life. Her little children were the burden of her sorrow. That all this should come upon them! A father who had disgraced them — who did not love his home! For this was certainly what it would come to be, even though he maintained all outward proprieties. She told herself that it was probable this had not been going on long. She forced herself to think back to the exact date when her husband began to stay away to dinners and to be out late evenings. How could she have been so easily satisfied in her safe, happy belief that her peace was to last forever, and go off to sleep before his return, often and often?

And then her conscience, arising from a refreshing sleep, began to take up its neglected work and accused her smartly. It was all her fault. She could see her mistakes as clearly now as if they had been roads leading off from the path she ought to have kept. She had allowed her husband to become alienated from herself. She could look back to the spot where she ought to have done something, just what she did not know. She did not even stop to question whether it had been possible in her state of health, and with their little income, which was eaten up so fast in those days by doctor's bills and little shoes. But all that was past. It could not be lived over. She had been a failure — yes, she, Miriam Hammond Winthrop — who had thought when she married that she would be the most devoted of wives, she had let her husband drift away from her, and had helped on the destruction that was coming surely and swiftly to her little children. Was it too late? Was the past utterly irretrievable? Had he gone too far? Had he lost his love for her entirely? Was her power all gone? She used to be able to bring the lovelight into his eyes. Could she ever do it again?

Suddenly she laid down the little white garment with the needle just as she was beginning to take the next stitch and went to the mirror over the mantel to look at herself.

She turned on all the gas jets and studied her face critically. Yes, she looked older, and there were wrinkles coming here and there. It seemed to her they had come that afternoon. Her eyes looked tired too, but could she not by vigorous attention to herself make her face once more attractive to her husband? If so it was worth doing, if she might save him, even if she died in the attempt. She took both hands and smoothed her forehead, rubbed her cheeks to make them red, and forgot to notice that the tears had burned themselves up, leaving her eyes brighter than usual. She tossed her hair up a little like the handsome woman's she had seen in the park. It really was more becoming. Why had she not taken the trouble to dress it in the present style? Then she went back to her chair again and took up the work. The buttonholes that she had expected would take several evenings to finish were vanishing before her excited fingers without her knowing it. It was a relief to her to do something; and she put all her energy into it so that her hands began to ache, but she was only conscious of the awful ache in her heart and sewed on.

If there were some one to advise her! Could she do it? Could she make a stand against the devil and try to save her Eden? Or was it more than one poor shy woman, with all the odds of the gay world against her, could accomplish?

She longed to have her husband come home that she might throw herself at his feet and beg and plead with him for her happiness, to save their home; she longed to accuse him madly, and fling scorching words at him, and watch his face as she told him how she and his baby had seen him that afternoon; and then she longed again to throw her arms around his neck and cry upon his breast as she used to do when they were first married, and any little thing happened that she did not like. How she used to cry over trifles then! How could she, when such a world of sorrow was coming to her so soon?

She was wise enough to know that none of these longings of her heart must be carried into effect if she would win her husband. In his present attitude he would laugh at her fears! She seemed to understand that her anguish would only anger him because he would feel condemned. Her own soul knew that she could not take him back into her heart of hearts until she won him back and he came of his own accord confessing his wrong to her. But would that ever be? He was a good man at heart, she believed. He would not do wrong, not very wrong, not knowingly. Perhaps he had not learned to love any other woman, only to love society, and — to — cease to love her.

If her dear, wise mother were there! But no! She could not tell her. She must never breathe this thing to any living soul if she would hope to do anything! His honor should be hers. She would protect him from even her own condemnation so long as she could. But what to do and how to do it!

Out of the chaos of her mind there presently began to form a plan. Her breath came and went with quick gasps and her heart beat wildly as she looked the daring thing in the face and summoned her courage to meet it.

Could she perhaps meet that woman, that outrageous woman, on her own ground and vanquish her? Could she with only the few poor little stones of her wits and the sling of her love face this woman Goliath of society and challenge her? What! expect that woman, with all her native grace and beauty, her fabulous wealth, and her years of training to give way before her? A crimson spot came out on either cheek, but she swallowed hard with her hot dry throat and set her lips in firm resolve. She could but fail. She would do it.

But how? And with what? It would take money. She could not use her husband's, at least not much of it, not to win him back. There was a little, a few hundreds, a small legacy her grandmother had left to her. How pitifully small it seemed now! She cast a glance at a fashion magazine that lay upon her table. She had bought it the day before because of a valuable article on how to make over dress skirts to suit the coming season's style. How satisfied with the sweet monotony of her life had she been then! It came to her with another sharp thrust now! But that magazine said that gowns from five to seven hundred dollars were no longer remarkable things. How she had smiled but the evening before as she read it and curled her lip at the unfortunates whose lives were run into the grooves of folly that could require such extravagance. Now she wished fiercely that she might possess several that cost not merely seven hundred but seven thousand dollars, if only she might outstrip them all and stand at the head for her husband to see.

But this was folly. She had only a little and that little must do! It had been put aside for a rainy day, or to send the children to college in case father failed. Alas! And now father had failed, but not in the way thought possible, and the money must be used to save him and them all from destruction, if indeed it would hold out. How long would it take, and how, how should she go about it?

With sudden energy she caught up the magazine and read. She had gone over it all the day before in her ride from the city where she had been shopping, and had recognized from its tone that it was familiar with a different world from hers. Now with sudden hope she read feverishly, if perchance there might be some help there for her.

Yes, there were suggestions of how to do this and that, how to plan and dress and act in the different functions of society; but of what use were they to her? How was she to begin? She was not in society and how was she to get there? She could not ask her husband. That would spoil it all. She must get there without his help.

If she only had that editor, that woman or whoever it was who answered those questions, for just a few minutes, she could find out if there was any way in which she could creep into that mystic circle where alone her battle could be fought. She had always despised people who wrote to newspapers for advice in their household troubles and now she felt a sudden sympathy for them. Actually it was now her only source of help, at least the only one of which she knew. Her cheeks burned as the suggestion of writing persistently put itself before her. She could hear her husband's scornful laugh ringing out as he ridiculed the poor fools who wrote to papers for advice, and the presumption that attempted to administer medicine — mental, moral, and physical — to all the troubles of the earth.

But the wife's heart suddenly overflowed with gratitude toward the paper. It was trying to do good in the world, it was ready to help the helpless. Why should she be ashamed to write? No one would ever know who it was. And she need not consider herself from last night's view-point. She had come to a terrible straight. Trouble and shame had entered her life. She no longer stood upon the high pinnacle of joy in happy wifehood! Her heart was broken and her idol clay. What should she care for her former ideas of nicety? It was not for her to question the ways or the means. It was for her to snatch at the first straw that presented itself, as any sensible drowning person would do.

With firm determination she laid down the magazine and walked deliberately to her desk. Her fingers did not tremble nor the resolute look pass from her chin as she selected plain paper and envelope and wrote. The words seemed to come without need of thought. She stated the case clearly in a few words, and signed her grandmother's initials. She folded, addressed the letter, and sent her sleepy little maid to post it before the set look relaxed.

Then having done all that was in her power to do that night she went up to her room in the dark and smothering her head in the pillow so that the baby would not be disturbed she let the wild sobs have their way.

Chapter 2

A Trip Abroad

"It is just barely possible I may have to take a flying trip to Paris," Claude Winthrop announced casually, looking up from the newspaper which had been engrossing his attention.

It was the next morning and his wife unrefreshed from her night's vigil was sitting quietly in her place at the breakfast table. She looked now and then at the top of her husband's head, thinking of his face as she had seen it in the park, and trying to realize that all round her was just the same outwardly as it had been yesterday and all the days that had gone before, only she knew that it was all so different.

She made some slight reply. He had said so many times that he hoped his business would take him abroad soon, that she ceased to reproach him for desiring to go without her and the children as she had done at first. She began to feel that he would not really go after all. It had been a source of uneasiness to her many times, for she had a morbid horror of having the wide ocean separate her from the one she loved better than all on earth besides. But this morning, in the light of recent discoveries, she realized that even this trouble of the past was as nothing beside what was laid upon her now to bear.

How often it is that when we mock at a trouble, or detract from its magnitude, it comes upon us suddenly as if to taunt us and reveal its true heaviness. Miriam Winthrop felt this with a sudden sharp pang a little later that day when she received and read a brief note from her husband brought by a messenger boy. For the moment all her more recent grief was forgotten and she was tormented by her former fears and dread.

"Dear Miriam," he had scrawled on the back of a business envelope, "I've got to go at once. The firm thinks I'm the only one who can represent them in Paris just now, and if I don't go there'll be trouble. I'm sorry it comes with such a rush but it's a fine thing for me. Pack my grip with what you think I need for a month. I don't want to be bothered with much. I may not get home till late and fear I shall have to take the midnight train. Haste. Clause."

She did not stop now to study the phraseology of the hastily worded note, nor let the coldness and baldness of the announcement enter her soul like a keen blade as it would be sure to do later when the trial began in dead earnest. She did not even give a thought to the difference between this note and those he used to write her when they were first married. It was enough to realize that he was going across the terrible ocean without her and talking about it as calmly as if he were but going downtown. Other people let their husbands go off without a murmur. There was Mrs. Forsythe, who smilingly said she intended to send her husband on a tour for six months so that she could be free from household cares and do as she pleased for a little while. But then she was Mr. Forsythe's wife, and Claude was — and then there came that sudden sharp remembrance of yesterday and its revelation, and her sorrow entered full into her being with a realization of what it was going to mean. Yes, perhaps she ought to be glad he was going away. But she was not — oh, she was not! It was worse a hundred-fold than it would have been if it had come two days ago. Now she was plunged into the awfulness of the black abyss that had yawned before her feet, and Claude was going from her and would not be there to help her out by any possible explanation, nor even to know of the horror in her path, for she knew in her heart that she could not and would not tell him her discovery now before he went. There would not be time, even it if were wise. No, she must bear it alone until he returned, if he ever did. Oh, that deep awful sea that must roll over her troubled heart for weeks before she could hope to begin to change things. Could she stand it? Would she live to brave it through?

A ringing baby laugh from the nursery, where Celia was drawing a wooly lamb over the floor, recalled her courage. She closed her lips in their firm lines once more and knew she would, she must!

Just one more awful thought came to her and glared at her with green, deriding, menacing eyes of possibility. That woman, could she, was she going abroad? There had been such things! Her brain reeled at the thought and with fear and wrath she put it away from her. She would never think that of Claude. No, never! She must go about making preparations for him, for there was much to be done, some mending, and where had that package of laundry been put? and, of, the horror of having to doubt one's husband! Claude might have been injudicious, but never wicked! No! She was unworthy to be his wife when she could think such things with absolutely nothing to found them upon save a simple everyday ride in the park. She hurried upstairs to bureau drawers and sent the nurse and the maid-of-all-work flying about on various errands and herself worked with swift, skilled fingers. But all the time the ache grew in her heart till it seemed it must break.

He did not come home to lunch. She had not expected that. She scarcely stopped herself to making a pretence of eating. So eager was she to complete the little things she had thought of to do for his comfort during the voyage before he should return that she forgot herself entirely in her present duties. The stinging tears welled up to her eyes without falling as they had done the night before, and burned themselves dry, again and again, and still she worked on feverishly, adding other little touches to the preparations she had made. He should not have cause for impatience that she had forgotten anything in his thought of her during the trip. She even put in his old cap that he was fond of wearing in traveling and which heretofore she had always struggled to secrete safely before they set out for a journey. There was a fine disregard of self in all that she did about the suit-case and a close attention to details for his liking. If he had any thought left for her at all he could not fail to note it.

She carefully placed a leather photograph case, a present from the children on last Christmas, containing all their likenesses with hers, in an inner pocket with his handkerchiefs, and then on second thought took it out to remove her own face and put in its place a new pose of the baby. She would not seek to remind him thus of her. He should see that she no longer put in any claims for his affection. Just why she did this she could not explain to herself, but she felt a triumph over herself in having done it. Was it revenge or love or jealousy or all? She did not know. She sat down beside the completed work and let great drops fall on the heavy, unresponsive leather, and groaned aloud, and then got up hastily to wipe her eyes and flash them in defiance at herself in the mirror. She would not give way now. She must act her part till he was gone. Then she would weep until she could get relief enough to think and know what to do.

He came late to dinner and brought his secretary with him. During the meal they were going over certain business matters which were to be left in this young man's charge. Miriam presided over her table and supplied their needs and held her tongue, feeling in this brief time of quietness and inaction how weary she was, how every nerve quivered with pain, how her eyeballs stung, and how the little veins in her temples throbbed.

They went to the library after dinner, where there was more business. The wife went up to her nursery and hovered over her daily cares, which suddenly seemed to have lost their necessity, so much greater was her need of some word with her husband.

It was not till ten o'clock that the front door closed upon the young man of business and she heard Claude coming upstairs. Her heart leaped then. Would he possibly say something comforting to her, some word of love for her, now that he was leaving, some little regret that she could not go too? Something, perhaps, that might explain that awful sight of yesterday, and wipe this day out of existence for her so far as its suffering had been concerned? Oh, if that might be she would never murmur again at sorrow or loneliness or anything that could come upon her, so long as she could have her husband her own.

But no, that could not be, she knew, for there was that look that she had seen her husband give to the strange woman, and even as she thought she heard him go into the bedroom.

"Miriam," he called, without waiting for her to come to the door, "I'm going right to bed. I'm just about played out, and I'll have to start early in the morning. Have you got everything all fixed up? All right, then I'll turn in. Don't let any one disturb me. I've told Simmons about everything, and if any call comes from the office folks you can refer them to Simmons."

Her low murmured "All right," was followed by the quick closing door. She stood in the hall and heard him move about the room, and knew that she might go to him and tell him all, or get some word from him more than this before he slept to wake and rush away from her, but she would not. She heard the click of the light as he turned it out, and the silence that followed his lying down, and reflected that she might at least go and kiss him good-night, and yet she had not the power to move.

How long she stood there she did not know. It seemed to her that every action of her life since she had known her husband came and was enacted before her, that every word he had ever spoken or written to her was spoken distinctly in her ear. She felt again his power over her when he told her how he loved her, and the gladness that enwrapped her like a garment as she knew that she loved him. It turned to a pall now as the other thoughts of yesterday trooped up, death-faced and horrid, to mock at those happier times.

She roused herself by and by to see that the house was locked for the night and the children sleeping quietly as usual. Then she made a careful toilet for the morning. It would need to be freshened a little she knew, if she could manage it, but the main points must be looked after now when her mind was clear. She must leave upon her husband a fair memory, a pleasing vision, if indeed this poor heartsick body of hers could be made to look pleasant to any one.

She put on a more elaborate gown than she had been wont to consider proper for a morning dress, but it was her husband's favorite color. She disregarded all her former prejudices and scorned her economies. What were economies when life was at stake? She also arranged her hair in the new way, taking a long time at it and being very critical of herself. All the while this was going on she was conscious of trying to stop thinking and to absorb herself in her occupation. The color was high in her cheeks. Her night of vigil and her day of labor, followed by the disappointment that her husband had said no tender word to her, had brought a feverishness which heightened the brilliancy of her eyes. She could see that she looked young again, and drew a little hope from the fact.

But a toilet cannot last a night-time even with such precious ends at stake, and when it was finished she took a candle and stole silently into the bedroom.

She had known that this moment must come. Her heart would not let her let him go without it. She must look down upon him and remember all the past and know the present with his face in sight. She had been dreading it and putting it off ever since he had shut the door. Now she stood and looked at him as he lay sleeping.

He was handsome even in his sleep. His heavy dark hair was tossed back against the pillow and his broad forehead looked noble to her even now with all the turmoil surging in her heart against him. She noted the long black lashes, the same his little children had. He looked so young as he lay asleep, and she could see their oldest child's resemblance to him as she had never seen it before. She made herself take in every feature. The pleasant curves of the lips, those lips that had said kind words, tender words of love to her, and had kissed her — and alas, could frame themselves in impatience. She could see them now as they looked during a recent disagreement. The remembrance struck like a blow across her heart. His arms were thrown out over the bed in the abondonment of weariness, and his hands seemed to appeal to her for a kindly thought. Those white hands, so symmetrical, and yet so firm and strong, how she had admired them as a girl. How proud she had always been of them as his wife. How they had helped her own hands when they first began their life together. She fain would stoop and kiss just his hand. She could not let him go without. He was tired, so tired; and she was sorry, so sorry; and he was her husband! She set the candle down softly upon the floor at a little distance and stopped, but started up at a suggestion. Had that hand ever touched in gentle pressure the hands of other women? Did that other woman know those shapely hands, that were hers, and yet were not hers now? She bowed her head amid the draperies of the bed and almost groaned aloud. She would fain have prayed, as there was no other help at hand, but she was not a praying woman. True she had a habit of kneeling to repeat a form of words, but even that form failed her now, though she tried to find some words to voice a cry to the Unknown.

Was ever sorrow like unto hers? Were there in the world other women who suffered this sort of thing? Yes, of course there were, there must be, poor wretches; she had read of them and known of them always; poor creatures who could not keep, or never had, their husbands' love; but not such as she, and such as Claude; no, no, that could not be! This never had happened before. It could not be true! She would not believe it. There must be some mistake.

The long night passed at last, and the toilet given its final touches, though the face it was meant to set off was wan with sorrow and exhaustion. Very quietly she served the breakfast, which was a hasty meal, as there was little time. She nerved herself to be bright and unconcerned, as if the proposed journey was but a brief one for a few hours. She had been wont to grieve so deeply at thought of separation, that her husband wondered a little that she should take it so quietly, and if he had had more time to note her and less upon his mind he would have seen the abnormal state of excitement that kept her calm and smiling when her heart was so fiercely torn.

Miriam saw to it that the children were at hand at the last moment to be kissed good-bye, and then with a hasty word of some handkerchiefs she had forgotten to put in his grip, she flew up the stairs and locked her door. She could not bear the hasty farewell, the careless kiss she saw was coming. She preferred that he should leave her uncaressed.

"Come, Miriam, I must go. Don't wait for handkerchiefs. There's no time to look. The cab is at the door. Come."

But she did not come, and he called good-bye and went.

She watched him slam the cab door after him and drive away in the early morning light, and then the great sobs that had been so carefully choked down for hours came and shook her frame, and she hid her face in the pillows where he had slept but a little while ago and let her sorrow wave upon wave roll over her head and bury her face in the awful chasms between its breakers till kindly nature claimed the worn-out body and overwrought nerves, and wrapt her in a deep and dreamless sleep of utter weariness.

Chapter 3
An Important Letter

The days that followed were to her like a long struggle through the darkness of some deep valley by night. When she looked back upon them they were filled with horror. Every time she slept and awoke there was the same awful realization of trouble to be instantly remembered and realized, coming with the keenness of first knowledge during the earliest waking moments, as one remembers death or dread calamity and tries to weave the unaccustomed threads of sorrow into the hitherto happy web of life and make it seem a part of the daily fabric.

She plunged into work with all her soul and body. What was to come she had yet to discover. She felt that now her course lay clear before her, she had but to get out of the way any work that might be a hindrance to the plans when they should be formed. The children's clothes were first. She had been working at them leisurely for some time, taking pleasure in designing and executing the pretty, dainty garments which should make her children into picturesque little creatures. Now she set about finishing this work with feverish eagerness and conscientiousness. She foresaw that her tender care of these little ones must be much interrupted in future. What had been her duty and her pleasure must now be neglected for a higher, more insistent duty, which could not be delayed.

She put lingering, wistful touches on her work and a world of love and pent-up mother desires. This much she could do before the demand for action came and she would do it better than it had ever been done before. But there was also another reason for the care she put upon the little garments. When she remembered that her face was almost bitter in its stern determination and her fingers flew the faster. She was going out to fight the world, and the world, if she succeeded, would be free to inspect her life, her home, her children, everything she had. These same little chores of theirs would not escape the inspection. They were to be a part of her furnishing for the warfare in which she was to engage. Therefore she worked late and early, and in a surprisingly short time the garments were laid away complete for use.

One of the first things she had done during these days of work had been to write a letter subscribing for the "Fashion Magazine," to which she had sent her appeal for help. She felt that she simply could not go to a newsstand and buy it. Her shame, her disgrace would be written large upon her face. No, she must make sure to see to it if any answer appeared to her letter, but she must see it first in the quiet and seclusion of her own room with locked doors. Whenever, as she went back and forth to the city stores, she saw a copy of that magazine in a window or a notice of it upon a sign-board, she turned her face guiltily away. It was as if the name of it was shouted to her from afar. She dreaded the thought that any one should know to what depths she had descended, actually to have written to a public editor for assistance in her trouble. And yet, and yet in spite of it all and without her own consent, she was building greatly on the answer that should come to her. Would they understand what she wanted? And would they give her any help that she could follow? Or would she have to go blindly all alone? This thought gradually began to stand out clearly in her confused brain as she tried to plan while her fingers were executing wonders with her needle.

A month! And she must be ready for action when her husband returned. It might be he would be delayed longer, but she must be ready. Would the printed help come in time? How long did it take those things to get to headquarters and fall into line with other questions till at last an answer would come?

She watched the mail from week to week. The day of the arrival of the magazine was an anxious one. She shivered when it was put into her hand and tried to go about her household duties calmly, forcing herself to give the cook minute directions sometimes before retiring behind locked doors to scan the pages hastily and then more thoroughly. It must not be suspected that she had more than a passing interest in that magazine.

She read every word from cover to cover to make sure she did not miss her answer, though she knew such answers only appeared in a certain column. Meantime she was gaining much worldly knowledge as she read. There was a certain "shibboleth" spoken in those columns which she foresaw she must make her own if she would be the success she aimed to be. Unconsciously she weighed this and that question in dress, household decoration, manners, and customs. Without her own knowledge she grew to apply these newly acquired rules to her own home and life.

At last one morning she found the initials she had signed to her question staring her in the face.

For one brief instant she closed her eyes and drew a deep breath. Then her hand fluttered to her heart and she read with nervous rapidity:

Indeed, I have considered the situation carefully, for I know exactly what a complex problem you feel you have to face. But let me reassure you; many and many a wife and mother is in a similar predicament. How can it be otherwise when one has since marriage had little children to take care of and is occupied in the most natural, best of all ways that a woman can be occupied?

Miriam Winthrop caught her breath in a quick, dry sob at this, and then read on:

But I must congratulate you for the conclusion you have reached and your wise, wholesome desire to take up social life again and make a position for yourself and your husband, and, above all, for your children's future.

Ah, yes, for her children's future! But not in the way the writer meant.

It seems to me it would be unwise to start out to entertain elaborately even if you have the means for it. No, I should not advise you to give a big general reception, nor big dinners, nor anything of the sort. First of all, it would be inappropriate to entertain so in your small house, for you know there is proportion in everything. But what you could do is to send out cards for four days next month, let us say.

Then followed minute directions for the giving of informal little teas, with details of simple refreshments, decorations, forms, and costumes suggested. Nothing was forgotten, though there were no superfluous words used, from the garb and deportment of the maid who opens the door to directions about the proper garments for her husband to wear. Ah, her husband knew to an exact science how to dress well upon all possible occasions. That one suggestion was unnecessary, and a deep sigh breathed in her excitement as she read on, more and more convinced that the beginning of the undertakng seemed possible.

There was also a plan of further campaign of dinners and luncheons and a children's party hinted at, and the writer concluded:

Meanwhile you will probably receive invitations in return which you should accept, wearing pretty, becoming dresses to the entertainments and making as much of yourself as possible. This is every woman's duty, especially if she is a wife and mother. Try to read up on the subjects which are generally talked of, so that you will be an intelligent companion besides educating yourself, and try to find out what are the interests of the people you want to know. Return your calls regularly. When you have established a position for yourself it will be perfectly permissible for you, when you meet a stranger at a luncheon, or dinner, or any entertainment at the house of a mutual friend, to ask her if you may not call, as you would like to know her better, so gradually you will enlarge your circle without forcing yourself. I should advise you, if you have time, to go into some charitable work; join one of the societies of your church, and do what you can to help others outside of your home. By and by send out cards for a series of days and give during the winter some *musicales* or readings, if you can afford them. I am very certain you will succeed in your undertakings. It only requires tact and thought for others.

She closed her eyes and leaned back in her chair with another deep sign as suddenly the appalling magnitude of the work she had undertaken broke over her. She faltered at the thought of the wearisome way she must tread. Would it all pay? Could she do it? Would her strength and her money hold out till she had gained her point and won her husband to herself? Was it worse than useless to try? Might she not better give in at the start and accept the situation? Never!

She sprang to her feet, throwing the magazine down and walking excitedly to and fro, her hot brain fairly reeling under the whirl of plans for sandwiches and dresses and invitations and sundries which should cost but a trifle yet should hold their own with the best.

And from that moment she went forward and would not *think* the word defeat. She had a clue to the ways of the great world. It had been given her graciously and clearly. She could understand and obey. She felt in her heart that there would be results. If there was failure, it would be her fault in carrying out insturctions; but there *should not* be failure. She would see to that. Had she not always been able to make or do anything that she had set her heart upon? She recalled with a weary smile how she had patiently sewed white feathers on an old ivory fan frame as a girl, because her dearest wish had been to have a feather fan and her mother had not considered that their purse was full enough for such an unnecessary expenditure. There were other things too, small in themselves, but as she looked back upon them and recalled how she had carried her point despite all obstacles, they gave her courage to hope that what she had once done she could do again. Her purpose should be carried out to the end. It was her only hope. Then with a pitiful sob trembling in her throat as she drew another deep breath she unlocked her door and walked forth to begin her herculean task.

Downtown her resolves led her, to the great stores, where were wonders of the world of fashion in plenty. Her money was limited and she must use her wits.

It happened to be a good day for her induction into the science that began in the garden of Eden with a fig leaf. That was a brilliant exhibition of gowns, robes, dresses, frocks, or whatever the fashionable name for the outer covering a woman happened to be that week, and the display of more bewildering beauty of texture, color, form and fashion than perhaps had ever been seen in that city before.

She paused before the great glass cases containing these marvels of the dressmakers' art and began a systematic study, catching her breath at the enormous importance that the world placed upon clothes, and then shutting her eyes to her own stupendous audacity.

She went over all the beautiful display once and then returned to the beginning and began to take notes in minute detail. There was that great exquisite gray costume. There were possibilities in her own gray silk, out of date and somewhat worn. She noted carefully the little touch of elegance given by the vest of latticed gray velvet ribbon, the spaces filled by filmy spider's webs in silver thread. Being well versed in lace stitches she took courage. That vest which alone gave the costume its distinguishment would be unattainable to most women without a well-filled purse. To her it was quite possible. Her skillful fingers would help her here with little labor. The real outer material of the garment need not be expensive, some light wool with silken threads, and lined with her old gray silk. She drew a sigh of relief and passed on, mentally counting the few dollars that would represent this first dress. There would not be many such for she had but few silk dresses that would even do for lining. There was a black one which might work in, and that was all, unless she sacrificed her wedding gown. She almost blushed to think of its simplicity beside the billows of white satin she at that moment came upon, encrusted with priceless point lace. She passed it by with a mere glance and moved on to another simple-looking costume which scarcely seemed to belong to the elaborate collection, and appeared almost to be shrinking behind the card announcing its designer and executor. Mrs. Winthrop read the card. Not for nothing had she studied her fashion magazine. She knew the name of that house in Paris well by this time, and stood in awe before the model of cloth that was representative. She looked from the card back to the gown and began to see detail such as she had read about and until now had not understood. What gladdened her more than anything else was to discover that most of the distinguishing features of these wonderful dresses were bits of needle work which could easily be attained by one who understood embroidery and lace making and all the many little arts and secrets of fancy work of the higher grade as did she. She blessed the days gone by when she had let her happy fingers learn this cunning while she framed wonderful stories of bears and fairies and poppy-garlanded nymphs from the land of sweet dreams for her little ones. Oh, in those days, she had never conceived of the terrible need in which these accomplishments would bring her aid!

But she must not pause to let these thoughts sweep over her and bring that terrible grip of her heart which seemed almost like a piercing dagger. She must control her feelings. She would have need of a heart strong and active for her work. She must not let it break down for lack of self-control. She had heard that great trouble would bring on heart disease. She would not let it come to her. Her will should lay an iron hand upon her feelings and keep her laughing and bright in spite of the shadow that lurked just over her head. She would force her body to perform all the physical part of being glad. It might be there was something in the mind cure. She had read of such things. She would try it. Not try, she would *make* it succeed. Steadily on she went around that array again, growing interested as she progressed, putting down in a little notebook, items to be remembered, relating to certain things she might do with old material or with her ability to embroider and sew.

She ignored many showy wax ladies in imported attire as being out of keeping with her needs. There was one sentence in her mentor's letter she had not forgotten: "for you know there is proportion in everything." It should never be said of her that she was inappropriately dressed for her position. Everything should be quiet and yet — and yet — cunning planner — she meant to have the distinguished, inimitable something about her clothes that would mark the woman of good taste in the art of dressing well, and give a dim idea of studied plainness which every well-dressed woman knows is purchased at far greater price than the more showy garment. Once she paused beside a lovely creation of point lace whose pattern was faintly outlined in the tiniest possible ruched ribbon of pale pink, like a dream of roses in winter frost, and examined the pattern, while the wax-cheeked bridesmaid who wore it graciously held out a wilderness of pink roses before her unnoticing eyes, and surveyed her staringly from under her thick auburn eyelashes. She studied the lace carefully and wondered if she could achieve its like for the garnishing of one of her gowns with a collar and handkerchief of fine point she possessed, and some of that delicate ribbon work. How effective it would be on black!

Weary at last of the long strain she turned to go back. She would just see that gray suit again and be sure how the white chiffon was arranged under the gray and silver lattice and the exact shade of the canary colored breast knot of soft satin, and then she would go home for that day. She was too tired to do another thing, and really she had accomplished much. She must have a sample of her own gray silk before she could get the outer material. What a blessing that the gray silk waist fitted her so beautifully. All the better that it was plain. It would make a most delightful lining. Of course the skirt must be remodeled but that would not be difficult with a good pattern. She could do the underpart all herself and not have a dressmaker till she was ready for the outside. Ah! perhaps she might even accomplish this one gown alone entirely. She was sure she could do all the particular parts if she gave herself up to it, and that would leave more money to pay for the other things, for the dressmaker would have much to do and she must go to a very good one to have her linings made, and perhaps to a tailor for some things. She must economize all she could.

Thinking which she arrived before the gray gown.

Then from above her, somewhere on another floor of the great store and floating down through the open rotunda, came soft, sweet, swelling music, like angelic voices from afar.

It seemed to come nearer and surround her being and float about her naked soul and bathe her in its restfulness.

In a distant gallery there was some newly invented instrument, by whose mechanism a thousand harps and voices seemed to be set free at once and soar aloft in blended harmony.

The melody was familiar. It had been dear to her when it first came out. She knew the words. Each note spoke to her heart now. It had grown tiresomely familiar during her stay in this part of the world, by the constant grinding of it out by the poor wheezy street pianos and hand-organs, as if a common barnyard fowl should attempt the thrush's roundelay. But now the song seemed to come to her with new significance.

> Last night I lay a sleeping,
>   There came a dream so fair,
> I saw the Holy City
>   Beside the temple there,
> I heard the children singing

> And ever as they sang
> Methought the voice of angels
> From heaven in answer rang,
> Jerusalem, Jerusalem.

The burdened woman looked up, startled suddenly from her intricate busy plans for earth, realized almost with a sort of mingled horror and longing that there was another world than this. Would what she did now and here affect her happiness there? Would these poor paltry dressed count? Would her trouble be over ever?

Her throat choked up and she stood leaning against the glass case unheeding the people who passed and looked curiously at her absorbed, listening face.

When the music was over she went home.

Chapter 4
Her Rival Disclosed

That night she dreamed a single dream the whole night through. The scene reminded her of the background of some posters. There was a sky of clearly defined blotches of inky blue and dead white, with strange angels outined against it. They seemed to be constantly warning her against something, at command of heavenly music that floated above, now soft, now clearer, as the need became greater. And she below, was striving to obey, with anguish in her soul. Gradually the face of her husband appeared a little way off, smiling, glad, gay. He was talking with a throng of beautiful women and evil men. Then it became clear that the danger was to him, and the angels were bidding her save him.

With all her soul dragging her down in heaviness she sought to get nearer to him and to attract his attention, but his expressive eyes rested on all faces but hers. He did not see, or would not recongize her. Her soul longed for one loving smile such as he used to give her in the old days when they were in a company of friends and could not speak save with their eyes. But now he could not look. He seemed to be another being and yet the same. At last she could lay her hand upon his and then she thought he surely would look, and she poured out pleading words into his ear of warning and entreaty. But he shook her off with anger, passed on from her grasp, and with a cry which seemed to rend her heart she awoke to live the whole scene over again.

Out from a night thus spent she went to her task, with white face and set lips. That gray dress should be bought to-day and begun.

She wasted no time in looking that morning, But as she sat waiting at the counter for a package which she wished to take home with her, a woman, tall and elegantly gowned, moved slowly down the aisle and stopped close beside her to examine an exquisite piece of lace that was being displayed.

Some sudden memory made Mrs. Winthrop look up at her face, and there she saw before her the one who had sat beside her husband in the park but a few days before.

Her heart fairly stood still to think that that woman was beside her. A great wave of hate and horror rolled over her and threatened for a moment to take away her consciousness, but her self-control that morning was tremendous, and she compelled her eyes to look steadily at the one who had won her husband from her, perhaps, but who, after all, was but a woman, another like herself. She would see what it was that had attracted. Oh, if she could but find out who she was!

And as if in answer to her wish came a smiling saleswoman, saying: "Good morning, Mrs. Sylvester. Is any one waiting upon you?"

Miriam, quietly waiting for her package, sat watching her supposed rival as she tumbled the laces about ruthlessly as though their yards were priced in pennies instead of dollars, and at last ordered home two pieces that she might the better decide which suited her. As she moved away the smiling saleswoman said, "Let me see; the number is 1820 is it not? I cannot remember anything this morning," and the proud lady bent her head and smiled condescendingly in reply and then swept by and was gone.

Mrs. Winthrop turned feverish eyes to the busy pencil that was rapidly writing down the address and noted carefully the name of the fashionble square where Mrs. Sylvester lived. Then she gathered up her packages and started home, her knees trembling under her as she walked and a quiver ran through her as if she had faced her worst foe.

Suddenly she stopped in the street and a light broke over her face. There was a rift, just a little rift in the dark clouds over her head. And now she knew that down deep in her heart she had harbored a fear which she would not let be put into thoughts even, that this woman, this enemy of hers, this Mrs. Sylvester, was on the wide ocean. Nay, even that she might be in the same ship with her own husband, Claude. Now that she knew she was not she saw the absurdity of the idea. That a woman who calmly purchased such costly lace would give up her great orbit for the sake of a comparatively poor man was ridiculous. Still, there were women who liked to play with hearts, and who took care never to play the game too long with any one. And after all, what mattered it whether she played it well or ill, so long as the other player had been willing. Ah! That was the hard part. Her Claude was hers no longer. He had given another woman the light of his eyes, and his wife's heart was breaking. The tiny gleam of light in the clouds above closed blank and dull once more and she went on her way with a tumult of feelings running riot in her breast.

An idea came to her as she took her way home which startled her with its daring. What if she should try to use this very woman to help against herself? How could she do it? What sort of woman was she? What if she should invite her to one of these little teas for which she was preparing? What if she should? What if she *should?* Then would she not be going forth to meet Goliath the Great with her little sling and stones?

But the thought could not be got rid of. Thereafter every gown she planned, every fabric she bought or fashioned, every arrangement of the little home was done as under the surveillance of the haughty, beautiful woman with the scornful mouth and unscrupulous eyes.

The days that followed were weary ones, scarce begun ere ended, it seemed to the poor woman who was toiling to achieve a multiplicity of works before a certain time. She worked with breathless energy, never daring to stop and rest lest she should give up and faint beneath the load, or lest the tragedy of her life should wreck her mind.

Letters came from her husband as he went from place to place. A few directions were given her about matters of business, but they always seemed to be written in haste. Her fingers trembled when she opened them and her heart grew colder at each one she read. He complained of not receiving her letters and she set her lips grimly, which ill became the softly rounded lines of mouth and chin. She had written none, nor would she. The questions he asked might be answered when he came. They seemed to be of moment to him, to her they were as trifles. The questions he did *not* ask were a whole volume of the tragedy she was living. The fact that he did not think or care to ask them made her excuse for not writing; though her heart was sometimes bursting with the words she would send him, still she restrained herself. It was not time yet. She must bide and work and be ready when the moment came.

A goodly array of "soft apparel" was gathering in her wardrobe. Under constant supervision the housemaid was growing silent and dextrous in the matter of waiting upon doors and tables. She wondered in her heart why her mistress had suddenly grown so punctilious about the wearing of caps and aprons and a silver tray for the cards.

There were various changes made in the house. The amount of money spent was not large but the changes were an improvement. A carpenter and an upholsterer for a few hours, with some yards of effective material, a good supply of paint and an artistic eye had really metamorphosed the home into a charming spot. Mrs. Winthrop visited noted decorators, and wandered with attentive eye through the model rooms in housefurnishing establishments until she was well versed in the effects aimed at by the highest artists in that line. She had faithfully followed the advice of her magazine to study her rooms from different points of view and make them express something beautiful from every one, and the effect was really lovely, although to her it spoke of but one thing — her great sorrow. There was nothing gaudy or imposing about the pleasant little house. All was in keeping with its surroundings, but there was not a spot that did not suggest restfulness, brightness, a cheery place in which to chat, an inviting nook to read a book. She certainly had succeeded beyond her highest hopes in making her home an attractive one to the guests she proposed to bring there, but the wonder was that she had succeeded when the real feelings in her heart had been anything but restfulness and peace and joy, the elements of a true home.

And then came the question of guests. Ah, those guests. Who were they to be? It had seemed easy to get into society by the purchase of a few gowns and the arrangement of her house, with the sending out of the mysterious bits of white pasteboard which meant so much in society. But first, who was society, the society into which she must get to win her point? And how was she to find out? Her husband could tell her. Of course he knew all about it, but it would not do to ask him. If she had done as he wished when they were first married and gone hither and yon and entertained, all might have been different. Perhaps she would have held her own with him if she had done so. Doubtless their money would have been inadequate for such a life, but then too, doubtless many things would have been different. It was too late to think of what might have been. It was too late to go to her husband for help to undo her past. She must accomplish her task alone.

Then she sat down with determined mien to surmount this new difficulty in her path. She thought over the list of her acquaintances. There was just one person, and she could scarce be called an acquaintance, upon whose presence she was determined, if it was possible to compass it, and that person was Mrs. Sylvester. What sort of woman she was, how she would accept society — such society as Mrs. Claude Winthop could offer her — and how society — the kind of society that was Mrs. Winthrop's ideal — would accept Mrs. Sylvester, were questions that forced themselves upon her thoughts continually and which she compelled herself to put away. She could not answer them. It was better for her that they were not answered, for have Mrs. Sylvester she would, and after all, when danger and chance of mistake were on every hand in this unknown way, what mattered a few little questions like that? She had nothing to lose and everything to gain. Therefore Mrs. Sylvester's name and address, carefully remembered, headed the list when she set herself to make it out.

Then there were her neighbors. She thought them carefully over. Not one of them was what she could call a society woman, for theirs was not a fashionable street. There was the woman across the way who slapped her baby and the woman on her right who wore such a horrible bonnet and the one on her left who borrowed butter and sugar and eggs over the back fence and talked bad English and called her husband always "He." The would-be hostess shivered and let her mind travel rapidly up the street and down again on the other side, and decided that there was only one eligible neighbor on it and she a quiet, sweet-faced, elderly woman, who dressed plainly and lived alone with a niece, a pretty girl whose tasteful fingers allowed her always to be dressed well. With a defiant thought toward Mrs. Sylvester and a remembrance that her husband had once said they were the only really intellectual people on the street, she wrote down the name of the Winslows.

Then she bit her pencil and thought again. There were the ladies of the church who had called upon her when she first moved to that place several years ago, and who had continued to call at long intervals apparently from a sense of duty. They were not society people, but were wealthy and dressed well and would do her no discredit. She certainly owed them a social debt if she owed it to any one in the whole city. One after another she wrote their names hesitatingly, her face troubled meanwhile. These were not the kind of people who could help her much in what she had to do. There were others in the church where they had gone, regularly at first and then more seldom, till now they scarcely went at all. It was a large church and fashionable. Yes, there were society people in it. Religion was fashionable sometimes. She had met a few, but would she dare invite such people on so slight acquaintance? Mrs. Sylvester was different. She was to be invited anyway. But these others. There were the Lymans and the Whartons and the Bidwells and a dozen other families. Stay, did not her magazine help her there? It suggested that she attend some of the charities of her church. Perhaps there she would become better acquainted. But what were they and how was she to find out? She must go to church and discover.

She leaned wearily back in her chair and drew her hands nervously across her eyes. It was Saturday evening, and she had been feeling thankful that it was a disgrace to sew on the Sabbath and she could have a little time to rest, but here came another duty looming up for that day also. There was no help for it, however. She saw that she must go and begin to get acquainted.

Back flew her pencil to her paper and down went the names of the best families in her church, with an inward resolve to come home from the service the next day with an introduction to some of them, if it were a possible thing, and a list of all the meetings of the church at which she would be likely to meet them. Poor little woman. She did not know how few, how pitifully few, of these best families attended the diffeent meetings of the church. Well for her that she did not, for she counted much on those "charities" that she was to take up for bringing her friends, and one more straw that night might have broken her down, she was so near to discouragement.

There came a memory now of men her husband called great, men he had met and some he wished to meet. She wrote their names all down, wondering gravely if there was any way in which she could get to know them well enough to invite them to her home. One in particular, a man well known in political circles and whose speeches in the United States House of Representatives had become famous. She suddenly remembered a much-neglected cousin of her mother's living in another part of the city who had an intimate acquaintance with this great man, being an old schoolmate of his sister. Perhaps she could help. At any rate she must be invited. Her cheek crimsoned at the thought that she had been forgotten, and she drew her breath quickly as she wondered what Aunt Katherine would think of Mrs. Sylvester.

Then there were a few literary people well known to Aunt Katherine. Down went their names and up came Aunt Katherine in her niece's estimation as her heart began to lighten. Counting up, she saw she had a goodly list if — that great if — if they all came.

The little cuckoo clock that had been a cherished wedding gift came out and sang twelve times in the hallway, and Mrs. Winthrop, remembering with a sigh the hour of church and that morning was already upon her, put the list in her desk and went to bed, wondering as she closed her aching eyes if the days would ever be over when all this horror would be a thing of the past and she could lie down in quietness and peace and truly rest.

Chapter 5
An Unexpected Service

Mrs. Winthrop had hurried to church late and seated herself a little flurried over a new gown she wore, which seemed to her not to fit just right. She was anxious to put on her bravest front before the world in this her first approach for its favor. She bowed her head in reverent attitude, but her mind was still intent upon the problem which had occupied it on the way to church — whether she could achieve the making of a certain gown described in her last fashion magazine without any more help than the picture and her own wits. She raised her head and sat back in her seat as the text was announced:

"See, saith he, that thou make all things according to the pattern shewed to thee in the mount."

The words startled her. They could not have sounded to her soul more loudly if they had been, "See that thou make all things according to the patterns showed to thee in the fashion magazine."

Indeed, when the sentence first reached her ear, her overstrained imagination fancied the preacher was speaking to her, had read her thought, and was about to administer a reproof. Her color rose and she glanced nervously about.

But there was on every face about her a well bred apathy that betokened perfect trust in the ability of the speaker to perform his part of the services without disturbing them.

Mrs. Winthrop tried now to center her mind on what was being said. Perhaps she had mistaken his words and her own silly brain had falsified the text to suit what was in her mind.

When a third time came the words: "See . . . that thou make all things according to the pattern shewed to thee in the mount!" it began to seem an awful sentence, though without any very distinct meaning.

The sermon which followed was eloquent and learned. There was an elaborate description of the tabernacle, and the main point of the sermon, if point there might be said to be, was an appeal for certain styles of church architecture. But of all this Mrs. Claude Winthrop heard not a word, except it might have been the name of Moses.

In her younger days she had been taught the Bible. She knew in a general way that "the mount" was something holy. She did not wait to puzzle her brain about Moses in the mount nor wonder what it was he had been given a pattern of. She might have recalled it if she had tried. But instead she simply took the text as spoken to her. There had been something unearthly, almost uncanny, to her weary brain in the way the words had been said out of the stillness that came after the singing had ceased. In her uneasy state of mind it was brought home to her how far from any patterns given in any mounts had been the things that she had made of late.

Following close upon the benediction came the bewilderment of a familiar greeting. Mrs. Winthrop had been so beset by her thoughts during the sermon that she had thus far lost sight of her object in coming to church that morning. True, she grasped in her hand, as if it were something precious, the church calendar containing the announcements of all meetings of the church to be held that week, but she had forgotten to look out among the congregation those who might help in her schemes. Therefore she stood in amazement at the torrent of words spoken by the young girl who had sat in the seat before her. She knew that the girl's name was Celia Lyman and that her mother belonged to an exclusive set of people. She had barely a speaking acquaintance with Mrs. Lyman, and had never felt that she would be likely to recognize her outside of the church.

"I beg your pardon," the sweet voice said, while a detaining gloved hand was laid gently on Miriam's arm, "but mamma told me to be sure and give you a message. She was unable to get out this morning. She has one of her miserable headaches, and is all worn out. But she wanted me to tell you that she was anxious to have you come to our house Thursday to the *musicale*. She supposed she had sent you an invitation with the rest, but this morning she found it had slipped down behind her writing desk against the wall. She remembers laying it out for Miss Faulkes to look up your street and number, for mamma had quite forgotten it — she never remembers such things — but there it lay with only your name on it. And now Miss Faulkes says she couldn't find your address and forgot to speak to mamma about it. She is becoming careless about things. So as it was so late and mamma could not find the paper with your address she thought maybe you would just take the invitation informally this time, for there is to be some really fine music which mamma is sure you will enjoy. You won't mind this once, will you?" and a pair of violet eyes searched her face as if the matter were of great moment.

Mrs. Winthrop endeavored to veil her amazement and murmured her thanks, saying that the manner of the invitation did not matter, and was rewarded by a most ravishing smile.

"Then you'll be sure to come. Four to six is the hour. Oh, and I had almost forgotten, mamma told me to be sure to get your street and number so it would be on hand for another time of need," with a dainty silver pencil and a silver mounted memoranda was lifted from a collection of small nothings that hung on tiny chains at her belt, while the lovely eyes were lifted to her face inquiringly.

Mrs. Winthrop was conscious of a slight lifting of Miss Celia's eyebrows as she repeated the street and number after her and wrote, and was there a shadow of surprise in her voice? It was not a fashionable locality, and Miriam Winthrop suddenly saw a new difficulty in her way.

Then she turned to go down the aisle and bowed here and there mechanically, scarcely knowing whom she met. How strange, how very strange, that Mrs. Lyman, after almost two years of utterly ignoring her since they had first met, should suddenly invite her to her home and her wonderful *musicales,* for their fame had reached even her ears, stranger almost though she was. It must be that a Higher Power was enlisted to help her to-day, for here was opening to her the very door the key of which she had despaired of finding. A superstitious feeling that the text was meant for her in some way as a warning, kept clinging to her, and made her go to her own room as soon as she had reached home, and after bolting her door kneel down and whisper a few words that were meant for a sort of prayer, an attempt to placate some unseen Ruler in whom she believed with a sort of nursery-fairy-tale credulity.

In the meantime Miss Celis Lyman was detailing her encounter to her mother.

"Yes, I saw Mrs. Preston, mamma, only I completely forgot her name when church was out, but I just turned around and talked hard, and I don't think she noticed in the least that I didn't speak it. I knew her at once, because she was so sweetly gowned. There were three other ladies in the seat behind us, but they were all strangers. There seemed to be lots of strangers there to-day; we had a man in our own pew. I told her all you said, and put a nice little compliment about her being so fond of music, though I couldn't quite remember whether you said that or not, but it pleased her awfully for I saw her cheeks get as pink as roses. She said it didn't matter in the least about the invitation and she would be so glad to come, So now you needn't worry another bit about that lazy Miss Faulkes. I would dismiss her if I were you."

"Did you get Mrs. Preston's address, Celia?" asked the mother from her luxurious couch; "you know I must call upon her if possible before the *musicale.* She is a stranger and a new-comer, and I wish to show her some attention on account of her father knowing your grandfather so well.''

"Yes, mamma, I did remember it, though it was just a hairbreadth escape. I had to call her back to get it. You know I never can remember more than one thing at once; but really I deserve a good deal of credit, for I was dying to get over to the other side of the church to speak to Margaret Langdon before she got away. She is expecting her cousin home from Europe soon, you know, and I wanted to make sure he would be in time for Christobel's house party, because if he isn't I'm not going to accept, for there isn't another man going that I care a cent about except Ralph Jackson, and he's so overpoweringly engaged, there is no comfort for any other girl now in him. Let me see, where did I write that address.''

The sweet voice tinkled on like a babbling of some useless little brook.

"Oh, here it is, mamma, Hazel Avenue — 1515 Hazel Avenue. Say, mamma, isn't it rather queer for a Preston to live on Hazel Avenue? Are they poor? Her gown did not look like it. I should say it was imported. No one but a master-hand could have put those little touches to her costume.''

Mrs. Lyman sat up regardless of her pillows that slipped to the floor.

"Hazel Avenue! Are you *sure,* Celia! You are so careless. Perhaps you have some other address mixed with it.''

"No, mamma, I'm sure this time for I said it over after her, and I remember thinking it was a very dull part of town for that dress she wore to have come from.''

"Celia, are you sure you got the right woman?''

"Sure, *perfectly* sure, mamma. I studied her sidewise during the closing hymn, for she didn't sit directly behind me. You said she had brown eyes and hair, and anyway, I remember seeing her in the seat before. I'm sure it was the right woman. Now quiet down, mamma; if it had not been the right one she would surely have told me, wouldn't she? She was the perfect pink of refinement in manner and dress.''

"Well, I suppose she would," said the mother, as her daughter rearranged the pillows for her, "but you are very careless for a girl of your age, and I should have to call upon her to make sure it is all right. There is really no telling what you may have said to her, after all. And it does seem queer to invite some one from Hazel Avenue.''

The house on Hazel Avenue which the Winthrops occupied had been just like all the rest on that street until three weeks before. One of Miriam's first moves toward a new way of living had been to have a conference with their landlord, the result of which had been that he agreed to make certain changes if she would make certain other changes. She had carefully considered and inquired the cost before she began and had put the matter in immediate operation as soon as she had the landlord's permission. A little carpenter work and painting, and some large panes of plate glass, and the house was transformed outwardly as well as inwardly. The neighbors regarded the curved bay window that occupied the place of the former two common windows with envy. A new front door and tiled vestibule had taken the place of their dingy predecessors, and a queer little odd-shaped window with leaded panes over the front door broke the straight, solemn line of the monotonous row, making an altogether pretty and dainty looking abiding-place.

The carpenter and painter had finished their work but the day before, and Miriam carefully arranged the filmy curtains and graceful palm branches, and was hovering over a newly filled window box in the second story curved bay window, which was aglow with bright blossoms and rich greenery, when she saw a carriage turn into Hazel Avenue from Fifteenth Street and stop before her door.

She did not wait to see who it was, but slipped to her bedroom, where lay on her bed a pretty house gown just finished, all but a few stray hooks which were waiting to be put on. It was the work of but a moment to slip into it, and she blessed the fates that had made her leave it there close at hand. She had tried it on but an hour before and so felt sure that it looked all right, and when her wondering but demure handmaid came to her door with the silver tray bearing Mrs. Lyman's card she found her mistress already fastening the waist of her gown and quite calm outwardly, although quaking inwardly. She was about to make her first entrance into real society, a genuine call from a society woman, and through no effort of her own. She rejoiced in that fact.

"Isn't it sweet here?" murmured Celia, who had begged to come along because she had fallen in love with the supposed Mrs. Preston.

"Very," said her mother with a relieved air, "quite modest and unassuming, but all that is required," and she settled back to await the coming of her hostess.

Miriam trembled as she crossed the little hall and wondered if she would be able to imitate the fashionable handclasp of the day which she had observed of late and had feared to attempt, but she came forward quite naturally in spite of her trepidation and welcomed her caller graciously. There was less assurance in Mrs. Lyman's manner than she had expected. In fact that lady seemed almost ill at ease as she rose to meet her, and she turned with relief to the fair-haired daughter who immediately began to gush about the house which she called "sweet."

Mrs. Winthrop at once spoke of the kindness of Mrs. Lyman in inviting her to the *musicale,* expressing her delight in fine music, and an indescribable look came over Mrs. Lyman's face, while Miss Celia began to say something about all the Prestons being so fond of music, which her mother immediately drowned by plunging wildly into a conversation about something as far from music as she could think of.

It was a rather interesting call, altogether considered. The hostess felt herself to be on trial and was therefore not quite natural. The caller too was evidently somewhat distraught. Her daughter could scarcely wait until they were out at the carriage before asking her what was the matter. But Mrs. Lyman paused at the very threshold, a sudden thought reminding her that she did not know the name of this guest-to-be of hers.

"Is Mr. — that is, is your husband at home now?" She asked it hesitatingly, and Miriam, because of her tragic thought of her husband, felt herself flushing to the roots of her hair.

She made a great effort to control herself, for she knew she was blushing, but answered quietly enough:

"No. Mr. Winthrop has been obliged to go abroad on business. I am expecting him home soon."

"Ah, indeed. Then you must be lonely," murmured the caller, turning satisfied to go down the steps.

"Winthrop, Winthrop? Where have I heard that name? I know her face and I think I can recall his, but who are they? Celia, my child, into what have you led me?"

By this time the young lady had begun to suspect what was wrong, but she was not struck with the serious side. Instead she burst into a peal of laughter, whereat her mother laid a reproving hand upon her mouth.

Hush, Celia, she will hear you," she said, and looked anxiously back at the little house fast vanishing from sight through the carriage window. "It really isn't so bad a house and she seems refined. I suppose it can't be helped now."

"And why should it?" said Miss Celia, sobering down. "She is perfectly lovely and had the sweetest little home. What does it matter who they are if they are nice, I would like to know? She looks as if she was perfectly happy. I should just enjoy such cozy love-in-a-cottage as that. I saw the dearest baby in white in the maid's arms up at that pretty window behind the flowers. I'm going to take her up. I don't care who she is and I don't see why you care. Aren't you 'who' enough yourself without bothering about other folks? It can't hurt you any, mamma, if her grandfather didn't know yours."

"Celia," said her mother severely, "you are very young and know very little of the world."

Chapter 6
The Campaign Opened

Altogether the day seemed slightly brighter to Miriam Winthrop than any that had preceded it since her trouble fell upon her. She had not failed at the first step. Marvelous help had come to her. It was a good omen. Unconsciously she took on a somewhat more cheerful attitude. It was not that the way was any less dark, but far ahead of her she thought she caught a glimmer of hope. It might fade as she approached, but it was there now and to it she would go.

She set her armor in array, and looking it over decided which bravery to wear to the *musicale*. Then as the shades of evening dulled the lustrous folds of silk and satin, she hung them all away and went to the nursery. She had been so weary that she had put aside her motherly duties often, and now she heard the baby's voice pleading for a story. Her heart pierced her that she had neglected her darling little one, and she came swiftly and took her from the nurse and in the old-time way snuggled the curly head in her arms and began to rock.

The baby looked up with a joyous smile and never a reproach.

"Oh, 'oo dear, pitty itty mommmie. I so glad oo tummed. Sing me pitty song, mommie, sing poppie's song."

She almost stopped rocking, and a choking came into her throat. She could not sing that. It was a song she had woven out of her own happy heart when her first baby was in her arms, and night after night she would lull her to sleep, their little Pearl, their oldest child, while Claude lay on the sofa nearby in the gloaming and listened, telling her it was the sweetest music earth could hold for him. The song had been sung to the other children and Claude had loved it until the children had come to call it "Papa's song." She thought of those happy, happy days, and the ray of hope that had dawned, vanished and left her in darkness once more. To think that he, after his devotion to her, could ever look like that into another woman's eyes! How could she take him back and forgive him, even if she succeeded in winning him once more to herself? It must be done for the children's sake and for the world's view, but how for her own heart's sake could there ever be any hope.?

But the baby was pleading and the tears must be choked back. She would not grieve the little one unnecessarily.

"Mamma will sing 'Little Bo-Peep,' " she answered as brightly as her voice could compass.

"No, no; baby want poppie's song; mommie sing poppie's song." She was crying now, with her tender puckered little lips held up irresistibly sweet. How could she refuse? After all, 'twas no harder than all the rest she must bear and do.

She caught her voice through the tears in her throat and began:

> The birdies have tucked their heads under their wings
> And nestled down closely, the dear little things
> And my dear birdie is here in her nest,
> With her head nestled close on her own mother's breast.
>
> The wind whispers soft sleepy songs to the roses,
> And kisses the buds on the tips of their noses;
> Shall I sing a sleepy song soft to my sweet,
> And kiss the pink toes on her dainty wee feet?
>
> The butterflies folded their silver gauze wings,
> And now sweetly sleep with all fluttering things.
> Will you fold your paddies, my dear little girl,
> And rest your tired footies, my precious wee pearl?
>
> The violet's closed its pretty blue eye
> That has gazed all day long at the clear summer sky,
> Now droop the dark lashes over your eyes,
> They are weary with holding great looks of surprise.
>
> The flower bells have dropped their tired little heads,
> And laid themselves down in their soft mossy beds,
> Your golden head droops and your eyes are shut tight,
> Shall I lay you down sweet on your pillow so white?

She crooned the song to a little tune that had woven itself out of the years of her singing it, and seemed to fit the words as no other melody could do, and the sleepy little child in her arms nestled closer and closer, folding her hands and closing her eyes as the song went on, until with the last words the soft regular breathing told the mother the baby was truly asleep. Still she sat and held her, humming the melody, not daring to stop so soon lest she should waken, and trying to make real again the dear days when she had sat happily and sung thus. But the dark rolling of deep waters was between her and her husband, and a darker and more awful roll of trouble separated them still farther from one another.

The other two children, sitting in the wide window seat, had dropped their books as the light faded too much for them to see, and sat listening to the song. Pearl crept to her mother's side, slipped her soft little hand inside her mother's and laid her head against her lap.

"Oh, mamma," said Carroll from the window in a whisper that tried to be soft for the baby's sake, "when will our father come back? It seems as if he had been gone for years. Will he ever come back?"

And the poor mother's heart echoed the yearning cry, "Will he ever come back?"

The days that followed were filled with toil, and plans developed rapidly now, for hourly Miriam was growing wiser in the ways of the world. The *musicale* was a great help to her, for while she knew few present and kept herself unobtrusively in the background, she had good opportunity to take notes. Mentally she went over her first list of her own teas and marked off some and put down others. She began to see possibilities of asking many of these others. The young girl, Celia, fluttered over to her and introduced her here and there, and with an enthusiasm characteristic of a young girl expressed her intention of coming to see the baby. Before she drifted away she had made an early appointment to call on Baby Celia, being delighted that they bore the same name. As Miriam Winthrop watched her move gracefully from this group to that and smile and say a pleasant word she saw the possibility of help in that girl and resolved to follow it up.

The days that followed the *musicale* opened up a new world for Miriam Winthrop. She began to grow in the good graces of many people whom she might not have met if she had not first been invited to the Lymans'.

Meantime letters from her husband announced positively that he would be at home at a certain time, now very near at hand, and Miriam in all haste gathered her forces and went over her visiting list. The list was very different now from the one she had first made out in her ignorance. Only one name had she blindly clung to throughout, which strict adherence to society etiquette would have ruled out for the present, at least, because of her being an entire stranger, and that was the name of the woman who headed her list. Just why she wanted her there she herself could not understand, but she felt as if she must meet her to begin the battle. With fearful heart and strong purpose that never once wavered, she sent out her cards.

There would be plenty of time for her husband to understand the new state of things after he reached home and no possibility of his upsetting her plans if the invitations were already out when he returned. The fashion magazine had made it plain that her husband must be in evidence. Her own heart made it plainer that he must witness the fray from beginning to end if he was to be won over.

The invitations out, she set about her preparations for the day, which in general had been made long ago, but which she now planned out in every minute detail, so that the domestic wheels should move smoothly without the possibility of a hitch at the trying time.

She invited Miss Lyman and one or two other young people to lunch informally and practiced on them without their knowledge. She sent the maid with Pearl to a child's party and bade her keep her eyes and ears open. The maid returned demure and said little, but showed that she had learned several lessons. Miriam began to feel that she could afford to rest and store up strength for the day of the first reception, when a new anxiety rose. Another letter from her husband announced that he would be delayed several days later than he had supposed and would now reach home on the day, the *very day,* of her first tea. What if he should be delayed? What if he should not come until afterward? How miserably she had planned! How her work would all be for naught! She foresaw in a flash the dreary anxiety of the day, of awaiting his arrival till the hour, of the having to dress and meet the people with her mind upon his arrival. And then what would he think? He might be angry to come home and find the house full of guests. There was no telling in these days what attitude he might take toward her. She drew a sign of relief as she remembered that whatever he felt toward her he would veil till their guests had gone.

Just as she had foreseen it came to pass.

The simple flower decorations were all in place just where they would look the most natural and effective, the rooms were in perfect readiness for the guests. The maid attired in black with cap and cuffs and apron, the children disposed of in quietness for the afternoon, the refreshments at hand and the hostess exquisitely gowned.

And yet Claude Winthrop had not arrived. His wife looked anxiously from the window now and again. She had fortunately forgotten to wonder what he would say to the changed appearance of the outside of the house. She was only anxious to get him upstairs and ready for the company. She surveyed herself in a full-length mirror. Her cheeks were flushed with the unusual excitement, and her eyes almost feverishly bright. The gown was becoming, fitted her perfectly, and was worn with an air of perfect ease that did not convey the idea of its being an unusual thing for the wearer to be thus dressed. It may have been the one great absorbing thought that kept all others out, that made this possible, for she was naturally a timid woman, shrinking into herself and becoming painfully self-conscious at times in the presence of strangers. But love had transformed her into another being for the time. Not all the worldly wisdom of society, not all the habits of generations could present a better front than this simple unassuming ease which love and a question of life and death had made it possible for her to wear.

She glanced at her watch. Five minutes to the hour. She must be ready now. Some one might come at any minute. What if no one should come! For a moment she stood still at the thought of such dumb defeat. But no! She must not think of such a thing. Time enough for that trouble if it should come. She must go down and see if the rooms were just right. With haste she laid out her husband's clothes on the bed in the nursery, and gave orders that he be told at once where to find them when he came in. Then she heard the sound of carriage wheels and a panic lest he had come, and she would have to face him with all that was unspoken in her heart, she fled to the parlor.

It was only Celia Lyman, who had promised to help her pour tea, and who had arrived early and chattered gleefully. She was young yet and looked at everything in a delightfully childish manner. She condoned with her hostess over the absence of her husband, and said ten times that he would be sure to get there soon, and she fluttered from one corner to another and called the rooms "perfectly fine" and "dear," and a hundred other adjectives her enthusiastic heart suggested, and told Miriam that she looked as sweet as a girl and that her husband would "just have to kiss her" when he got there, right before them all, she was so beautiful. Miriam's cheeks glowed for an instant over this approval. She cared not a straw whether Celia Lyman admired her, but she cared with her whole soul what her husband thought of her. In fact, she had come to feel that the whole matter depended largely upon the first impression, and now she began to think that it was a good thing he should have arrived too late for them to have any talk over the matter. The transformation would thus be the greater — if only he came in time to see it at all.

The callers began to drop in by ones and twos. They really came. Miriam found herself wondering why they had cared to come and if they were surprised that she had dared ask them, but they seemed quite pleased and decorously unsurprised over the lovely spot when they got there. They lingered too, and declared she had been unkind not to have let them come before, and numerous pretty compliments. There was plenty to be done. Miriam was not used to the position of hostess. It taxed her brain to keep track of her guests and she felt that she ought to have given more attention to this one and that. She almost forgot about her husband's non-appearance for a new minutes, until the maid approached and said in low tones:

"Mr. Winthrop is here, ma'am, and says he will be down in a few minutes."

After that her heart thumped painfully and all sorts of questions began to bestir themselves. How had he taken it? What would he think of her and the house, and the people? She cast a hurried glance about and felt satisfied with those who had come. There were others — there was one other — who had not yet arrived, who might come — ah! She caught her breath with one of those quick signs that told of high tension in the nerves and which had become habitual with her of late. Ah! then would come the crucial moment!

At that instant an elegant carriage had stopped before the door, a coachman and footman in livery mounted guard. The footman opened the carriage door, and altogether overawed the demure maid at the door whose education had not as yet included footmen, and a tall and beautiful woman in costly apparel stepped curiously into the house.

Chapter 7
A Challenge To The Enemy

The hostess had been trembling but a moment before at thoughts of the possibilities of the next few minutes. But when the arrival paused in the doorway of the pretty reception room with eye-brows slightly uplifted, and glanced about superciliously as if to take in the entire situation, new strength seemed to come to her. All the puzzling questions that had troubled her for the past weeks vanished. She forgot that the woman who was entering the room was an entire stranger to her, that she had dared to invite her without introduction or the usual formalities of calling. Her mind bravely rose above the thought of broken laws of etiquette and ignored everything but the mere fact that the woman was here, in spite of it all. What motives had brought her were not her concern now. That she had chosen to come to the house of an obscure stranger was enough. There might be, there doubtless were, curiosity, condescension, amusement — and worst of all, an interest in the house of Winthrop — mingled together as an incentive. Nevertheless she had accepted the challenge and was here.

As though she had been all her life accustomed to such functions the hostess calmly finished her sentence to the fine, erect, white-haired old lady of undoubted respectability to whom she was talking. It was a satisfaction to her afterward that Mrs. Sylvester had entered just at the moment when Mrs. Carroll stood by her side. The visitor would see that her other friends were not altogether unknown.

Then glancing up as though she had just become aware of the new arrival, she came forward a step to greet her, unconsciously assuming a graceful, condescending manner. She wondered why her heart did not palpitate and why stumbling apologies did not frame themselves on her lips. But no! she seemed not to be herself.

"So glad you could come," she said graciously, and quite as if she had been saying those things for half a century, and not a hint of what was running through her mind, "I wonder *why* you came? I wonder why you *came?*"

The caller viewed the hostess as Goliath might have looked at David, and so well was the role assumed that she could not decide whether Mrs. Winthrop was wholly innocent or wholly subtle.

Others arrived just then, Mrs. Winthrop was obliged to turn to greet them. Therefore she was enabled to turn away without being either embarrassed or effusive. Mrs. Sylvester drifted a little farther away speaking to one or two whom she knew slightly. As a whole the assembled company were not intimates of Mrs. Sylvester's. She still wore a half-amused, half-curious expression, and kept her eyes fixed upon the hostess, even while talking with others. She studied her face, the becoming arrangement of the soft hair on the shapely head, then the dress, and a look of surprise grew in her eyes.

All these expressions were noted by another onlooker who had not yet entered the room.

Claude Winthrop had stopped before his own door and looked up at the house in bewilderment. What had happened since he left? The street was surely the right one. He glanced across to make sure. Yes, there were the familiar landmarks. Had Miriam moved away? Strange. Then the door was opened by the demure Jane in garb of black with immaculate linen, the insignia of her office, who explained in low tones that Mrs. Winthrop had some guests and would be glad if he would dress and come down as soon as possible. He would find everything prepared for him in the nursery.

With a hasty vision of elegant bonnets and silken robes he slipped quickly through the back stairs, and went up to the nursery in no pleasant frame of mind. What could all this mean? It was very careless of Miriam to have such a state of things going on when he arrived, and after so long an absence. it was not like a loving wife to be so thoughtless. He was weary too, and what kind of people were downstairs? A lot of relatives of hers perhaps. He would just let them understand that for the present it would be more convenient for them to postpone any further visits. He had come home and wanted his house to himself, and a chance to rest. These and like ill-natured thoughts passed through his mind while he impatiently went through the details of his toilet. But who could the people below stairs be? They wore bonnets many of them. It must be they were not here to stay. What in the world could it all mean? He was baffled in any attempt to answer his own questions. He grew angrier as his toilet progressed. He half resolved not to go down. It would serve his wife right for not coming to meet him. This had been what she had feared he would do. But his curiosity, as much as anything else, made him go down. He came in from the back hall, that he might view the room before entering. His first glimpse showed him rooms quite unfamiliar in arrangement, and filled with well-dressed, well-bred people who were chatting pleasantly and sipping cups of tea. Over in the center, near the front of the house, he caught a glimpse of a beautiful woman. The oval of her face seemed familiar and reminded him strangely of something he had once loved. She was exquisitely dressed in a gown all gray and shining with soft touches of sunset pink about it, that recalled the rosehue in her cheek. He was glad that he was well dressed himself. Who could that woman be? A dart of memory brought a shaded lane with wild roses growing on either hand, roses the color of that soft pink stuff in the front of her gown, and the flush on the oval cheek — and Miriam turned her face to the front and raised her eyes, bright with excitement, for the moment deep with the brilliancy they had worn long ago on that summer evening in the lane of sweetbrier. Her husband's heart stood still. Was that Miriam, or was it some wraith of his bewildered vision? That beautiful woman his wife? Strange he had forgotten, during his absence, how lovely she was. It was worth while going away to come home to such enchantment. How lovely, how graceful, how perfectly gowned! Oh, the joy of his young love returned to him! With one heart's throb he was a youth again and Miriam more beautiful than ever before him. He stood entranced in the doorway or his own parlor, gazing at his own wife.

And then what evil spell was this that brought a memory of the times when he had forgotten her? Who was that? Could it be? He rubbed his eyes. Mrs. Sylvester! In his home! In *their* home! The thought of her was repugnant to him just now, for his heart had been recalled to the days of simple joys and innocent love. Her haughty, supercilious bearing, her lofty, commanding smile, so familiar, were suddenly grown hateful. He saw her look at his wife — *his wife!* What did she mean by that amused, quizzical expression? She was not worthy to touch so much as a finger of his spotless Miriam, and yet — there came his wife forward to greet her. He caught his breath and was conscious that he was glad she paid no further homage to that guest than a mere greeting. His brows contracted angrily. It was not pleasant to think that he had paid sweet compliments to Mrs. Sylvester. He would rather forget that part now. What a fool he had been! He distinctly remembered that he had considered her beautiful. So she was, with a certain style of beauty, but — compare her with that flower-like loveliness of his wife! Two sides of his nature were fighting in the man's heart. He did not wish to meet that other woman now. He would wipe out some experiences of the past from his mind. Mrs. Sylvester had been well enough to while away an idle moment with, but why had he ever wished to leave Miriam's side?

But these thoughts went like flashes through his mind as he watched. A moment after a group standing close to the door turned and recognizing him drew him at once into the room and he began making his way toward his wife, for he had a sudden longing to be near her — to protect her from the woman whose friend he had been glad to count himself but a little while before.

He spoke to this and that one, answering questions with little knowledge of what he said, his eyes always as much as possible, like Mrs. Sylvester's, upon his wife. People looked after him and noticed his gaze and murmured, "How fond he is of his wife! A most charming couple," and then dropped back to themselves and their own petty themes.

He had almost reached his wife's side now. He could see the fine tendrils of hair as it waved up from her neck, just as he used to admire it long ago. How was it that he had not noticed her beauty lately? Was it all because of his little while away from her? There was but a divan between him and his wife now. He could reach over and touch her arm. He could see the texture of her gown and see the crystal of her clear eyes.

And then she turned, just in front of him, to speak once more to Mrs. Sylvester.

"It is good of you to be so unconventional as to come to us," she said brightly. "You have been so kind to my husband. He did enjoy his drive with you so much the other day. Do let me give you another lump of sugar in your tea? Miss Lyman, have you the sugar there?"

It was the inspiration of the moment. Just what, in her desperation, she hoped to accomplish, she was hardly sure herself. She did not know that her husband was within hearing, though she had seen him coming toward her a few moments before, and her heart had stood still, knowing that the next few minutes would tell much for or against her cause.

Miriam was perfectly at her ease. She wondered at herself as she heard the words that dared come to her lips, and knew that a smile was upon her face whose import was not felt in her cold, frightened heart. She chatted on brightly.

Mrs. Sylvester was nonplussed. How did Mrs. Winthrop learn about the drive? Had her husband been giving his own version to prevent trouble? Was she so very innocent, or was it consummate skill? She regarded her hostess critically. Claude Winthrop, standing just behind and a little to one side, felt angered by her expression.

Just then she turned, saw him, and came forward, still with the same curious expression on her face, regarding him half-quizzically.

"Ah, Sir Claude," she said, her eyes lighting with a new interest.

At the sound of her husband's name spoken so familiarly, Miriam also turned and saw him, and then facing her guest and opponent flashed one look, a challenge to the enemy. It was but an instant that the clear eyes looked into the hard, unscrupulous ones, but the other understood. With a half-amused smile still upon her face she accepted the challenge, and Miriam moved quickly to greet a caller, a silver-haired gentleman of distinction to whom she talked eagerly, thinking the while how he had weathered the storms of youth and was coming near the end of the toilsome journey, and she searched in his face for some trace of peace at the thought of victory.

The little by-play between the two women would not have been noticed by an observer. Only they two understood. Claude Winthrop, looking on with disturbed mien, comprehended only vaguely. He greeted Mrs. Sylvester coldly, suddenly aware that his own wife had met him after weeks of absence without so much as a look of greeting.

His eyes followed her as she moved toward the man with white hair, and his face grew rigid as he saw her eagerly talking with him. He knew the handsome old face crowned with the silver of honor to be but the white sepulchre covering of a reprobate, a man without a conscience, who had no scruples whatever against satisfying his selfish nature. This was the weary, sainted pilgrim to whom his wife thought she was talking. He wondered once more over this strange gathering. How came these people here? Where did Miriam get to know them all. The scoundrel was a man of influence and reputation, not easily secured outside certain circles of society, because though he was bad, he was also rich, influential, graceful in society, and withal knew how ingratiate himself into the favor of women.

Claude Winthrop was suddenly recalled to himself by the voice of Mrs. Sylvester.

"I wish you would tell me what it is all for," she said playfully.

"I beg your pardon?" he said coldly, not understanding.

"Why all this?" answered the lady, waving her hand toward the roomful of people. "Why did you make her do it? Were you not satisfied with things as they were?"

"I do not understand you," he said, beginning to feel with rising anger that perhaps he did.

"How exceedingly obtuse you are this afternoon, Claude," she replied, laughing lightly and touching his sleeve with the tip of her fan as she darted a glance at Miriam, who seemed not to see it, but turned her deep eyes to the white hair and gold spectacles, her face fairly glowing with a pleasure in his company which she did not feel. Instinctively she knew she must not seem to care.

Claude Winthrop drew back slightly at sound of his name. He felt a shame creep into his face at thought of the pride he had felt when she had first called him thus. What had happened that had made things so different? How far had he gone? What a fool he had been! Did Miriam suspect? And how did Miriam know about that ride?

"Where have you been all this time, Claude?" said Mrs. Sylvester in her pleasantest tone. "You have not been near me for ages. I actually accepted your wife's invitation this afternoon to hunt you up. I have sent two or three notes and invitations to your usual city address but have heard nothing from you. I suppose she found you out from the fact that she knows about the ride. Poor boy, won't she let you have a little innocent amusement?"

Her tone had in it that caressing quality with which she had first subdued him to her feet. Its spell might have worked fully once more had it not been for that contemptuous, covert sneer as she spoke of his wife. His beautiful wife? He glanced over again at Miriam.

"Oh, she won't hear us; she's thoroughly engaged with Senator Bradenburg. She certainly cannot object so long as she amuses herself with such as he."

A certain shame rolled over him that he did not have the courage to knock this woman down for speaking in such terms of his wife, or at least to condemn her with words, as she was a woman and could not for that reason be knocked down. But he was silenced by the thought that he had given her ground for speech of this kind. Had he not dishonored Miriam by admiring this woman, another man's wife, nay by visiting her often and making sweetly turned speeches to her, amusing himself by writing bits of poems about her eyes, likening them to all the stars and jewels of the universe, when his own Miriam's eyes held depths unknown to Mrs. Sylvester? For very shame's sake his tongue was tied.

"I have been abroad for eight weeks," he replied weakly, and instantly saw that he was making apologies for not having been to see Mrs. Sylvester. Also he knew that he had felt called upon to make this apology, and he further added: "I have not yet been to the city office, as I just returned to-day, and therefore I suppose the mail you sent there is still awaiting me."

Then he could have kicked himself for having made the explanation as he saw the light come into Mrs. Sylvester's eyes.

"Truly I am glad there is some such reason. I thought you had grown weary of —" she paused and added "us." Then she laughed lightly and looked into his face as if to make it plain that she meant herself by the pronoun.

To Claude Winthrop this intimacy had suddenly become hateful. He longed for courage to tell the woman by his side so, but his dissembling heart said, "Wait, treat her pleasantly and show her that you have meant nothing by your former actions but mere friendship. You can gradually make her see that you love your own wife."

But even as he thought this, the memory of a certain night — when, as it seemed to him now, he must have lost his senses, he had bent over the woman beside him and kissed her lips, letting his arm linger about her waist as he did so — brought the waves of red blood over his face.

He had not gone long or far in the treacherous way or he would not so suddenly have been brought to see himself in this light. The absence from home, the changed aspect of everything, Miriam's beautiful appearance and the contrast between these two women brought thus unexpectedly together before him had combined to effect it. And yet he had not the courage to do anything. he despised himself even while he answered Mrs. Sylvester's low spoken questions in a distraught way. He was thankful when she made her adieus, and was only half aware that his last word had been a promise to come to her the next evening.

Chapter 8
New Views of Things

'Tis not to cry God mercy, or sit
   And droop, or to confess that thou has failed;
'Tis to bewail the sins thou didst commit,
   And not commit those sins thou hast bewailed.
He that bewails and not forsakes them too,
   Confesses rather what he means to do.
                                  — *Francis Quarles.*

Claude Winthrop noticed with relief as he turned back to the parlor that most of the guests had departed. He would not get a chance to speak to Miriam. And yet he was not half so sure that he wished to see her alone as he had been a little while before. Her mention of that ride of his with Mrs. Sylvester had made him uneasy in her presence. How much did she know? How did she know anything?

He was almost relieved to find that the end was not yet, and that Miss Lyman and a friend of hers were to remain to dinner. His wife took no notice of him than if she had seen him but the hour before and arranged the whole programme with him. Indeed, now that he began to observe carefully he saw that she skillfully avoided saying anything to him except in the most general way.

He began to notice the changes in the rooms. How exquisitely everything was arranged! What a difference had been made. How had it been accomplished? All these years with Miriam he had not known that she possessed such capabilities. There positively had been nothing that even Mrs. Sylvester could have sneered at, though of course there was not such a display of wealth as one beheld in her house. But everything was in keeping. It did not suggest unlimited income, but it must have cost something and where had the money come from? He frowned and wondered if Miriam had been running into debt. But a glance at her graceful form made him forget possible bills.

With the inconsistency of a man who has long indulged himself in selfishness he forgot that he had been anxious to see Miriam during the whole latter part of his journey that he might find fault with her for not answering some of his important business questions, and indeed for not writing to him at all during his absence. He had gone about so much that at first he had not noticed it, laying it to failure of mails, but as the time drew near to get home and some business questions still remained unanswered he began to feel the grievance of her unwifely action. He had intended giving her a sound going over for allowing him to be so anxious concerning her health and the children's all that time, and he actually thought, poor blind fellow, that he had been anxious about her, even while he was preparing some wounding sentences for her ear on the subject.

But now as he sat at his own well-appointed table with the sort of guests about it he had always craved, and his beautiful wife opposite, he told himself that he had been eager for days to see her once more, to have her to himself, and here he was being kept from her for hours by strangers. He forgot Mrs. Sylvester for a time, forgot everything save the latest impressions of his wife. He watched her constantly and admiringly, comparing her favorably with a certain famous actress he had seen in Paris. There was something fresh and unsullied about the purity of his wife's face that reached his better self and touched the feelings that had first attracted him to her. Some men need always to have their best joys kept constantly at a distance in order that they may appreciate them at anything like their full value.

Claude Winthrop began to grow anxious for the dinner guests to depart, and turned from the door as he bade them good evening with a sign of relief and anticipation.

He turned, intending to clasp his wife in his arms. He expected to find her blushing shyly and smiling behind him, as had been her wont in their early married days when guests had broken in upon their close companionship. But he found empty air behind him. He took a step forward into the little reception room, thinking she had coyly stepped in there lest some lingering servant should witness their glad meeting. But she was not there. He peered into the little music room beyond, and came back into the hall blankly looking for her. Above, in the distance he heard the cry of a child and the quick stir of rustling, and then a door closed, and subdued voices murmured at intervals.

He called but there came no answer, until he called again. He was becoming angry. It was no way to treat him on his home-coming. Other women did not treat their husbands so — at least other women did not treat him coldly. He was about to mount the stairs when the maid appeared at the head of the stairs, and said, in low tone, that Mrs. Winthrop had been obliged to go to the baby who had cried for her.

He frowned slightly that she was delayed again, but doubtless the guests had kept her from the baby a long time and she would soon be able to soothe Celia to sleep and would come to him. He stepped back to the parlor and looked about him. Miriam certainly had good taste. He walked from one end of the room to the other, touched a cushion here, smoothed the broad cool leaf of a palm that stood near him and then glancing down, a prism of light caught his eye. He stooped and picked up the glittering object. it was a slender hoop of jewels, and as he looked at it there seemed something familiar about the setting of it. Where had he seen it before? Ah! it was Mrs. Sylvester's, for he had seen it upon her wrist again and again. He could seem to remember its gleam in his eyes as he came to himself after that guilty kiss. A coldness came into his fingers, a horror at himself and the shadow of wrong that he was beginning to realize in his life. He dropped the bracelet from his nerveless fingers, and then as quickly picked it up. Miriam must not see it. It seemed to him the pretty jewel thing would tell his secrets to her by the light of its piercing gems that could reveal only the truth. He turned the bracelet over and saw engraved initials inside, S.S. Sylvia Sylvester from — those were Senator Bradenberg's initials, but of course it was not likely; still — and a feeling of loathing came over him for the woman in whose company he had stood in that very spot but three hours before. With sudden resolve he hid the bracelet in his inner pocket. Miriam must not see it. He must return it. He saw at once that the call he promised would have to be made. It never occurred to him that it would be decidedly better for Miriam to send the bracelet herself. He dreaded to speak to her of that other woman, and how else would Miriam know to whom the bauble belonged? How indeed! and what would she think of him for knowing so exactly to whom it belonged with only initials to guide him?

He sat down to wait for Miriam, resting his head against the sharp back of a chair and feeling as if the bracelet pressed against his heart and hurt it as the chair did his head.

Upstairs he could hear a low murmur of a lullaby interspersed with the wail of a baby in protest. The soft tapping of a trotting foot came regularly. This went on for a long time. Claude Winthrop was impatient. He had waited already long enough.

At last the maid came downstairs.

"Ms. Winthrop says please not to wait for her. Little Miss Celia is not well and she must stay by her," she said with respectful tone, and was gone. He remembered afterward that she had been carrying a hot-water bottle. The baby must be unusually out of sorts. He yawned impatiently and went upstairs to his room. It certainly was very awkward and disagreeable in Miriam not to give him a chance to even kiss her on his return. She might have slipped away from the baby for a minute. But no, women always thought of their children first before their husbands. It made no difference how much they slighted the one whom they had professed to love above every other earthly creature, if only a baby cried. It was the old grievance he had had before he went abroad. By use of it he managed to forget the bracelet and its uncomfortable reminders for a little while.

Before he undressed he listened at the door. All seemed quiet in the hall. He tiptoed softly toward the nursery door. The light was turned down and only the rays from the street electric light outside showed the dim outline of his wife sitting at the further end of the room. She had slipped off the reception gown and wore a soft loose pink garment with little frills of white. In the dusk it took on the softness of a cloud at evening. The little curly head nestled in the hollow of her arm gave the touch of madonna to the picture. Miriam's head was turned away. He could only see the profile, against the flaring light outside, sweet and pure and sad. What had she to be sad about? His ever-ready anger rose, even while his conscience reproached him. Yes, she was lovely. She was lovlier even than in the promise of her youth when he had first loved her. He would go in softly and stoop over and kiss her as he used to do long ago, so softly that the sleeping baby would not wake, kiss that sad look away and bring her lovely loving smile. He half made a movement to start and then the baby stirred and gave a hoarse cry. He recognized at once the croupy cough, and saw Miriam's strong white hands move quickly as she replaced the cold wet compress from a dish of water at her side.

The maid was coming too with hot water to make steam in the room. It was an all-night job he knew at once. But it was not serious. He could see that already the worst barking roughness of the cough was checked. They knew what to do and he was better out of the way. He tiptoed silently back to his room and closed the door just as the maid reached the top landing of the stairs. It was just as well for him to go to bed at once. Miriam could not get away.

And Miriam sat the long night through and thought.

Even after the baby was breathing naturally again and tucked in her little warm crib, and could as well have been left to the experienced nurse, she sat with her head bent over the rail of the crib and did not sleep.

The die had been cast. She had made her first entrance into society! And it had not been altogether a failure, though she was not sure how much of a success it had been. Time only could tell that.

She forced herself to go over the details of the afternoon and evening. She felt again her heart freeze at sight of the graceful, dreadful woman who entered her home in bodily presence — who had entered it in spirit as a serpent sometime before. She shrank once more from meeting her husband's gaze. She knew she had not done so yet. She wondered if he knew it. She had felt the surprise in his face ever since he had come. She knew that he was pleased with her appearance and the house. She recognized a change of tone toward herself. She might if she chose be on a more intimate footing now than she had been for some months back. The coldness and harshness that had characterized him were gone. That she knew intuitively. So far she had scored a point. Her longing, loving heart had told her this even without looking him clearly in the eyes. But the great gulf that was fixed between their hearts was kept there at her command, not his, now. He might be willing to bridge it, for a while at least — her heart winced as she bravely added that last clause; but for her it could never be bridged until all possibility of his ever crossing it away from her again was removed, if it ever could be removed.

She wondered at herself that could love and yearn, and long to lay her sick child down and go to him and lay her head upon his breast and tell all her aching heart-full to him and let him comfort her as he used to do; and this while she knew that his friendship with that graceful, unprincipled woman with the steel eyes was as yet unreckoned for. And yet her pride and her poor hurt love would never let her yield to all her yearnings till the fight was fought clear through to the end and she had won, if win she might. And she was weary, weary unto death, she thought. Life looked very black at best. What good was she to accomplish by all this worldly panorama in which she had become a puppet? And then her aching heart cried out against the husband who could be so weak as to bring all this suffering and distress upon her he had professed to love. What was love anyway but a passing phase of the emotions? She thought with a shudder of a bit of rhyme; where had she read it? a scrap at the head of a chapter of some book. It had grated on her when she read it, and she had thought with pity of the one who would write it, and contrasted his circumstances with hers. That had not been her happy experience of love, but that was before —

> Oh, love's but a dance,
>   Where Time plays the fiddle!
> See the couples advance,
>   Oh, love's but a dance!

> A whisper, a glance —
>   "Shall we twirl down the middle?"
> Oh, love's but a dance,
>   Where Time Plays the fiddle!

Was it true? Was love but that? Was there nothing real nor lasting?

And then what strange absurdity of the mind brought back the text of that sermon she had heard, the only sermon or text she seemed ever to have heard in her life as she thought of it now: "See that thou make all things according to the pattern shewed to thee in the mount."

If one did all things according to that pattern, would it make a difference? Would love be true while life lasted?

And at last with the burden of all she must do pressing heavily upon her, and with the dread of the morrow and what it might bring forth hanging over her, she fell asleep, one hand upon the baby's hand and her cheek resting uncomfortably on the little flannel double-gown folded against the crib rail.

Chapter 9
At Mrs. Sylvester's

Was she a maid, or an evil dream?
Her eyes began to glitter and gleam;
  He would have gone, but he stayed instead;
Green they gleamed as he looked in them:
"Give me my fee," she said.
— *Christina G. Rossetti.*

Miriam presided at the breakfast table the next morning in an elaborate little morning robe the like of which she had been wont to consider too fine for everyday use. Now nothing was too good. All, all was put into her venture. She would exchange it for a simpler one as soon as her husband was out of the house, meantime it had its use.

On one thing she had forgotten to reckon. The children met her in the hall and began to exclaim joyously on her appearance, but she hushed them before their father heard. She did not care to reveal any of the machinery of her maneuver by having him suppose it was unusual for her to be dressed in this way. If he noticed it, well and good, but better not wear it than to have it remarked upon.

She had managed to put on with the dress her fine distant manner of the evening before. Her husband felt that the moment he entered the breakfast room. It seemed like a sweet, far-off mist that enveloped her, through which, try as he would, he could not break. She looked a little pale after her night's vigil, but she had chosen her gown with regard to her pallor, and so it but made her the more interesting. A little while before she would have despised herself for such small subterfuges, now they seemed all important.

She smiled behind the coffee cups over her night of watching and said she would be all right after a few hours' sleep, and then told her husband of a concert for which she had tickets that evening.

He looked surprised, but her manner was so assured, quite as if they had been going out in society for years together, that he said nothing, especially as the maid and the children were present. He was more puzzled than ever over the new order of things. Miriam mentioned the hour of the concert, and suggested that he be sure to come home early to dress for it.

The bracelet in his pocket suddenly recalled to him his half-engagement for the evening. He became somewhat abstracted and fell to wondering if he could possibly have the face to call at the Sylvester house and get rid of that annoying bit of jewelry as well as its owner before going to the concert. He tried to recall whether Mrs. Sylvester had said anything about afternoon tea. What day was it? Yes, she was always at home on that afternoon. He could call late, when others had gone, get the disagreeable business out of the way forever and then he could breathe freely and enjoy the concert with his wife.

He was so engrossed in these thoughts that he forgot to feel aggrieved when Miriam left the table before he was through on the excuse of going to Celia, and said as she paused at the door that she would lie down in her room for a couple of hours and she wished they would try not to disturb her.

She vanished and he had the memory of a pretty vision in the doorway. He had meant to see her alone for just a moment anyway before going downtown, but she was gone now and perhaps it was just as well. He would get the Sylvester matter out of the way before he kissed her and then he would feel his conscience clear. Old scores would be wiped out. He would take good care to warn Miriam against that woman. She was not fit company for her. Whatever possessed her to invite her? How did she ever meet her? Pondering, he came to feel quite as if his friendship with Mrs. Sylvester had been through no fault of his own, but wholly owing to her malign influence, to which in some hour of mental aberration he had weakly yielded, scarcely realizing what would be the outcome and so was not so very much to blame after all. He would make a clean breast of it to Miriam sometime and that would show her that she must have nothing further to do with Mrs. Sylvester.

He finally managed to cajole his conscience into the belief that all this sophistry was true and actually settled to his morning paper with something like a pleasant anticipation of the evening. That Sylvester part would be hard to get through with but he meant to do it, and it was pleasant that he need not rebuke himself for keeping his promise to her. He was glad of that, for now he had a real reason for going, a legitimate one.

And Miriam doffed the pretty gown and crept to her couch in the darkened chamber with heavy sobs shaking her frame. She would not allow them to break into the outburst of tears that would have relieved the tension. There would be traces of that on her face and she could not afford to show any such emotion now. The concert was a link in the chain. It was to be a great society affair, a brilliant performer and the last night. The tickets had been held high and she had paid dearly for the seats she had secured among the high and mighty ones. She would not have been able to compass such places at all, but for the opportune inability of some friends of the Lymans who were called to a distant funeral unexpectedly and could not use their own seats. Celia Lyman had heard of it and eagerly offered to get her the seats two days before. The concert was to be the next movement in the plan of campaign, which now that it was started seemed to grow of itself. Mrs. Sylvester would be sure to be there. Miriam tried to think how she must do and what she should wear for that evening, but at last nature took her revenge and she fell asleep.

Claude Winthrop managed to get through a tolerable toilet at his club — he had borne the call in mind when he dressed that morning — and a little before six o'clock, without having yet gone home, he rang the bell at the Sylvesters'.

Mrs. Sylvester's footman had been accustomed to his calling frequently, often at this hour. Without announcing him in the reception room, where Claude could hear several voices and the clink of late tea things, he led him to a small reception room to the right of the doorway heavily hung with *portires*. He sent word that he would like to see Mrs. Sylvester immediately, if possible, for just a moment. In a few minutes he heard the soft rustle of her dress and her white hand drew back the heavy folds of drapery.

She came in with her most confidential air and a light of welcome in her eyes.

"So good of you to come the first possible minute," she said holding out both hands to greet him, "But let me tell you, Claude, I knew you would!"

There was assurance in her tone and a favor that stirred the lowest in him. He writhed inwardly. It was going to be very hard to do what he had planned to do. He could not broach the subject at once. He wished she would be a little reserved as she knew well how to be.

"You mistake," he said and tried to say it coldly, but somehow his voice sounded strange to himself, "I merely ran in on an errand. I cannot stay. I am due at home now. I promised to take my wife to the concert at the Academy."

"Oh, what a pity!" She said it sweetly, but there was a hardness under the surface tones and a sharp glitter came into her steel eyes. Her mouth always wore a determined look; the pretty curve of red set itself in thin lines of compression now.

"I must excuse myself from the others, then, and attend to you at once." She said it and was gone before he had time to demur. He was searching for that annoying bracelet. It would help to open the way for the further remarks he had to make, though now he was ready for them he could not think for his life what he had meant to say. Ah, there was the bracelet in his inner breast pocket. How annoying! She would think he had placed it over his heart on purpose. It was a bad beginning but — and then he looked up and realized what she had said and that she was gone. He was angry and relieved all in one, angry that he had not got the matter done with while she was there without further delay, glad that he had time to think what to say. He wanted her to understand that he was sorry for his foolishness — say that he had been but playing, how would that sound? He could soften it by saying he knew she meant the same, and then a vision of Miriam looking at him with her clear eyes while he made his "clean breast" came and made him tremble. His throat grew dry and hot. He could hear Mrs. Sylvester's voice in the distance in farewells. He knew that sound, having waited for it more than once in this same room. She knew how to dismiss people in a way that sent them home thinking they had made the move to go themselves. She would soon get rid of them all. He heard the front door close and a pause, and low voices for a few minutes and then steps and the front door closed again. She did not come. He looked impatiently at his watch and felt feebly in his brain for suitable phrases to clothe his message.

At the farther end of Mrs. Sylvester's long reception room in the shelter of a window seat, sat Senator Bradenberg and Mrs. Sylvester. They were talking in low tones. There was about their manner a freedom as of two who understood each other fully. Each recognized the power of the other in certain directions. Each trusted the other because each was to a certain extent in the power of that other and knew it. This made the basis of a friendship that was not unpleasant, at times, when it suited the convenience of the two concerned. Each had about the same amount of unscrupulousness. They were well suited.

"I will do it," she said looking him straight in the eye, "if you will do something for me. It is about as pleasant as the task you have given me, so we are even again. You said a little while ago you would go to the concert to-night with me. Now I want you to go instead with Mrs. Winthrop. She is pretty and she is new. It would not be hard work. Never mind what my object is. Just be on hand a little before the appointed hour, and gracefully — as you well know how — make her understand that her husband was detained, and that you have come in his place. Stay. You may make it

more complete. Say he will meet her at the concert to take her home. I will
see that he is there. You understand how to do it perfectly. I need not tell
you.''

The silver hair was bowed.

''Thank you,'' he said, touching his heart suggestively with his hand on
which a rare diamond glittered, ''and in return?''

Her hand was on the bell. She touched it and turned with a satisfied
smile.

''In return I will invite your awkward, clumsy congressman to my house
and endeavor to charm him long enough at least for you to get your
precious vote taken.''

She turned and spoke a word of command to the footman, and they
rose and walked slowly up the length of the parlor, the white head bowed
low once more, and this time he touched her hand with his lips, and she
returned the salute with a playful little tap on his pink, wicked old cheek.

It was just as they had reached the door that Claude was ushered into the
larger room by the footman. The senator understood at once. He shook
hands graciously and declared he was glad to see Mr. Winthrop at home
once more, that he was looking well, and he had enjoyed the few minutes
spent yesterday in their delightful little home with his most charming wife
for hostess.

Then he bowed himself out. He was a wise and wily old serpent.

Claude drew himself up. He knew Senator Brandenburg. All the men
knew him. What was he doing here with Mrs. Sylvester? And that bracelet!
— were those really his initials? Then he winced as he remembered that this
was no concern of his now. He was not jealous for Mrs. Sylvester. What a
contrary thing was human nature. It was Miriam for whom he was jealous.
He did not want her pure name on lips so sullied — and he felt a soothing
qualm of righteous wrath pass over him.

Mrs. Sylvester had given an order to the footman in a low tone.

''Now Claude,'' she said in her *tete-a-tete* tone of voice, ''I have kept
you such an unconscionable time that you will not get home in time for
dinner before the concert, so I have told Warner to have dinner served at
once and we will go right out to the dining room, and you can talk while we
eat. I am absolutely alone to-night. Mr. Sylvester is in Chicago for a week,
perhaps longer, and Miss Page dines in her room. She complains of sick
headache this afternoon.'' She did not add that Miss Page had been informed, but three minutes before, that her dinner would be served to her in
her room.

Claude looked helplessly about him. It was late. There seemed no way out of this tangle into which he had inadvertently strayed. He had a wild thought of flinging the bracelet down and starting for the door, but instead he bit his lips and followed his voluble hostess into the brilliant dining room.

It was not a pleasant dinner. The gurest was *distrait*. The hostess talked without interruption giving him details of a small scandal that had been enacted during his stay abroad, about which neither cared a whit.

Claude ate hurriedly, hoping to hasten the courses, and then waited impatiently for Mrs. Sylvester to finish. She seemed to be in no haste now that they were seated, and the courses came with unusual slowness for a well-regulated house. He glanced in dismay at the great carved clock as the silver chimes rang half-past seven, and shoved his chair back in alarm. What had he been about? Not a word of his errand had he spoken, and it was already too late to reach home in time to take his wife to the Academy at the time she had named.

He drew the bracelet out of his pocket and threw it down on the fine deep linen between them, but before he had time to explain Mrs. Sylvester had arisen and taken it quietly, as if she had expected it to be there. Long afterward he wondered if she had dropped it on purpose. But now he did not think of that as she quickly clasped it on her white arm. There was a determined look in the red cupid's line of her mouth and her eyes burned a cold blue flame, as if she knew she had come to a critical moment and meant to tide herself well over.

"Claude," she said, and coming over to his side she placed the white hand on his arm, "you need not look so frightened. Just enjoy yourself. I have fixed it all right. Your wife is not expecting you. I sent her word some time ago that you were detained — you were, you know — and that entirely against your will," and she laughed a silvery laugh of assurance.

Claude had grown white around his mouth.

"You sent my wife word —" he said hoarsely trying to rise and shake that hateful hand from his arm. He suddenly saw his crime in all its enormity. It was as if he saw it through Miriam's eyes.

"Yes, I did," she answered laughing, "and you need not look so frightened. It is all right and proper. You are to meet her at the Academy. I sent her a charming escort, who was delighted to be of service, and he has explained it all. By this time they are starting and very soon we will start too. Come, be a good boy, and talk to me while I finish my coffee."

Chapter 10
The Plot Thickens

"And what you leave," said Nell, "I'll take,
And what you spurn, I'll wear;
For he's my lord for better or worse and worse;
And him I love, Maude Clare.
Yea, though you're taller by the head,
More wise and much more fair;
I'll love him 'till he loves me best,
Me best of all, Maude Clare."
— *Christina G. Rossetti.*

Miriam had awakened from her long sleep to accomplish many things. The dinner which awaited her husband would have been much more enjoyable to him than the one which he tried to choke down at Mrs. Sylvester's. His wife had remembered his every like and dislike and the appointments of the table were exquisite. She had resolved that he should find no pleasanter place than his own home in so far as it was in her power. Therefore she took as much pains about the setting and decoration of the dinner table as she had done the night before when they were entertaining guests. It was hard to have to treat one's husband like a stranger, and she sighed as she remembered the cosy little suppers taken on the kitchen table on the girl's "day off," when she and Claude had not taken time to eat in a regular way but had brought the baby's high-chair out of the kitchen and she had ransacked the pantry and refrigerator for nice little tidbits and sent a savory smell forth from the gas-stove while Claude quoted a verse of Riley's poem, "When mother gets the supper," and the baby crowed over the delightful informality of the occasion as she drummed on a tin pan. But that was oh, so long ago! And now she was putting touches to the fern dish that had just come from the florist's little shop around the corner exactly as if Claude were an outsider.

The supper was perfectly cooked and was ready at the appointed hour. After that it stayed in a continual state of readiness until it had depreciated its value more than half and finally the cook declared sulkily that it was "intoirly spoiled." Then the children were given their dinner and sent off to bed, and Miriam took a few mouthfuls, her mind in such a state of uneasiness that she scarcely tasted what she ate. But she knew she must eat if she would go through the evening. What could have happened to Claude? Would he not come at all? Had he forgotten?

For the hundredth time she walked to the mirror to see that everything was right about her costume.

It was an exquisite creation of filmy black over clear white that she had chosen for the evening, which could not have been accomplished save by her skillful needle, without a vast outlay of money. She knew this, and again and again looked it over critically to be sure there was no mark of "home-made" about it, and again felt sure that no one would know it was not made by a master hand.

She put up her hand to her throat to still the choking sensation that would keep rising as the minutes flew by and her husband did not appear. She touched the string of pearls, a wedding gift, from a maiden aunt. She half smiled as she remembered the laughing prophecies made by her girl friends of a tear which she must shed for every pearl the bride wore. How sure she had been that they would not come true, how little fear of the old superstition! And yet she had shed tears enough, and about such petty things. So many that she had not any left now wherewith to water her first, her only, her awful sorrow when it did come!

Ah! that clock! The hands were painfully near to half-past seven. And Claude must eat his dinner, and the distance to the Academy was not short, and she so dreaded going late at this her first entrance into that charmed circle.

But hark! There was a carriage! And steps! Had Claude waited perhaps to get the carriage and come home in it that he might not have to keep her waiting so long! How good of him to think of it! She had not ventured a carriage. She had known the expense must be saved wherever possible if she would not run short in her venture into the world.

Why did he not come in quickly? She was so glad over the carriage that she forgot for the instant all that had gone before, and the reason for her cool demeanor toward her husband. it was so hard to play this distant unconcerned role toward one who had been a part of herself for so long.

Why, there was the bell! Claude had forgotten his latch-key perhaps, or lost it. She rushed forward to the door. There was no time to waste now. She laid grip upon her self-control and remembered she must not give way to her feelings as she put her hand upon the knob and then she opened the door to come face to face with — not Claude as she had expected, but the smiling face of the silver-haired senator.

Her cheeks had grown pink during the last half-hour with excitement. She was really a beautiful woman and she struck the senator so as he greeted her deferentially. He was glad he had come. The prospect before him was a pleasant one.

Miriam stood speechless for an instant, so sure had she been that it was Claude's step she heard. Then she recovered her self-possession and held out her hand in greeting. She was conscious of relief that the caller was an old man and would not therefore see through the disguise she would put over her uneasiness. But she liked the senator. All women did when he chose to have them do so. Her smile was genuine, though she wondered as she explained her acting as door maid, whether he would stay long, and whether Claude would not come soon. Also she was conscious of a disappointment about the carriage and realized how near she had been to forgiving Claude all just because of a paltry carriage and a little supposed thought of her convenience.

And then she became aware that Senator Bradenberg was not coming in, that he was trying to explain something to her.

"I have come in your husband's place to take you to the Academy," he was saying, "and I do hope, my dear madam, that you will let me do all in my power to make up for his loss. It is certainly a privilege to be allowed —"

Miriam in quick alarm put her hand on her heart, crushing as she did so some exquisite white rose buds that rested there among the lace.

"Has anything happened?" she said in a frightened voice. "Is Claude hurt? — or ill?"

The senator decided that she was a very beautiful woman and that he would not object to seeing her color come and go on his account like that. It would be worth working for.

"Oh, no indeed, Mrs. Winthrop," he said in his most suave manner. "Nothing is the matter at all. He was merely detained longer than — ah — he expected to be — and — ah — we made this little arrangement. He expects to meet you, I believe, at the Academy, when I suppose I shall unfortunately have to surrender in his favor. Meanwhile I am delighted to be so fortunate as to have your company, if you will permit, and the carriage is at the door."

With beating heart and eyes bright with tears that seemed scorching to get out, Miriam hastened to be ready. Her gloves and wraps were at hand. She had expected to have to hurry. But somehow this new move made things so hard. Where was Claude, and what could be the matter? Oh, was there to be some new, terrible revelation! Why had she started out on this fool's attempt to conquer what she did not know?

But she was glad it was Senator Bradenberg and not some younger man her husband had sent. She could talk politics to him and he would never notice how preoccupied she was. He was a good, kind man, old enough to be her father. And thanks to the hint in her magazine she had read enough of the questions of the day not to quake over the thought of a talk with even this noted man. There were subjects enough to talk about. She would ask him questions thick and fast and let him do the talking, that was the way to make people think you a good conversationalist, just be a good listener. But when would Claude appear, and how should she discover what had kept him? Would he tell her of his own free will? She must not forget again the manner she was maintaining toward him. If she once let him see that she was acting all would be lost.

How pleasant it was that she was to have the escort of so distinguished a man as the senator if she could not have Claude. It would surely give her prestige, for he seemed to be spoken of as a talented man who stood high in the political as well as the social world, and could command much influence.

Then she went down to her escort, ready, trying to smile and thanking him for being so kind as to come. She feared that she had not been so cordial as she might have been at first, she had been so taken aback.

"Where did you say you met Mr. Winthrop?" she asked as the carriage door slammed shut and they started on their way.

The senator cleared his throat and spoke with a pleasant unconcern. He was used to such situations. In fact he rather enjoyed them.

"At Mrs. Sylvester's. He was, I believe, on for a little dinner there and found it impossible to make both engagements fit, hence I am here. I do hope you won't find me a very great bore!"

"At Mrs. Sylvester's!" said Miriam and her voice sounded like death, even to herself. The carriage was passing a brilliantly lighted square and her white face was lit up for the moment. She turned piteous eyes of entreaty toward the senator as she spoke.

"You poor child!" said the senator in his graceful, caressing tone. "It is terribly disappointing to have one's husband off with another woman while you have to take up with any one that comes along, isn't it? but it is the way of the world, you know."

A flood of crimson concealed the pallor on Miriam's cheeks. There might be anything or nothing in these words, but instantly she was on the alert. Even an old man, old enough to be her father, should not see and pity. She had felt that he had meant pity for her, real pity in that sentence, though he was too polite to really say it, and had turned it off with pleasantry. But no one should suspect the torture she was passing through. Instantly summoning all her self-control she responded with a gayety that surprised herself:

"Not at all. I quite enjoy the prospect. I shall ask you a hundred and one questions whose answers I have been aching to know this long time, if you will not mind. Yes, of course, Claude is at Sylvester's. I ought to have remembered — she is quite a friend of ours you know — didn't you see her at our house yesterday? I fear you thought me quite ungrateful, but I assure you I am only too delighted to have this opportunity of talking with you."

And then she summoned to her bidding all the reading she had been doing lately, all the talk of the daily papers about leagues and intrigues, all the confusing tangle of subject that have two sides to them, and sometimes three sides, and began to ply her questions.

Senator Bradenberg watched her closely as well as he could do for the dim lights that flashed past as they rode. Here was certainly a marvelous woman, a woman worth cultivating. She was evidently acting. He was too well versed in the world not to know beyond a doubt the meaning of that tone when she had first said, "At Mrs. Sylvester's!" But how quickly she had rallied, with a beautiful color she had summoned to her aid. That he could detect beneath the mask of smiles a pain too deep for utterance, only added zest to the occasion. His sated emotions would have a pleasant little treat. For many a day all pleasures had palled. Now there was something new to live for. He straightened up in the carriage and threw his whole magnetic self into his answers, that self that carried bills through the senate at all odds; that self that had made the conquest of many hearts and ruined many lives. It was not for nothing he had gained his reputation. He knew how to talk. He knew how to make one forget that time was flying. Miriam under cover of the darkness had tried to listen and think at the same time, but in the brilliancy of the Academy she drew her breath and resolutely set herself to listen to all that was said to her. Here she could be seen and she must not let the senator suspect, never, never, never, that she had any trouble. And so she put her whole self into her questions and listened with her eyes as well as with her ears, and more and more as he looked down into those clear, thoughtful eyes and saw the quick play of expression he was pleased that he had come.

There were a few about her whom she knew, and to these she nooded. Her companion bowed and smiled right and left and she knew that she was a center of observation.

She was glad when the first strains of the great orchestra in the opening selection made it possible for her to sit back and keep still. But even then she knew she must keep strict guard over her face. She had often been told that her thoughts were all plainly written there. Claude used to say so. He must not read her heart now. No one must read it. She would lock it away and be false in her face for this night at least. She must think quickly and be ready to act. Senator Bradenberg had said that her husband would meet her at the Academy. When would he come? Would he come alone? He was at Mrs. Sylvester's at dinner. He would likely come with her. She must be expecting that sight and not faint, nor even show the slightest change of expression that it was anything to her. Mrs. Sylvester's box was just opposite. She would be able to see them without lifting her eyes, without showing that she saw them.

And even as she thought it two figures appeared in that box, and she knew without looking that it was her husband and beside him, tall and fair and handsome in a clinging dress of heavenly blue, was Mrs. Sylvester. Her white silk opera cloak was over Claude's arm, and her white glove touched him on the shoulder and pointed something about the arrangement of the chairs where they were to sit. But Miriam was listening with rapt face to the music — music which she did not hear — and apparently saw them not. Several eyes were turned toward her as the smiling beauty and the dark-haired man with the set face entered the box, and Miriam bore the scrutiny well. Even the man by her side, watching her narrowly, could not decide whether she had seen them yet.

Not until the music had ceased and the applause was over did she raise her eyes in a studied circuit and let them travel unconcernedly over the boxes, and rest for just an instant on the face of her husband as he sat uncomfortably in the background, and then pass on as if she had taken no note. But her heart was freezing, freezing, and she was glad that she could turn to the senator and begin to talk or she felt sure she would lose consciousness.

She wondered vaguely what Claude would do if she should faint and then she forced herself to listen to what was being said.

Chapter 11
At Cross Purposes

Oh, we're sunk enough here, God knows!
   but not quite so sunk that moments,
Sure though seldom, are denied us,
   when the spirit's true endowments
Stand out plainly from its false ones,
   and apprise if pursuing
Or the right way or the wrong way,
   to its triumph or undoing,

There are flashes stuck from midnights,
   there are fire-flames noondays kindle,
Whereby piled-up honors perish,
   whereby swollen ambitions dwindle;
While just this or that poor impulse,
   which for once had play unstifled,
Seems the sole work of a lifetime that away
   the rest have trifled.
                —Robert Browning.

Claude Winthrop's face was stern and his nerves were tense as he seated himself on the edge of a chair and began to search the audience for his wife's face. He would not even rest his whole weight upon the chair, but as people do when under excitement he seemed to think that he could help himself by working with every muscle of his body. He paid little heed to the beautiful woman by his side, and saw only to be chagrined by it, the attention that was called to their box, as this one and that, even those who were not friends of Mrs. Sylvester turned and gazed, or bowed across the sea of hands.

He was so confused that he could not distinguish persons. One face melted into another in a dizzy whirl. In vain he searched impatiently for the one face that he desired to see. He could not find it. Once he thought he caught a familiar expression but some one leaned forward and hid it from his sight, and he searched without avail in the same spot for several minutes. His brows drew down in a decided scowl. Mrs. Sylvester began to fear that she would not be able to coax him into being agreeable. She leaned toward him and made some laughing remark but he only scowled the harder and did not reply. He had begun a systematic search of the audience. Mrs. Sylvester had not told him whom she had sent as an escort for his wife. She had laughingly put him aside saying he would see in good time, and he was too angry to ask her again. He tried to recall where his wife had told him their seats were located, but everything of the morning except things that he did not wish to remember, seemed dimmed by the happenings of the day. She would not have chosen expensive seats he felt sure. He began in the humbler seats and went from face to face looking carefully, lest by any chance he should miss her. He dreaded, as he hoped, to find her. What did she think of him? Did she know where he had been detained? What message had Mrs. Sylvester sent? It was likely she had done it up all right, and thrown Miriam entirely off the track, for she seemed to suppose that this was what he wished, and he, fool and weakling that he was, had not had the courage to tell her it was not. It was likely Miriam would not suspect anything, nevertheless he felt that this state of things was not conducive to the confidential relations which he wished to re-establish with his wife. How glad he was that the music kept up. He would not have to talk until he found her. He could not tell from his wife's face whether she was angry or grieved. He hurried his eyes along the next row and morbidly fearing he had missed a few faces went conscientiously back over it again.

"Claude, you positively do look too bearish to endure. You really must moderate that frown," said Mrs. Sylvester leaning toward him again. "If you don't I shall be sorry I brought you."

"I am sorry already," he wished to say, and bit his lips that he had not the courage. He had never known before what a coward he was. After regarding him for a moment the lady added:

"If it is on your wife's account you are glaring into the audience in that style you are wasting time. I assure you she looks very happy and is perfectly oblivious of you and me. She seems to be enjoying both the music and her companion hugely. Come, cheer up!"

He followed the direction of her glance and suddenly saw his wife. It was just as she raised her eyes in that sweeping survey and looked him full in the face. There was no recognition in hers — there was placid enjoyment in her expression. This might have restored his equilibrium had he not instantly recognized her companion. That silver head was noticeable in any audience. It seemed to the enraged husband as if it shone with unusual brilliancy to-night, as if to call attention to his shame. With an exclamation half under his breath Claude started from his chair. He felt that he must rush down at once and rescue Miriam from the clutches of that vile man. Hardly knowing what he did he threw Mrs. Sylvester's long white cloak away from him to a distant chair. It had slipped down in front of him from the seat where he had put it in his pre-occupation.

"Claude!" Mrs. Sylvester turned with alarm instantly covered by an amused smile, such as an indulgent nurse might wear over a child's antics. "Claude, every one is watching you! For pity's sake remember where you are! Do sit down here beside me and hand me my programme. See, I have dropped it, and be careful, the music is very soft just now. People will hear you if you move the chairs in such a reckless fashion. Senator Bradenberg won't bite. You can safely trust your wife down there until the programme is over. I did not know you were so impulsive!"

She had talked on softly, bringing him back to a sense of his position, until she saw him seated in the chair on her other side and felt reasonably certain that he would remain there for a little while at least. She had not counted on his being so stirred, and felt chagrined at her lack of power to make him forget his wife. It was unfortunate that she had had no one else by but the "bad senator" to send on this errand. She might have known Claude would be squeamish about having his wife's name associated with his. He was a little notorious, but she had not thought it would matter much. She bit her lip in vexation that she had let him know that she had sent the senator. She might have found a way to let him suppose that it was his wife's own choice to go with him. Stay! Could she not do it yet?

"Your wife has resources of her own," she said in a low voice, amusedly. "I see she has scorned advice and chosen her own escort."

With a quick look at her Claude asked:

"Whom did you send, may I ask?"

"Oh, dear me! Don't put on that tremendous voice," was her laughing response, "no one you could possibly object to in the least, but it seems she prefers the senator. There is no accounting for tastes." He looked sharply at her for a minute. It had never occurred to him to doubt her word before, but now he felt uncertain of her. Was this true? Had Miriam refused to go with the person Mrs. Sylvester had sent and preferred Senator Bradenberg? If so things were a thousand times worse than he supposed. Of course Miriam did not know the man she was favoring. Her pure, true nature would shrink from him, he felt sure, if she knew all. But to have her name linked with his before others was gall and wormwood to her husband. For the time being his own offenses became as nothing to this. Men could do a great many things that would not be forgiven in a woman. Woman's nature was pure and true — here he glanced at the woman by his side and was uncertain — and when she fell, great was the fall!

And all this time the senator had watched every movement of the box above him. He knew a jealous look when he saw it. How interesting! A flirtation with a married woman was twice as spicy if there was some opposition, a little intrigue necessary, and even an effort, just at first, to win her attention from her true liege lord. With a glitter in his eye he settled to his pleasant task, in no wise deterred by the unhappy look of Claude Winthrop above him. Was not that young man in company with another married woman? Why should he object to his wife's receiving attention?

And Miriam, while she kept perfect control of her face, knew every movement of her husband. She saw the change at Mrs. Sylvester's command to the seat nearer to her. She saw the apparent good understanding between them — thought she saw, because imagination was all at work on that side, that Claude avoided her eyes, and that he was all deference to his companion. So blind is love sometimes. So wise is wickedness — temptation.

Miriam became aware that Senator Bradenberg was telling some interesting stories to her. She thought he had kind eyes and a pleasant face. She must not for the world let him suspect that she would rather be anywhere else in the world than by his side at that minute. He was a dear old man who was exerting himself to the utmost to make himself agreeable and he would be pained if he knew how she longed to be at home and bury her face in the pillows and weep in the darkness. The phantom of those restful pillows came between her and the singers whenever she dared raise her eyes to see her husband there beside another woman.

The old plunderer of hearts was meditating whether he would venture to ask her to let him accompany her back home, or whether it would be wisest for his purpose to surrender her to her husband this first time, when she turned to him of her own accord with a coaxing smile on her pretty face such as she used to wear as a child when she wanted something very much, before the days came when she was not so sure of having all her wishes.

"Take me home, please, won't you. I want to hear the end of that story you were telling me. My husband will have to go home with Mrs. Sylvester you know, and anyway I want to hear the rest."

He was quick enough not to show his surprise. He was delighted and he was puzzled. Was that all acting, that innocent pleading look, or was she really interested? He had always flattered himself on being able to win a woman if he tried, but he had supposed this one harder to reach just at the very first. Or was she possibly piqued by her husband's action? Ah! That must be it. He would have to go slowly for a woman with that pure curve of brow was usually wedded to certain narrow laws of life and it was not easy to persuade her that no possible harm could come from the breaking of them.

He acquiesed with charming grace, and because he knew husbands and the world in general, he joined with her in hastening their steps just a trifle at the close.

And so it happened that they were well down the wide staircase on one side when Claude and Mrs. Sylvester appeared high above them at the top of the opposite stairs. Claude had hurried Mrs. Sylvester beyond all endurance. She felt thoroughly vexed with him, and began to think that this was the end of her intrigue after all. He would rush to his wife and confess all, perhaps, and find out that she had not spoken the truth and then farewell to him. Well! Why not! Why did she care? There were others handsomer, with more wealth and standing — let him go. But a tightening of her heartstrings made her feel that she was not ready for that — not yet. Therefore it was with a certain triumph that she watched Miriam descend below them. She looked up, indeed, and nodded her recognition coolly too, as if she had known they were there all the time and did not mind, and went on talking with bright, animated face that her enemy could but acknowledge was beautiful.

They stood in the full light of the main entrance as Claude again appeared in sight at the food of the stairs. He was just in time to get a glimpse of his wife's face turned smilingly toward her escort's as she stepped into the shadow of the carriage. A moment more and the senator's white hair made a gleam of light as he entered the carriage, and the door was slammed shut. Claude could hear the rumble of the wheels and the subdued clatter of the horses' hoofs as they moved away.

To think of his wife shut into a carriage with such a man incensed Claude more than anything had ever had the power to do before. He felt as if he must rush after them down the street, crying Help! Murder! Police! Anything to overtake them and get her away from that man.

But what he did was to control himself. His face was deathly white and his eyes, as Mrs. Sylvester looked into them, were angry eyes.

"How silly of you!" she laughed softly in his ear as they waited for her carriage to be called. "She is perfectly able to take care of herself. Didn't you see how well she worked it to get away from you? You ought to be willing she should have a little pleasure, when you are enjoying yourself. I thought that last movement was well done. She will make quite a success in society if she keeps on as she has begun. I am not sure but I shall take her up myself. You surely are in no position, Claude, to object to a little giddiness on her part,'' and she tapped him familiarly on his arm with her fan as the carriage drove up.

He gravely helped her into the carriage, then giving the word to the footman, ''To Mrs. Sylvester's home,'' he bowed and said to the lady:

''I wish you good evening, madam,'' closed the carriage door, and turned away into the dark street, walking as rapidly as possible.

Chapter 12
More Complications

What so false as truth is,
  False to thee?
Where the serpent's tooth is,
  Shun the tree —

Where the apple reddens,
  Never pry —
Lest we lose our Edens,
  Eve and I.
                    —*Robert Browning.*

Miriam had got rid of the senator gracefully, leaving him with a glow of satisfaction about his *blase* old heart, and locked herself into the guest chamber with her grief. This room was as far from the other bedrooms as the house would allow. Here she could not be heard if a sob escaped her.

The house was still and dark when Claude after his long, breathless walk reached it. He had been too agitated to trust himself in any kind of public conveyance. He wanted to be alone and to have the physical exertion of walking to help him grow calm. Inaction was more than he could bear. He had had enough of that during the evening. Before he reached home he had gone over the miserable matter in every possible phase. He had excused all his own wrong-doing again and again, only to see himself the next moment in a more miserable, despicable light than ever. He had blamed Miriam, and excused her. He had raged with both the senator and Mrs. Sylvester until he was weary of the thought of them and still he did not come to any conclusion. He began to dread to meet his wife as he approached the house, for he knew that she could use scathing words if she chose, and his own heart told him she had reason. Still, the fact that he had left Mrs. Sylvester as he had, just now stood for a great deal in his favor in the summing up of himself by himself. He almost felt that it undid the past completely. He had been angry, of course, or he would not have had the courage to do it. But that he did not recognize now. He thought himself strong and noble to have dismissed her as he had done.

It was the end of any relations with her, for she would consider that he had insulted her. He thought he knew Mrs. Sylvester well enough to be sure that her pride was the strongest thing about her. He had yet to learn that he did not know how little he knew about women — some women.

He was almost relieved to find the house dark when he reached home. Miriam had retired. Would she waken and speak to him? He struck a match and glanced about the hall and parlor. Miriam's long wrap, a white glove and a programme of the evening's concert lay on a chair near the door, proving that his wife had really reached home. She was not still out in the drakness with that awful man. In anguish of soul he went upstairs and found all dark there save a little light in the bedroom. Miriam, then, had gone to another room. She was angry or she did not care for him any longer. Which? The terrible thought that Miriam could possibly ever be weaned from him suddenly struck him with heavy force. It had not seemed strange to him that he should amuse himself with a beautiful and attractive woman for a little while when Miriam was busy at home with the children and could not give him all the attention he wanted, but to have her, whom he had always been wont to consider his devoted slave, relax in her great clinging devotion to him was another thing. A wife was menat for a life-long adoration of her husband. It was an indignity to him that she should have any desire for pleasure in the company of others than himself. His indignation waxed at the thought, as his vanity was hurt by the reflection that he might not be sufficient for all her earthly needs. He was not naturally a vain man but he had certainly always supposed that he was Miriam's ideal of all the manly virtues. It was terrible to think that this might be otherwise. For once in his life the very depths of his nature were stirred to their utmost. He did not sleep well. He began to tremble over meeting his wife on the morrow. How could he say what he wished to say about Senator Bradenberg when she had seen him in the company of Mrs. Sylvester? How could he open such a subject? How could he justify himself?

With thoughts like these he tossed the long night through and only fell into an uneasy doze as morning was beginning to dawn. The long delayed home-coming kiss to his wife had not yet been given and it began to seem unlikely that it would come soon. He had even forgotten it in the graver questions that were arising.

Miriam forced herself into a sort of gayety in the morning. The long night watch had been a desperate one for her. She had been trying to find out what to do, but her final conclusion had been to bide her time and go on in the way she had set for herself.

There were letters on the breakfast table. She busied herself with them when Claude came in, an thus they met in a constrained calmness that neither felt.

There were invitations. Miriam read them and passed them over for her husband to see. He frowned as he read them and wondered how they came to be sent to them. This belonged to the new order of things of which he did not wish for more until the trouble between himself and his wife was settled. He was puzzled too, at the kind of people that seemed suddenly to have become aware of their existence. They were people who did not often take up the quiet and obscure. He wondered vaguely if Mrs. Sylvester had a hand in it, or the senator, or who?

Then he tried to frame a sentence of warning to his wife, but the words would not come. At last he asked lamely:

"Do you know anything about the man who was with you last evening?"

She looked up with cool dignity.

"Why he is the most delightful old gentleman, and he is a very warm friend of your Mrs. Sylvester, is he not?"

The children came trooping in just then and the maid opened the opposite door and brought in the coffee. Claude's face grew deeply red. There was no more to be said then. Miriam did not seem to notice that anything had happened. He ate the very few mouthfuls of breakfast that he took hurriedly, and left the house.

The day was spent in a round of worry. He dreaded to go home because he had not yet decided how to settle matters with Miriam and yet he confidently expected to bring the matter to some kind of a settlement at once.

But there were guests. Miriam explained in a low tone at the door that he had hurried away so in the morning she had forgotten to mention them, and then she slipped back to the parlor and left him scowling. Was it ever to be like this? Were outsiders to invade his world, even in his own house, forever?

During the days that followed the same state of things prevailed between husband and wife. There was always a cool distance, always some one else present, always some invitation or some guest or some excuse. Claude began to understand that it was of a purpose. Such things could not happen continually without a cause. Miriam was showing him that she wished to stay at a distance. She was pleasant, always attentive to his needs, but not with the loving, caressing touch, nor the joy of service for him in her face. He could see that it was simply a part of her housewifely duties and she performed it gracefully as she had grown to perform all her duties of late.

The little afternoon teas that had begun so bravely the day of his arrival in accordance with the advice received from the magazine letter went on. They grew popular. There was a charming informality and simplicity about them that was not always to be found.

Contrary to Claude's expectation the matter with Mrs. Sylvester was not yet ended. After some weeks' silence he received a note from her at his place of business. it read:

> DEAR CLAUDE: I hoped you would have recovered from your fit of childishness before this and come to apologize. But I suppose matters are somewhat complicated and it is not so easy to do. However, I forgave you without the asking. You were excited and I know you are sorry for your rudeness.
>
> Please run in this afternoon. I want to see you about something very important. If you don't want your wife to find out everything you had better obey this invitation.
>
> > Yours as ever,
> > SYLVIA.

He tore the note into shreds and then sent his office boy on a fool's errand while he burned it scrap by scrap. He ground his teeth angrily and sat down to think what he should do. He did not wish to go near that woman again. His conscience told him that he ought not to do so. But what was he to do and what did she mean by her hint about his wife's knowing? He wished she did know, he told himself, and then spent the remainder of the afternoon in trying to plan how he could prevent her from knowing. At the end he took his hat and hurried, as he had known from the first he would do, to Mrs. Sylvester's. It was a trifle after five o'clock, the hour named, and he rang the bell hastily. He hoped no one was with her. He would get through with her in short order this time. He had planned just how he would do it. He meant to be sharp and to the point. If she threatened to reveal anything he would tell her to go ahead and do her worst, and then he would go home and have it out with Miriam. He wished he had done that long ago. That was what he ought to have done. It was his mierable hesitancy that had made all the trouble. He would be firm this time as he had been at the carriage door that night.

He had just reached this conclusion for the fiftieth time that afternoon when the door was opened — it was too soon for his ring to have been answered unless the footman was in close attendance on the door as during calling hours — he heard the soft rustle of a woman's garments and his wife stood before him!

One instant they stood there face to face, she deadthly white, he crimson to the hair and looking as if he had been caught in the greatest crime the world can know. He could not get his voice nor command his brain. He felt stunned. Before he could come to himself she had forced a smile — such a wan, wild smile — and flitted by him like a spectre.

He turned, coming to himself. A carriage had driven up to the curb. He had noticed it in the street before. Miriam was getting in.

"Miriam!" he called in anguish and ran down the steps at a bound, but she was in and had closed the door with a click, and the driver started up his horse. It was a hired carriage from the livery around the conrer from them. Miriam had not looked up nor given any sign that she knew him since that glance in the doorway. It contained reproach and wounded pride and hurt love and sense of deep injury received, all in one. It seemed to him he could never forget that look.

He suddenly became aware that Mrs. Sylvester's footman was standing with respectful curiosity in the door waiting for him to enter, and there he stood looking after that vanishing carriage and knowing not what to do.

For an instant his impulse led him to go in and tell that false woman exactly what he thought of her, and then the sight of the carriage as it turned the corner drove all else from his mind. He must not let Miriam get out of his sight. With a mad idea of overtaking her he started down the street. Afterward it seemed to him he had fled from the house which had stood for temptation to him.

He grew calmer soon and realized that he could never overtake that swift carriage. it had turned and turned again, and he had lost sight of it. To the best of his ideas it did not seem to be on the way home. But he must go there at once. He must be there when Miriam came home if possible. He would meet her and tell her all. There should be no weak delay any more. This must end at once. He was being well punished for all the sins he had ever committed, he told himself.

He had passed through moods enough for a year of time before he reached his home. He felt more weary than he remembered to have felt for years when he applied his latch key to the door and let himself in.

The light was turned low in parlor and hall as if awaiting the moment when it would be needed, and there was a reassuring whiff of something savory from the regions of the dining room. There was something substantial and sweet in the home atmosphere, all light and warmth, with a chatter of children's voices above like the babbling of a merry little brook, that gave him confidence. Strange he had not noticed before how sweet and safe it all was. Strange he had ever cared for anything else than this that was all his! But *was* it his? The question brought a twinge of fear. Was it possible he was about to lose, nay, had already lost, the center and source of all this — his wife's love?

He settled down in a large arm-chair and rested his head back against the cushiony top. How tired he was! He dropped his eyelids with a sense of relief and wished that he might also drop his burdens as easily. Oh, if Miriam would but come softly up behind as she used to do and kiss his eyelids — so! How sweet, how infinitely sweet, it had been! And he had scorned it for the touch of that other woman's proud lips even for a few days! How impossible it seemed to him now to choose such a course.

He waited a few minutes with his overcoat still on thinking to hear the carriage drive up to the door, for he had been sure when he entered that Miriam was not yet in the house, by a hundred little signs and sounds. He could always tell when his wife was near without needing to see or hear her. The children's voices sounded weary and not glad as when with her. What a mother she had been! Why had he never taken time to be thankful for that? For he loved his children though he had paid very little attention to them lately.

But it occurred to him that he had been out of touch with Miriam for some time. Perhaps his senses for detecting her presence were not so keen as formerly. She might be in the house and he now know it, after all. He rang the bell to inquire, but when the maid appeared she said Mrs. Winthrop had not yet returned from calling.

He tramped up and down the pretty parlors, his watch in his hand, and looked first from one window and then the other. At last he took his hat and went out again. He could not stand this inaction another minute. A hundred frightful fancies were surging through his brain. He remembered Miriam's intense, impulsive nature in her youthful days. There was no telling but she had been led to do something desperate. Of course that was all fancy, but he must set his mind at rest. He could not have her out in the dark alone with such thoughts of him in her heart as he knew she must have. Down deep in his innermost soul he began for the first time to have some twinges of shame and sorrow for the way he had brought her to this agony, began to despise himself just a little, as he would have despised another man who had done the same thing.

With troubled brows drawn together he paused on the street corner and looked this way and that, trying to stop even the beats of his heart that he might listen if a carriage was coming. But no such welcome sound greeted his ear. Then he formed his plan hastily. He must go back to where he had last seen the carriage and try to trace it. Perhaps she was in need of his help somewhere at that minute.

He walked rapidly now, forgetting his weariness, not thinking to gain time by taking a car or calling a cab. It seemed to him he was more likely to accomplish something on his feet. It was a relief to his tense, strained nerves to be on the move.

When he arrived at the corner near the Sylvester mansion all was still and dark, with twinkling lights glimmering down among the shadowed street. There was nothing to show where the carriage had passed a little over two hours before. Of course there was not. He might have known that. Why had he come here — of all places? He was losing his head.

He looked toward the wide windows of the beautiful house in the next block where the soft roseshaded lights proclaimed a life of ease, and as he turned his head quickly away he breathed in his heart a great curse on the woman who had wrought this mischief, and immediately after upon himself for having been so weak as to have been led by her.

Back he took his weary way once more, following every turn which the carriage might have taken, as a dog follows a lost scent, and always back to the main way home again. And behind him followed on his trail those horrid wolves of fears and fancies — the thought of what might have happened to Miriam.

Chapter 13
In The Serpent's Toils

Poor little heart!
  Did they forget thee?
Then dinna care! Then dinna care!
Poor little heart!
  Did they forsake thee?
Be debonaire! Be debonaire!
  — *Emily Dickinson.*

When Miriam gave the hasty order to the driver to go to her aunt's house on the west side of the city she had it in mind merely to make time to think before there would be any possible chance of seeing her husband or children or even her servants again. It was a long drive to Cresson Avenue, and her mind might become clearer by the time she reached there and she be able to mark out some course for herself. At the moment she was conscious of but one thing, and that was that the worst had happened. Her fears, which she now knew to have been but fears and not certainties, were confirmed at last, and in such a way that there was no more room left for hope. She knew that in all the weary work of her carefully planned campaign she had been upheld by one great, strong hope, and that was that her husband was true to her after all and that in some mysterious way the trouble would be all explained so that there would finally come a glad morning after her night of sorrow. Now hope was stricken, never to rise again, she felt sure. Could the enemy have been permitted then to look into Miriam Winthrop's heart she would have exclaimed in joyful triumph that her victory was complete.

Miriam sank back in the carriage, having first drawn the curtains, hid her face in her hands and shuddered — shuddered until she felt she was going into a nervous chill. Then suddenly she remembered that there was a great affair on hand that evening — one of the first of the really great functions to which she and Claude had been invited since her venture into the world. It was to be an affair of hundreds, not of tens, and its greatness consisted in the home in which it was held and in the very select company who were invited. It meant much to the success of her schemes that she had been invited there. She had not dared to hope for an invitation, and had wondered ever since it came to whom she owed the honor.

This gathering, which a few hours before had meant so much to her, had suddenly become as nothing. But somehow the memory of it recalled her to the exact situation and enabled her to gain command of herself and look things in the face.

Gradually the whole thing became clear to her. She must hold down her feelings till she was sure what she ought to do and not act rashly. In the meantime, it would not do to let her enemy see her defeat. She must wear a brave front and not give up the battle even though she felt that all was lost. Better to die fighting than that. The party, at least, must be gone through with, till she could get time to think. Mrs. Sylvester, who would be sure to be there — and a sudden thought like a dart made her sure to whom she owed her invitation — should see her smiling and unabashed, even though Mrs. Sylvester might have looked from her richly curtained windows but a few minutes before and seen the last prop swept from her hope.

But how could she go with Claude after what had happened? Of course she had ridden many times in a carriage with him during the last few weeks in a silence that was painful to both, or in constrained conversation of which neither took much account. She had been able to keep him at a distance when nothing had passed between them to give tangible expression to the chasm that lay between their love. But now, after what had happened, she felt she could not ride with him that night. It would be impossible for her to control herself. Besides, she doubted if he would come home at all, much less accompany her to the party. Some other way must be thought out. Could she take the maid? But no, she was not trained, and the nurse was away with her sick mother. The children must not suffer, whatever happened.

Could she inveigle her aunt into going with her? No; for her aunt would ask a hundred troublesome questions, and she was noted for sharp eyes and a sharper tongue. She would pry something out of her niece before she granted any favors. Her aunt would not do.

She pushed up the silken curtains of the carriage and looked into the street. She was surprised to find how dark it had grown. They were driving more slowly now over a rough pavement by tall houses. It was some minutes before Miriam could make out the locality.

Then a great club-house loomed up, brilliant with its many windows and its lavish display of electric lights. In the arched marble entrance night was made into day. A profusion of flowers and palms veiled some of the windows, and the liveried servants moving here and there, at the doorways or in the distance behind the windows, gave some hint of what man's idea of a heaven upon earth might be.

Miriam's notions of a club-house were vague and a little fearful, but it was a part of the world into which she had entered, and she looked curiously, and wondered if Claude had found his way in there, and if this grandeur had made him dissatisfied with all that his home could give. Her sad eyes looked intently at the windows, noted the elegance and ease that seemed to prevade even the entrance-way to the place, and her heart sank. How little and how ignorant had she been to think to go against a world such as this was. Even for her one previous love she had been worse than foolish to try against such odds.

Then, just as they were passing the last window she saw a gleam of white hair, and a familiar face below coming down the marble steps.

A quick resolve came to her aid. Here was help. She would make an appeal to Senator Bradenberg.

She stopped the driver and explained to him that she wished to speak to the gentleman just coming down the steps, and the gallant senator was by her side in an instant, his hat lifted in deference.

In the brilliant light that came from the arch over the entrance Miriam's face shone distinctly. There was not a trace in the lustrous eyes of the storm through which she had been passing, save a feverish light that but made them brighter. The excitement of the moment had brought out the clear red of the cheeks, and the senator voted her for the hundredth time a very beautiful woman.

There was a childlike innocence in her appeal that saved her from any hint of suspicion of motives not the highest.

"Are you going to the Washburns' to-night, and have you promised to escort any one? Because if you haven't won't you please take me? Circumstances have arranged themselves in such a way that it will be impossible for my husband to accompany me. I shall be ready to start at nine o'clock. Now tell me frankly, please, if you have another engagement, or I shall never ask you again. You have been so good a friend, you know, that I have made bold to appeal to you, as I happened to see you in passing. You see I began to fear I might not get there at all."

The senator beamed. If he had other engagements he chose to keep them in the background. he was a man whose engagements were always subject to his own pleasure in the matter. He felt that Miriam's appeal gave him a decided advantage over this beautiful woman, and his eyes gleamed with a light that was not wholly saintly as he responded graciously that he would be charmed to accompany her to the Washburns'. He blessed the happy circumstances that had made him her choice.

He studied her face keenly with his hawk eyes to see if there was aught between herself and her husband that could give him more advantage with her, and he pressed her hand with a lingering tenderness wholly unnecessary as he paid her a pretty compliment. Then the carriage moved on, and Miriam was wrapped in the darkness of her thoughts once more, giving no heed to the lover-like words that had been murmured in her ear by the "dear kind old man," as she phrased it to herself.

Miriam reviewed with burning brain the nerves held in control like a vise, the movements it would be necessary for her to make. The gown she was to wear lay at this moment in her dressing room, the crowning creation of her skillful fingers. On it had been put more expense than all her other wardrobe together, and into it was woven the most careful and laborious needlework of which she was capable. In her own mind, after the experience she had had so far, it compared well with the costly imported robes the rich ones wore. It was filmy and encrusted here and there, not too much, with the frost-like lace-work carefully chosen and curiously blended with the lace-work of the owner's own daring fingers. It was white, all creamy white, and out of it her well-set shapely head had risen like a queen's when last she tried it on. Her dark, rich hair would set all off. She was almost sure the garment would be a success. But a daring thought for her was hovering in her breast. It was to bare her neck and arms. She had not done it before, for all the prejudices of her up-bringing in a country town where tradition did not call such dress modest, had been against it, and though she had deferred to inexorable custom by having her evening dresses made low, she had invariably managed to fill the vacant space with something soft and white which, while a cover, was yet a concession. And for her arms, gloves and lace made it quite possible to keep one's ideals even in a world where such notions were at a discount.

But now her eyes gleamed in the darkness. It seemed to her a devil perhaps might be whispering the suggestion. A daring like none she had ever felt before came to her. She would do it. Claude should see her in the same way in which he saw Mrs. Sylvester. He should see that his wife's neck was as white and her arms as well rounded as those of her adversary. For once she would appear as did others. If she was to die fighting, and she felt it was near the end of the battle now, whatever the result, she would die brilliantly. Any scruples she might have had before had fled. What were scruples at such a time? If it was this that Claude admired he should see that his wife could be as beautiful as any. She would die leaving him with the pain of regret in his heart.

The turning of the carriage from the smooth asphalt pavement to the cobblestones reminded her suddenly that she was nearing her aunt's, and that now she had no desire to see that excellent woman. She leaned forward and by the light of the passing street lamps examined her watch. It was growing late. She must hurry home to dress or she would not be ready when the senator came.

She gave the direction to the coachman, who occupied his homeward ride in some very uncomplimentary reflections on "parties who never knew their own minds," and settled herself to relax perfectly and rest during the homeward ride.

It was an evidence of the wonderful control she had acquired over herself during the last few months that she was able to do this in the face of all she had gone through and all that was yet to come.

Arrived at home she went at once to her room, and the first thing she did after locking her door and turning up the gas, was to cut with determined hands the carefully arranged white drapery from the neck and sleeves of her dress. She held her breath as she did it lest her courage fail, and she crushed the soft mass into a hopeless heap in the waste-basket lest she should be tempted to replace it. Then with bated breath she set about her preparations.

There was no thought of the untasted dinner. She did not remember it till the maid, coming at her summons to help fasten her gown, spoke of it. Then she answered that she was detained elsewhere and could not get home for dinner. She did not question if her husband had returned. It did not occur to her that he might have done so. She felt almost certain he had stayed with Mrs. Sylvester. She had not permitted herself one backward glance from her fast-moving carriage that afternoon.

The discreet maid said nothing. She saw that her mistress was at high pressure. She noticed with satisfaction that the shrouding white had been removed from the neck of the dress. She was glad that at last the world would have a chance to see that Mrs. Winthrop was a handsome woman, and knew how to dress as well as any one.

The toilet was interrupted only by the arrival of a box of most exquisite white orchids with Senator Bradenberg's card. With the light of battle still in her eyes, Miriam fastened them in place as one more weapon wherewith to dazzle the enemy, and as she did so blessed the "kind old man" for having selected these costly flowers, which otherwise she could never have hoped to wear.

It was the one touch the costume needed. Miriam stood a moment and gazed startled at her own beauty. She scarcely knew herself. She seemed to be looking at some other person critically, and to be more than satisfied. The color in her cheeks from intense excitement was more beautiful than any artist could have painted it, the lustre of her eyes beyond the power of any drug to produce.

"You should let the children see you, ma'am, before you go," said the maid in admiration. "Miss Pearl is likely to be awake yet, and Celie would soon hush off to sleep again."

But Miriam shuddered. Let her little innocent children look upon her so? Never! The white neck and arms that gleamed at her from the glass seemed dreadful to her when she realized that she was throwing in what conscience she had left. She had staked all, and it must be win or lose to-night. This she said to her heart as she looked steadily into her own eyes in the glass.

She turned away and let the maid wrap about her shoulders the long, white cloak, and said:

"No, don't waken the children. I would rather they would sleep. You need not sit up for me, I may be late, Be sure the baby is well covered."

Then she went down to meet her escort who had arrived and take her seat in the carriage, and the door was slammed shut and she whirled away in the darkness.

Five minutes afterward Claude once more reached his own door, weary and faint and frightened.

Chapter 14
The Washburn Party

Hold me but safe again within the bond
Of one immortal look! All woe that was,
Forgotten, and all terror that may be,
Defied — no past is mine, no future: look at me!

. . . .

When I saw him tangled in her toils,
A shame, said I, if she adds just him
To her nine and ninety other spoils,
The hundredth for a whim!
                                    — *Robert Browning.*

Claude Winthrop's sharpened ears had caught the sound of carriage wheels as he neared his own street. It was a welcome sound, and he began to berate his wife in his heart for giving him such an evening of suspense, and, in spite of his own repentings, he forgot at once that he was the cause of the trouble and put it upon her.

He heard the carriage door shut and the rumble coming toward him, and looked keenly at the driver as the dark object came in sight. Was it the same carriage in which Miriam had gone out that afternoon, and where had she been all this time? Then just in front of a street lamp the carriage passed him and he caught the gleam of white hair and a graceful head bent in deference as only the bad senator could do, and caught a gleam of something white beyond him, and a face out of the darkness, and then sudden fear took hold of him.

He hastened his steps with renewed vigor, and fairly shook the door open when his fumbling key refused to give him entrance at once.

"Where is Mrs. Winthrop?" he demanded of the startled maid as she appeared in answer to his ring.

"Why sir, she's gone. She told me you were detained, and the carriage has come and she's gone."

"Gone?" he echoed the words wildly, his blood-shot eyes and haggard face making the girl wonder if he had been drinking.

"Why, gone to the Washburn party, of course," she answered, edging nearer to the dining-room door.

Claude Winthrop tore off his overcoat and went upstairs two steps at a time. He rushed from room to toom as if he hoped to find her there. Gradually it was dawning upon him that they had been going to the Washburns' this night. He had forgotten until now. But Miriam had not. It seemed she had gone despite what had happened that afternoon. It came to him bitterly that she was able to face society with what there was between them. It showed him plainly, he thought, that she had long understood all that his call that afternoon upon Mrs. Sylvester had meant to her. In sudden sharp fear the possibility that she did not care so much as he had supposed she would was presented to his mind.

The light was still burning brightly in her dressing-room, and on the dressing table lay the paste-board box from which she had taken the orchids. One poor flower had been slightly bruised, and she had left it lying with the senator's card, carelessly, on the tissue paper of the box. Claude caught up the card and read, and horror choked him, and a fire flamed up into his eyes. If Senator Bradenberg had been present just then it might not have been well with him.

Half frenzied the husband tore through the rooms again, in the vain search for something to prove that it was not true, that she was yet there, and he might explain and all be made right between them, for he seemed to know that he would never be at rest again until that peace had come. It was a sign of the stirring of good in his heart that he now began to have a little doubt as to whether this might ever be.

He went to the nursery at last. He touched the cool foreheads of his boy and girl as they lay in their first sound sleep, and then bent over the crib where lay his baby. And it was in her soft neck, with her gold curls folding all about his hot, tired eyes, and her sweet breath coming and going regularly like the breath from a meadow at evening when the cows are coming home, that he was first able to think, and that a kind of repentance for what had happened began to stir him to better things.

It was not long he stayed there, but he gained strength to think, and then knew that he must get him to the Washburn house with all possible speed. The gay throng was the last place he would have chosen in his present state of mind, but he felt it imperative that he see his wife at once and bring her home. After that all should be made straight before he slept.

He kised little Celia tenderly and went swiftly to make his own toilet.

It was not the careful, prolonged affair that Claude Winthrop's toilets were usually, even for an everyday function, and yet this was one of the great crushes of the season. But he did not care now. He was going in search of his wife. A certain amount of care must be taken to gain him entrance and prevent comment, but what mattered the set of his necktie now?

Nevertheless he was delayed by little things, his hands were nervous and trembling with excitement. In his haste he had to undo and do things over again, and he began to feel the lack of his dinner, yet he would not stop to get anything.

And at last he was out on the street and started toward the Washburns'. Even then it seemed to him as if he were treading over and over the same ground like a horse set to saw wood, and did not get on in spite of all his efforts. And when he came in sight of the great house with its canvas-guarded entrance and its many twinkling windows it seemed to him the glitter of a hateful, treacherous trap that had snared his beautiful wife.

The music and the dancing and the pomp and ceremony and feasting were in full sway when he at last entered and began his search.

Then, after all, it was not his wife but Mrs. Sylvester who first met his searching gaze.

She was all in black to-night, black velvet, rich and sweeping and simple, and out of it her white shoulders rose in all their loveliness. The only jewels she wore were a string of diamonds about her throat, and diamonds in the aigrette in her hair. The effect was startling. Claude had never seen her all in black before, for she affected much the dainty shades of blue and pink or white and gold. But it seemed to-night as if she had chosen her costume with a view to dazzling all who beheld her.

In her hand she carried — and Claude could not help but notice — a great handful of delicate lilies of the valley, the flowers he had given Miriam on their wedding day. And alas, the flowers he had often given this other woman woo.

It angered him that he noticed her at all, that he saw how beautiful she was, that he did not hate the white hands that held the lilies, the scornful lips that smiled at him, and the treacherous eyes that summoned him so imperatively. It amazed him that in his present state of feeling he could notice details like flowers and recall clearly all the sweetness and the bitter connected with them.

He did not answer her summons. He did not respond to her unspoken greeting across the roomful of unnoticing people. He only drew his brows together in a heavy frown — the frown that some people had remarked upon as being "interesting" — and glowered back, and then turned his restless eyes to search the great ball room once more.

He did not look her way again. He would not, though he was long conscious of her amazed gaze still fixed upon him as she talked to a circle of admiring men. It occurred to him that with that same amused smile would she greet death and destruction if they should chance to come her way.

As soon as he could, for the crush, he made his way slowly around the room, but not toward Mrs. Sylvester. Always he kept it in mind to avoid the place where he had seen her, to avoid it even with his eyes. And thus moving suddenly she spoke to him, startling him, as one will start at finding the evil so carefully avoided in front standing just behind one.

How she had come there he did not stop to question. He turned upon her angrily.

"Claude, you are a perfect bear! I have come to warn you to take that frown from your face or you will presently be the subject of comment. What is the matter? That little meeting with your wife on my doorstep seems not to have agreed with your fine temper, my dear. Was she so very angry?"

There was pity in the well-modulated tone, the alluring pity that Mrs. Sylvester knew so well how to use upon occasion, and it roused the soul of the half-frenzied man nearly to distraction. He could have struck her as she stood there in all her insolent beauty, speaking of his peerless wife with such disdain. He could have struck her, yet the hand that strikes was fettered by the tender pressures he had once given to her hand, by the waxen blossoms he had disloyally brought to another than his wife; and the white lips that would have uttered withering words to her were sealed by the kiss he had once placed upon her lips. Oh, horror of agony! How that kiss burned into his lips now and to his very soul, like the sting of a venomous serpent!

There she stood before him with all her power about her, all her beauty, all her unscrupulousness, and dared to be what she was and to look him in the eyes and bid him follow her.

He turned from her as one would have turned from some hideous, loathsome sight, and would have moved away without a word but that she laid her hand upon his arm and walked beside him, and he could not rid himself of her except by shaking her off and bringing the eyes of the assembled multitude upon them both. He was forced to walk beside her, but he did it with his angry eyes fixed straight ahead, and so soon as they were come to an alcove where it was possible he stepped out of the crowd and led her to a vacant seat.

She saw that for some strange reason he was proof against her wiles tonight. He meant to leave her here alone. He had not yielded to her startling beauty. She knew it was startling, she had studied for days to make it so. And yet it had failed!

Failed? Should she entertain such a thought? Not for an instant! Summoning all her arts she said with a piteous little sigh:

"Claude, you must bring me something from the supper room. The heat has made me dizzy and faint. To tell the truth I have been ill for a week, and I only made the effort to get up and come here that I might see you about something very important, and you declined to come and see me, even though I warned you —"

"What shall I bring you?" he cut her short with his icy words as if impatient to have the disagreeable duty done.

"Claude," she said reproachfully, her voice trembling, "you are acting abominably. But I forgive you. Get me something quick, at least a glass of water —" and she leaned back against the cusions and dropped her delicate eyelids for an instant with a flutter of weakness, though her color was too bright for one about to faint.

He cast one glance into her face and thought he detected deceit in her very attitude. But he went at once. Strange he could see so plainly now what but a few short weeks ago had been so charmingly veiled.

He scarcely knew what he got from the supper room, anything to have the hateful duty done and be free, but when he brought it to her Mrs. Sylvester smiled faintly and asked him to sit down beside her for just a minute until she felt better. She took the glass he brought her and sipped a few swallows.

"Wait!" she commanded impressively, suddenly dropping all her smiling ways and taking a new tone with him, "I have something most important to tell you. It will take but a moment, and indeed I must tell you though you do not deserve it."

He waited beside her impatiently. He could do no less after her request although he felt that she was deceiving him merely to keep him there. His natural politeness seemed to make it necessary that he remain for a few minutes at least, and his cowardly spirit saw no way to leave. But as she talked his eyes searched the brilliant moving throng. He scarcely heard what Mrs. Sylvester was saying, till he became conscious that she was speaking of Miriam:

"Have you seen her yet? She is magnificent. That gown of hers must have been a fabulous price. It is perfect. Only the greatest artist could have turned it out. And right there lies her trouble. She is so constantly with Senator Bradenberg —"

Claude's icy voice broke in upon her voluble talk:

"You will be kind enough to leave my wife's name out of the conversation."

She had never heard him speak like that. She looked up at him half-frightened and was not reassured by the angry eyes that met hers. Her scheme was in danger of failure, and there was nothing in the world that she hated worse than failure; besides she had found this flirtation so altogether interesting and so hard to pursue that her heart — as much of a heart as she possessed — was affected by it, and when a heart is involved, and there is no conscience behind it, there is nothing a woman will not do. She dashed in boldly:

"But I must speak of your wife. Don't you see she will bring a scandal upon you? You surely are not blind. I feel it my duty to warn you. I did not dream her innocent baby-face covered so wise and old a head. It has not taken her long to learn the ways of the world. She has cast aside the last vestige of her country prudery to-night, and her gown is irreproachable —"

At that moment there was a stir among the throng near them, and the music burst forth loudly. Instinctively Claude leaned forward to catch her words, though they were making his soul rage within him. Encouraged by this Mrs. Sylvester went on:

"She had made a wonderful success with nothing to start on, but she should be warned to go a little slower. There are other men with whom she might amuse herself, but she is all taken up with the senator and does not understand. She ought to know that when Senator Bradenberg plays, he plays to kill!"

Trembling with rage, white with horror and fury, Claude essayed to stop her and bent low to speak the words. He felt so angry he would have liked to throttle the white neck in its setting of diamongs.

"Take care what you are saying of my wife, Mrs. Sylvester!" He said the words so quietly that she scarcely realized how intensely he was feeling until she looked into his face and he met her eyes steadily.

What it was just then that made them both look up at the people passing near them neither knew. There was nothing in their coming to attract attention, more than in those that had passed before, but Claude found himself face to face with his wife coming calmly toward him on the arm of the senator, the senator's orchids on her breast, and the senator's glances for her face.

For a moment he looked without knowing what he saw. It seemed to him that she had died and this was her white angel come to reproach him. The filmy robe which he knew not, seemed some angel garment. The bare neck and arms to which he was so unaccustomed, all made her seem unreal.

He gazed and gazed as she came nearer, lost in admiration of her beauty, until she was near enough to touch him, and then she looked up unconsciously, took in coolly the situation, nodded to Mrs. Sylvester, passed by her husband's searching gaze as though he had been a stranger, and with slightly heightened color, her small white hand resting confidently upon the soft broadcloth of the senator's arm, passed on into the conservatory.

Chapter 15
Villainy Foiled

I took my power in my hand
And went against the world;
'Twas not so much as David had,
But I was twice as bold.

I aimed my pebble, but myself
Was all the one that fell.
Was it Goliath was too large,
Or only I too small?
— *Emily Dickinson.*

When Miriam had felt herself shut into the carriage on the way to the Washburns' two hours before, she leaned back against the cushions and closed her eyes in a momentary relief. She had been on so intense a strain for so many hours that she was glad of the minute's relief from glaring light and necessity for action.

It was before she had opened her eyes that the senator bent over her with his tender: "You are very weary, poor child!" and the carriage passed Claude in the uncertain lamplight.

She roused herself to be an interested listener to her companion, wishing all the time it had been possible for her to take this ride without an escort. What a relief it would have been to just shut her eyes and rest without even trying to think, all the way. For she felt instinctively that the evening was to be an ordeal.

"I *am* tired," she said smiling and trying to rally her forces to seem gay. "I have been having a full day."

"Well, lean back and rest. You need not mind me. Don't feel that you must keep up now to hide your feelings. I know through what a strain you are passing. You are a brave woman."

Horror froze Miriam's veins. Her heart almost stopped beating for the moment. A numbness crept up from her finger tips tingling through her whole being. She started upright in her seat and her face grew white in the dim darkness of the carriage so that her companion wondered if perhaps he might have gone too far.

He knew? He had seen her trouble? Then the whole world must know. Then her secret was out, and her defeat was an accomplished thing already, without the evening's test. Claude was fallen and her heart was desolate! And yet she found that she had still been clinging to that poor dead hope that she had declared gone forever so many, many times.

For the instant she longed to return home and hide her heart where no eye might look upon her defeat, no scornful lips speak to others of her shame. Then the steady control into which she had been schooling herself for weeks took command and she rallied. Not for the world would she give sign that she recognized her defeat. She would go through this one evening with her head held as bravely as though her heart were crowned with happiness. She would not give a sign or quiver, though the knife went twisting through her heart again and again. So would she at least make glorious her defeat.

"Oh, 'tis not so bad as that!" she laughed gayly, and wondered at herself that her voice could assume so much; "but I have been accepting too many invitations perhaps, and the sudden change from my quiet life with my children during the last few years has been a little hard."

The worldly wisdom that covered all the meaning of her companion's pity had not been acquired for nothing. It was better after all that she should spend her time in mental fencing with the senator than that she should have time to rest and think, as think she must, however much she might wish to cease.

Senator Bradenberg admired her bravery, wondered if it were wholly brave or wholly innocent, and pleased himself all the more with the prospect of the conquest of this charming woman in the near future.

He had put to play his cards well, and she would be won — all the more interesting that she was not easy to conquer. Once she found out that her husband was on intimate terms with a woman like Mrs. Sylvester she would turn to him for comfort. Then he would have it all his own way. In his long career there had been few that he had cared to smile upon who had been able to resist him.

He saw that she did not intend to give him her confidence at present, and gracefully led the conversation from the dangerous point, yet always keeping in it that tender personal note, whose main impression was that he was ready to do anything in her service.

He told her how it had touched his heart that she had chosen him to take her out to-night, that he had felt from the first moment of meeting her that there was something drawing them toward one another, she reminded him so strikingly of a dear lost sister. Oh, that dear lost sister who had never existed except in her fertile brain, and oh, the long list of beautiful women who were like her! He told her how he had been watching her, and how beautiful she was, and what a success in society, and how pleased he was that she had chosen to wear his poor flowers on her heart — "as a shield, my dear, use them as a shield, if you please, against anything that might trouble you," and then, as she murmured her thanks for words she had only half heard because her mind was traveling on ahead of the carriage and she was planning the last scene of the conflict, he took her little hand and pressed it gently and stroked it with his well-tended fingers and told her she was to turn to him when anything arose to give her any trouble, that he could always be relied upon. And could he have known that Miriam was thinking much more about how she could get her hand away without hurting the kind old man's feelings than she was of his words, he would not have smiled so confidently as he handed her from the carriage, nor would his sensual eyes have looked at her with half the light of triumph that they held.

He was kindness itself during the evening. He did not keep her entirely to himself for it was not his way to call too much attention when he was in the way of a conquest. There were people who delighted to warn young innocents against bad wolves. He had no desire to have anything interfere with his plans. Therefore he kept them to himself, and played the quiet, elderly escort to perfection. He so managed that Mrs. Winthrop was always the center of a group of people worth knowing; he seemed to be not too much in evidence, and yet he was on hand at the right moment to serve her. He sent her down to supper with another man on purpose, and watched her from afar with gloating eye. When she had appeared from the dressing room and he saw that she had modified her way of dress to suit the most exacting laws of society his heart had leaped in something like the way it did in youthful days. She was learning fast. One more barrier was broken down. How lovely she was, and what incomparable arms and what finely modeled shoulders. Could Claude have seen his evil gaze just then he would certainly have knocked him down.

All the evening the senator watched for his moment, not sure yet that it would come to-night or even in many nights — watched until he saw the weary look coming more and more into the beautiful dark eyes; watched until the pitiful, white quiver became more distinct about the firm, sweet mouth; watched until he saw Claude enter, and saw Mrs. Sylvester's maneuvers, and until those two went to the alcove by the conservatory entrance. Then he felt that his time had come.

Slowly and with careful calculation he made his way to Miriam's side and murmured low to her that there were some beautiful orchids, rarer even than those she wore, in the conservatory, and as she looked tired would she like to come and see them? And she assented eagerly. She had caught glimpses of Mrs. Sylvester on one side of the room and her husband on the other a few minutes before, and every instant since had been of agonizing expectation. The crisis, she felt, was just at hand. Almost she felt her heart fail her. She fain would get a minute away from all this glare and noise before it came. And then they passed the alcove and she saw her husband apparently in deep converse with her enemy.

The senator, watching her closely, saw the magnificent way in which she passed the ordeal, and then saw the white stealing about her mouth in deadly, haggard lines. Almost he thought she would fall and he led her to a seat behind some palms in a turn of the walk, out of the way of most of the guests.

It was a true lover's retreat where he had placed her, in a chair of many soft cushions, and he took the delicate fan from her hand and wafted it gently till she seemed to gain a little courage to look up, a piteous appeal in her eyes.

He did not quite understand that appeal. He took it as the signal for his own plans to begin.

"My dear," he said placing an arm on the back of her chair and letting his fingers touch the white shoulders near them, "don't look so pitiful. There are other loves in this world, even if one has failed. I told you you might turn to me and I have felt from the first that you would do so. My dear, I love you as he, whose name you bear, could never do. Will you come with me and let me comfort you?" and then he leaned over her and pressed a kiss upon her horrified lips.

If all the terror of all the women in this world who have been sinned against could have been concentrated in one look, that look was Miriam Winthrop's. Consternation, dismay, loathing, and alarm were mingled in one mighty, fascinated gaze. It was the look of one who, having fled from pursuing terror, encounters a beast of prey more fearful than anything that could have gone before.

Miriam had shuddered as his evil fingers touched her cold shoulder. It was a liberty which even an old man should not have taken, she thought; and then as the meaning of his words became clear at last to her she watched him with horrified, wild gaze, seeming to see the very glare of the lower regions in his wicked eyes. Noticing as one will the details of insignificant things at such a time, she saw a miniature, reflected in the crystal discs of his eyeglasses, the ballroom beyond, with its gayly moving throngs, the dancers, the flutter of fans, the turning of heads, the slow walk of couples near the entrance of the conservatory, the sharp-pointed palms towering all about, and two tall figures in black coming toward them. All the time she saw these things she felt that the minute for this human tiger to spring was coming, and her life would depend upon whether she was able to evade his horrid clutch.

She was utterly unprepared for the kiss, but her senses were on the alert. All these months of agony and silent self-control had been, as it were, schooling her to meet this awful minute. All the sorrow she had suffered as she came up, step by step, this long dark way of trouble had been as nothing to the torture of the present development. Just where she had trusted the most had she found treachery the basest.

One instant she crouched in the chair after that shameful touch of his lips and then, darting upward with all the litheness of her girlhood days, she raised her firm hand and struck the elegant and ardent senator in the face; struck him full in the eyes where the two fragile discs balanced on their slender nose-piece of gold across his aristocratic nose, and sent the glasses shivering in a myriad pieces on the marble floor, and a trickle of blood down the senator's baffled, astonished face showed that the glass had done its work before it reached the floor.

Then Miriam turned and, panting, wildly fled.

The senator, wiping his blinded eyes and stinging cheeks in bewilderment, looked up to see two people standing at the entrance to their retreat. And one was fair and tall and clad in black velvet and wore a devilish smile of amusement on her face, but the other had angry eyes that blazed from a face as white as death.

The senator was searching vainly in his fertile brain for an explanation that should allow him to assume his usual careless ease. It is safe to say he had not been many times slapped in the face for a kiss. He would have given much to know how long these spectators had been present.

But Miriam, flying down between the palms, all white — white face, white arms, white gown, the light of holy anger springing from her sorrowful eyes, like some desecrated angel, tearing, as she flew, the hateful blossoms from her breast and stamping on them, looked up and saw her husband standing before her, and beside him saw her enemy and knew her hour had come and her defeat complete, with all the witnesses present. As though she had been struck to the heart, she dropped silently at his feet, striking her head heavily on the marble floor.

Darting one awful look of imprecation and revenge, Claude stooped and gathered her in his arms and felt the unresponsive heart.

And behind him stood that silent figure in black velvet, with the same scornful smile upon her lips, the only witness of the first flush of humiliation on the face of the usually complaisant senator, and the first white agony of the terrified husband.

This was her work, and she viewed it with the cruel scorn of a heartless woman.

Chapter 16
Fighting Death

The small neglect that may have pained,
A giant structure will have gained
When it can never be explained.
— *A.D.F. Randolph.*

They were all sympathy in a moment, the crowd outside that surged about to help, but some glanced curiously at Mrs. Sylvester and then at Claude, and others looked beyond to where the senator searched for the frame of his eye-glasses, the while he concocted a fine tale of how they were broken as he tried to save Mrs. Winthrop from falling, and told it too, to those who came to help him look. For he was shut in from escape at present unless he crawled behind the palms, which he would have been glad to do.

A doctor was found somewhere in the hushed throng, who cleared a space for air and gave opportunity for the abashed old scoundrel to slip away.

But Mrs. Sylvester did not move. Claude once, on looking up, while the doctor was listening to the heart to see if there was any movement at all, saw her standing there and hated her. He wished she would go and leave him alone with his misery and his dead life, she who had brought him here to meet his just punishment and who had stayed to see it meted out to him stroke by stroke.

Some one gave an order for a carriage and Celia Lyman brought the soft white cloak that Miriam had ingeniously made to imitate a much costlier one, and Mrs. Sylvester still stood and watched, not offering to be of any assistance, only smiling that perpetual amustment which almost seemed as if her eyes were glad of all this mischief.

They carried Miriam to the carriage by a side entrance and the doctor went with them to take her home.

And as long as she could see them down the long palm arch of the conservatory, Mrs. Sylvester watched them. Then she turned and went back to the ballroom, but her hands were empty. She had lost somewhere her lilies of the valley.

Back through the darkness of the streets rode Miriam, resting at last from all the weary way and in her husband's arms; back from her glorious defeat, where she had come out from the world's smirching as white in soul as were her garments.

The doctor kept his practised finger upon the place where the pulse should have been, but only a feeble, occasional flutter gave any hope that there was life. The long day's strain, with the tremendous happenings, added to the months of agony, had secured the inevitable result. The poor weak body and tortured soul had given way and were almost at the parting place.

They carried her in and up the staircase down which she had come so beautiful and so sorrowful but a few short hours before, and the household was awakened to that hushed excitement that prevades the home where death is lingering on the threshold.

The frightened servants obeyed orders, went on errands, brought stimulants and blankets and hot water.

All night they worked, the doctor and a nurse and another doctor, who had been summoned to their aid. The husband stood helpless at the foot of the bed and watched his wife's white face that seemed to be modeled in marble, so still it was and unearthly in its spotless reproach. And was this the end then? Was he no more to see her on earth? Never to have a chance to explain — no, there was no explanation — but to tell her that he loved her? Was not this punishment too great for all he had done, for his weakness, his cowardice? Nay, but what had he made her suffer! spoke the white face on the pillow to his shrinking heart.

And little Pearl stole from her bed in her long nightdress and crept her soft little hand in his and whispered:

"Is our mamma dead, father? Why doesn't she wake up?"

And even the sorrowing, gentle little voice seemed to accuse him of the deed.

The long hours dragged away and still there was no sign from her that she lived save an occasional flutter of the heart, and once a gasping sigh. But at last, just as the morning broke, the large eyes opened upon them unknowingly, as though they had been looking on great mysteries, and then dropped shut again as she moaned softly, "Oh, I am so tired!"

They said she slept, but it seemed more like death than sleep.

And suddenly, in the midst of it all, the face on the pillow seemed to fade out of Claude's vision and he found himself clinging to the foot of the bed and the doctor trying to persuade him to lie down. And some one discovered that he needed attention too. But he came to himself again soon with the sharp reality that comes always in sorrow after a moment's unconsciousness, which robs it of its pain, and insisted on coming back where he could see his wife. And the morning wore away.

Then silently there entered one of the death angel's sentinels that he posts where he may have occasion to return. Fever took up his stand beside that bed, all fire-clothed and mocking. The patient began to moan and toss and mutter of things all troublous, and out of the chaos of heart-rendering sentences, that showed her husband much that otherwise he never would have known, there came one sentence again and again until it became the one sentence that the poor troubled brain could communicate:

"The pattern, the pattern, the pattern on the mount. Oh, give me the pattern on the mount!"

"What does she mean?" asked the doctor, puzzled after the hundredth attempt to quiet the restless one with answers that would set her at peace. "Had she been sewing much before she was taken ill? There is usually some little occurrence, or some big one, back of the trouble of a delirious mind, I believe," he said, "and if one is only bright enough to find out what it is, it can sometimes be removed." He looked at Claude with the light of enthusiasm for his profession in his eyes, but the husband's haggard face responded only with a hopeless compliance. He was taking his punishment bitterly.

Then Claude went out to the maid to get, if possible, some solution to the question that was troubling the patient, for the doctor felt much would be gained if her mind could be set at rest on this point and she be induced to sleep again.

Careful questioning brought out the facts from the demure maid. Yes, Mrs. Winthrop had done a great deal of sewing since when Mr. Winthrop went to Europe. She had finished all the children's clothes herself without the usual help from a seamstress, and she had made many of her beautiful gowns with her own hands. The tears flowed freely as the maid went into details. She brought different dresses from the wardrobe and showed Mr. Winthrop the exquisite needleword, the rare lace and *applique,* and danity outlining of pattern in curious ribbon-work and embroidery.

Claude listened to it all helplessly, with agonized expression. He fingered the beautiful handiwork clumsily. It seemed something sacred to him. This, then, explained why no bills had come to him for all the rare garments she had worn. Then he remembered his mission.

"Did she have any patterns?" he asked awkwardly enough.

"Oh, yes, sir, a whole box full, besides those in the fashion book. I have them put by carefully," and she brought forth a large pasteboard box containing patterns of every imaginable garment a woman could put on. Her husband turned the leaves of the pile of fashion magazines without purpose. Just to touch these things that had been a part of his wife's precious life while he in his blindness had been separated from her, seemed good. (Perchance the book he held was the very one containing the letter that gave Miriam imspiration for her gigantic undertaking.) But finally he brought the box of patterns to the doctor and tried to tell him all.

They carried them to the bed and laid them out one by one and let the sick one touch them. She looked at them without interest and the paper crackled gratingly between her fevered fingers. They were the things of a life with which she seemed almost to be done. And still her lips repeated: "I want the pattern on the mount. Can no one show me where to get the pattern on the mount?"

"Is there anything in the house that she calls a 'mount'?" asked the doctor, but they shook their heads.

"It's my opinion it's a minister she needs," said the silent nurse at last. "There's something like what she's saying in the Bible, if I ain't mistaken."

The doctor's face brightened. "Surely," he said, "it must be that. Have you a minister whom she knows well?"

But Claude shook his head sadly. They had not been frequent attendants at church of late. He was unacquainted with his wife's recent attempts at identification with the church. He shrank from the strange minister who had preached the last time he was there.

"Then may I bring my brother?" said the doctor. "He is studying for the ministry and he is here on a visit. He has a lot of sense, if he is my brother, and I'd like to put him in the next room and see what he makes of all this."

Claude's heart was too heavy to care what was done. He was wrestling with the conviction that Miriam was going to die. It was traditional that dying people talked of religious things. That was what this talk of the pattern on the mount meant, of course. Strange that it had been only the uneducated nurse who had been able to think of it! And he sat at the foot of the bed, his haggard face almost the counterpart of his wife's, so unceasingly did he watch her.

They had sent for her mother to come, Claude's mother-in-law, with her decided ways and her dainty cameo face that Claude used to like to think Miriam's would be like when he and she grew old together. And she would come, and perhaps read the awful tale of his shame and her daughter's sorrow from his eyes. He felt that it was written there.

His mother-in-law had always liked him, and he had returned the affection, but now she would despise him. He shrank from that like a blow.

Then tropped back one by one the years which he and Miriam had spent together. The little house where they first began housekeeping — how foolish and how happy they were there! The tiny parlor that they furnished bit by bit as they could spare the money and how they would go hand in hand to look at each new purchase and he would tell her she had a new idol now to worship, and she would blush and tell him, No, she never worshipped things that had no life.

The days when she did the work and they ate breakfast on the kitchen table to save trouble and also to save coal! The very taste of the buckwheat cakes and syrup that she piled upon his plate hot from the smoking griddle was in his mouth. So keenly can the suffering nerves smite back the aching heart by a sight, an ordor, or a taste.

Then there was the day when her aunt sent the lovely little crib and its fixings, all dainty with broad blue satin ribbons, for the expected little one that was coming to gladden their hearts. How they had hovered over that little nest, smoothed down the fine white coverlet, patted the little ruffled pillow and admired the softness of the pretty blankets. And he would remember now with what curious blending of emotions he had bent again over that crib, alone, a few days later, and turned down the wriggling blanket to look upon his first-born, his little Pearl, all pink and sweet and sleeping with her rose-leaf hands tight curled and her tiny mouth set firmly as if she meant to face and conquer this world into which she had come!

That look of a madonna Miriam had given him! How it was burned into his soul now beside that changed face on the pillow, and beside it came the wraith of her as she had been that night, the last he had seen her conscious and well, her beautiful, sad face, and her reproachful eyes. Oh, horror of horrors! Oh, pity of pities! that any life could bear such punishment as his! God had no need to make a hell hereafter for such as he if this could be for all who sinned that way.

And over and over he thought it all out, the story since the day she must have known about his drive in the park. All the changes he had seen in her, and yet had not noticed at the time. The little things that she had done so carefully for his comfort on his voyage. The true meaning of her silence during his absence, the picture of the children with her own taken from frame.

He pieced together bit by bit her carefully hidden plans, her almost superhuman effort, and its reason.

That she had had marvelous success he did not stop to wonder at. She was Miriam. No other woman could have achieved what she had, no other was worthy of it. She was peerless. So, as his old love for her grew into a new and more understanding love his sin grew in enormity, until its weight threatened to overpower him.

Then came his wonder over her treatment of Mrs. Sylvester, how she had found out, and how she succeeded in getting into the society in which that odious woman moved, and to crown all there came that last night at the Washburns', Miriam's startling beauty, and perfect self-control and the scene in the conservatory which both he and Mrs. Sylvester had been witnesses throughout. Sometimes, for a moment, he forgot even his sorrow, to glory in the fact that Mrs. Sylvester had seen Miriam repulse the wicked man who had sought to do her harm. Almost it was worth the horror it had cost him to see those hateful lips touch his wife's, that the evil woman might know how pure, how true, his Miriam had really been.

And then he would to live it over again and all the time that sweet monotonous voice would repeat:

"The pattern in the mount! The pattern in the mount!"

Chapter 17
The Ministry of Song

Adrift! A little boat adrift!
And night is coming down!
Will no one guide a little boat
Unto the nearest town?
— Emily Dickinson.

When Dr. Carter drove back to the Winthrop house with his brother they found Celia Lyman standing at the door, just about to enter. She had called to know how Mrs. Winthrop was.

The doctor, whose keen memory was one of the means of his success in his profession, recognized the young girl as the one who had been of much assistance the night that Mrs. Winthrop was taken ill, and according to his habit of making all things that came in his way bend to the purpose he had in hand, he asked Miss Lyman to come in a few minutes, saying he would then be better able to tell her how his patient was doing. He had it in mind that this young girl might be able to give them a clue, or at least render some help in quieting the restlessness of the sick one.

On the way to the house the doctor and his brother had talked the case over carefully. The doctor had not much religion to boast of himself, but he had all faith in his brother, and together they had arranged a little plan whereby they hoped to gain the attention of Mrs. Winthrop for a moment and get her mind quieted.

"Did you ever try music to soothe one in delirium?" asked the brother. "When I was sick in the South that winter it would put me to sleep even to hear a street hand-organ. There seemed to be something in the rhythm of sound that did all the tossing and tumbling and twisting for me, and let me rest for a few minutes. Couldn't you get her attention if some one would sing softly, some one with a sweet voice that she knew well?"

"That's a good idea, George," responded the doctor heartily; "you ought to have been a doctor yourself. It's a pity to waste yourself on the ministry."

"Won't it be as well to be a doctor of souls?" had been the answer.

Now that Doctor Carter saw Miss Lyman this conversation suddenly came back to him.

"Ask her if she can sing, George," he whispered after having introduced his brother, as he left the two in the parlor below and went upstairs.

And so it happened that a half-hour later Celia Lyman sat near the door of the room adjoining the sick-room, an old hymn book in her lap and her heart throbbing in frightened beats, ready to sing if the doctor should give her a sign to do so.

She hoped in the depths of her heart that it would not be considererd necessary. She had never been so near to death before as even this, and she was afraid her voice would not respond when she tried to sing. She wondered why she had promised when that handsome stranger asked her. Of course it was nothing for her to sing that old song that she had heard a hundred times in church, and there was the music just before her; but how would her voice sound without any accompaniment but that ceaseless murmur of the monotonous voice in the next room, the voice of the woman whom she had admired, and who they said was near to the awful door of death? She shuddered as she thought of her loveliness in the beautiful gown she wore when she had last seen her. It seemed impossible that one who but a few days before was so full of life and the brightness of the world should now be all but within that mysterious shadow.

From where she sat she could catch a glimpse now and then of the bowed head and shoulders of Mrs. Winthrop. She kept her face the other way. It was terrible to see deep grief in a man. She remembered how his eyes had watched his wife every time she had seen him, and girl-like she had woven of her fancies a cord of tender romance binding these two wedded souls together. All these things did not make it easier for her to sing.

When Mr. Carter first asked her if she would sing if she were needed, she had begged him not to speak of it, and shrank from going upstairs even, but when she looked into the calm eyes of the stranger and saw that he was in earnest about it, and that he expected her to be as ready to sacrifice as he would be, her pretty color came and went, and before she knew it she had consented to try. She did not like to say "No" any more than she liked to do what she was asked. But finally, with trembling heart, she followed them upstairs and took her seat with the old hymn book. She had hoped very much that no music would be found and she might have that for an excuse, but the maid at last produced from the nursery bookcase and old hymn book and the young minister had found the hymn he was looking for, and now he had gone into the sick-room and left the door ajar.

She could see Mr. Winthrop raise his head and bow as the minister came toward the bed. She could see the hopeless droop of his mouth, the heavy sadness of his eyes.

Mr. Carter stood a moment looking into the restless eyes that did not notice him, and then he said quite clearly, so that Celia could hear every word in the other room:

"I know the pattern in the mount. I can get it for you, my friend."

The low muttered ceased for a minute and the hallow eyes turned upon the speaker.

"What is the pattern in the mount?" said the high, unnatural voice. "Give me the pattern in the mount."

"Jesus Christ is the pattern in the mount," answered the clear voice once more, every word spoken as one would speak to a very little child. "And he has sent you a message to-day. He wants you to put your work away and rest."

"But I can't; I spoiled it all. My life is all cut up and it won't fit that pattern. I can't get any more to begin over again."

The restless head began once more and the low moaning that struck such terror to the hearts of the watchers.

"Jesus will make it new again if you will just rest in him. You are tired, you know, and he wants you to rest. Listen!"

The doctor gave the signal and Celia, with fluttering heart that almost threatened to choke her, sang:

> " 'Come unto me, ye weary,
>   And I will give you rest,'
> Oh, blessed voice of Jesus,
>   Which comes to hearts opprest!"

Then, with slight pause, she went on:

> "Just as I am, without one plea,
> But that thy blood was shed for me,
> And that thou bid'st me come to thee,
>   O Lamb of God, I come!"

Celia's trembling voice ceased.

The eyes of the sick woman had kept themselves fixed upon the strange young man in a kind of wondering joy, but as the music died away she showed signs of restlessness once more.

"Now," said the clear voice commandingly again, "if you will shut your eyes and go to sleep till you are stronger, then, when you are well enough, I will tell you all about the pattern in the mount. Now, just lie still and listen.''

She let him lay her hands down straight upon the white bedcover and obediently closed her eyes with the faint shadow of a smile, and Celia, her courage growing with her need, sang on:

> "Just as I am, and waiting not
> To rid my soul of one dark blot,
> To thee, whose blood can cleanse each spot,
>   O Lamb of God, I come!"

On through the rest of the hymn she sang, her voice growing low and tender.

The doctor, coming up behind, with perspiration standing on his brow and the tears in his kind eyes, whispered quickly: "Don't stop for anything till I tell you. Sing on, sing something, sing anything.''

And Celia, feeling as if she were a part of a great life-saving machine that was wound up and could not stop, sang on. There were three other hymns on the same page set to the same music, tender, beautiful words. She sang them all, her instinct telling her to make her voice gradually softer, and at last the nurse whispered, "He says you may stop," and Celia went downstairs, threw herself into a cozy corner, buried her face in the pile of cushions and cried as if her heart would break.

It was so that Mr. Carter found her a little later when he came down. She tried to smooth her rumpled hair and wipe the tears from her pretty face as she sat up quickly on his entrance. But he came over toward her eagerly, the light of a pleasant comradeship in his eyes.

"She is quiet now," he said with a glad ring. "Your singing soothed her wonderfully. God has given you a rare gift in your voice.''

Then, noticing for the first time her tear-stained face, he said anxiously:

"It has been a great strain upon you. Of course it would be. She was your dear friend, you said.''

Out into the sunshine they went, those two, who had never met before until that morning, and whom God had brought together in a bit of task for him, and talked and walked into a new world all their own.

"Oh, but I'm afraid you are mistaken about me," said Celia softly when she could get her breath to speak. "I am not — I don't know about these things. I am not —" she hesitated for a word.

"You don't mean you are not a Christian?" the young man asked anxiously. He had been so sure he detected the sympathy in her voice as she sang. He thought no one could sing like that without knowing the meaning of the words.

"Oh, no," said Celia, relieved; "I'm a Christian, I suppose. That is, I'm a member of the church. I joined when I was a little girl and all my Sunday-school class were joining. Mother thought I was too young and maybe I was. I'm not very good. I never heard anybody talk as you've done this morning and I never went where there was any trouble before. I couldn't do what you did and I didn't think I could do what I did. Oh, isn't it awful that everybody has to die?"

Her face turned grey in the sunshine and she shivered visibly.

"Yes, if that were all," the young man answered solemnly; "but when you think of eternity and heaven it would be more awful if we couldn't die, if we had to go on living in this world where trouble and sin are everywhere."

"But sin and trouble are not everywhere. This is a lovely world, the one I live in. I have been in society where there isn't any of that. I suppose of course there is sin and trouble among wicked people, and probably it is just as well for those to die and get out of it. But take for instance Mrs. Winthrop. She has a lovely little home and charming children and a husband who adores her. The last time I saw her, the night she was taken ill, she was at one of the most conservative gatherings to be found in this city. She has the *entree* among the nicest people now, and she has perfect taste in dress. It is so dreadful for her to be in danger of dying. I think dying is cruel!"

"But sin and trouble are in the world even though they have not touched you," spoke the young man tenderly. He longed to strike an answering chord in the soul of this beautiful girl. He had come from among earnest Christian workers to visit his brother and he found the world about him chilly for his warm enthusiasm.

"I come from a recent college settlement work. I could take you to homes where little children are crying for bread and mothers are working from day to day for a few pennies to buy it, and because there is not enough for all they work on without, and give the crying, unsatisfied children their share. I could show you deathbed after deathbed where souls go out into a darkness that is not broken by any whisper of the light that Jesus can give."

Celia looked up at the glowing face as he walked beside her, and thought that she knew how the face of a saint looked. And yet he was only a plain young man doing his Master's work with the fervor of a consecrated spirit.

Celia Lyman took no account of the length of the walk as she listened with absorbing interest to the story fo the young man's work in the slums, and of the Christian work that a band of his college men were carrying on. It opened a new world to her, a world that appealed to her and invited her, while it yet repulsed her.

Long after the others were asleep in the Lyman home that night Celia sat by her window looking up at the stars and thinking. And the still stars answered her with their unerring steadiness that there was another world than the one of laughter and pleasure in which she had been living, and there might be more earnest living yet, even for her.

Then she knelt beside her bed and tried to pray, but the only words that would come were, "O Lord, don't let me die — not till I'm good."

And thus the task she had performed for another that day was bringing its good to her own soul, for Celia Lyman's prayers had of late been few and far between.

Chapter 18
An Unwelcome Visitor

A worthless woman, mere cold clay,
    As all false things are; but so fair,
She takes the breath of men away
    Who gaze upon her unaware.
        — *Elizabeth Barrett Browning.*

The almost solemn hush that pervaded the pretty reception room of the Winthrop home where even the palms seemed to hold up warning fingers to be still, affected the beautiful woman who entered with almost a chill of dread.

Just why Mrs. Sylvester had finally decided to call and inquire concerning Mrs. Winthrop it is not easy to say. First of all, it was because she never liked to be balked in anything she undertook, and she had sense enough to see that the situation as it stood at present was against her. It was not altogether that she disliked to lose an admirer. That was unpleasant, certainly, and she knew she had all but lost. But to lose him and know that he held her in light esteem was worse. Her pride was involved and her pride was her main virtue. She had lost many an admirer by quietly turning him down when he became troublesome, and had not felt discomfort thereby, because she was assured that he would go off in some corner and dream for a little while of her beauty and grace, and sigh over the impossibility of ever possessing her, and then forget gradually; but always she would remain a pleasant picture to be thought of when alone, smoking, or when by and by the wife of his choice should annoy him in any way, as inevitably she would.

But Claude Winthrop had by no means reached the point when he was troublesome. To tell the truth he had been hard to win. From amusing herself with him one evening as a business acquaintance of her husband's she had gone on to admire and then to try to win his admiration. It had played no small part in the affair that Claude Winthrop had taken her for a pure and true woman. She had played well the part of innocence, had used her lovely eyes to advantage, and felt a thrill of exultation the first time when she succeeded in catching his eyes upon her in admiration.

Her own had dropped modestly at first and then been raised shyly with a lovely sweep of color over face and neck as she had let him see a little, just a very little, of an answering admiration in them.

Of course he was not rich nor great, but then what did that matter for a married woman? She was not after position, and she was not afraid of hurting her own because she knew well how to plan her campaign so that her meetings with him would not be under any prying eyes.

It had been a long time before she had been able to win more from him than that look of admiration, but all the more earnestly had she tried, because that fact gave the affair the nature of a young, forbidden, first love, and it was worth while to win when the odds were great.

If she had made the advances they had been so delicately and naturally made that he had not suspected, and in his private conferences with his conscience during those first days when it had not been lulled to sleep, he had blamed himself, not her.

Gradually she had let him suspect what was really the truth, that her marriage was not one of love, but this was done in such a way as to leave him free to suppose that she was very unhappy over it, whereas it had been a marriage of her own planning, and in whose achievement she had secretly exulted much. It was a marriage that gave her all she wanted and left her free to be admired by whom she would. And then the pity that is akin to love and put her hands over the eyes of his conscience while he had given that kiss of comfort — that kiss that now he would have given worlds to call back to him. The kiss that was his wife's and that he had thrown away.

The beauty of his wife and her grace and success had maddened Mrs. Sylvester into vowing she would win in spite of everything. But strongest of all now was the fact that she was at the point where, if she could have won Claude Winthrop, she would be willing to leave her husband and home and everything she counted worth while in this world, for with what heart she had she loved him better than she had ever loved any man before. His touches upon her fingers had been all too few, his one kiss she treasured beyond the many she had received from others.

And now it seemed that even as her rival was fallen she was going to lose. If she would save the situation it must be done before the enemy died, if die she did. Mrs. Sylvester, riding toward the Winthrop home had allowed herself for one moment to think of the possibility of what might be if Miriam should die, and her face had softened, but only with selfishness.

And she sat down in all her elegance in the carefully wrought reception room while she waited for Claude to come down, as she had requested.

With cold, critical look she let her eyes rove from one object to another, and admitted to herself that it had all been well done though there had evidently been a pitiful lack of money to carry out the plan.

Then she heard heavy footsteps and collected her faculties for the next act in the tragedy which she had willed to play.

Claude Winthrop stood before her, the full, agonized expression of the sick room not yet faded from his face. His eyes were heavy with loss of sleep, his collar was awry, and he wore no tie. His hair was tumbled carelessly as though it had been smoothed with his fingers on the way down. His caller wondered if he had not seen her card nor known who it was that wished to see him. She had never seen him careless in his dress before, but somehow, so perverse is human nature, he seemed all the more interesting to her because he made a sight so unfamiliar. And yet, with her cool consideration, she decided that it would not be pleasant to have a man around the house looking like that, if one were married to him.

He stook looking at her bewildered for a moment as she advanced to meet him, her delicately gloved hand outstretched to greet him, her voice sweet and sympathetic. But his hands were in his pockets, and he gripped to the lining and kept them there. The delicate little rose leaf of a hand, clad in gloves so soft as to be like a baby's skin, and so exquisitely perfumed as to leave the impression of a warm touch of a flower, that she had counted so much upon, was held out in vain. Claude looked at it as though it had been a poisonous reptile, and as she spoke the scorn grew in his eyes.

"Claude, poor fellow, I have been so sorry for you," she murmured, "I have waited from day to day in breathless eagerness to hear news. At last I could stand it no longer and came to see. How is she? She was so beautiful; I know how hard it has been for you; I do not blame you for the cruel things you said to me that night. I had a hard task and an unnecessary one, but I have felt it, oh, I have felt it these days —" There were tears in her eyes now, she had those weapons well trained and could call them ever at a moment's notice, and Claude's attitude showed her that if she would keep any influence for herself in future she must act well her part now. "I want you to forgive me for what I felt I ought to tell you about her that night. I felt I could not stand it if she should die —"

She paused to bury a well-suppressed sob in her fine handkerchief, and Claude spoke in cold deliberate tones. He was looking at her as he might have looked at the devil who had come to take him to the place of eternal punishment.

"And so it is you!" he said, scorn in his voice, "and you have dared to follow here, and at this time! Well, I have been a fool and worse, I know, and my punishment has begun, and is perhaps none too great for me, but so long as it is in my power to prevent, it shall not include further friendship with such as you!''

Then he turned and walked out of the room and up the stairs with head erect and eyes shining with a desperate flame of anger.

Mrs. Sylvester had been prepared for almost anything, but not for this. She had never seen Mr. Winthrop any other than a perfect gentleman. She had presumed much upon this fact. She felt sure she could make him hear her out, and was reasonably certain of the final impression she would leave. But to have him go in this way was baffling beyond endurance. She bit her lip at his insolence and with rising anger declared that if she could not bring him to his senses she would at least have her revenge. Was not his position in the business world dependent upon her husband's word? How easy it would be to give a hint, a suggestion, a mere shadow of what had been this man's attentions to herself — and too, without in the least implicating herself — and her husband would fly into a mighty passion. The gleam of revenge, the malicious gleam, grew in her eyes as she looked about for some means of conquering this embarrassing situation. She must call him back for a moment if it were but to suggest this thought to him. Quickly she stepped outside the door and closing it, rang the street bell.

"Will you say to Mr. Winthrop that I have forgotten one most important thing and have come back to tell him? I will detain him but a moment." This was the message she sent by the servant when she appeared, and once more this persistent woman seated herself in the parlor.

If she had not been so wrapped about with a sense of self and her own purposes she would have felt that a hush of expectancy was prevading the very house itself, the hush of solemn crisis.

Into the chamber above, where death waited to claim his victim, where the eyes of the watchers were turned in quiet sorrow upon that white face on the pillow, and where the only sound that could be heard was the faint breathing that had come to have so portentous a sound, came her message, borne by the troubled, reluctant maid who hesitated at the door.

Claude, kneeling in his old place at the food of the bed, his head dropped upon his folded arms, did not see the maid at the door, nor hear her half-whispered, "Mr. Winthrop, please sir —"

His mother-in-law, who had come but a few hours before, motioned the maid to her and listened to the message. She glanced at Claude, saw the agony of his very attitude, and set her determined lips. He should not be disturbed now. Her own sorrow was a thing to be expected and accepted.

Claude's was different. She knew what it would be, for had she not lost her husband in her youth?

She left the place beside her daughter's pillow and went with swift, determined step out of the door and down the stairs.

Her prim black silk and soft lace, her fine silver hair and cameo face, lit by eyes that needed no spectacles to see the minutest detail in the face of the woman she had come to cow, dawned upon Mrs. Sylvester in wonder.

"You surely cannot know that you are calling my son from the bedside of his dying wife?" she said in clear unflinching tones and fixing her piercing eyes upon the visitor fearlessly.

"Oh, I beg pardon, it was merely a matter of business," said Mrs. Sylvester sweetly, the while her soul raged within her at the way things were going after all. "I did not mean to intrude, of course I had not heard that Mrs. Winthrop was so ill."

Mrs. Hammond's fine patrician face trembled with dignity as she cut short the voluble words.

"You will do us a favor by leaving us to ourselves at present."

And there was nothing left for Mrs. Sylvester but retreat, but as she rode away in her luxurious carriage she planned a revenge as cruel as it was sweet to her baffled heart.

Chapter 19
Getting Toward the Pattern

I was tired yesterday, but not to-day
I could run and not be weary,
This blessed way;
For I have His strength to stay me,
With His might my feet are shod.
I can find my resting-places
In the promises of God.

— *A. C. S.*

The slow minutes dragged themselves into hours. The watchers never knew when the dark fell outside and the lights were turned on.

The doctor had taken off his overcoat and did not look as if he intended to go away again. In the next room his brother waited in the dark, for it might be there would be need for him, at least so the doctor thought. The family had not been told that he was there. Somehow the doctor always felt more hope of any desperate case when he knew his brother was near by praying, for that his brother would pray he felt sure. Though Doctor Carter did not pray himself, he sometimes took comfort in the fact that his brother did.

No one had told Claude Winthrop that the moment of the crisis was near at hand, but he seemed to know it, and his quivering heart waited for the blow hour after hour and shrank at every sound or change in the patient.

Yes, she was slipping away from him into the shadows with that awful cloud of estrangement between them and no opportunity to make it right before she went. He hardly looked for any recognition from her. It was more than he dared hope. And if it came, what could he say? Could he call, "Forgive me!" down into the shadows of the valley and hope to get even an answering gleam of forgiveness from her eyes, the dear eyes that had spoken so eloquently to him in days that were gone?

Then suddenly the doctor, who with finger on the pulse had been hovering near the bed, warned them all to silence with cautioning hand, and the eyes of the sick one opened and looked upon them intelligently and her own clear voice said:

"I have seen Jesus and he is going to help me make it all over according to the pattern."

Then she smiled upon them and slept once more.

Claude remained as he had been, looking at her face. It had come then and gone, the moment which he had waited for, half hoping, yet with fear. And now it was over and the blackness was shutting about him once more. What she had said, though in so natural a tone, was something he could never understand. It showed that she had already entered a world where he did not belong. He did not doubt that the end was in sight and that this was the last word she would ever speak in the world.

He noted not the swift departure from the room of all but doctor and nurse nor the silent preparations for the night. Dazed and heavy-hearted, he followed the doctor, as he drew him away. He scarcely took in the meaning of the words, spoken low and with a ring of triumph out in the hall, "Mr. Winthrop, she will live." The words did not seem to convey their ordinary meaning to his brain. He had it firmly fixed in his mind that she would die, and he answered the kind doctor with a patient smile that showed he did not take the joyful news for truth.

"She will live, I tell you, man! The crisis is past! I hardly dared hope it would turn out so, but now I feel sure. If all goes well to-night we shall begin to go uphill instead of down. Now the next thing is for you to get a good sleep."

He made Claude lie down and tucked him up as he might have done with a baby and then slipped away, sighing to himself, "Poor fellow. He hardly understands yet. The strain has been hard on him. I wouldn't have imagined he was that sort of man."

Claude Winthrop had been passive in the hands of the doctor, but he had no idea of going to sleep. Sleep, thought he, was a thing that would never visit his weary brain again. But nature was stronger than his intentions. Placed in a relaxed position, it was not many minutes before he sank into unconsciousness, and it was not until morning was high in the world that he woke once more to the heavy burden that he carried.

For the first moment he could not remember how he came in that room nor anything that had happened. Then he concluded that his wife must be gone, else they would not have brought him away. But he saw beside him the doctor, smiling, and he knew that he would not look like that if all were over. Gradually there came to his memory the doctor's words of the night before, and a light broke over his face. He looked into Doctor Carter's eyes anxiously to read if the hope was still there.

"Doing well," he nodded reassuringly. "All she needs now is perfect quiet and perfect nursing. She will not need you for a while. She must stay, if possible, in a quiescent state. There must be no talking, no excitement. Nothing to remind her of life, or in her weak state she may have a relapse. You'd better rest yourself completely for a few days. You have been through a heavy stain. I'm going to take you in charge or we'll have a case of nervous prostration before we know it."

The doctor might have talked in a foreign tongue for all that Claude heard of what he said. His mind could take in but one thing and that was that Miriam would live. He must adjust himself to that before there was room for anything else.

His impulse was to go at once to his wife and make his full confession, for he shrank from the burden of it any longer, but gradually his common sense and the doctor's words asserted themselves. There was then hope, but he must be patient and wait for the burden to be removed, days, perhaps weeks.

After the doctor went out he lay still and listened to the distant hum of the city outside, the sound of the world to which they had come back, he and Miriam, to live over again the life they had failed to live aright. No, not they, but he. Miriam had been all right. Miriam had been true through all. To him now came the picture sharp and clear of the way she had struck the senator in the conservatory. He had not heard all he said, but he had seen the kiss. He gloried in Miriam's righteous wrath. He had not been true to her, but she had been absolutely true to him, and that in spite of knowing of his weakness.

Hour after hour he reviewed the story, taking up details he had not remembered before, and always coming up against the blank wall of his own defenseless weakness — no, *sin,* for that was the name by which he had learned to call his own conduct.

By and by he slept again, but now came dark dreams to trouble him, and always the face of his wife, cold, sad, averted from him. He woke with the sweat of agony on his brow.

They let him into the sick-room but seldom now, and only when she was asleep. He must not come near her or touch her or do anything to take her out of that restful world into which she had slipped. It was their only hope for her recovery that she might remain untroubled by anything, not even the joy of seeing her loved ones, until her heart had grown a little stronger and she was able to bear emotion of any kind.

The husband hovered about the door of the sick-room, haunting the halls like a gaunt spectre and asking anxiously for any news of the nurses or the doctor as they passed. He seemed to feel it a part of his just punishment that at this time, when his place should have been close beside his dear wife, he should be thus shut away from her, more shut away than he had ever been in his life before. he grew almost to hate the nurses whose presence kept her he loved so secluded from his view.

Doctor Carter pitied him from the depths of his heart, but he dared not let him come into the presence of his wife yet, lest his haggard face should startle her and she become aware of her own serious condition. She was entirely herself now when awake, and seemed to be perfectly content to lie still and do as she was bid. She had not asked for any one, and did not seem to care for anything but just to lie and rest. The time had not come to rouse her from this state. Until then her husband must wait and be patient.

But Doctor Carter spoke to his brother about it.

"I wish, George, you would see what you can do at doctoring the soul of that man if you know anything about the business," he said, one afternoon as he came out from the house to the carriage where his brother was waiting for him, "he needs something to soothe him a little. If religion is worth anything at all it ought to be able to do that. Sometime when you're in there just see if you can't get him to talk with you. He is taking life as hard as he did last week when there was practically no hope. If he keeps on he'll break down before she gets to the point where he will be needed."

And the brother pondered in his heart what he might be able to say to this older man who seemed to be locked so firmly within his sorrow.

With Miriam the world had receded so far, and all things grown so dim, that she was a long time in coming back to the things that had been hers once more. Her memory of her illness was like some horrible journey over stormy seas, over rapids and dangerous rocks, with thunder and lightning all about, until suddenly a voice had said, "Peace, be still," and her little bark which was about to sink amid the tempest had drifted into quiet waters, where the sunlight glinted through leafy shadows, and a great peace arched over all. There was rest, deep, sweet rest. And in that haven she was content to stay.

She swallowed what they gave her obediently, and she lay and rested and forgot.

Gradually there came order out of the chaos of her mind. She did not remember the song nor the words that had been spoken to her when she was under the power of the fever, but she knew that a new influence had taken hold of her life that would make all wrongs right. To this thought she fixed her heart. She had left the problems of her life all unsolved, but they did not trouble her any more. They were in hands that knew well how to control them. Where she got this faith she did not know, did not question. That it was in her heart gave her comfort. She would not let herself think about the old troubles, as her mind grew stronger and memory, always a poor nurse, rushed in with pictures filled with old troubles. She did not question about anything. She tried as much as possible to keep from wondering how she came here and where her husband and children were.

But there came a time at last when she could no longer put by memory. She awoke one morning to find the walls of her mind all hung with pictures, fresh and vivid, of the weary way she had trod before she had found this haven. They pierced her with their darts of evil. And about three portraits her gaze lingered longest. One beautiful, scornful face crowned with golden hair, another old and wicked, topped with silver white, and a third, the face averted with indifferent aspect, with soft sweep of dark hair, and handsome, manly outlines. Ah! here was her world all back again, and whither was her peace flown?

She looked up and seemed to see a light and to hear a voice speaking to her soul: "Come unto me, and I will give you rest."

Why had that rest not meant death for her? What other rest could there be but that? And yet it had not been, and still the voice insisted, "I *will* give you rest." And gladly, gladly she took hold once more upon a faith that had come to her out of the dark of her forgotten childhood when her mother's teachings had fallen on unheeding childish ears.

There is much perplexity and sadness about whether a soul taken from this earth out of the midst of life not lived for God, and spending its last moments in delirium, can be saved. But why does not comfort come to such questioners from the thought of the power of the God who made that soul, to speak to it even in delirium? It is not strange that God should speak to one of his creatures now any more than that he spoke to Adam or to Moses.

It was in some such way that Miriam came back to life, knowing that henceforth if she lived her life at all, she must live it hand in hand with God. And thus she came to herself, feeling content to lie in God's hand, but dreading to come back to a life which had baffled her on every side.

It was then the doctor began to be uneasy. She was not gaining fast enough, but seemed to have come to a standstill.

Something more was needed to rouse her to an interest in the world and give her an object for getting well. Doctor Carter thought at once of her husband, and had decided to bring him in to see her for a few minutes, but when he went in search of him he found him with a drawn and haggard expression upon his face, so much worse than it had been during the days that had passed that he changed his mind and decided to try the children. A woman would do more for her baby anyway than for any one else on earth.

It had been thought best that Miriam should not know that her mother was in the house yet, lest she should guess how ill she had been, therefore the grandmother had taken up her place in the nursery, to the delight of the children, who had sorely missed their mother's devotion of late.

Little Celia was brought to her mother first, and nestled down shyly beside her on the pillow, and touched the thin hand wonderingly, and the other children came and kissed her softly in awe, for her face was changed by her illness, white and almost unearthly in its beauty, and then they trooped away glad to get back to the cheer of the nursery and grandmother's stories, while Miriam lay still, feeling that she had drifted out away from even her children, that they had learned to do without her while she was ill, and that she was not needed back among them now.

On the whole the doctor's experiment had not succeeded so well as he had hoped. He sat down and studied the problem in perplexity. To have brought his patient out from the shadow of death thus far and then to see her slip slowly back again was more than he could endure.

"George," said he impatiently, as his brother came into the office, "why don't you pray this thing out for me? What's the use of prayer if you can't work a miracle now and then?"

And the result of that conference was that once more George Carter stood beside that bed and spoke.

He came in quietly as if his coming were an every-day affair.

"I came to see you once before when you were so ill, Mrs. Winthrop," he said, smiling pleasantly. "You don't remember me, I suppose? You were troubled about the 'pattern on the mount,' and I promised to tell you more about it when you were stronger. Would you like to hear it now?"

Miriam's face lit with a half-smile of remembrance.

"I heard a sermon once —" she said and paused. Speech seemed long and hard to her yet.

"Yes, and you were so tired and were troubled that you had not made your life according to the pattern?"

She nodded understandingly.

"I told you then that Jesus wanted you to rest. I bring you another message to-day. It is this, "Be *strong* in the Lord.' He wants you to get well and begin to live after the pattern that he has set for you. You need not be troubled that you think you have spoiled it all. He will make that right.

When you are strong you will find the pattern with careful directions in this book. Now will you obey the message and get well?''

Wonderingly she answered, "Yes." It seemed to her that some strong angel had been sent down to speak to her and give her heart of life again. And she was near enough yet to the other world not to be much amazed over it.

The young man knelt beside the bed and closed his eyes:

"Dear Lord," he said, "help this child of thine to get strong for thee, and show her how to follow thee. For Jesus' sake."

Then he was gone, and Miriam lay thinking of it all, and in her heart there grew again determination to make the fight anew, this time with the God of battles on her side, and win.

Chapter 20

In the Devil's Grip

Fool! All that is, at all,
Lasts ever, past recall;
Earth changes, but thy soul and God stand sure.
— *Robert Browning.*

Claude Winthrop had paid little attention to his business since the night his wife was taken ill. He had sent a message down to the office to the effect that his wife was in a serious condition, and that he could not leave home. Twice the private secretary had been out to consult him about some important affair that he only was familiar with, but beyond that and friendly notes of sympathy from different men in the house — which he had scarcely read — he had heard nothing. It had not seemed strange to him that things were going on just the same without him, nor had he stopped to think that the notes he had received from the heads of the firm had been curt and formal.

He knew that he had left affairs in such shape that the man just below him could manage everything until he went back, and beyond that he had not troubled himself. What was business at such a time as this?

And then, three days after the crisis had passed and the little world of their friends came to know that Miriam was better, and ere he himself had as yet been able to move out from under the shadow that had settled upon him, there came a letter which brought him suddenly to his senses.

It was on the afternoon that Doctor Carter intended to take him in to see his wife that the letter had come. He picked it up from the desk where the maid had placed it after the two o'clock delivery and read it, idly at first, and then starting to his feet, read it over again trying to understand the words. They danced before his eyes and would not stand still for him to understand. But at last he comprehended. It was a firm but courteous dismissal from the business house where but yesterday he had supposed he was in a fair way to become second only to the head in a few years, and perhaps if all went well, even one of the heads by and by.

How had his ambitions crumbled at his feet? How had he fallen? What could it mean? Was it a dream? What had brought it about? They surely had not dismissed him for the brief absence when his wife hung between life and death. They were good men. They would not do that. He must go down and see about it at once. There was some mistake. They had sent the letter to the wrong man or some clerk had blundered. he started to his feet and found that he was trembling from head to foot. He must not go in this way. He must steady himself. This long nightmare of sickness and trouble had upset him. But he must set this thing straight at once. Why, where would he be if he lost his business connection? What would Miriam and the children do? How precious had they become? How terrible it be if this were true, but of course it could not be. It was some mistake.

Just then a maid tapped on the door and handed him a special delivery letter. He frowned at the interruption, signed his name in the book, and sat down impatiently to see what the letter contained.

It was a dainty envelope that bore the large blue stamp, and filled the room about it with a subtle fragrance that carried a hateful memory with it. It was the fragrance of lilies of the valley. His heart stabbed him that the perfume of his wife's wedding flowers should have power to bring a hateful memory. But he tore open the thick envelope and read, his eyes growing dark with anger and understanding.

> DEAR CLAUDE: — I am sorry for you in your humiliation. I would have done something for you if I dared, but my husband was very angry. But though I have cause to be angry with you, still I forgive you, and if you will come to me I will yet put you in the way of something far better than the position which you occupied.

He read no further, but tearing the letter in tiny bits put it in the flames of the fireplace until every atom was consumed. Then he rose and began to pace the floor. He knew now whom he had to thank for his dismissal. This, then, was her revenge!

It was just at this point that the doctor looked in and changed his mind about taking Clause to see his wife.

And while the angel of peace was taking up his abode with the wife, the husband wrestled with the adversary.

All that long afternoon he paced his room inside locked doors. He did not go down to the office as he intended. He knew now that it would be of no use. If Mr. Syulvester had spoken the word it was final. There was no appeal from that. And Mrs. Sylvester had arranged it so. He followed carefully every thread of evidence. Things that he had said and done and forgotten came up now to haunt him. The case was against him. And what could he do or say? He could not go to Mr. Sylvester and say that his wife's insinuations were false, because there was enough of truth for their foundation to make that impossible. He could not tell the man that the fault had been the woman's in the first place because that would be as useless as it was pitiful, for after all, would it better his case to say that he had been weak enough to be led by a woman into temptation? And how well he knew that that woman could make herself appear as pure and unsullied as a star in the heavens. He was caught in a net. He was bound hand and foot. It was too late to even try to extricate himself. And why had she done it? Was it her cruel desire to subjugate, that she still wished to keep him a slave to herself and so, though having shown him her power over him, yet show him her tenderness by offering help just now when she knew his extremity? Or did she really care for him? He recalled looks and actions more meaningful than mere coquetry. How they would have made his foolish heart throb in some of the days gone by to have recognized what they meant. But now it was a sort of fear of her that filled him. She was determined to have his love, and it seemed that he was powerless to keep her from it. What had he left but to go to her for help — or let Miriam and the children suffer? — and what would that be but to begin again the double life which had caused him so great misery during the past weeks?

Then it was given to him at last to look into the open mouth of the horrible pit of wickedness into which his feet had almost slipped beyond reclaim. He saw things as they were. He called things by their names. His own soul appeared cringing before his sharpened judgment, all blackened with dishonor. And in that lurid place where abode the evil thoughts and careless actions of his past days, each one an evil spirit come to haunt him, he thought he was going insane. What ugly creatures were these that menaced all hope of peace, these little evil-faced imps that mocked at him as if they had a right? Was it possible that they were his own thoughts? Had he really entertained such creatures and taken pleasure in them when they had appeared as angels of light?

Cold sweat stood upon his forehead and he pressed his burning eyeballs for relief from pain. Almost he seemed to see a vision of eternal fires prepared for such writhing souls as his who had dared to fashion a torture so exquisite for a soul so pure as Miriam's.

And he had ventured to hope for a reconciliation. He, blackened as he was with the evil he had harbored in his thoughts? He to expect once more to touch her sweet hand, and have the honor of pressing her precious lips against his own dishonored ones — his lips that had promised and had not performed, his lips that had deliberately been untrue to her! He to think ever to have her look with clear and trustful gaze into his eyes with eyes of love!

The knocks that came to his door from time to time, the call to dinner, the messages that came to the house, made no more impression upon his mind than if they had been the moaning of the wind outside. At first he only answered that he was busy, but as he became more and more absorbed he did not respond at all, nor even lift his head from where it had sunk upon his arms on his desk.

Life in the future looked too black for him to face. He seemed to have reached the end of all things for himself. Now and again he would bring himself to consider the possibility of going to Mrs. Sylvester and taking the business chance she offered for Miriam's sake, but the thought of bringing help to Miriam through the one who had caused her so much sorrow was intolerable. Then he would try to consider what he should do. It was useless to think of attempting to get something else in that same city with a tarnished character. Neither could he ever face his wife with all this upon him. They would be better off without him. He was now but a sorrow and humiliation to them, his wife and his children. Through sharpened memory he knew as clearly how Miriam had felt about his relations to Mrs. Sylvester as though he had been able to read her heart. It was like looking at his shameful self through eyes that saw as the eyes of God see.

There was nothing for him but that horrible torture into which he had been looking, or the worse torture of going on with life.

It had grown dark in his library now, and the room felt chilly. Some one had turned the heat away from the room, but he had not noticed it before. If they should find him lying here to-morrow cold and dead, they would hide it from Miriam until she was better, and when she was strong enough to hear it, it would be to her but a fit ending for the sorrowful story she had begun many months back. He could never hope now to win back her love and favor again. Even a "clean breast" of it could never undo the past. He would not even be able to support her as he had done of late, and there would be disgrace too, attached to him, which would be harder for her to bear. If he ended it all to-night there would at least be pity. There was always pity for one who went out of life by his own hand. Perhaps they would say he had lost his mind through worry over his wife's illness. And perhaps he had! He felt as if it were gone.

Only one thing was clear. He saw it shining before him now out of the darkness of the room; though its cruel metal form was shut away in a locked drawer, it gleamed with swift and irrevocable relief.

He struck the light to find the key of the drawer. The key had been put away from other keys because Miriam was afraid of the wicked instrument of death. It had been one of the purchases of his younger days when the possession of a revolver was synonymous with manhood. He had argued that it was necessary to have one to protect his family in case of burglars, and he had proudly slept with it under his pillow until in deference to Miriam, it had gone, first to a high shelf in the closet near the bed, then to this secret drawer, where it had stayed. For as the little ones had entered their home and his fatherhood had grown more deeply protective he had feared the revolver himself, lest the children should by mistake play with it some day.

It was not loaded. He had cleaned it carefully and unloaded it, and showed it to Miriam one day when she was worried and fearful of it, and had put it where he had scarcely looked at it since.

There was a sort of morbid fascination in handling it now. Clearly, out of the shadows of the room came the picture of his wife as she had sat there sewing while he put it away. Ah, she never dreamed how it would be with them both when he should take it out as he was doing now, and load it that he might end his own wretched existence with it.

And after? Yes, there might be more to life than what appeared, but it could scarcely be worse than was his here. He did not think of it. It seemed to him that in ending his life he was at least showing his own remorse for the folly that had made of their happy home a place of misery.

Slowly, deliberately, he opened the box containing the tiny things that would bring swift healing to his sick soul and wipe out all this horror. He was as calm about loading that revolver as if he intended to kill a squirrel instead of himself. And when his work was complete he carefully closed the drawer and locked it again and put all the little articles on his desk straight. Then he placed the cold steel to his temple, moving it carefully to the vital spot, and raised his trembling finger to the trigger.

His senses were on the alert. He knew perfectly what he was about to do. There was in his face a light of triumph. He saw the end in view and blessed relief from the terrible self-condemnation.

The house had been still for a long time. He realized it too, with all the rest that came before him now in this one clear moment of vision. He felt the silence of the street and all the neighborhood, in the anticipation of the loud report that would presently ring out. He was glad the library was so far from Miriam's room. She would not be disturbed by the sound. They would keep all quiet for her sake, and he would be gone!

His finger was touching the trigger now. In an instant more all would be over.

Suddenly on the stillness of the room there came a sound and the revolver dropped from the nerveless finger of the man standing upon the threshold of another world.

Chapter 21
After the Storm, Peace

Behind the dim unknown,
Standeth God within the shadow, keeping
watch above his own.
— *James Russell Lowell.*

Strange what creatures of habit and memory we are! An odor will carry us back over scores of years into scenes we have not thought of for many a long day. A touch will set vibrating in us chords that we thought dead. The sight of the curve of a cheek, like that of a lost loved one, will bring back to us old impulses and change our plans in a moment, while a wound will call us into sudden action and set every nerve a-throbbing.

The sound which broke the stillness of that room of agony and brought Claude Winthrop from a suicide's act to one of frightened ministration was commonplace enough to have passed with other sounds of the night, and yet one that had never lost its power of striking fear to his heart.

It was the hoarse, shrill bark of croup, and the sound came from the room overhead, where his baby, Celia, slept in her little white crib, close by the register, whose flue was also connected with the library register.

The cough was hoarse enough to have alarmed one less preoccupied than Claude, but it came to him with the sharp arrow of memory. He saw himself as he was those few short years gone by, when that sound had first broken upon his terrified ear and their first child struggled for breath. He could feel again, as he felt then, the impossibility of fastening the buttons of his clothes with his trembling fingers and the frightful sense of the agony of time that would have to pass before he could get the doctor there. He could see Miriam white and frightened, with the tears streaming unheeded down her cheeks and her long hair falling about her white gown, as she frantically searched the index of an old medical book her mother had given her, along with a recipe book and the Bible for their first setting-up of housekeeping. They had recognized croup at once as the much-talked-of-terror, which, like death, one hears of and dreads but yet never really expects to come his way.

Claude's first realization when he heard that sound was that the last time he had heard it was the night he arrived home from Europe. Then the mother had been there and the cough had not been severe. Now the mother was lying asleep, weak and frail, unable to go to the little one, just having crept back from the dark valley of the shadow. And the father, the other one upon whom the little one depended, had been hovering in that valley too, but by his own wish and cowardly purpose.

It was almost strange that the weary brain, which during the day and evening had been subjected to so many varying sensations, and the eyes that had looked so clearly into his past life and his present, had yet strength left to look in the face the cowardly portrait of himself as it appeared after the last two hours in his library.

This all went through his mind like a flash when he locked the revolver away from sight, and then bounded away up the stairs to the nursery.

The nurse had already been roused and was on her way to the bath room for hot water. The little one sat up in her crib crying and coughing frightfully. She held out her hands piteously to her father and he gathered her up, all swathed in her blankets, and held her in his arms, the wildness melting out of his eyes and a tender light growing there instead.

The nurse was sleepy and did not like being roused from her slumber. Moreover, she knew in her heart that the cause of this attack was her own carelessness for having allowed Celia to stand in the keen draught of an open door while she flirted with the grocer's boy the day before. She worked only half-heartedly, and the father finally sent her to telephone for the doctor and himself arranged the cold compress on the struggling little throat and covered it carefully with many folds of flannel. With one free hand he lighted the alcohol lamp under the kettle of water that was always kept in the nursery for such a time of need, and soon the steam in the air and the frequent applications of the cloth wrung from cold water relieved the little girl so that she was able to speak.

She slipped a hot hand from the folds of blanket and patted his cheek feebly.

"Good, good poppie, take care Celie," came the hoarse whisper. "Dear, good poppie won't leave Celie 'lone any more?"

He assured her he would stay with her and snuggled her close to his breast, and in this safe shelter behind his little one, with the everyday domestic atmosphere about him, a great peace came into his heart. The other life, that life which he had been about to take, seemed so far away, so impossible. How could he ever have sinned with the sweetness, the purity of his little ones in his keeping?

The thoughts of the world, the struggles he had passed through during the afternoon and evening, the tortures that had been his, were all outside this little room. He could even put them from his mind. They did not belong here, where love reigned supreme.

The grandmother came frightened from her room, with a gray look about her face. She had forgotten the days when her own children were ill, and croup had taken on a new terror for her. She offered to hold Celia, but the father shook his head and held her close, and was comforted by the little hand that clung to his neck and the hoarse voice that fretted, "No, poppie keep Celie."

He held her all night long, even after the doctor had come and the disease had been controlled and the household settled to quiet.

And then was fulfilled anew that prophecy which said, "And a little child shall lead them."

Through that little sleeping girl the heavenly Father spoke to the weary, sinsick soul of the earthly father. All the long night did he feel the love and tenderness of the infinite Fatherhood that bears with the sins and follies of his earthly children. And as a penitent child did he judge himself. And now it was not so much horror for what he had done as sorrow that filled his heart.

When morning came the little one smiled and patted his face again, and cooed gently: "Oo did stay, poppie, oo stayed wiv Celie."

They had their breakfast together on the little round white table which he had fashioned in his evening hours about Christmas time during the days of Pearl's babyhood, when money with which to buy toys was not so plentiful as of late years. He ate bites of her poached egg and toast, that she fed him, and took sips of her milk obediently, and each ate more than they would have done alone.

The other children gathered about their father with surprise and delight. The tired grandmother saw that she was not needed and retired to rest.

He let himself be taken by storm and be soothed by their fluttering hands. He reveled in their clear eyes and direct speech. He told stories of adventure and fun. He read the Mother Goose books through as many times as the young tyrants demanded, and he built houses of blocks for them to overthrow. There was nothing, even to dressing Celia's doll, that he stopped at, though the costume when finished presented a most remarkable combination.

But when at a call from the nurse he was forced to go downstairs to see about having a prescription filled for the doctor he shivered visibly. Here in the light, cheery nursery, which everywhere spoke of Miriam's presence, he had been able to forget the nightmare of the days that were passed, ending in the almost tragedy of the night before.

Cold chills crept down his back as he passed the library door, and he was glad to find it closed. It seemed as if all the evil thoughts that had visited him the previous night must be shut within the walls of that room.

And it was necessary after all for him to enter the library to get the prescription the doctor had written the day before, which must be renewed. He knew it was lying on his desk next to the letter of dismissal that had come to him. The doctor had hurried away to his lecture at the medical college to which he was already late, leaving his brother, who had kindly offered to save Claude the trouble of going out, and he stood there waiting now.

As he watched the haggard look creep into Claude Winthrop's face he prayed in his heart for some opportunity to help him and followed to the library door.

Claude was glad of his companionship. He dreaded to look about him. He breathed a sigh of relief as he remembered that he had locked the revolver out of sight the evening before. It seemed as if it would but tell the tale of his cowardice and sin if it lay there in sight.

As they entered, to Claude's fevered imagination, the shadows seemed to shrink into the corners and take the forms of all the fiendish tortures that had been here dealt out to him a few hours ago. The little gold cup on the mantle, innocent in itself, had somehow reminded him last night of the first tiny cup of tea Mrs. Sylvester had handed him when she began to weave her spell about his unsuspecting heart! There were the ashes in the grate that spoke of the partly read letter he had burned! There was the whole dreadful mistake of his life again all standing about in the pictures, the chairs, the drapery, everything that he had looked at in his march about the room. So memory uses commonplace hooks to hang their deeds upon, and we may not take them down and put them out of sight however much we try.

"I wish that I might do something more for you."

It was George Carter who spoke, wistfully, as he lingered by the door with the prescription in his hand.

Claude looked up surprised out of his absorption. It did him good to see the other man still standing there. It dispelled some of the shadows from his mind. It was like medicine to hear the sympathetic tones. His heart went out in longing for that sympathy. He liked this wholesome man whose coming seemed like some strong, life-giving breeze from the mountain-tops. It brought relief from the stagnant, humid depths of what his own nature had come to be.

The look on his face drew the younger man back to the desk again, and the two pairs of eyes met in a recognition of their brotherhood as it is given for spirit to speak to spirit without the use of words.

"I wish you could give me a prescription that would cure mistakes," said Claude earnestly, thinking of the days when he was this young man's age, and wishing he could go back to that time and begin over his life. He felt sure he could live it better in the light of all he now knew.

The light of longing came into the eyes of the younger minister. " 'As far as the east is from the west, so far hath *He* removed our transgressions from us!' " repeated the young man reverently. "Won't that apply to mistakes too, don't you think, if we ask him?"

A hopeless sorrow settled into the face of Claude.

"It wouldn't apply to the inevitable results," said Claude hopelessly.

"God controls all results," said George Carter. "He is able to make even the result of terrible mistakes work together for good to them that love him."

"But I am not one of those," said Claude sadly.

"It is your privilege to be."

There was a great silence in the room. And all those shadows in the corners gathered about and drew together, and hovered over and behind Claude Winthrop contending for his soul. Almost they had succeeded last night. Now another Power, greater than themselves, was here. A light of hope was shining into that room.

By and by Claude broke the stillness which had been with his guest one silent prayer.

"Will you pray for me?" he spoke in husky tones.

Broken and contrite he knelt beside the same chair in which he had sat and planned to take his life. He wondered as he listened to the simple, earnest prayer that any man could come so near to God. Ah! if he had been like that he never could have gone so far astray.

"Father, thou knowest this man's heart. Thou knowest his sorrow, his mistakes, his failures —" and to Claude came a realization that God had known all the time, had watched him when he put the revolver to his temple, had stayed his hand by the cry of his child, had been guarding him from himself.

One by one the evil spirits were exorcised and slunk away from that room, forever. And in the heart of the man bowed low before his Maker there grew a "light that never shone on land or sea."

He gripped the hand of his guest as they rose from their knees.

"I would give worlds," said Claude, "if I began this way, as you have done."

When George Carter was gone and he was left alone he had no more fear for the haunting memories of the night. He could even quietly open the drawer where lay the revolver and remove the cartridge and put it away in safety without a shaking hand. In his heart was a great thankfulness that he had been saved from himself and allowed one more chance. His life that he would have thrown away was saved and then gently given back that he might try it over again and see if he could not better it with God's help.

He could not see ahead. He did not know what he should do nor how he should do it, but he knew that whatever he did was to be done in a different way from any that he had ever tried before, and with different motives. And please God, if he ever stood with his life at the mercy of a revolver again, it should be held in the hand of another, and he would not have the regret for his past that had held him so fast last night.

Chapter 22
Reconciliation

O heart! O blood that freezes, blood that burns!
Earth's returns
For whole centuries of folly, noise and sin!
Shut them in,
With their triumphs and their glories and the rest!
Love is best.
— *Robert Browning.*

And now at last Miriam began to wonder about her husband. She searched her mind for any memory of his presence in the sickroom during her illness, but could not be sure of it. Had he then deserted her entirely? And they would not tell her of it till she was stronger!

Little by little the incidents of that last awful afternoon and evening came to her mind. She stood again upon the Sylvester doorstep and met her husband face to face. She met him at the entrance to the Washburn conservatory, and she lived over the shameful scene with the senator, and her flight, until it ended in unconsciousness at her husband's feet. Had he turned upon his heel and spurned her then before the world? He knew what the senator was. He had tried to warn her once, and she had resented it because she felt he had no right to call her to account when he was so much more at fault than she; but now she saw her own part in sinful colors. She should have been more careful. She had been so blind, and so wrapped up in her own purposes! To think that she could go against the whole world and win back her own! No, she had but brought shame and disgrace upon herself!

But God had forgiven. He would help her to begin over again, only how could she ever bear it without Claude? If only it could have been right that she should die. But there were the children. Then her new purpose came back to her, and a portion of the comfort, but she set her eyes restlessly upon the door and knew all who entered before the door was fairly open.

She would not ask one question, for if there were shame to tell and more humiliation, she did not want them to watch her bear it. It was for

132

her and God. She kept hoping the suspense would be over, and some word would show her just how matters stood with regard to her husband, so that she might have opportunity to adjust herself to the new state of things during this resting-time when she could keep her eyes closed and shut out the world of other beings and be alone with God.

There came a night when the night nurse was suddenly taken ill. The day nurse had been going home at evening since Miriam had grown so much better. There was no one to call upon but Claude.

The nurse was too ill to hesitate long. She called Mr. Winthrop and asked him to stay with the patient for an hour or two until she should feel better. There was nothing to be done. The patient was sleeping quietly, and would probably continue to do so all night. If she should stir there was the medicine to be given, and there was water in the pitcher in the window. Mrs. Winthrop would not notice the change even if she should waken.

Then the nurse betook herself to a couch in the next room with her aching head, and Claude stole softly into the darkened room with bated breath as though he were entering a sacred temple.

It was a precious privilege, this of sitting once more beside her whom he loved better than his own life — who had been given back to him from the dead. There was a future into which he dared not look as yet, which might hold sorrow and estrangement still from her, but the present was his and she lay here for him to guard.

Silently he took his seat as though he had been asked to sit in an antechamber of heaven, and counted not the hours slow while he heard the music of her regular breathing, and blessed God with every breath that she was here alive and getting well.

How he longed to stoop and kiss the sweet brow. But no, he must never do that until she had forgiven him. And could she ever forgive him?

Her white hand lay like a lily against the whiteness of the bed covering. He knelt and reaching out one hand laid it near to hers. And by and by it crept a little nearer, till one finger touched hers.

It was like feeling warm and living the hand of one who had gone out into the land of the dead. It thrilled him with a deeper joy than even when he had touched it long ago in the rose-bordered lane where they had wandered together when first he took that hand in his and dared to hold it, and they both walked silent, neither letting the other see by look or motion what each was feeling over that hand-clasp.

When the morning broke gray and pink in the eastern window, and the heavy-eyed nurse, somewhat refreshed from her sleep, came back to take his place, he went out from that room and knelt beside his baby's crib and prayed, prayed that God might make him better and more worthy to have and keep the precious wife who had once been his so fully.

Thereafter he made a habit of stealing in at night and sending the nurse to lie down, while he watched beside the bed, and the nurse, nothing loath, obeyed.

Then he would look at the sweet face upon the pillow, softly shaded in the darkened room, and let his whole soul go out to her in a caress. And more and more he dared touch the hand that lay upon the bed beside him, to even lay his own hand closely over it as if it were a little, lost, cold bird.

She never spoke nor stirred, nor wakened in the least. And so he would continue to kneel beside her till the morningtime and he knew the nurse was coming back.

And in these vigils he told her all again and again. He bitterly blamed himself, and then told her how he loved her. How the love he had given her before was as nothing to the new love that had blossomed here beside her sick-bed.

And all the time she lay there in her weakness asleep, and answered him not by so much as the fluttering of an eyelash.

His heart cried out in agony at last that he might speak to her, might roll this awful burden of confession at her feet, and let her know that in those terrible moments when he had been made to appear before her in the wrong, he had not been so very wrong as it looked; let her know that her fears were greater than the truth, and that he had not ceased to love her, but loved her in his repentance with an aching love that could never be satisfied — no, not if they should have an eternity to live and love each other.

And once when he was holding her hand close and thinking so, and praying, she drew a long, quivering sigh, and that was all. And then he moaned softly to himself, and laid his face down on the hand that lay in his so still and strengthless.

And Miriam dreamed a dream, a sweet, sweet dream. She had not dreamed the like since first her sorrow had pierced her soul. She dreamed her husband was beside her and that his hand touched hers, and she smiled in her sleep, and would not stir lest she should wake and find him gone.

Claude saw that smile, and wondered if when grown people smiled in their sleep it was because they were in pain, as nurses said of little babies in their sleep.

When the morrow came and Miriam remembered her dream she hugged it close to her heart, and all that day would not look toward the door nor listen to the nurses, lest she should hear some word that might dispel it.

She longed for night to come that she might dream the sweet thing over once more. And with the memory of his touch, his loving touch once again, she forgot, as foolish, loving woman will, the misery and the shame he had brought her to bear, and found she loved him still. And from that time the portraits of the woman and of the senator began to fade in memory's gallery until they took on the natural color of the other pictures there.

Night came, and Miriam sank to sleep in a blessed anticipation which wafted her to unconsciousness like a breath from a bed of glowing poppies. Would the dream come again, or would it not?

And again it came.

The next day the doctor thought her decidedly better, and wondered if it would not be a good plan to let her husband in in daylight to have a bit of a talk with her, but she seemed so content to lie and smile and do as she was bidden that he hardly dared to break the spell yet for any experiments. His brother had told him of his conversation with the husband and he felt a little uneasy about the effect that his appearance might have on his wife. So he held his peace for one day more, and thought about it.

Miriam came to sudden consciousness that night in the midst of her dream. The dream was there in all its reality. She felt the strong hand holding hers, she knew the long supple fingers, and the smooth texture of the skin. And that was his face touching her palm, his cheek, as he used to lay it in her hand long ago. But she was awake and not dreaming. Why did the dream not go? She dared not stir, but lay there trying to make her breath come regularly as in sleep. She dared not lift her eyelids lest the dear dream should pass.

Her quivering heart reviewed all she knew of the tragedy of their lives once more, and she judged him before the bar of her soul as guilty, and yet she loved him. It stood much in his favor that he had still some love for her, for he would never lay his cheek so in her hand unless he had. 'Tis sad a woman will forgive all else save lack of love for her. And that she cannot forgive.

And then herself — she was not so worthy of his love as in the past. For had she not sinned also? — though without intention and unthinkingly. But he had a right to question her conduct with the senator. Perhaps, perhaps, there was something too, to plead on his side. Perhaps he was not all wrong or weak or wicked as she feared!

And then a drop fell on her hand, and straightway she knew it for a tear.

At once the motherhood in her, that is a part of all true wifehood, rose. A great love and pity swept over her. He was sorry. And as she would have done with a sorrowful, repentant child, she reached out arms that were suddenly made strong by love and gathered her dream to herself.

"Miriam, my darling, can you forgive?" He spoke the words brokenly. He was frightened that he had waked her, but the moment had come and she had enfolded him in her arms and his face was resting in the old place on her bosom.

Her answer was a kiss.

When the nurse came to take his place that morning she thought the glory in his face was from the rosy reflection of the eastern sky, and she blamed herself that she had slept so late.

Miriam lay with closed eyes and face turned away and apparently slept still, but the joy that glowed in her consciousness would hardly be kept within bounds.

Chapter 23
New Paths Opening

Great feelings hath she of her own,
Which lesser souls may never know;
God giveth them to her alone,
And sweet they are as any tone
Wherewith the wind may choose to blow.
— *James Russell Lowell.*

Dinner in the Lyman home was strictly a family affair the evening of the arrival home from abroad of Celia's only brother, and they lingered late over the dessert, enjoying the luxury of asking all the questions that one forgets to put in letters, or to answer when they are found there.

"By the way, father, have you opened up the new department in the business that you were speaking of when I left?"

"Well, no, we haven't," answered the father passing his cup for more coffee and helping himself to another stem of the luscious hothouse grapes. "The fact is, I haven't found the right man to take charge of it yet. When you come to think of it, my son, the right man is a rare commodity in market now-a-days. If you had not the other department in hand so thoroughly I should be almost inclined to put you in there for a time till I could find some one else. I believe the time is ripe for such a business, but the right man has not appeared yet, and without him it would be worse than useless to attempt it."

"I wish you could get the fellow I met over in Paris. He would be just the man. A keener eye for business I never saw, and I happened to know he made several points for his house when he was over there. He was a mighty fine fellow. I got in with him on the voyage by a little accident that made it rather necessary for me to give up my stateroom to a lady who was suddenly taken ill and wanted to be next her friends. I could not exchange with her and so I sought the only other place left, which was to share a stateroom with Winthrop. And he was good company, I tell you. We grew so intimate that we took lodgings together while he stayed in Paris, which wasn't long, so that I got to see more of him than simply as an acquaintance."

"Winthrop, did you say?" asked Celia, turning her bright eyes toward her brother. "Did he live in this city? I wonder if it was my Mrs. Winthrop's husband?"

"Yes, he lived here — is confidential everything at Marshall & Sylvester's, or was when he was over. His name is Claude Winthrop. But how would you ever know them?"

There followed a merry laugh at Celia's expense.

"Oh, she picked them up by means of her unfortunate habit of always rushing ahead without knowing what she is doing," said her mother resignedly.

"Now mamma, you know you approve of Mrs. Winthrop, quite."

"Well, she is not so bad as some; I must admit, Celia, she is quite presentable, though I don't know but it would encourage you in your carelessness to say so, for the next one you take up may not be."

"The next one she's taken up is a *man,* mamma," said Marion, a fourteen-year-old girl who inherited her mother's face and many of her tastes and qualities, and was not easily disconcerted. "And you'd better look out for her or she'll soon be putting on black and going as a missionary. He's a minister this time."

"Marion!" said Celia reproachfully, her cheeks growing all too rosy for comfort.

"Well, didn't I hear you promising to go slumming with him tomorrow? and to a meeting the next evening? It seems to me you're getting pretty thick when you come to think that is the night of the Grahams' theatre party. If I was in society you wouldn't catch me running off to any college settlements if I could help it. You needn't get mad. I thought I ought to tell mamma before it was too late, and this is a good time for it when you can have the opinion of the whole family on him. I have only done it for your good."

Celia's cheeks were very red indeed now and a suspicious moisture was in her eyes, though her father and brother were laughing over her sister's pertness.

Mrs. Lyman looked searchingly at Celia. Anything extraordinary was entirely consistent with her elder daughter's character and she appreciated to the full her younger daughter's worldly common sense.

"What does she mean, Celia?" asked the mother commandingly.

"I suppose she means Mr. Carter, mamma," said Celia, almost ready to cry with vexation. She had not intended to have her plans flaunted thus before the whole family. "He is Doctor Carter's brother and he is a theological student. He has been making some sociological studies in the lower quarter of the city, in the college settlement. He walked home with me from Mrs. Winthrop's to-day when I took the flowers to her, you know, and I was very much interested in the account of his work. He asked me to go with him and the doctor tomorrow to visit the settlement house."

"No doubt!" answered the mother. "Of course you were interested. I never knew you not to be where it was a case of needed discretion. And I suppose you proposed to go down there and run the risk of bringing home the smallpox and typhoid fever and a few other pleasant diseases, did you?" She spoke sternly and Celia felt there was no hope for her plans, but she put in a protest.

"Indeed, mamma, it is perfectly safe there. The doctor goes every day, and he said it was all right."

"Yes, and I was coming in from school when they stood at the steps fixing it all out, and I saw them smiling and made up my mind somebody better kept watch out, for he has been here before, and so I just stayed in the vestibule behind the door till they —" put in the irrespressible Marion, her eyes lit by triumph that she had brought the culprit to justice. She could always depend on her mother to do the right thing.

"Marion! you may leave the room," was the unexpected command from the father, and Marion stopped suddenly with her cake half-way to her mouth.

"But papa, I —" she began with assurance.

"Leave the room! Put down that cake, and leave the room without another word," said the father sternly.

And Marion obeyed.

But the mother was bent on searching Celia through and through. She did not intend her plans for a brilliant marriage to be upset by any theological student.

"Celia, answer me," she went on, " did you really intend to go down into that awful part of the city?"

"I should like to, mamma," was the meek answer. All she wanted now was to get quietly out of the room.

"I can see no possible harm in her going down there if Doctor Carter is along," spoke up the father unexpectedly. "Let her go if she wants to. It can't hurt her."

"Mr. Lyman, do you know what you are saying?" asked his wife in horrified tones.

"I certainly do, Mrs. Lyman. I went down there myself once to see a miserable old tenement I owned. Some of their people came after me and told me what a rat-hole it was, and kept at me till I went, and the result was

I had to tear it down and build it all over. It isn't a very pretty spot, but you'll certainly find it interesting, if that's what you want, Celia.''

Celia looked her gratitude to her father, and her mother sat back compelled to be resigned, but not content.

"And what was this about a meeting on the night of the theatre party?" she questioned, taking new fire at thought of Marion's words.

"It was nothing but an evangelistic meeting in the Academy of Music," faltered Celia.

"And you promised to go?" demanded the mother.

"Yes, mother."

"And with a nobody of a theological student?"

Celia's gaze was on her plate where she was trying to hide her confusion, but at this probing she roused with a flash in her eye that reminded one of her father, and answered:

"Well, mother, I didn't see any reason why I shouldn't. The doctor's wife is going too. I have seen that play a hundred times, and I'm bored to death with it anyway, and besides I can't endure Dudley Fenwick, and I know if I went I should have to, all the evening."

"And you can endure this poor theological student, can you, little sister? There's nothing like being frank. I guess I shall have to look him up."

The brother's tone was sympathetic in spite of the twinkle of fun in his eyes.

"Do," said the father. "Look him up, Howard. And meantime, mother, I think we can trust Celia not to be indiscreet. Let the child go to the meeting if she prefers, and let the matter rest until Howard gives us his verdict. There are worse people than theological students in this world, and worse places than religious meetings. It strikes me she looks a little thin these days. One theatre party less won't harm her."

"Oh, very well, if you'll answer for the consequences, Mr. Lyman," said his wife with compressed lips, and she gave the signal for leaving the table.

But Celia did not follow her mother immediately, having no desire for a long lecture which she knew would be hers. She was not prepared for her mother's searching questions. There were some things which must be answered in her own heart first before they were brought to the light of her mother's practical worldly tests, and she had not allowed herself to ask these questions as yet. So she turned aside and lingered in the library with her father and brother, and slipped a loving hand into her father's as she sat on a hassock at his feet and rested her head on the arm of his leather chair.

He laid his hand lovingly on her head in recognition of a silent bond between them and went on with his talk, while the brother, watching her, thought how pretty and graceful she was growing.

"Tell me more about this fellow Winthrop. Do you think he could be had if we made it worth while to him?"

The young man entered into a detailed description of some business enterprises in which Claude had acted wisely and well, and the father listened, growing more interested with each new incident.

Finally he turned to Celia.

"And so you know the Winthrops, do you, daughter? Tell me all you know about them. It sometimes takes two or three witnesses to establish a fact. Are you as enthusiastic as your brother?"

Celia launched into a full description of her first conversation with Mrs. Winthrop in church, and the misplaced invitation.

Over the call that she and her mother made later upon Mrs. Winthrop the father and son laughed long and loud, and Mrs. Lyman in the parlor heard it and moved her daintily shod feet uneasily. What new folly were those two encouraging in Celia, now? she wondered.

Celia could talk well when she was interested, and she felt just now that she had her audience, so she went on to describe Mrs. Winthrop in her home, her beauty and her grace and sweetness, the evening at the Washburns', her own private opinion of her friend's successes and triumphs in society, her manner so free from all artificiality. Then her fall and illness. Here she hesitated. This had been the turning-point in her own life she now began to feel. Should she, or should she not speak of that morning and her song beside the sick-room door? With sudden resolve, glancing up quickly to see if both were interested, she dashed in. Her cheeks were glowed crimson, for she was speaking of things she had not been taught to think much about, and there was a constraint about both her listeners, but their interest evidently did not flag.

She began on the doorstep that bright crisp morning when she had called to see how Mrs. Winthrop was, and Doctor Carter and his brother drove up to the door. She let them feel the hush of the sad home that had so deeply affected her. From their own knowledge of her they read between the lines how hard it had been for her to accede to the doctor's request and sing. She even told them of her glimpse of the sorrowing husband and the droning monotony of the voice that went on and on in that one dreadful sentence about the pattern.

Inadvertently each of the listeners noted how well she told what the young minister had said, and laid it up in his heart for future reference when that young man should come in for his reckoning. They did not interrupt her till she came to a sudden halt, at a loss how to explain the various walks and talks with Mr. Carter, to which she found herself confessing.

But they were kindly eyes that searched her face, as much of it as could be seen, and her father patted her gently on her head again, and she was soothed.

"Well, now I've been thinking of a plan," said the father when they had sat for several minutes in silence, "and I guess it may prove of some benefit to both them and us. I like all you say about that man. I believe he may be the man for our business. But the next thing is to get hold of him. We must work it gently. Of course if he is a fixture with Marshall & Sylvester, or bound to them by honor in any way, there will be no use in trying. But that will be to find out. He has a right to better himself if he can, and perhaps we can put him in the way of it. Now, daughter, isn't it almost time for Lent to come when you gay butterflies of fashion are allowed a little rest? What? Next week? Why, I didn't realize the winter was so nearly gone. Well, that suits admirably. Mother won't have so many plans for you, Celia, and so it won't bother her any. And by that time your invalid ought to be able to travel. They'll be sending her away I suppose for a while."

"Oh, yes," interrupted Celia eagerly, "I heard Doctor Carter tell Mr. Winthrop yesterday that if she kept on improving as she had done the last two days he would soon be able to send her off to get a breath of sea air. But I don't believe they can go anywhere for I saw his face get awfully sad when the doctor said it and he didn't answer a word, just went and stood by the window and looked out at nothing."

"Ah! excellent!" said Mr. Lyman, looking pleased, "All the better for our plans if he can't afford it. Now what I propose is this: Celia, you and Howard take one of the servants, take Jane, mother won't miss her much, you know, and run down to the shore for a couple of weeks and invite your friends to come and stay with you a little while. It can be done in such a way that they won't feel uncomfortable about accepting the invitation. Probably Mr. Winthrop may not be able to be there all the time, but he can run up and down morning and evening with Howard, and that will afford you, son, an excellent opportunity for studying him and also for bringing things to the proper point for a business proposition if we consider that wise. I will run down myself if I can, for over Sunday, and meet him. Then we can talk things over at our leisure. How would you like that?"

Celia's eyes danced with pleasure. There had not been anything so pleasant proposed to her since she left the days of dolls houses and had a real fire in her cookstove with permission to cook anything she pleased for her dolls. Besides, it would give her a respite from the endless round of irksome society duties, which her mother kept her working at so constantly. She had been as eager as any girl about the gayeties of society, but when it came to the duty part, the calls and teas at the homes of stupid people about whom she cared not a row of pins, Celia was very loath to obey.

They talked so long about the new plans that Mrs. Lyman sent to know if they were coming up to the sitting room that evening at all, and reluctantly they closed the subject with a whispered word from her father to Celia that she might open the subject with the Winthrops and the doctor as soon as she saw fit.

Then the three went upstairs mutually agreed to say nothing about it that night to the mother.

Howard and his sister went at once to the piano. On the music rack lay a collection of some of the finest compositions of sacred music. Howard took it up and turning the leaves read the name "George H. Carter," written at the top. Celia saw the quick look he gave her and her cheeks burned again, but she was pleased when he laid the book open on the piano and said: "That's very fine music, all of it, little sister. I admire his taste. Let's try this one."

They sang on and Mr. Lyman and his wife sat and read. But Celia felt that something had been recognized between herself and her brother that made things more definite in herself than she had planned to have them. She wondered why it was that she was glad that Howard liked the music.

Chapter 24
Seaside and Heartside

And the eyes forget the tears they have shed,
The heart forgets its sorrow and ache;
The soul partakes the season's youth,
And the sulphurous rifts of passion and woe
Lie deep 'neath a silence pure and smooth,
Like burnt out craters healed with snow.
— *James Russell Lowell.*

To Miriam Winthrop the days now became one long, sweet dream. Her husband came into the room and kissed her the next morning quietly, as one would expect a husband to do the first time he had seen his wife after a long illness. Very little passed between them save looks, but they spoke volumes. Neither nurse nor doctor knew that that kiss was anything more to the two they were watching then any kiss between a husband and wife might be.

They had feared lest the excitement of her husband's coming might be bad for her, lest his haggard face might disturb her, and now, behold, she lay as quiet as a spring morning under the first rays of the rising sun, and the face of the man was changed, joy-touched, glorified. They could not know that that look meant forgiveness and peace for each, that the kiss meant the recognition of all the sorrows and fears and separation — and the healing of them.

Only a few minutes he stayed, for the doctor was still uneasy. And they pressed each other's hands and looked once more each into the depths of the soul of the other and he was gone again. They complied with the laws of the doctor and nurse but each seemed to say to the other that it was only a little while and then they could have each other all the time.

Claude went away again in the light of his wife's smile, but their eyes seemed to promise of the trysting hour, and Miriam slept much during the day and thought as often as she waked of the dream, the dear dream, that would be hers at night when he came to sit beside her once more.

Doctor Carter told him how absolutely necessary it was that his wife should not be excited in any way nor hindered in the least from the rest and recuperation that she was undergoing.

That night, as soon as the nurse had gone from the room and her hand stole out to meet his, he whispered that she must not talk or think, but just sleep and let him sit beside her, and she pressed his hand in happy submission. She did not wish to talk or think, only to breathe in the joy of having the old pain gone. Explanations were for stronger days than these. Faith and a kiss were heaven enough for her now.

And so the days slipped into brighter ones and she grew stronger.

Claude lingered much about the nursery with the little ones and took them on long walks on bright days now. Their chatter seemed to help him fight back the depression that more and more was settling upon him.

He had told no one yet about his trouble with the firm. They did not seem surprised that he was not tied down to the office as in former days. No one had time to think. If they thought anything, they supposed he had arranged matters with a substitute so that he was not so much needed downtown. Sometimes he went out at the old morning hour and wandered aimlessly about in parts of the town that were not familiar to him, past rows and rows of little new brick houses with continuous porches that looked like an unending sleeping car, and yet with their pretty windows and white curtains presented a simple picture of home that Claude almost envied. Here lived men with very small salaries indeed, lived and were happy, and brought up their families to be good men a women. Here might he and Miriam have lived and been content in the first days of their youth. But to take her here now from the more spacious quarters, spacious in comparison with these tiny cottages of four and six rooms, seemed awful to her husband.

It must not be supposed that Claude had not gone near his old business firm. He had mustered the courage and faced them, but they were obdurate. Mr. Sylvester had given the order and had put his own nephew in the place to learn the business. They regretted deeply that it was so. They missed him sorely, one member of the firm even confided to him, but what could they do? Sylvester was the head, after all, and he would have to find out his own mistakes. If he thought it was worth while to see Sylvester, he would be back from Chicago in a few days.

Claude had no desire to face Mr. Sylvester. He knew that anything he might say would be utterly useless. Mrs. Sylvester had power to paint the character of even her husband's dearest friend in colors of the blackest to him. He adored her and she knew well how to retain that adoration.

Day after day he tried to formulate some plan for his future life. There was a little money put away in the bank. Not much besides what was in Miriam's name. That he would never touch. It occurred to him that she must have used it for her society venture, for no bills had come to him for anything beyond the ordinary expenses of the house, and he had left her very little money when he went abroad.

Something definite must be done before she should get well enough to notice that he did not go to his business and begin to ask about it. But what it should be remained from day to day more and more of a problem. He would think until the very room swam before him and then he would retreat to the nursery and forget for a little while his troubles in a merry romp with the little ones.

One or two futile attempts he made with other firms in his line of business, but when they raised their eyebrows on being told that he was no longer with Marshall & Sylvester and answered coldly that they had no opening at present, he would slip away feeling as ashamed as if he had been whipped.

He even ventured the thought of an attempt to borrow money and start in business for himself, in a small way, perhaps in another city or a large, growing town. But this move was too decided to be taken without consultation with Miriam, and she was in no condition to be told anything at present. Besides, where would he borrow the money if he wanted to?

Whenever the thought of telling the family of his severed relations with Marshall & Sylvester occurred to him, he would start out again on a search for something to do. He came to the point where he would have been willing to accept a very humble position indeed with a small salary just for the sake of earning something and being able to tell Miriam, when he should be allowed to talk with her freely, that he had something with which to support her.

But when he attempted to find such a position, he found also that the applicants for it were many and were skilled, and that the salary was so exceedingly small that it would be a question if they could even afford one of the little six-roomed cottages.

The fact that he had been dismissed so summarily from Marshall & Sylvester's was against him. It would have been possible, of course, for him to go to some of the friendly members of the firm and request commendatory letters, but his pride was against that. Besides, he felt that by the order of Mr. Sylvester any commendation from the firm officially had been forbidden. This had been conveyed to him by kindly hints. He felt sure that Mr. Marshall thought that the matter was merely a personal one with Mr. Sylvester, and that nothing had been said against his character in a public way. Mrs. Sylvester laid her plans well. She did not care to make anything public that could so much as breathe her name in its connection.

It is probable that the Claude of six months ago under these circumstances would have risen above circumstances, would have outcunninged Mrs. Sylvester, would have brazened his position through and secured something even better than he had had with Marshall & Sylvester. But he was not the Claude Winthrop of six months ago. He had not the fine opinion of himself that he once held. He had passed through fires, and saw yet more ahead of him to be passed through, which crushed his ambition and filled him with depression.

It was therefore like the proverbial last straw added to his burden when the doctor told him that in two weeks or three at the most he might take his wife to the seacoast. His heart throbbed in dull aches and his eyes did not light with joy as the doctor had expected.

Miriam must go to the shore, of course, if that was what she needed to bring her back to health and strength. But where and how was it to be accomplished? What a fool he had been! That day and the next he alternately sat in depressed sadness in his library and walked the streets for some hope of a business position.

It was in one of these wild aimless walks toward evening that he passed George Carter, whose cheery bow and smile set astir thoughts of the prayer that had been uttered for him. And one phrase came back and was reiterated over and over to him, "God is able."

Was God able? Could he, would he do aught for him, when he had been all these years indifferent?

When he reached home he went again to his library where he had spent so many lonely hours lately, and in desperation flung himself upon his knees.

"O God," he cried, "show me what to do." Again and again he said the same words over. And then he knelt there silent, not knowing why he waited, but feeling that he had cast the burden at the feet of One able and willing to bear it.

Before he had risen from his knees the maid knocked at the door. Miss Lyman was in the reception room, and would like a few words with him, if convenient.

Long afterward Claude read the verse, "Before they call I will answer, and while they are yet speaking I will hear," and his thoughts reverted to that hour in his library.

Celia gave her invitation in a most charming way, as she always did such things. She made him feel that it would be a favor to them if he would accept. If there had been the slightest patronage about the invitation, or if he had suspected that they looked upon him at all as a subject for charity his pride would have induced him to decline at once; but as it was he found when she was gone that he had promised to take Miriam to the Lyman cottage by the sea just as soon as the doctor gave permission, and his heart grew light as he looked about him and drew a long breath. That would give him time to find something to do and know where he stood. How blessed that would be. And he would have a chance to talk with Miriam and feel the sweetness of her forgiveness. He was looking forward to that time as he remembered he had looked forward to his honeymoon long ago.

After that he began seriously to meditate going back to the little town from which he had wooed and won Miriam, and starting in business for himself. He could at least earn a modest income, and if there must be sacrifices, why, in a small town they need not be so great as they would have to be if they stayed in the city. But this would have to be brought before the clear lens of Miriam's judgment by and by. In the meantime he must do all in his power to find something better before they went. Nevertheless, his heart was lighter than it had been since the receipt of the company's letter.

Miriam's eyes grew bright over the prospect that was before her, and sooner than they had dared hope she was able to sit up and be made ready for the journey.

It was down beside the sea, in sheltered corners where a wheeled chair found retreat and the sun kept things warm even in March, and where the few stragglers on the boardwalk were like themselves absorbed in themselves and heeded them not, that Claude and Miriam talked it all over.

Not an experience, not a heartache did they leave tucked away in a forgotten crevice of their hearts to cause trouble at some future time. They confessed everything — and forgave. As rapidly as possible, but without smoothing it over, Claude told all, and later answered all his wife's questions until each felt satisfied, and they had no future fear of the past.

Gently and sadly Claude told her also of that dreadful day when heaven and hell seemed contending for his soul, and as he came to the place where he had to tell of his own intention to take his life, she clutched his hand tight and bit her lips and pressed her eyelids close over her eyes until the tears were crushed beneath the lashes.

Then there were the new experiences to tell, of the day when God had spoken to each of them, and forgiven, and promised to help. They looked back into the past and saw how all might have been different if they had but followed the pattern sooner.

Claude had not told Miriam yet of his business troubles. He judged, and rightly, that she ought not to have more to bear just yet than what she must know to set her heart at rest. So he let her go on thinking that he was having a long vacation for her sake, and she murmured once how good they were not to worry him to come home all the time he was there.

It was the day that she said this that he began once more to feel the old depression stealing over him, and as he wheeled her back to the cottage he did not talk much nor answer with the light-heartedness that had been his of late. Miriam felt the shadow of his mood and grew sad herself.

But that evening Mr. Lyman came down from the city with his son, and after dinner, when Miriam was resting on the couch and Celia singing soft melodies to the accompaniment of her guitar, the three men went out to the piazza together, and walked and talked.

The murmur of the waves mingled with their voices, and Claude's thoughts were sad and troubled. How could he bear to tell Miriam the added trouble? which while in comparison to the other trouble was nothing, was yet one which had an immediate bearing on their lives.

Mr. Lyman asked a number of keen questions, which Claude answered, his thoughts only half on the conversation, and of which he did not see the drift until suddenly he aroused to the fact that a most flattering proposition had been made to him.

He straightened up, every sense on the alert at once. His keen business instinct told him that this was a rare offer even to a man older and more experienced than himself.

They talked along and in the midst of their conversation the moon rose full and grandly over the waters, touching every ripple and furrow with a glory as of myriads of jewels. Claude wondered as he looked if it were typical of the waves of sorrow that had gone over him and Miriam, and that were to be by and by glorified into joy.

It was all settled before the chill of the early spring evening had driven them inside the house once more, and Claude went over to Miriam's couch with a lighter step than had been his for years.

"Sweetheart, I've something beautiful to tell you to-morrow," he whispered in her ear, before the others came in, and immediately Miriam's sadness was turned into joy again.

And the next day was Easter. The sea seemed to have put on an added blueness for the day and the sky matched it in clearness.

Doctor Carter had come down to the shore the night before, with his wife and baby and his brother. Perhaps it was this fact that made Celia's eyes shine brighter than usual as she waited demurely by the window for her father to be ready for church, and saw from the hotel door across the way the doctor and his brother emerging. She had hoped for this but had not dared to think much about it.

That afternoon when all the world passed by on the boardwalk to show its garments gay, as the great world of fashion had decreed — contemptible in its vanity beside the rolling majesty of the sea, that has worn its silken robes and lace of foam for age on ages, and never needs a new — Miriam and Claude sat in a sunny nook once more and talked.

He had told her all the plans and they had looked beyond the crowds that surged by them to the billows of God's everlasting sea, and recognized something in their majesty that called them. Then hand in hand under the great traveling robe that was thrown over Miriam's lap they registered their vow to follow Jesus Christ in all their future life.

There were tints of rose and gold beginning to glow in the green of the sea, and the nook was growing chilly since the sun had left it. The board-walk was almost deserted, for fashion had gone to the evening meal. Up the sand, walking slowly, came Celia and George Carter, walking as if every step were too precious to be hurried through, and they were talking as those talk who hold sweet converse one with another.

Miriam watched them for a few minutes and then sighed.

"Oh," said she wearily, "will they have to make the mistakes and go through the sorrow that we did, Claude?" and there was a quiver in her voice that touched his heart with an exquisite reproach.

"No, dear," he answered gently, "for they have begun 'according to the pattern.' "

Chapter 25
The Pattern Followed

True love is but a humble, low-born thing,
And hath its food served up in earthen ware;
It is a thing to walk with, hand in hand,
Through the everydayness of this work-day world,
Baring its tender feet to every roughness,
Yet letting not one heart-beat go astray.
— *James Russell Lowell.*

They did not stay in the house that had been the scene of so much sorrow and conflict. It soon had another occupant and the landlord raised the rent five dollars a month on account of Miriam's bay window, and the new occupants moved through the street under the halo of its distinction.

It was quite possible to secure a house in one of the semi-suburbs of the city with some ground about it, not too far away from the office which was to be Claude's headquarters.

Miriam rejoiced in the change and the children shouted for joy.

"There's woses, an' vi'lets, an' dandylines, an' butcherflies, an' butchercups, an' birdies," explained small Celia to her nurse.

And the other children clapped their hands over a "real live weeping willow tree" on the lawn.

"And there is a stable at the back of the lot," said Claude, his face as bright as his children's; "sometime we'll have a horse and take drives every day."

At this there was a chorus of glee from the children, and so bright a smile on Miriam's face that Claude was thoughtful for some time after.

It was a lovely spring day. The air had in it that subtle fragrance that lures all who breathe to come and revel in the sunshine. There were hints of blossoms to come on every twig and bough, and the grass seemed leaping up to meet the light.

Miriam was looking wistfully out across her pretty lawn, noticing all the beauty and breathing in the sweetness. She was thinking of the days like these when she and Claude had wandered over the hillside and hunted for the first wild flowers. She was weak enough yet to long for those days back again. As she looked, a carriage drew up in front of the gate and her husband sprang out and came up the walk.

He had come to take her for a drive he said, the air would do her good, and she must hurry and get ready, for they must make the most of their first "afternoon off," as he called it.

She paused by the hat rack and reached for her hat and coat and then with sudden impulse she went on upstairs and slipped into another gown. She must not lose all her worldly wisdom just because she had greater motives to work by now, and a different pattern.

It did not take long to make herself pretty and her husband stood admiring her as she came down the hall fifteen minutes later, his face as bright and eager as a boy's. There would be always something half-boyish about Claude that was very winning, so thought his wife.

"We will go to the park," he said as he headed the horse toward the river drive, "It is just the day for the park."

It was one of those days when fashion has ordered "all out on parade." And they were there, the jingling silver-mounted ones, and the quieter rubber-tired ones, looking weary and bored in their spring array. It was a part of their day's doing, this drive, and many of them had the look as if they were taking medicine.

Miriam had not been here since the day that her heart had been pierced. Now as they swept into the wide smooth drive and became one of the double procession that curved about the river's edge and up among the hills, she smiled to think how happy she was, and how her heart was bubbling over as light as had been her little child's, almost a year ago when she had brought her here to play.

Claude grew joyful. He felt the sweet air like new wine mounting first to his heart, then to his head. He was proud of his wife, sitting in her quiet beauty beside him. He was pleased over his business prospects, and withal there was a great, deep peace in his soul. He felt that this world of nature into which they were driving was his Father's world and he was glad to be in it.

On they drove, past the little canoes on the river; past the old pebble-dash hotels that advocated catfish and waffles for light refreshment, on their signs; past the old covered bridge, and the little rustic abiding-place of the park guards; past the spring and the grotto, into the winding drive all arched with brown branches and tender green feathery tips beginning to peep through; on till they had out-distanced most of their driving companions and were rolling along on the hard road alone, except for an occasional one who had gone farther than the rest and was turning early home again. They could look down now on the brook as it rippled along over the glistening stones below, and the little rustic bridge that crossed it, where a boy stood earnestly fishing — past them all. And now they were approaching the curve where she and Celia had climbed the bank and looked down on the world below.

Claude had been speaking, talking of the beauty of the drive and the sunlight glinting through the boughs down into the water. Then he had looked at her, but her heart had been going back over the year to the moment when she had stood up there on the bank and looked down here — where she was now, safe and happy with Claude.

But the words he was now speaking to her, were sweet and tender, and showed perfectly how he understood her feelings, full of a nobler, deeper love than any they had expressed before. She could not forget her thoughts and look up into his eyes which were compelling hers. And then he bent and kissed her.

It was a long, clinging kiss, and the look he gave her after it was one of tender meaning.

All softly just then there swept around the curve another driver. Her horses were finely blooded, her equipage the latest, and her silken robes were rich and fair to see. Beside her sat a man who looked at her adoringly, as she held her horses with a graceful skill, but she was not talking to him, nor did she once glance toward him, and it was not on her horses that she kept her gaze so earnestly nor yet upon the landscape, though it was passing good to see.

Miriam, her face flooded with the glory of her love and the joy of perfect harmony, looked up to see this woman, her enemy, with the eyes of hate gazing upon her.

She did not stir, nor cry out, as she might have done at another time, or did her fair face flush the slightest perceptible rose color. Her steady eyes all clear with dews of heaven looked full upon her enemy, and knew her fight was won.

They passed as in the flash of sunlight that lit the pool below and Claude had not looked up nor recognized his friend and enemy of old. Miriam, her joy rushing over her anew as the tumult of her heart subsided, hid her glad face upon her husband's shoulder and wept tears of joy.

So they drove out from the arching branches into the late spring sunlight of the upper road that led home, and Miriam smiled to think the last shadow of her sorrow had been swept from her path, for her enemy had been met and was conquered.

When they reached home and the evening meal was over, Claude brought a Bible out and called the children round their mother.

"Miriam," he said, and his voice was constrained with feeling, "if we are going to follow the new Pattern, hadn't we better begin right? I don't want the children to make the mistake we did."

And Miriam, her cup of comfort running over, assented with joyful eyes.

The little ones with wondering, reverent faces, knelt beside their mother while their father prayed his first faltering prayer in the presence of others.

Down upon her knees was Miriam, her heart filled full of praise, and upon her life a peace that passeth understanding. This was the new way and it was good — to follow the pattern, Christ Jesus, and evermore "believe on him to life everlasting."

> "Oh, the little birds sang east, and the little
>   birds sang west,
> And I smiled to think God's greatness flowed around
>   our incompleteness —
> Round our restlessness, his rest."

An Unwilling Guest

Chapter 1
Outside Quarantine

The gray horse stopped by a post on the other side of the road from the little wooden station as if he knew what was expected of him, and a young girl got out of the carriage and fastened him with a strap. The horse bowed his head two or three times as if to let her know the hitching was unnecessary but he would overlook it this time seeing it was she who had done it.

The girl's fingers did their work with accustomed skill, but the horse saw that she was preoccupied and she turned from him toward the station a trifle reluctantly. There was a grave pucker between her eyebrows that showed that her present duty was not one of choice.

She walked deliberately into the little waiting room occupied by some women and noisy children, and compared her watch with the grim-faced clock behind the agent's grating. She asked in a clear voice if the five-fifty-five New York train was on time, and being assured that it was she went out to the platform to look up the long stretch of track gleaming in the late afternoon sun, and wait.

Five miles away, speeding toward the same station, another girl of about the same age sat in a chair car, impatiently watching the houses, trees, and telegraph poles as they flew by. She had gathered her possessions about her preparatory to leaving the train, had been duly brushed by the obsequious porter who seemed to have her in charge, and she now wore an air of impatient submission to the inevitable.

She was unmistakably city bred and wealthy, from the crown of her elaborate black chiffon hat to the tip of her elegant boot. She looked with scorn on the rich farming country, with its plain, useful buildings and occasional pretty homes, through which she was being carried. It was evident, even to the casual onlooker, that this journey she was taking was hardly to her taste. She felt a wave of rebellion toward her father, now well on his way to another continent, for having insisted upon immuring her in a small back-country village with his maiden sister during his enforced absence. He might well enough have left her in New York with a suitable chaperon if he had only thought so, or taken her along — though that would have been a bore, as he was too hurried with business to be able to give time and thought to making it pleasant for her.

She drew her pretty forehead into a frown as she thought the vexed question over again and contemplated with dread the six stupid weeks before she could hope for his return and her release from exile. She pouted her lips in annoyance as she thought of a certain young man who was to be in New York during the winter. She was to have met him at a dinner this very night. She wondered for the hundredth time if it could possibly be that papa had heard of her friendship with this young fellow and because of it had hustled her off to Hillcroft so unceremoniously. Her cheeks burned at the thought and she bit her lips angrily. Papa was so particular! Men did not know how to bring up a girl, anyway. If only her mother had lived she felt sure she would not have had such old-fashioned notions, for her mother had been quite a woman of fashion, from what people in society said of her. There was nothing the matter with this Mr. Worthington either — a little fast, but it had not hurt him. He was delightful company. Fathers ought to know that their daughters enjoyed men with some spirit and not namby-pamby milk-and-water creatures. Probably papa had been a bit wild in his youth also; she had heard it said that all men were, in which case he ought to be lenient toward other young men and not expect them to be grave and solemn before their time. Mr. Worthington dressed perfectly, and that was a good deal. She liked to see a man well dressed. Papa was certainly very foolish about her. With this filial reflection the young woman arose as the train came to a halt and followed the porter from the car.

Several passengers alighted, but the girl on the platform knew instinctively that the young woman in the elegant gray broadcloth skirt and dainty shirt waist, carrying on her arm her gray coat, which showed more than a gleam of the turquoise blue silk lining, and unconcernedly trailing her long skirt on the dirty platform, was the one with whom she had to do.

Allison Grey waited just the least perceptible second before she stepped forward. She told herself afterward that it made it so much worse to have that porter standing smiling and bowing to listen. She felt that her duty was fully as disagreeable as she had feared, yet she was one who usually faced duty cheerfully. She could not help glancing down at her own blue serge skirt and plain white shirt waist, and remembering that her hands were guiltless of gloves, as she walked forward to where the other girl stood.

"Is this Miss Rutherford?" she asked, trying to keep her voice from trembling, and hoping her mental perturbation was not visible.

The traveler wheeled with a graceful turn of her tall figure that left the tailor-made skirt in lovely curved lines which Allison with her artist's eye noted at once, — and stared. Evelyn Rutherford's eyes were black and had an expression which in a less refined type of girl would have been called saucy. In her it was modified into haughtiness. She looked Allison Grey over and it seemed to Allison that she took account of every discrepancy in her plain little outfit before she answered.

"It is." There was that in the tone of the answer that said: "And what business of yours may that be, pray?"

Allison's cheek flushed and there came a sparkle in her eye that spoke of other feelings than her quiet answer betokened:

"Then will you come this way, please? The carriage is on the other side of the station. Your aunt, Miss Rutherford, was unable to meet you and I have come in her place. If you will give me your check I will see that your baggage is attended to at once."

"Indeed!" said the bewildered traveler, and she followed the other girl with an air of injured dignity. Was this some kind of a superior servant her aunt had sent to take her place? Her maid, perhaps? She certainly did not speak nor act like a servant, and yet — Then her indignation waxed great. To think that her father's sister should treat her in this way, not even come to the station to meet her when she was an entire stranger, and had never even seen her since she was three years old! In New York, of course, she would not have expected it. Things were different. But she had always understood that country people made a great deal of meeting their friends at the station. Her aunt had spoken of this in her letters. A fine welcome, to be sure! She could not be ill or this person would have mentioned it at once.

She entirely forgot that a few moments before one of the greatest grievances had been that she feared her aunt would bore her with a show of affection, for she remembered the many caresses of her babyhood indistinctly, and her nature was not one that cared for feminine affection overmuch.

Allison showed the porter where to deposit the bags and umbrellas on the station platform, and taking the checks given her she left the elegant stranger standing amid her belongings, looking with disdain at the pony phaeton across the road and wondering where the carriage could be. She was growing angry at being left standing so long when she became aware that the girl across the road untying the pony was the same one who had gone away with her checks, and it began to dawn upon her that she was expected to get into that small conveyance with this other girl.

She submitted with what grace she could, as there seemed to be nothing else to be done, but the expression on her face was anything but pleasant, and she demanded an explanation of the state of things in no sweet manner.

"What is the meaning of all this? Is this my aunt's carriage? Where is her driver?" she asked imperiously. Having made up her mind that this girl was a servant she concluded to treat her accordingly.

It was characteristic of Allison that she waited until she had carefully spread the clean linen robe over the gray broadcloth skirt, gathered her reins deliberately, and given the pony word to go before she answered. Even then she did not speak until the phaeton was turned about and they were fairly started spinning over the smooth road under the arching trees. By that time her voice was sweet and steady, and her temper was well under her control.

"I am very sorry, Miss Rutherford, that you should suffer any inconvenience," she said. "It certainly is not so pleasant for you as if your aunt had been able to meet you as she planned. No, this is not her carriage. It belongs to us, and we are her neighbors and dear friends." She forced herself to say this with a pleasant smile, although she felt somehow as if the girl beside her would resent it.

"Really!" interpolated Miss Rutherford, as one who awaits a much-needed explanation.

"Yes, your aunt was expecting you, 'looking forward with great pleasure to your coming,' she bade me say," went on Allison, reciting her lesson a trifle stiffly, "and only two hours ago she discovered serious illness among her household which they are afraid may be contagious. They cannot tell for some hours yet. She does not wish you to come to the house until they are sure. She hopes that it will be all right for you to come home by to-morrow, or the next day at most, and in the meantime we will try to make you as comfortable as possible. Your aunt sent us word by the doctor this morning asking me to meet you and explain why it would not be safe for her to meet you. I am Allison Grey. We live quite at the other end of town from Miss Rutherford, so you will be entirely safe from any infection should it prove to be serious. Miss Rutherford was kind enough to think my mother could make you a little more comfortable than any one else."

Allison was almost in her usual spirits as she finished speaking. It would not be so bad after the stranger understood, surely. She did not add what Miss Rutherford had said about having her niece with herself, Allison, as she hoped another girl's company would make her feel less lonely and strange, for Allison saw at once that this was not a girl who cared for other girls' company a straw, at least not such as she.

Evelyn Rutherford's face was a study. Chagrin and astonishment struggled for the mastery.

"I do not understand," she said. "Who is ill in the family that could prevent my aunt meeting me? I thought she lived alone."

"She does," said Allison quickly, "except for her two servants. It is one of them, the cook. She has been with Miss Rutherford for fifteen years, you know, and is almost like her own flesh and blood to her. Besides, she has taken care of her all night herself, before she knew there was any need for caution, and if it is smallpox, as they fear, she has been fully exposed to it already, so it would not be safe for her to come to you until they are sure."

"Horrors!" exclaimed the stranger, and Allison saw that her face turned a deadly white. "Stop! Turn around! I will go right back to New York!"

"You need not feel afraid," said Allison gently. "There is none of it in town and this case is entirely isolated. The woman has been away on a visit to her brother and probably took the disease there. She came home only yesterday. She came back sooner than she intended because you were coming and Miss Rutherford sent for her. There is really no cause for alarm, for the utmost care will be taken if it should prove to be smallpox, and by morning we may hear that it is all right and she is getting well, and it is not that at all. Besides, there is no New York train going out to-night. The last one passed yours about ten miles back. You will have to stay until to-morrow anyway."

"Mercy!" said the stranger, seeming not to be able to find words to express her feelings. She was certainly taking the news very badly, but her hostess hoped she would behave better when she was fully possessed of the facts.

Miss Rutherford asked a few more questions about her aunt, commenting scornfully upon her devotion to a servant, which brought an angry flush to the other girl's cheek — and then settled down to the inevitable. Upon reflection she decided it would be better to wait and write or telegraph to her friends in New York before returning to them. Indeed, there was no one in town just then — for it was early for people to return to the city — with whom she felt sufficiently intimate to drop down upon them unannounced for a prolonged visit, and she knew that her father would utterly disapprove of her being with any of them, anyway.

"Do your people keep a boarding house?" she asked, turning curious eyes on Allison, who flushed again under the tone, which sounded to her insolent, but waited until she had disentangled the reins from the pony's tail before she replied gently:

"No."

"Well — but — I don't understand," said the guest. "Did you not say that my aunt had arranged for me to board with you?"

A bright spot came in each of Allison's cheeks ere she replied with gentle dignity:

"No, you are to *visit* us, if you will. Your aunt is a dear friend of my mother, Miss Rutherford." She resolved in her heart that she would never, never, call this girl Evelyn. She did not want the intimate friendship that her old friend had hinted at in telling her first of the coming of this city niece.

Allison was favored with another disagreeable stare, but she gave her attention to the pony.

"Really, I'm obliged," said the guest in icy tones that made Allison feel as if she had been guilty of unpardonable impertinence in inviting her. "Was there no hotel or private boarding house to which I could have gone? I dislike to be under obligations to entire strangers."

Allison's tones were as icily dignified now as her unwilling guest's as she replied: "Certainly, there are two hotels and there is a boarding house. You would hardly care to stay in the boarding house I fancy. It has not the reputation of being very clean. I can take you to either of the hotels if you wish, but even in Hillcroft it would scarcely be the thing for a young girl to stay alone at one of them. We sometimes hear of chaperons, even as far West as this, Miss Rutherford."

Allison's eyes were bright and she drew herself up straight in the carriage as she said this, but she remembered almost immediately the pained look that would have come into her mother's eyes if she had heard this exhibition of something besides a meek and quiet spirit, and she tried to control herself. Yet in spite of the way in which she had spoken, her words had some effect on the young woman by her side. She had been met by the enemy on her own ground and vanquished. She had a faint idea that her brother Dick would have remarked something about being "hoist with his own petard" had he been by, for she was wont to be particular about these things at home. She felt thankful that he was several hundreds of miles away. She said no more about hotels. She understood the matter of chaperonage even better than did Allison Grey, and strange as it may seem, Allison rose in her estimation several degrees after her haughty speech.

There was silence in the phaeton for some minutes. Then the driver spoke, to point out a dingy house close to the street with several dirty children playing about the steps. There was a sign in one window on a fly-specked card, "Rooms to Rent," and a card hung out on a stick nailed to the door-frame, "Vegetable soup to-day."

"This is the boarding house," said Allison. "Do you wish me to leave you here?" Her spirit was not quite subdued yet.

Evelyn Rutherford looked and uttered an exclamation of horror. Her companion caught the expression and a spirit of fun took the place of her look of indignation. In spite of herself she laughed.

But the girl beside her was too much used to having her own way to relish any such joke as this. She maintained an offended silence.

They passed the two hotels of the town, facing one another on Post-office Square. There were loungers smoking on the steps and on the long piazzas of both and at the open door of one a dashing young woman, with a loud laugh and louder attire, joked openly with a crowd of men and seemed to be proud of her position among them. Evelyn curled her lip and shrank into the carriage farther at thought of herself as a guest at that house.

"I fear I shall have to trouble you, at least until I can communicate with my aunt or make other arrangements," she said stiffly, and added condescendingly, "I'm sure I'm much obliged."

Then the carriage turned in at a flower-bordered driveway with glimpses of a pretty lawn beyond the fringe of crimson blossoms and Miss Rutherford realized that her journey was at an end.

Chapter 2
Contrasts

They stopped at a side door which opened on a vine-clad piazza. The house was white with green blinds and plenty of vines in autumn tinting clinging to it here and there as if they loved it. A sweet-faced woman opened the door as they stopped at the steps and came out to meet them. She had eyes like Allison's and a firm, sweet chin that suggested strength and self-control. Apparently she had none of Allison's preconceived idea of their guest for she came forward with a gentle welcome in her face and voice.

"So you found her all right, Allison dear," she said as she waited for the stranger to step from the carriage, and Evelyn noticed that she placed her arm around her daughter and put an unobtrusive kiss on the pink cheek.

"This is mother," Allison said, all the sharpness gone out of her voice.

That Mrs. Grey should fold her in her arms and place a kiss, tender and loving, upon her cheek was an utter astonishment to Evelyn Rutherford. She was not used to being kissed. Her own mother had long been gone from her, and the women in whose charge she had been had not felt inclined to kiss her. In fact, she disliked any show of affection, expecially between two women, and would have been disposed to resent this kiss, had it been given by one less sweet and sincere. But one could not resent Mrs. Grey, even if that one were Evelyn Rutherford.

"My dear, I am so sorry for you," was what she said next. "It must be very hard for your journey to end among strangers after all. But you need not be anxious about your dear aunt, she is so strong and well and has often nursed contagious diseases without contracting anything."

Allison, as she went down the steps to take the pony to his stable, could not help waiting just the least little bit to hear what this strange girl would say, but all the satisfaction she had was a glimpse of her face filled with utter astonishment. She felt in her heart that the least of Miss Rutherford's concerns was about her aunt. She wondered if her mother could not tell that by just a glance, or if she simply chose to ignore it in her sweet, persistent way. There were often times when Allison Grey wondered thus about her mother, and often had she suspected that

8

behind the sweet, innocent smile which acknowledged only what she chose to see, there was a deeper insight into the character before her than even her shrewd daughter possessed. Allison puzzled over it now as she drove to the stable, flecking the pony's back with the end of the whip that was almost never used for its legitimate purpose.

In the house Miss Rutherford was carried from one astonishment to another. The gentle, well-bred welcome, she could not repulse. It took her at a disadvantage. She was ill at ease. She followed Mrs. Grey silently to her room. Something kept her from the condescending thanks she had been about to speak, thanks which would have put her in no way obligated to these new, and, as she chose to consider, rather commonplace strangers. Why she had not uttered the cold, haughty words she did not know, but she had not.

The room into which she was ushered was not unattractive even to her city-bred eyes. To be sure the furnishings were inexpensive, that she saw at a glance, but she could not help feeling the air of daintiness and comfort everywhere. The materials used were nothing but rose-colored cambric and sheer white muslin, but the effect was lovely. There was a little fire in an open grate and a low old-fashioned chair drawn up invitingly. The day was just a trifle chilly for October, but the windows were still wide open.

"Now, dear," said Mrs. Grey, throwing the door open. "I hope you will be perfectly comfortable here. My room is just across the hall and Allison sleeps next to you, so you need not be lonely in the night."

Left to herself Miss Rutherford took off her hat and looked about her. The room was pretty enough. The low, wide window-seat in the bay window, covered with rosebud chintz and provided with plenty of luxurious pillows, and quite charming; but then it had a homemade look, after all, and the girl scorned home-made things. She had not been brought up to love and reverence the home. Her world was society, and how society would laugh over an effect achieved in cheap cottons with such evident lack of professional decorators. Nevertheless, she looked about with curiosity and a growing satisfaction. Since she must be thus cast upon a desert island she was glad that it was no worse, and she shuddered over the thought of the possibilities in that boarding house she had passed. However, she was not a young woman given to much thanksgiving and generally spent her time in bewailing what she did not have rather than in being glad over what she had escaped.

Presently the lack of a maid, who was to her a necessary institution, began to make itself felt. Her aunt had servants she knew, for they had been mentioned occasionally in the long letters she wrote at stated intervals to them. Her father had most emphatically declared against taking a maid with her from New York. This had been one of her greatest grievances. Her father said that her aunt had all the servants that would be necessary to wait upon her, and it was high time she learned to do things for herself. All her tears and protestations had not availed.

But in this house there had been no word of a maid. Mrs. Grey had told her to let her know if there was anything she needed, but had not suggested sending a servant. Of course they must have servants. She would investigate.

She looked about her for signs of a bell, but no bell appeared. She opened the door and listened. There was the distant tinkle of china and silver, as of some one setting a table; there came a tempting whiff of something savory through the hall and distant voices talking low and pleasantly, but there seemed to be no servant anywhere in sight or sound.

Across the hall Mrs. Grey's wide, old-fashioned room seemed to smile peacefully at her and speak of a life she did not understand and into which she had never had a glimpse before. It annoyed her now. She did not care for it. It seemed to demand a depth of earnestness beneath living that was uncomfortable, she knew not why. She went in and slammed her door again and sat down on the bay-window seat, looking out discontentedly across the lawn.

Presently a wagon drove into the yard carrying her two large trunks. She heard voices about the door and then the heavy tread of a man bearing a burden. She waited, thinking how she could get hold of a servant.

Allison's light tap on the door soon followed and behind her was the man with a trunk on his shoulder.

"Wal, I kin tell yew that there trunk ain't filled with feathers!" ejaculated the man as he put down the trunk with a thump and looked shrewdly at its owner.

"You ought to bring some one to help you, Mr. Carter," said Allison's fresh, clear voice, with just a tinge of indignation in it as she looked toward the stranger, "that was entirely too much of a lift for you."

Miss Rutherford curled her lip and turned toward the window till the colloquy should be concluded.

"And now," said Mr. Carter, puffing and blowing from the weight of the second trunk which was even worse than the first, "I s'pose you want them there things unstropped. You don't look like you was much more fit to do it yourself than one o' these ere grasshoppers, er a good-sized butterfly."

"Sir!" said Miss Rutherford in freezing astonishment.

"I said as how you wa'n't built for unstroppin' trunks," remarked the amiable Carter with his foot against the top of the trunk and his cheeks puffed out in the effort to unfasten a refractory buckle.

"Your remarks are entirely unnecessary," said the haughty young woman, straightening herself to her full height and looking disagreeable in the extreme.

The buckle gave way, and Carter taking his old hat from the floor where it had fallen looked at her slowly and carefully from head to foot, his face growing redder than when he had first put down the trunk.

"No harm meant, I'm sure, miss," he said in deep embarrassment as he shuffled away, mumbling something under his breath as he went downstairs.

"The idea!" said the young woman to herself. "What impudence! He ought not to be employed by decent people." Then she heard Allison's step in the hall and remembered her wants.

"Will you please let your maid bring me some hot water," she said with a sweet imperiousness she knew how to assume on occasion.

"I will attend to it at once," answered Allison in a cold tone, and it became evident to the guest that her sympathies were all with Mr. Carter. It made her indignant and she retired to her room to await the hot water.

She stood before the mantel idly studying a few photographs. One, the face of a young man, scarcely more than a boy, attracted her with an oddly familiar glance. Where had she seen some one who had that same peculiarly direct gaze, that awakened a faint stir of undefined pleasant memories? She turned from the picture without having discovered, to answer the tap on the door with a "come" that was meant as a pleasant preface to her request that the entering maid would assist her a little and met Allison with the hot water.

"Oh, how kind to bring it yourself," said the guest a trifle less stiffly than before. "But would you mind lending me your maid for a few minutes? Can you spare her? I won't keep her very long."

The color crept into Allison's cheek as she answered steadily: "I am very sorry to say we are without any just now, so I cannot possibly send her to you; but I shall be glad to help you in any way I can as soon as mother can spare me."

"Oh, indeed!" said the guest with one of her stares. "Don't trouble yourself. I shall doubtless get along in some way," and she turned her back upon Allison and looked haughtily out of the window.

Allison reflected a moment and said in a pleasanter tone:

"If there is any lifting to be done or your trunks are not right, father will help you when he comes in for supper. And I'm sure mother would want me to help you in any way I can, if you will just tell me what to do. Would you like me to help you unpack?"

"Oh, no, thank you," said the guest with her face still toward the window, "I can do very well myself."

Allison hesitated and then turned to go. As she was half out the door she said helplessly: "We have supper in half an hour. If you want me just call. I can easily hear you."

Miss Rutherford made no answer. After the door had closed she began elaborate preparations for a dinner toilet. She belonged to a part of the world that considered it a crime to appear at dinner in any but evening attire. In her life atmosphere it was thought to be a part of the unwritten code of culture which must be adhered to in spite of circumstances, as one would wear clothes even if thrown among naked savages. In her eyes Hillcroft was somewhat of a cannibal island, but it never occurred to her that it would be proper for her to do as the savages did. Therefore she "dressed" for dinner.

It was decidedly over an hour from that time before the guest descended. Mr. Grey had waited as patiently as possible, though he had pressing engagements for the evening. The bell rang twice, loud and clear, and Allison tapped at her door once and asked politely if she could be of any assistance as supper was ready; but in spite of all this the guest came into the dining room as coolly as if she had not been keeping every one waiting for at least three-quarters of an hour, and spoiling most effectually the roasted potatoes, which had been in their perfection when the bell rang.

Mrs. Grey had been as much annoyed by the delay as she ever allowed herself to be over anything, for she did like to have potatoes roasted to just the right turn, and prided herself upon knowing the instant to take them from the oven and crack their brown coats till the steam burst forth and showed the snowy whiteness of the dry delicious filling.

But potatoes and engagements alike were forgotten when Miss Rutherford burst upon them in her glory.

She had chosen a costume which in her estimation was plain, but which by its very unexpectedness was somewhat startling. It was only a black net with spangles of jet in delicate traceries and intricate patterns here and there, but the dazzling whiteness of the beautiful neck and arms in contrast made it very effective. She certainly was a beautiful girl, and she saw their acknowledgment of this fact in their eyes as she entered the room.

But she could not know of the shock which the bare white shoulders and beautifully molded arms gave to the whole family. Hillcroft was not a place which *décolleté* dressing was considered "just quite the thing" among the older, well-established families. It was felt to be a little "fast" by the best people, and it happened that Allison had never in the whole of her quiet, sheltered life sat down to a table or even moved about familiarly in the same room with a woman who considered it quite respectable to use so little material in the waist of her dress. It shocked her indescribably. She could scarcely understand herself why it should have such an effect upon her. She was a girl who had read widely, and in the world of literature she had moved much in the society of women who dressed in this way, and so far as one can be, through books, she was used to society's ways. But she had moved through that airy world of the mind without even noticing this feature of the fashions, except to disapprove them, because her parents did. Now she looked for the first time upon a beautiful woman standing unblushing before her father in a costume that his own daughter would have thought immodest to wear in his presence. After the first startled look Allison turned away her face. It was a beautiful vision, but one that she felt ought not to be looked upon. It seemed that the girl before her must be shielded in some way and the only way she could do it was by averting her gaze.

If Allison had been a frequenter of the theatre she would not have felt in this way; but Hillcroft was not a place where many artists penetrated, and if it had been, Mr. Grey disapproved of the theatre and so did his wife.

The feeling which Allison had about the white neck and arms extended in a less degree to her mother and father. There was a tinge of embarrassment in their greeting as they sat down to the evening meal, which they could hardly have explained. It was not so much embarrassment for themselves as for their guest, for they felt that she must inevitably discover how out of place she was in such surroundings, and then what could she feel but confusion? They forgot that her home surroundings had not been theirs.

Chapter 3
The Maid-of-All-Work

It was well for the Grey family that their custom was to drop their eyes and bow their heads upon sitting down to a meal, while the head of the house asked God's blessing.

On this occasion it was a great relief to all concerned to close their eyes and quiet their hearts before God for a brief instant. They were people who lived close enough to their heavenly Father to gather strength from even so brief a heart-lift as this was.

As for the guest, it was actually the first time since her little girlhood that she had sat at a table and heard God's blessing asked. There could scarcely have been brought together two girls whose lives had been farther apart than those of Allison Grey and Evelyn Rutherford. Miss Rutherford slightly inclined her head as good breeding would dictate, but she kept her eyes wide open and looked about on the group, half amused and a trifle annoyed. She did not care to have such an interruption to her little triumph of entrance. Besides, she now thought she knew why these people were so awfully placid and unusual in their behavior, — they were religious. She had never known any very religious people, but she felt sure they were disagreeable and she decided again to get away from them as soon as possible. Meantime she was hungry and she could not help seeing that a tempting meal was set before her, even though, in the house-keeper's notion, it was almost spoiled.

When the blessing was concluded she noticed, as she waited for the plate containing a piece of juicy steak to be handed her, that the tablecloth was fine and exquisitely ironed, and that the spoons and forks, though thin and old-fashioned, were solid silver. She happened to be interested in old silver just then, on account of a fad of a city friend, so she was able to recognize it. This fact made the people rise somewhat in her estimation, and she set herself to be very charming to the head of the house. It had never seemed to her worth while to exercise her charms upon women.

She really could talk very well. Allison had to admit that as she sat quietly serving the delicious peaches and cream, and passing honey, delicate biscuits, and amber coffee with the lightest of sponge cake.

14

The guest did thorough justice to the evening meal, and talked so well about her journey to Mr. Grey that he quite forgot his hurry and suddenly looked at his watch to find that he was already five minutes late to a very important committee meeting.

Allison did not fail to note all these things, nor to admit the beauty and charm of their visitor as she from time to time cast furtive glances, getting used to the dazzling display of white arms. Her face grew grave as the meal drew to a close, and her mother watching, partly understood.

They had just risen from the table when Mrs. Grey, stepping softly from the hall, folded a white, fleecy shawl about the guest's shoulders saying gently: "Now, dear, you must go out and watch the moon rise over the lawn, and you will need this wrap. It is very cool outside."

Allison noticed with vexation that the shawl was her mother's carefully guarded best one that her brother had sent last Christmas. Allison herself always declined to wear it that it might be saved for mother. Yet here was this disagreeable, haughty, hateful —

Allison stopped suddenly and tried to devote herself to clearing off the supper table, realizing that her state of mind was not charitable, to say the least. She went with swift feet and skillful fingers about the work of washing the supper dishes, and her mother, perhaps thinking it was just as well for Allison to have a quiet thinking time, did not offer to help, but sat on the piazza with their guest, talking quietly to her about her aunt, though she must have noticed that the girl did not respond very heartily nor seem much interested. By and by Allison slipped out with another shawl and wrapped it about her mother and the stranger saw in the moonlight the mother's grateful smile and the lingering pressure she gave Allison's hand, and wondering, felt for the first time in her life a strange lack in her own existence.

"Are the dishes all washed, dear?" said Mrs. Grey a little while later, when Allison came out and settled at her mother's feet on the upper step.

"Yes, mother, and I have started the oatmeal for breakfast. You wanted oatmeal didn't you?"

During the few words that followed about domestic arrangements it became evident to Miss Rutherford that the other girl had actually washed the supper dishes and done a good deal of the work of the house that day. She looked at her with curiosity and not a little sympathy. She felt a lofty pity for any girl who did not move amid the pleasures of society, but to be obliged to wash dishes seemed to the New York girl a state not far from actual degradation. And yet here was this girl talking about it as composedly as if it were an every-day occurrence which she did not in the least mind.

She wondered what could be the cause of the necessity for this state of things. Probably all the servants had decamped at once, it might be on account of the fear of smallpox. In that case it might be that even she was in danger of contagion. It would be well to investigate. Mrs. Grey had gone into the house and Allison sat on the step quietly looking out at the shadows on the lawn.

"You said your maid had left you, I think," said Miss Rutherford, trying to speak pleasantly. "Have all your servants gone? What was the matter? Were they afraid of the smallpox?"

"Oh, dear no!" said Allison, this time surprised out of her gravity into a genuine laugh. "There isn't any smallpox in town, only perhaps that one case you know. No, we never keep more than one servant. I did not say she had left; I said we had none now. She's not a maid in the sense you meant; she's the maid-of-all-work. She has been with mother since we were little children, but she is away on a vacation now. She always goes for a month every fall to visit her brother in Chicago, and during that month mother and I do all the work, all but the washing. She went only to Chicago day before yesterday, so we are just getting broken in, you see."

"Oh!" said Miss Rutherford slowly, trying to take in such a state of things and the possibility that anybody could accept it calmly. "And you only keep one servant? I'm sure I don't see how ever in the world you manage. Why, we keep four always, and sometimes five, and then things are never half done right. I should think you would just hate to have to do the work. Don't you?"

"Why, no," said Allison slowly. "I rather like it. Mother and I have such nice times doing it together. I love to make bread. I always do that part now; it's a little too hard for mother."

"Do you mean to say you can make bread?" The questioner leaned forward and looked curiously at the other girl, as though she had confessed to belonging to some strange tribe of wild people of whom she had heard, but whom she had never expected to look upon.

"Why, certainly!" said Allison, laughing heartily now. "I can make good bread, too, I think. Wasn't that good you had for supper?"

"Yes, it was fine. I think it was the best I ever ate, but I never dreamed a girl could make it. Don't you get your hands all stuck up? I should think it would ruin them forever. I've always heard work was terrible on the hands," and she looked down at her own white ones sparkling with jewels in the moonlight as if they might have become contaminated by those so lowly near by.

"I have not found that my hands suffered," said Allison, in a cold tone, spreading out a pair as small and white and shapely as those adorned with rings. Her guest looked at her curiously again. Sitting there on the step in that graceful attitude, with the white scarf about her head and shoulders which her mother had placed there when she went in, and the moonlight streaming all about her, Miss Rutherford suddenly saw that the other girl was beautiful too. The delicately cut features showed clearly with the pure line of profile against the dark foliage in shadow behind her. Evelyn Rutherford knew that here was a face that her brother would rave over as being "pure Greek." What a pity that such a girl must be shut in by such surroundings, a little quiet village wherein she was buried, and nothing to do but wash dishes and make bread. Curiosity began to grow in her. She would try to find out how this other girl reconciled herself to such surroundings. Did she know no better? or had she never heard of any other world, of life and gayety? What did she do with her time? She decided to find out.

"What in the earth do you do with yourself the rest of the time? You only have to wash dishes and make bread one month you say. I should think you would die buried away out here? Is there any life at all in this little place?"

If Allison had been better acquainted with her visitor she would have known that her tone was as near true pity as she had ever yet come in speaking to another girl. As it was, she recognized only a scornful curiosity, and it seemed an indignity put upon her home and her upbringing. She grew suddenly angry and with her habit of self-control waited a moment before she answered. Her questioner studied her meanwhile and wondered at the look that gradually overspread her face. She had lifted her eyes for steadying to the brilliant autumn skies, studded with innumerable stars. Did they speak to her of the Father in heaven whom she recognized, of his wealth and power and all the glories to which she was heir? Did it suddenly come to her how foolish it was that she should mind the pity of this other girl, whose lot was set, indeed, amid earthly pleasures, but whose hope for the future might be so lacking? For suddenly the watcher saw a look almost of triumph mixed with one which seemed like pity, come over the fair young face before her, and then a joyous laugh broke out clear and sweet.

"Why, Miss Rutherford," she said, turning to look at her straight in the face, "I would not change my lot for that of any other girl in the world. I love Hillcroft with all my heart, and I love my life and my work and my pleasures. Why, I wouldn't be you for anything in the world, much as you may wonder at it. As for life here, there is plenty of it if you only know where to look for it."

Miss Rutherford about made up her mind that the investigation was not worth pursuing. It was not pleasant to have pity thrust back upon one in this style. She straightened back in the comfortable rocking-chair and asked in an indifferent tone:

"Then there is something going on? I always thought from aunt's letters that it must be a very poky place. What do you do?"

"There are plenty of young people here, and we are all interested in the same things. I suppose we do a great deal as they do in other places," mused Allison, wondering where to begin to tell about her life which seemed so full. Instinctively she felt that she must not mention first the pursuit dearest to her heart, her beloved Sunday-school class of boys, for it would not be understood. She thought a minute and then went on.

"We have a most delightful club," she said eagerly, her eyes kindling with pleasures past and to come. "I think you would enjoy that."

"Club?" said Miss Rutherford, stifling a yawn. "Girls or men?"

"Both," said Allison. "The girls meet early and do the real, solid hard work, and in the evening the boys come and enjoy and learn and give the money."

"You don't say?" said Miss Rutherford, with interest. "How odd! I never heard the like. What do you do? I suppose you make fancy work and the men buy it for charity and then you have a good time in the evening. Is that it? What do you do? Dance? Or perhaps you are devoted to cards."

She was quite at home now and began to feel as if perhaps her exile might be tolerable after all.

"Oh, no!" said Allison, almost shocked to see how far she had been from making her visitor understand. "Why it is a club of the young people of the church."

"Do you mean it is a religious society?" questioned the girl, a covert sneer on her face.

"No, not religious," answered Allison "but it is made up of the young people in our church. It is wholly secular and we have delightful times, but it is not a bit like society. We don't any of us play cards or dance, at least a great many of us don't know how and don't care anything about those things. But we have most delightful meetings."

Then Allison entered into a detailed and glowing account of the last meeting of their unique club of young people, wherein was combined the intellectual, useful, and social. She warmed to the subject as she went on till it seemed to her that her guest could not but see how fascinating such evening entertainments could be. She told how her hostess had contrived clever ways to make the entertainment of the evening bring in the subject which had been the theme of the afternoon's discussion; and described the dainty arrangement of tables, flowers, lights, and refreshments to suit the occasion until she felt sure Miss Rutherford would see that she understood how things ought to be as well as if she lived in New York. Then she turned at the close to meet cold unresponsiveness and hear in the tone of entire indifference the word, "Indeed!" from Miss Rutherford.

In truth the visitor had heard very little of what was said. It sounded to her like a country church sociable — though she had never attended such a gathering — and she was simply bored by the account. Her mind was not sufficiently awake as yet to appreciate the cleverness manifested by these village girls in supplying the needs of social life which in the city are ministered to by professionals as a matter of course. She had been idly studying the sweet face before her and wondering what haunting memory was awakened by the expression that flitted across it now and again. Where had she seen some one of whom these people reminded her?

Allison suddenly subsided. She was aware that she had been casting her precious pearls before — well, she was hardly prepared to finish the sentence. But she was a girl whose likes and dislikes were intense, and when she went into anything she put her whole heart into it. This young people's club was dear to her. She did not relish seeing it despised. She was glad that her mother came out just then and made it unnecessary for her to say anything more. Gladder still was she when she saw her father open the gate down among the shadows of the trees and she could flit down to meet him and come back slowly arm in arm with him, asking about his meeting and knowing that he loved to tell her all about everything. She drew a long breath of relief and felt she had gotten away from the interloper in her pleasant home for a little space.

Meantime the guest watched her in absolute amazement. She tried to fancy herself rushing at her father in that style, and walking arm in arm up the path. Why did this other girl do it? And what was the reason of that pleasant look of understanding and love that passed between father and daughter as the two reached the steps and paused to finish a sentence before sitting down?

Evelyn Rutherford felt for the second time that there was something missing from her life which might have been pleasant and wondered what it was. Whose fault had it been, hers or her father's?

Chapter 4
Allison's Fears

"Mamma," said Allison the next morning, as she put on the kettle she had just filled with fresh water from the spring, "Had you forgotten that Maurice is coming next week?"

The mother looked from the eggs she was beating as she said, with a bright smile: "Oh, no indeed, daughter! How could you think I would forget my dear boy for a minute?"

"But suppose — she — is here yet?" and the troubled expression in the dark eyes showed that this was not the first time she had pondered the possibility.

"Why there is room enough, Allison," said the mother, beating some cold rice into the milk and eggs for the delicate batter-cakes she knew how to make to perfection.

"Oh, yes, *room* enough," said the girl. "But, mother, think of it! How can we enjoy his visit with her here? She will just spoil everything and Maurice won't like it at all."

"I fancy I should enjoy his visit if there were a whole regiment of strangers here, dear," said her mother, laughing, "and as for one girl being able to spoil it, I think you are mistaken. Besides, your brother is not so easily put out as that."

Allison looked at her mother with the trouble still in her eyes. She was evidently not yet satisfied, though she went thoughtfully about setting the breakfast table. But as she placed the forks and spoons at the stranger's plate, a vision of that young woman in her bewitching black gown and gleaming white shoulders appeared and brought back her trouble in full force. She went to the kitchen door and stood irresolute a moment watching her mother, opened her mouth to speak and closed it again, and then went back to her cups and plates. She could not quite make up her mind to put her thought into words and wondered whether it was wise to trouble her mother with it, even if she could. If it could not be helped why give her mother the anxiety of thinking about it, seeing she had not yet thought of such a thing for herself? Or had she? Did the mother think of it and calmly put her anxiety aside because there seemed a duty in the way she was walking?

Allison drew her brows in thought and went to look out of the window. Twice she went to the kitchen door and began, "Mother," but when the mother answered she asked some trivial question about the table and turned away. At last however she threw down the pile of napkins she was placing and deliberately walked to her mother's side.

"Mother," she said, in a low, troubled tone, "I must tell you what I am afraid of. Didn't you notice how pretty she looked last night and how attractive she can be when she tries, with all those beautiful clothes and her city airs? I can't help thinking what a terrible thing it would be if Maurice should take a fancy to her, and — and — marry her — perhaps?" she finished desperately.

The mother stood erect and looked her daughter full in the face gravely.

"Dear child," she said, "do you think your brother is so easily influenced by a pretty face and a beautiful effect? You give him little credit of discernment. And besides, do you not recognize a higher Power in shaping our lives than a mere chance of meeting? Cannot you trust God when we are in the way of duty?"

"But is this the way of duty?" asked the daughter desperately.

"What would you have me do, dear? Refuse my old friend her request? Tell the girl to go?"

Allison turned to the window with tears growing in her eyes. "Wouldn't there be some other way? She doesn't want to stay, I feel sure, and we could just encourage her to go back home. I think that could be done without being any more impolite than she has been."

"Allison, have you forgotten her aunt? She is one of our oldest, most valued friends. She has come to our rescue in many a time of trouble and now she has asked us to help her. Is it less incumbent upon us to do it because it is unpleasant? Have you forgotten that this girl is a fellow-mortal, that your Saviour died for her? You may be doing her great injustice. You have let your prejudice influence you largely and you forget the wide difference in your home surroundings. Her ideas of what is proper in dress and everything else are built on an entirely different standard from yours. The life she has led is not Hillcroft life."

"I should think not!" said Allison, in a low, repressed tone.

"Allison, won't you try to know this girl's true character before you begin to hate her?"

"Mamma, I should think it was plain enough what her character is, and you know I don't hate her, only it is so hard to think of having Maurice's visit spoiled by her, and it would be just terrible to have her come between me and my brother. I could not bear it."

"I wish my little girl would learn to trust her troubles to her Burden-Bearer instead of carrying them herself. You may be carrying all this woe unnecessarily. It may be this sickness will not prove serious and she can go to her aunt's in a day or two. But, Allison, have you forgotten that you have been asked to make a friend of this girl and to help her?"

"Mother, I could *never* help her, and she would never take any help from me," said Allison with firm conviction.

"My daughter, you do not know what you can do with God's help, or rather what God can do with your help."

Then the fried potatoes demanded attention and Allison, unconvinced but somewhat softened by her mother's words, went back and finished her work quickly.

The guest, however, did not put in an appearance at breakfast time. They waited as long as possible for her and then went on without her, thinking she was weary with the long journey. To Allison it was a relief to have her father and mother to herself. Mrs. Grey realized this and tried to make the little time spent at the table as cheerful as possible, speaking of the expected arrival of the brother and son who had been away for nearly a year and who was to give them a whole week of his precious society before entering his professional career in an Eastern city. But the sister's face was not altogether unclouded and she looked eagerly for the promised message from the doctor which she hoped would bring word that their guest might leave them soon.

But the doctor did not come and as the morning wore on and he did not send a message, Allison began to have a growing conviction that there would be no good news, else it would have been brought before. Her mother tried to make her look upon the cheerful side, insisting that no news was good news, and trying to make her see how inhospitable she was to actually desire a visitor to leave; but her usually ready smile was slow to come. The mother grew troubled over this persistent feeling on the part of her usually sunny and helpful daughter. It seemed strange that Allison should take such a dislike to another girl. Perhaps she did not realize how deeply some of Miss Rutherford's looks and tones of evident scorn had cut the sensitive nature. Allison writhed inwardly again and again that morning over remembered sentences and glances. She worked grimly, taking the utmost trouble to prepare for dinner a dessert so elaborate that it was usually saved for high occasions. Her mother, smiling, understood and let her alone.

And while she worked with foamy eggs, rich whipped cream and gelatine, she made up her mind that she would show this city girl how much a country girl could do, and how useless was a frivolous life of mere pleasure. Forgetting that her chief aim should be to show her the adornments of a meek and quiet spirit she let her eyes flash many times as, according to her impetuous habit of mind, she plunged into imaginary scenes and discussions with this new girl from another atmosphere.

It was nearly eleven o'clock before the visitor came downstairs. She wore an elaborate white morning gown fastened at the belt with a clasp of gold in exquisite design. That dainty buckle worn on a morning costume accentuated the difference between these two girls to Allison. She would have kept such a rare ornament for her best gowns, but this girl doubtless had so many that it was quite common to her. Also, the stranger carried a novel in her hand and looked as utterly care-free and lazy as Allison herself would have liked to be, therefore she felt like a martyr and was filled with self-righteousness, and made a show of much bustle and haste. She plunged herself into an unnecessary piece of work which could not be left without spoiling, so that her mother had to carry the dainty tray with the lunch of rich milk, brown and white bread and butter, and a bunch of purple grapes to the guest.

Of this lunch Miss Rutherford partook leisurely, sitting in Mr. Grey's large rocking-chair, which always stood in the dining room that he might take a brief rest whenever he came in a little before a meal, and the while read her novel. Allison could see her through the open door and was offended anew. Her frame of mind was growing worse and worse. She resented the stranger's sitting in her father's chair; she resented her lying in bed and being daintily fed whenever she chose to arise; she resented the novel and the white gown and the beauty of the girl; and above all, she resented the fear that she would be there to share in her cherished brother's smiles and conversation.

It was not that her brother Maurice was given to being bewitched by any pretty girl that came along, that she was so worried about this particular one. No, it was rather the reverse with the young man. But he had his mother's gentle, kindly way of meeting every one pleasantly and giving every one a fair chance. It hurt Allison to think that this girl, who could be so hateful to her, would be given an opportunity to show how delightful she could be to others, and Allison was quick enough at character reading to know that her brother would be more likely to receive smiles than she had been. She began to recognize in her own feelings an element that she did not admire as the day wore slowly away.

At last, toward evening, came a message from the doctor. The symptoms were very grave. The case was decidedly smallpox. Miss Rutherford desired her niece to remain where she was until the danger was past and she could plan to take her to a safe place. She intimated that she had received instructions from her brother which made her anxious to have his daughter with her as soon as possible, and for the present she was to feel that she had put her in the safest, happiest home she knew in the world, where she hoped she would be more than contented until the danger was past.

This message was brought by a member of the doctor's family who had not been near the infected house and had received it over the telephone from the doctor; but the young lady to whom it came declined to see the messenger or to touch the paper upon which the message was written, preferring to take it from Mrs. Grey's lips. She was annoyed beyond measure at its import and retired to her room to consider plans for her own alleviation.

She was certainly in no enviable frame of mind as she sat looking out the window without seeing the glowing tints of autumn leaves in such profusion. The girl in the next room, who had also fled to a refuge to bear her disappointment, though she insisted that this was just what she had expected all the morning, had the advantage of recognizing in herself the evil spirit that was dominating her being and had a will to be free from it. Not only that, but she understood what to do in order to be free. It was not long before she knelt beside her bed to confess her sin and to beg forgiveness and strength. But her heart was yet hardened toward the intruder in her home.

It was perhaps not to Miss Rutherford's advantage that mention was made that evening of the expected home-coming of the son of the house.

It came about in this way. Mr. Grey asked his wife at the supper table about some arrangements in the house which were to be made in view of Maurice's coming and talk followed in which his name was used several times. Allison said little about him, but once or twice a sentence of hers showed the guest that whoever it was that was expected, his advent would give Allison great pleasure. She studied her curiously while she ate and the others talked, wondering if he were some commonplace rustic lover, and thought it a pity that this handsome girl should not have a chance among men who were of some account. She sat on the porch alone after supper until Allison and her mother had finished the work. It never occurred to her to offer her assistance. Indeed, she would not have known how to help if she had been so disposed. She looked upon all household tasks as menial, not for such as she.

She had decided that afternoon to write to one or two New York friends and beg for invitations. She had written several letters confiding her disagreeable position and she felt certain that the returning mail would bring her an invitation to quit this dismal place, believing that she had excuse enough to send to her father. Meantime she must while away the hours as best she might until her release. It would be but a week at most she felt sure. She yawned and wished for something to do. She had read until she was weary of it. She wondered if there were any fun to be got out of the town. She must find out who this expected Mr. Morris was, as she had settled it in her mind his name should be, though the family had spoken of him as "Maurice" merely.

Allison, in obedience to her mother's request, and in penance for her ugly thoughts of the morning, came to the piazza and dutifully sat down to talk.

"Who is this Mr. Morris you are expecting?" asked Miss Rutherford at once. "Is he interesting? Does he intend staying long? He isn't your especial property is he?"

"Mr. Morris?" questioned Allison puzzled, and laughing as she suddenly comprehended the mistake, then growing angry as she further realized the import of the last sentence, she said in a dignified tone: "I think you must mean my brother Maurice. He is coming home for a short visit. He will be here a week perhaps."

"Oh, indeed!" said the guest, losing interest at once. "He is away working, I suppose."

Allison hesitated before she answered, the color growing brighter in her cheeks and her eyes shining with the slightest bit of wickedness. Then she said in a strained voice:

"Yes, he is away — working."

Why she made such an answer she did not quite understand. It gave her real pleasure to feel that for a little while before he came at least this girl would not look upon her precious brother as a possible subject upon whom to exercise her charms. Ordinarily she would have resented the evident slight in the expression about his working and would have proudly hastened to state that his work was that of a physician in Bellevue Hospital, in New York, and that he was about to enter the profession for himself with a fine opening and every prospect of success in a worldly way. She was proud of her brother and would not have been willing to let this pass if he were not coming so soon to speak for himself and show this supercilious young woman that he was in every way superior to her. A little twinge of pride gave her pleasure as she thought of the surprise Maurice would evidently be. Meantime, the other girl was looking dreamily off into the garden.

"Maurice, you said? Maurice Grey. That's curious," she said musingly; "I know a man by that name and he is awfully nice too. He's fine!"

The girl on the step started almost imperceptibly. Had they then already met? There was all the more danger in their meeting in his home. And to have her call him "awfully nice!" It was intolerable.

"Where did you meet him?" she asked, in a cold tone which she forced to be steady. "My brother has been in New York."

"Oh, it isn't your brother, of course. He's quite a different person, I fancy. My Maurice Grey is quite a brilliant man. He is a young doctor and I hear his prospects for the future are remarkable. He's a good friend of mine, or was. I have not seen him for a year. I met him abroad," and in the moonlight her face took on a softened, dreamy, wistful look.

Chapter 5
The Arrival of Maurice Grey

The rush of thoughts into Allison's mind was suddenly checked by the sound of the gate clicking and a strong, manly step coming quickly up the walk. She started to her feet and looked down through the shadows. It could not be that any other step could sound just that way, and after poising one instant on the step to make sure, she uttered a smothered "Oh!" and rushed swiftly down the walk.

Miss Rutherford heard the sound of subdued greeting, and knew that the steps lingered while there was the murmur of low-spoken words. Then they came on and a voice that was strangely familiar to her ear said: "Where is mother? Yes, I found I could get away a whole week ahead and I thought I would enjoy giving you a real surprise for once in my life."

The mother's quick ear had caught the sound too, and she was out on the walk before he could reach the door, and had folded the tall form in her arms, saying tenderly, but so that the guest could hear, "Oh, my dear boy?" and Miss Rutherford knew again that she had missed something by having no mother. It made her heart ache with a strange new longing for just an instant, till Allison's clear, cold voice said precisely:

"Miss Rutherford, this is my brother, Dr. Maurice Grey, formerly of Bellevue Hospital."

Dr. Maurice Grey, wondering at the coldness and dignity of his sunny sister's introduction, turned in surprise to face the beautiful girl who stood in a flood of light at the top of the steps in front of the open door.

Was it only the hall light that illumined his face, or did Allison in her keen watch really notice a sudden lighting of his eyes as he smiled and grasped the white hand held out to his, saying, with true pleasure in his tones: "Why, Miss Rutherford! This is a pleasure, indeed, to find you in my own home. How comes it about? My surprise is double, is it not, mother? I have met Miss Rutherford before."

They sat down to talk while Allison, smarting under this cordial greeting to her foe, went to prepare a hasty supper for her brother. Her cheeks were glowing with a heat that did not come from the fire, over which she was making delicate slices of toast. She was covered with shame over the introduction she had given her brother. The instant the words were out of her mouth she had felt the bad taste and the low motive which had prompted her, and moreover, she anticipated her brother's dislike to being introduced in this way. She had felt his questioning look and the surprise in his face as he turned to greet the visitor. She knew he did not like it. She knew he preferred not to have any display made of his title or achievements. But worst of all was the feeling that she had done it for what her guest had said. She feared she was beginning to hate Miss Rutherford.

There was a verse somewhere in the Bible, she could not remember the exact words, which said you must not be glad when your enemy was brought low. Allison knew she would be very glad if Evelyn Rutherford could be brought very low before her brother so that he would despise her.

The household sat up unusually late that evening. There was much to be talked about, for the son had been away so long, and they could not bear to close their eyes upon the goodly sight of him even for a little while.

Miss Rutherford had the good grace and good breeding to take herself to her room early in the evening. Allison blessed her for this even while she recognized that it would count one with her brother in favor of the instinctive delicacy of their guest. But it was good to have him entirely to themselves, for the first evening at least.

Alone in her room Miss Rutherford lighted the gas, forgetting for once to wonder how people endured it to always have to light their own gas and have no maid to attend to such bothersome details. Then she walked to her mantel and contemplated the boyish face in the cabinet picture that stood there looking with frank eyes into her own, just as the young man downstairs had done to-night — and one other time. She understood now why his face had haunted her and stirred pleasant memories. It was like his present self and yet not enough for her to have recognized him, she decided, as she studied his features closely. She knew now why the faint memories had seemed so pleasant. How strange it was that for the third time she should be among strangers where she did not wish to be and should again meet him. Who was he? Her fate? Her affinity? The prince that every girl waits for, who will sometime come into her life and fill it full of joy forever? She was not a girl who spent much time in dreaming. The eager rush of doing and being and getting pleasure out of life had crowded out the sentimental. There had been little to develop the poetical. But her meeting, or rather meetings, with this young man had been so strange and unexpected that she could but be fascinated by the unusual.

She sat down in the low window seat, the picture in her hand, to think it over. Her first meeting with Maurice Grey — she shuddered as she remembered it. Her friend, Jane Bashford, had summoned her cousin from his den to attend her home one evening when nothing had been going on worthwhile and the two had spent the evening together. Jane and she were very close and spent much time at each other's home. It was an understood thing that Jane's cousin, or an old house servant, should see her home whenever she was out late and it was not convenient to send her in the carriage.

Jane's cousin had seemed exceedingly animated as they started out and when they were fairly on the street and away from the house, Evelyn, ignorant as she was in such matters, became aware that she was being escorted by a drunken man. She had not been much frightened at first, for she had known him since they were both children, and the way was short. She thought there would surely be some one passing in a moment to whom she might appeal for help if necessary; but it was later than she realized and when Jane's cousin became affectionate and attempted noisily to put his arm about her and kiss her, she grew alarmed and started to run, not knowing which way she went. She could remember just how her heart was beating and how the houses grim and tall looked down upon her, piling up in dark perspective whichever way she looked. Not a creature seemed abroad, no one to help her. Then suddenly there had been footsteps, a hand placed upon her trembling arm, and a strong manly voice had said:

"Miss Rutherford, can I help you?"

Even in her terror she had not thought to be afraid of this man, his voice seemed so strong and trustworthy. He had led her quickly through the streets to her home, saying with assurance: "Don't be alarmed. He has not control enough over his feet to follow," and had landed her safely at her own door, rung the bell, and waited until she was safely inside the brightly lighted hall with the mere explanation that he had known her brother in college and happened to see her in his company several times. It was all over before she had gathered her wits together to ask any questions. The man was gone and she did not even know his name. The brother, questioned, could not give any clue. He declared that he had a host of friends with strong, trustworthy voices and besides he believed that his sister would have considered almost any voice trustworthy, frightened as she was. She did not seem able to give any lucid description of the man, and so he dropped away from her life again and if it had not been for Jane Bashford's cousin, whom she had occasionally to meet in her world, perhaps she might have forgotten him altogether. She had kept away from

Jane's cousin as much as possible, he seemed willing that it should be so. Evelyn doubted if he realized how grave his offense had been. Sometimes, though, the dreadful night experience would come back to her vividly and she would live it over again and then hear that strong, clear voice and see the dim outline of a fine face in the darkness. She knew the face had been handsome, even though it had been too dark a night and she too perturbed to examine carefully. She felt certain she would know it again. She had often wondered why she never met any man who made her think of him and began to think she would not know him after all. Perhaps he walked the streets of New York every day and even passed her house and was kind enough not to embarrass her with having to thank him by ignoring the occurrence altogether.

It had been a year later — she started as she thought of it. It was just about a year ago now. How strange! A year apart each time. A year later she had met him again. She had known him almost at once, even before he spoke.

It was while she was traveling abroad. Her father had left her in care of friends who had a mania for seeing everything that was to be seen, and they had insisted upon dragging her with them. She hated it all. They were poky people, who went everywhere with a book and hunted up everything they saw in the book and read about it, and then told each other that it was here such a woman sat, and there such a man walked, and over yonder some one was murdered or buried or what not.

She had not cared for it. What were ancient battles and dead men and women to her? This was not what she had come to Europe for; she wanted some life and pleasure. Her father, doubtless, hoped she would imbibe some knowledge, but it had escaped from her like water off a duck's back. One afternoon they had taken her to visit a famous ruin. When they reached the ruin it was found that the excursion included a sail across a placid strip of water to a tiny island whereon was located something or other, Evelyn did not now know what, and was not sure that she had ever known. She had determined in her heart not to get into that leaky-looking boat, and the dirty sailor, and swelter in the hot sun while her guardians had all sorts of tiresome things pointed out and explained to them, and hunted out the items about them with slow, near-sighted vision in the volumes they carried. After the rest had embarked and the boatman essayed to help her in, she suddenly declared her intention of remaining where she was till their return, giving as her excuse a headache. There had been some demur. The boatman told her it might be some time. All the more reason why she felt she would not go. Her staying might hurry their return. Each of the party mildly offered to remain with her, but she had declined all their offers. She had longed to get away from them all for a little while. The day was sunny and the place entirely safe, with a comfortable seat under a tree by the water. At last they sailed away and left her.

She could remember now how unhappy she had been as she watched them go, and reflected that she must stay there alone until their return. She wished herself back in New York, wished her father had not come on this business trip, wished she ever could have anything but poky, commonplace happenings. She had longed for some adventure, and even looked about for some dangerous place to climb or some wild thing to do while they were gone. Suddenly in the midst of her thoughts there had come a tremendous storm.

She had not looked behind her until she heard the low rumble of thunder, and turning saw the whole mass of lowering ruins black against a blacker sky, with lurid flashes of lightning making great clefts and picking out every separate stone of the old castle with fearful distinctness.

She had been terribly frightened. She looked off to the place where her friends had but a moment before been a white speck on the quiet blue lake, and lo, there had been a transformation! The lake was no longer blue but a livid purple, with ghastly green lights over it, an ominous whirl and strange treacherous ripples blowing across it. The island seemed farther away, and the white sail had disappeared. Perhaps they had rounded the island. Perhaps they had landed. At any rate they were evidently not meditating an immediate return to her. She had sense enough to see that it would not be possible for them to do so now.

A terrible sheet of lightning blinded her eyes for an instant and sent her shivering from beneath the tree. She knew that a tree was a conductor of lightning. The rain began to fall in great plashing drops and she had fled to the ruin and wondered if that also were a place of danger. She had crept into an alcove with roof enough for protection from the rain and there, facing her in the companion alcove not three feet away stood a man, and his face she knew at once. She seemed to have seen his smile before, though that was impossible in the dark, and when he spoke, as he immediately did, she knew his voice. It all had been so strange. They had seemed good friends at once, as if they had known each other for years. He had seen that she was trembling, that she was afraid of the storm, and had led her inside to a place more sheltered, where the awful flashes that blazed through the whole sky could not be so distinctly seen and where the roar of the thunder and the sound of the dashing water in the thoroughly aroused little lake would reach but faintly through the great stone walls; and there they had talked.

She had told him how grateful her father was for his service to her a year ago, and how chagrined she was that she had not inquired his name, and how they had tried their best to find him and thank him. When he smiled and said he was glad she had not been afraid of him also, she felt that she had known him a long time.

Never once during the two hours they spent in the old hall of the castle, while the elements did their worst outside, did it occur to her to wonder if he belonged to the favored few who composed her world of society and who were eligible to talk and dance and play with such as she. It was only afterward that this question came to her, when her friends asked, "Who is he?" and "What is he?" for they came from the part of the world where these things count for much. Then she found she knew very little indeed from her three hours spent with him, as to either of these important questions, in the sense that these people meant. Afterward, when her brother Dick had been called in to help, she had been glad to know that he stood high in his profession, and could go anywhere, if he but chose. But he had not come her way again, though she had always been hoping that he would.

Their talk that afternoon had drifted to the old ruin and she suddenly found it peopled with real folks, breathing and walking before her, and she wondered why this man could make the people of history so interesting to her, when her friends had only bored her with talk of them.

Once when the lightning had been most vivid and she had shuddered involuntarily and covered her eyes with her hands, he had said, "Don't be afraid," in a quieting tone. Then she had looked up into his face and had known that he was not at all afraid.

She lay awake a long time that night after thinking the whole story over. A sudden thought had come to her. Was it, could it be because he belonged to this strange family and held peculiar beliefs, that he had not been afraid of that terrible storm? Or was it because he was a man? No, he had something more in his face than most men when they were merely brave. There was something in this whole family, some controlling, quieting force that she did not understand.

How very strange that he should have belonged to these people! And stranger still that she should be here.

Chapter 6
Maurice Grey's Vow

There were other vigils kept that night. The mother in her own room, though she put her light out quietly enough and knelt beside her bed as usual, prayed long and earnestly for her dear boy and added a petition for "the stranger beneath our roof." Then she lay down to wonder anxiously if she had done exactly right in bringing this strange unknown quantity into the house just now, when her dear boy was coming home, and to tell herself for the thousandth time that day that it had not been her doing. She had not even known that Maurice was coming this week. Finally she laid down her burden, asking her heavenly Father to make it all work out to his glory, and fell asleep.

Allison in her room was trying to read her Bible. She was reading by course and her chapter that night brought her to the thirteenth of First Corinthians. She had read two or three verses unthinking, when her mind suddenly became aware of the meaning of the words. Impatiently she closed her Bible, then opened it again. She would not read in her regular order to-night. She needed special help. Her soul was weary and hungry. She needed something like "Come unto me all ye that labour and are heavy laden," or "Let not your heart be troubled." Not that sharp upbraiding, and being obliged to examine her heart again.

She had done that all day. Besides, she knew that chapter by heart, "Though I speak with the tongues of men and angels and have not charity." She knew all the latest expositions, had read and even learned it, substituting the word "love" for "charity." The whole thing searched her too keenly to-night, hence she turned away.

But turn as she would to find comfort, that persistent Bible would open again and again back to the chapter in Corinthians. At last, unwillingly, she read it through, piercing her soul with every verse, and lay down to weary contemplation of her mistakes and failures, having tried to throw off her burdens in prayer, but picking them up and shouldering them once more. It was very hard for poor Allison to give up. When her will decided a thing she simply could not bear to hear things go the other way. She could not see how it was right. In theory she believed that God knew what would be best for all his children. In practice she had a strong

33

conviction that she knew pretty well what the Lord had intended in the first place and there was danger of its getting switched off the track if she did not watch the switch and worry about it.

Maurice Grey, in his own room, among the relics of his boyhood, his college days, and his early manhood, searched for a minute or two in an old desk drawer and brought therefrom a little black book labeled, "My Foreign Diary."

He hastily turned the leaves and read:

"At last I am afloat. New York has faded from our view. The last tie to *terra firma* in the shape of a dirty little boat has left us and we are bound for another shore. How I have dreamed of this day! Yet now that it has come I scarcely realize it. I have had so much to do the last forty-eight hours. I believe I felt more that my foreign trip was actually begun when I bade mother and father and Allison good-bye last week than I do now. It was hard to have to leave them behind. In my dreams of this they have always been a happy accompaniment to my anticipated pleasures.

"There has been nothing notable in the three days I have spent in New York, with the exception of my experience last evening. I was standing at the corner of West Sixty-fourth Street looking up Fifth Avenue and trying to decide whether it was too late to make a brief call on any of the fellows in that part of town, or whether I would go at once to the hotel and get a good night's rest. The clocks had just struck eleven and for New York there seemed to be a sudden quiet about that quarter. I could hear footsteps, a woman's and a man's. The woman's steps suddenly quickened into a run as they turned the corner below and she came in sight. I could see that the man was trying to catch her, and he did succeed in taking hold of her arm as she came nearer. Then he tried to kiss her, calling her name in loud tones, 'Evelyn.' It made me shudder to hear that lovely name spoken in the street so, and by a drunkard in a drunken voice! That has always seemed to me a name that speaks of a guarded, sheltered life. I soon saw that the man was beside himself with liquor, and as they passed under the street light I suddenly recognized the girl to be Dick Rutherford's stately sister. I never met her, but have seen her many times with Dick and other college men. She is a great society girl and very beautiful. I knew her at once. Her face was white with fear. She seemed as glad to turn to me as a little child in trouble might be. I think she was too frightened to talk much. I took her to her father's door, telling her I knew her brother. Perhaps it is just as well for my future peace of mind that she did not ask my name. She will never be bothered with having to thank me for the small service I did her, and I shall not be chagrined because I am not eligible to her 'set.' It might be some temptation to me to try to become eligible if I had not decided to live another kind of life. I have consecrated everything to Jesus Christ — myself, my talents, if I have any, my all. Miss Rutherford has other aims in life probably. She would not think twice of a young medical student. I wonder if she is a Christian. I wonder what our meeting last night was for!''

He turned the pages rapidly till his eye fell on the right date and then he settled to reading once more.

"I have had an adventure. Here in this strange land of wondrous beauty, where I did not expect to see a familiar face, I have met another human being to whom, indeed, I have spoken but once before, but with whom I have been conversing for nearly three hours. I was taking my second view of the old ruin before going away; and as I stood looking at the moss-grown turrets and imagining the old days back when knights and ladies walked and talked there and looked off across the lake to the blue mountains in the distance, it reminded me of Browning's poem, 'Love Among the Ruins.' I repeated a verse aloud as I stood alone in a grassy meadow that stretched away to a bit of ruin standing by itself:

> "Now the single little turret that remains
>   On the plains,
> By the caper overrooted, by the gourd
>   Overscored,
> While the patching houseleek's head of blossom
>   Through the chinks,
> Marks the basement where a tower in ancient time
>   Sprang sublime,
> And a burning ring, all around, the chariots traced
>   As they raced,
> And the monarch and his minions and his dames
>   Viewed the games.

"Just then I noticed the heavy blackness that was swiftly over-spreading the sky. I watched it grow dark all about the ruin till the gray turrets and the purply green-gray clouds blended and there were turrets and towers in the sky everywhere. Vivid flashes of lightning set forth this mighty spectacle. I withdrew to the shelter of a covered archway, and the rain began to pour down. I had not been under cover more than a minute before I heard the flutter of garments and looking out I saw — Evelyn Rutherford, Dick Rutherford's beautiful sister. The last time we met was in New York. How

strange that she should be here! We talked about many things, for there was
nothing for us to do but remain under cover until the rain ceased. I do not
think three hours ever went with greater swiftness. She is a fine conversationalist — or — no, is she? Perhaps she is a fine listener, for I can remember
hearing my own voice most of the time, now that I think of it. But if I can
judge by her face we certainly enjoyed the time together. We peopled the old
rooms and corridors with knights and ladies robed in rich satins, stiff with
gold broidery. I repeated Browning's poem again, for it kept running in my
head all day. She liked it, I think. At least her eyes seemed to say so, and her
comments were well-made and to the point. She showed a keen appreciation
of the poem's literary beauties, which was more than I expected from one in
her position in society. But then! It was but for an afternoon. What am I?
And what is she? We are as from two worlds. It may be we shall never meet
again. There are other poems of Browning's which might appropriately be
quoted just here, but I am too weary to-night to hunt them up, and besides, I
do not care to have the charm of the day lifted just yet. I never quite believed
in their sentiments either, and always revolted at the idea that two beings
who seemed to be affinities should meet and enjoy each other and then be
thrown apart and care no more, but I don't know but I understand better
now how the necessities of life compel one to adopt such a philosophy. But
somehow this adventure has unfitted me for the ordinary. It is well I am going back to work soon.

"I am reading the life of Moody. I have been making it a rule lately to do a
little religious reading every day, aside from the Bible, to keep in touch with
things most vital. I wonder I have never read this before. It is not a great
book as books go, but it is the story of a great life, a life near to God. Last
night I read that Moody made it a rule never to be alone with a person five
minutes without having by some little word or action left his testimony for
Christ, and found out whether his companion was a Christian. I was much
impressed by the story of his walking in the rain with a stranger on the street
to protect him with his umbrella and before the short walk was over asking
the question: 'My friend, do you know Jesus Christ?' I do not think I could
always do that way, perhaps; but I might be able to witness in some way if I
tried. I could not but marvel what a difference it would make in the world if
all Christians would do so. I lay awake thinking it over and resolved, after
much thought and prayer, to adopt this rule for myself. I made that resolve
only last evening and prayed for the necessary opportunity and courage.
Behold, it needed neither courage nor opportunity. Three hours were given
me in which to reach a human soul, and one with whom in all likelihood I
shall never come in contact again. If I loved Christ, as I had thought, would I

not have been anxious at once to do this little for him? I spoke of my father, mother, and sister, but of him whom I love better than all I breathed never a word. I cannot even comfort myself with the thought that there was aught in my conversation that indirectly showed her my purpose in life, not even so much as a hint that I ever attend church. And this because I was so absorbed in other things as to entirely forget. I do not think it would have required much courage.

"The thing I need to pray for first is watchfulness. My Master's words to his disciples apply to me now, 'Could ye not watch with me one hour?' I have been taking my ease, my pleasure, and never watching for words to say for him. And now the opportunity has passed. Oh, that I might have another! I judge this girl by her words and she does not seem to be a Christian. Does she judge me in the same way? I deserve it. Twice I have met this soul and missed my opportunity to carry a message for my Lord. I hereby pledge my word, God helping me, that if I am ever thrown in her company again I will do my humble best to show her that it is a sweet thing to have Christ as a Saviour. But so great a privilege is not likely to be awarded me again, seeing I have shown myself unfaithful. But I can and will pray for her. I will make it my daily practice, so help me God, to pray for her soul until I die or know that she belongs to Christ. She is nothing to me, perhaps; but the responsibility of three long hours misspent is upon me and I have been found wanting."

The young man closed the book which registered his vow almost reverently. He had kept that pledge for a year, and now he sat thoughtfully.

"Strange," he said, speaking aloud to himself as was his habit when alone, "strange and wonderful that I should have another opportunity given! It is a great privilege for a human soul to be given a third chance, having failed in two through utter thoughtlessness. Why I should feel so about this particular soul I do not know. There are doubtless many others whom I have passed by again and again, and never knew nor thought, but my meeting with this girl was unusual. And then, I believe one cannot pray for another without having a deep interest in that other. I am very happy. Can it be that I am to be allowed to do what I have left undone? It may be all my absurd imagination. I may not have been needed at all; but this I know, that if I live until to-morrow I shall endeavor to find out in some way if this young woman is a Christian."

He said the words solemnly as if registering a vow to an unseen witness, and then he knelt in prayer and offered a petition for this stranger beneath his father's roof, that she might know and love Jesus, and that if it were to be his privilege to show her the light that he might be guided by the Spirit.

Then he lay down with the joy of expectation in his soul.

Chapter 7
A Strange Love Story

For some reason best known to herself Evelyn Rutherford chose to appear at the breakfast table the next morning.

She was not expected. Without a word being said, mother and daughter and father too had taken it for granted that their guest would sleep and leave them to breakfast alone with the son and brother.

But she came in without any apparent hurry just as they were sitting down and the brother, who did not yet understand the state of the case with regard to their guest, hastened to draw out a chair and then looking about for his own seat, exclaimed:

"Why, Allison, you have counted wrong. You forgot so soon that I had come home. I did not think it of you, sister mine. You have but four plates."

Allison, whose cheeks were flaming and whose disappointment was great, murmured something about the waffles and that she was not going to sit down, which decision was arrived at on the spur of the moment, and vanished into the kitchen to hide her confusion and dismay. She had not counted on this possibility, and actual tears came into her eyes as she bent over the waffle iron to butter it, while it sputtered at the cool butter in much such a heated way as she would have enjoyed voicing her feelings.

In the dining room the young man carried the weight of the conversation, and strangely enough it was addressed to the guest almost entirely. He did not realize it, but his whole mind was largely filled with studying this girl with a view to gaining an influence over her for good, or at least finding out whether she needed it. He was not so conceited as to think that of course all people with whom he came into contact needed his help.

He was conscious of being quite happy. He was once more in his dear home, surrounded by those who loved him and whose smiles and voices could always make glad sunshine for him, and he was being given a chance to redeem the past.

But the gentle mother was troubled. She had watched her daughter's speaking face and knew the keen disappointment she was suffering, and she was such a mother that she thoroughly suffered with her. She knew Allison's delight in talking freely with her brother, in waiting upon him and asking questions; and she knew that the visitor made a complete bar to all these pleasures, for Allison was shy and reserved beyond most girls. Her daughter's feelings filled her thoughts so entirely as to leave little time to worry about her son; but occasionally, as she caught a bright look on his face and saw the beautiful face of the city girl light up with smiles as she replied, she began to fear that after all Allison was right and there was cause for worry.

Certainly Evelyn Rutherford was fascinating when she chose to be. She was dressed again in white, with the offending gold buckle, and as the morning had in it a tinge of frost, she had added a scarlet jacket which was exceedingly becoming. The mother could not deny that the vision was beautiful, and yet she had not thought there would be sympathy between these two. Neither could she wonder that the girl wished to please the young man seated opposite to her, as she looked with a mother's admiration on the fine form and strong, noble features of her boy.

But the boy suddenly became aware that, though the golden-brown waffles and amber syrup were vanishing rapidly and he had done his share of helping them onward, his sister, who came and went with very red cheeks, was not having any. When she came in with the next steaming plateful he suddenly arose and took it from her.

"Now sit down, Allison," he said, "and I will show you how well I remember my early training in waffle-baking, sister mine."

He took her, before she was aware of what he was going to do, and placed her in his chair, deftly gathering his own soiled dishes and placing before her a clean plate from the sideboard behind him. But his sister was in no mind to sit before the guest just now and try to eat. Swallow a mouthful she knew she could not and she did not wish the other girl to know it. She resisted her brother, urging several reasons why he must not bake the waffles, and finally followed him to the kitchen, only to be laughingly but persistently brought back and seated again. In a few minutes the young man returned with a plate of rather melancholy waffles, it must be confessed, compared with those which had gone before, but triumph on his face.

"They burned," he explained, "because I had so much trouble with Allison, but the next will be all right, now I've got my hand in," and he marched back to the kitchen looking very funny in his mother's big check apron he had donned, tied up high under his arms.

During all this pleasant home play Evelyn Rutherford looked on in amazement. It was as if she caught a glimpse of what her own childhood might have been if she had been blest with a mother and a true home. How pleasant it would be to have a brother who cared for one like that! It was not put on for show, she felt sure as she eyed him keenly. No, she had been positive from her first meeting with him that he was a man from another world than her own. Fancy Dick caring whether she had waffles or not, let alone taking the trouble to bake them for her, if he only had all he wanted for himself. As for baking waffles, either of them would be obliged to starve if it came to that, for they had no more idea than kittens what went into their make-up.

She began to look at Allison in a new light, with a lingering undertone of envy. True, this other girl had missed much of which her own life was composed; but did she not have some things that made for their loss that were even better, perhaps?

Allison, meanwhile, was having a very hard time with her breakfast, and her mother, perceiving this, made an excuse to send the rest away from the table as soon as possible. She sent her son from the kitchen, hoping he would go at once to his sister. She told him they must get up some pleasant occupation for them all for the morning, and he, nothing loth, went to the piazza in search of Allison. She had left the breakfast room and he supposed he should find her with her guest. His heart was light at the thought of his cherished sister with this girl, who was a queen in high circles. It was what he could have wished.

But Allison had fled to her room to let fall the pentup tears, and Miss Rutherford was standing on the piazza alone, fingering a lovely scarlet spray of the vine that covered the porch. He reached up and picked it for her, thinking what a crown it would make in her beautiful black hair. She accepted it pleasantly and fastened it in the gold clasp of her belt, where it well accorded with the crimson coat she wore with its moss-green velvet collar-facing.

The young man proposed a walk to the post office in the crisp October air, and searched for his sister to accompany them.

"Allison," he called, "where are you? Come down. We are going to the post office. Get your hat and hurry, dear. It is glorious out of doors."

A muffled voice that tried to sound natural answered from upstairs, "I can't come just now, Maurice. Don't wait for me." The while she frantically bathed her red eyes and swollen cheeks and scanned them hopelessly in the glass, her heart wrung with desire to go, and dislike of part of the company she should be in.

It may be that Maurice did not have his usual quick perceptions about him, or his mind was filled with another subject, for contrary to his custom he did not urge her and insist upon waiting, but turned to Miss Rutherford with an eagerness which would have made his sister's heart still heavier, had she been there to see.

She heard the steps go down the walk, and peeped out from the sheltering curtain to watch her brother and guest go slowly down the walk and out the gate talking and laughing together as if they did not miss her, and her much-tried soul threw itself into another abandonment of weeping, not caring now for the red eyes which would have plenty of time, she felt sure, to regain their wonted look ere they were called to meet a scrutinizing gaze again.

Evelyn Rutherford, as she walked down the pleasant shaded street with the handsome, well-built young man by her side, wondered at the beauty of the place and that she had not noticed it when she arrived. There were spacious grounds and houses comfortable and pretentious. There must be some life worth living, even in this place. Did all these homes know a life such as the Greys lived? What was it made the difference? She meant to find out. It was interesting, anyway, and she began to be glad she had come.

And now Maurice Grey had his opportunity, long coveted, at last. He was alone with her in a quiet, pleasant place with a reasonably long walk before him, and the one for whom he thought he had a message seemed ready to listen to anything he had to say. And yet he found it was not so easy after all. How was he to begin? He had thought much about it and planned the way he should say it many times, but somehow, with her beautiful eyes upon him and her bewitching laughter in his ears, none of those solemn sentences seemed to fit. He kept thinking back to the strange surroundings of their last meeting and feeling a sort of kinship of soul with her, and yet his longing for her salvation was just as great. He must not wait. He must not waste this opportunity. Already a part of the distance to the office had been traveled. Who knew how soon something would occur to break in upon the opportunity and it would be gone forever? Was he to waste this one also? With sudden eagerness he broke off in a sentence about some mutual friends they were speaking of and said:

"Miss Rutherford, pardon me for interrupting this line of thought, but my heart is so full of something I want to say to you, that I do not feel I can wait any longer."

Evelyn turned wondering eyes upon him. She was not without experience with young men. Not a few had told her of their undying affection, and asked for hers in return. These opening words sounded almost like some of theirs. Could it be that she was to add him to the list of men whom she rather despised in her heart for pledging their life and being ready to give their all to a pretty face without knowing much about the heart that was behind it? She had not time to reason this out. The idea merely flashed into being and flashed out again as it was quickly followed by the certainty that there was something of a vastly different nature to be spoken of, with a consciousness of satisfaction that this man was different from those others.

"I have blamed myself and have suffered for a whole year," went on her companion, "that I did not speak before, and have longed and hardly hoped for this opportunity."

In wondering silence Evelyn walked by his side. All sorts of possibilities went through her brain, none of which seemed adequate for the intensity of his language. She began to think that after all it must be a proposal and a sense of pleasure filled her at the thought. Then her pride rose in arms as she realized once more that his face did not look as if he were going to ask for her hand in marriage. She must not be blamed for making this the central thought of her life. It had been the only end to be attained, set forth to her from her babyhood. Even her father had unconsciously fostered it. Her nurses and teachers had trained her for the time when she would be married; her friends and associates talked of nothing else than their conquests. Naturally it seemed to her a thing worth boasting that she had won the love of many men. She was yet to learn that the love of one true man is worth a life's devotion, and the love of the hundred who fling their hearts about to the highest bidder or the prettiest face, and then furbish them up again for the next trial as good as new, is not worth a thought.

The young man had paused and Evelyn's eyes were lifted to meet such a hungering, tender gaze that she dropped them immediately. It was a different look from any she had ever met before. What did it mean? She had never yet met one in whose eyes blazed a passion for souls, that look that is the nearest reflection of His likeness earth can give. She did not understand it and it choked her.

It was not all what he had planned to say. The Spirit seemed to guide his low-spoken, impassioned words:

"I have a confession to make to you, and I am humiliated more than I can tell you at my shortcomings. A year ago I spent nearly three hours in your company. I talked of my family, my friends, my books, and my best life, but so far as I can remember I breathed no word of my best and dearest Friend."

The listener almost halted. Had he then brought her out here to tell her he was engaged? And for what? Did he fear she would expect his attention? Had she shown a particular delight in his society? The ready scorn mounted to her face, but melted as his words went on.

"It may seem strange to you, Miss Rutherford, that I love Jesus Christ better than my life, and have consecrated myself to his service. But I do, and I want you to know that he is a dear friend, and that his service is my highest joy. It seems incredible that feeling as I do I should allow myself to be in the company of any one for three hours without hinting anything that would lead that one to suppose that I knew Jesus Christ, and I can only say that I am ashamed and humiliated, and have resolved in future to witness for my Master wherever I may have opportunity.''

If the young man by her side had suddenly burst out in an eloquent tone in the Choctaw language, or in Sanskrit, or some other equally unknown tongue, Miss Rutherford would not have been surprised. A wild thought that he might be losing his mind flitted past her, but a look into the calm, steady eyes watching her so earnestly put that to flight. She looked down once more. There seemed to be nothing for her to say and she felt that he was not done.

"I am going to make a clean breast of it and tell you the whole story in as few words as possible. That night after I met you at the old ruin it all came over me that I had been with you so long and might never see you again, and yet I had not even found out if you loved my Saviour. We had compared notes about our tastes in books and many other things. We seemed in harmony on many questions. It grieved me more and more as I thought of it that I had not found out if you were planning to spend eternity in heaven, and that I had said no word to urge you to in case you were not thinking of it. And so I made bold to pray for you. I hope you will not feel it was presumption. And as I prayed I grew to long so for you to love Christ that sometimes I felt I must try to do something about it, though there seemed nothing I could do but go on praying. And so I have prayed for you every day since we last met." He paused and looked down at the silent girl beside him.

"Are you angry with me, Miss Rutherford, for presuming to take such an interest in your welfare?" There was a pleading in his tone which compelled her to answer, though all the haughtiness was gone from her voice and it was quite unsteady.

"No, I am not angry," she said softly.

"And you will believe that my Saviour was and is more to me than my very life, in spite of the fact that I have done nothing to prove it to you?"

"I have known from the beginning that you were different from every one else I ever met," answered Evelyn. "But I did not understand what made it — and — I do not think I understand now."

"And will you let me try to tell you? May I have the joy of bringing to you that great, great love that Jesus has for you?"

"And so 'twas a love story after all," mused Evelyn, and one in which her experience stood her in no stead.

The tall elms dropped the yellow leaves and the maples their crimson before them as they walked down the quiet streets. The interested neighbors looked out upon them and wondered, but the destiny of a soul was in the balance and the two who were most interested thought not of anything else.

"Maria, just come here, quick!" said Rebecca Bascomb, peeping through the closed blinds of the parlor where she was dusting. "Forever! If that ain't Maurice Grey! When did he come home? Ain't he grown? I never thought he'd be so grand looking. And who's that with him? His sister? No, you never saw Allison out in any such rig as that. A white dress in the morning! and a red flannel sack! I'll be beat! She looks for all the world like a circus rider. Did you ever? Who can she be, tricked out like that? He ain't been and got married has he? Maybe she's some actress he's brought home as his bride. I should think if that's so the fam'ly 'd never want to lift their heads again, as down on the theatre as they've always been. Step out o' sight, Maria, she's lookin' this way. I think I'll run over and take that recipe for fruit cake Mrs. Grey asked for last fall, and borrow her cookie cutter this afternoon. Ours is all worn out."

If our destinies could be affected by every word that is spoken about us or every glance of misunderstanding that is thrown upon us, how precarious would be our way. And how trivial will seem some of our thoughts about others when we realize at the judgment day that at the very time we were criticising them, eternal and momentous questions were being decided.

> God's ways . . . soon or late . . .
>   Touch the shining hills of day.
> The evil cannot brook delay,
>   The good can well afford to wait.

Chapter 8
A Promised Prayer

Meanwhile Allison in her room wept out her bitterness and knelt for comfort. Then she bathed her eyes and arranged her hair, and busied herself about little duties in her room till the traces of tears should be gone, wondering presently why her mother did not call her or come in search of her.

The loving mother, supposing Allison to be with the other two young people, patiently did the work in the kitchen, rejoicing that the shadow was lifted from her dear child's heart and hoping to see her bright and sunny when she returned. It was so unusual to have Allison other than laughing and sweet that it oppressed her. She was glad to have her out in the sunshine, and sang softly about her work the verse of a hymn which had lingered with her from last Sunday's service:

> Spirit of God, descending,
>   Fill our hearts with heavenly joy;
> Love with every passion blending,
>   Pleasure that can never cloy;
> Thus provided, pardoned, guided,
>   Nothing can our peace destroy.

Perchance the evil one wished to show her that this last line of her hymn was not true, for at that moment for some reason she was moved to go into the sitting room on an errand, and raising her eyes to the window she saw walking slowly up the driveway in deep and earnest converse, her son and their guest. The glimmer of the brilliant scarlet jacket flashed between the trees, and the mother looked for the duller blue of her daughter's to follow, but look as she might no Allison was in sight, and the two who walked thus together did not seem to need a third. She wondered what it could mean. Had Allison remained at the store on some petty excuse? Was the child carrying her ill feeling so far? The song died on her lips and peace picked up her fluttering garments and fled for the time being.

The guest went straight to her room. The mother sought her son with a troubled expression which the son could not fathom, and which in his exalted mood he soon forgot. Where was Allison? In her room, he thought.

She had asked them not to wait for her and they had been to the post office. He was reading letters, but his mind did not seem to be on them. His face wore an abstracted air, "illumined," was the word his mother thought of when he looked up at her in an answer to her question.

"My son, did I understand you that you had met Miss Rutherford before last evening?"

"Yes, mother, she is an old friend. I knew her in New York, and met her abroad. Her brother was in college with me," and so far had he progressed in his acquaintance with the lady in question that he actually thought as he spoke that his words, "she is an old friend," were true.

It was then her mother heart started up in fear at that look upon her boy's face. Oh, if he should put his heart in the keeping of one who was not worthy!

"Do you know her character, my boy?" she asked, and if Maurice had not been so abstracted he would have noticed that his mother's face wore an unwonted look of pain, almost agony. "Is she a — Christian?"

"Mother, she —" he hesitated, and then with his peculiarly winning smile put both his hands in hers just as he used to do when he was a little boy giving her sweet confidences, and looking frankly in her eyes finished, "Mother, she needs Christ. Will you help me pray for her?"

There was that in the reply that baffled the mother while it could not be resisted. She kissed him and gave her promise tenderly. She would not ask him further of his relations to their guest. She knew he would tell her if there was anything she should know. She knew she could trust him, and yet her heart was troubled until she took her worry to that never-failing source of comfort, her Saviour. She was a woman who, in an unusual sense, had learned to lay her burden at her Lord's feet and leave it there. Sometimes her friends did not understand this calmness and were wont to think her indifferent or blind to possible dangers; but those who knew her best had learned to believe that it was simple trust which smoothed her brow and kept her young and fair.

She went to Allison at last with the care gone from her face and found her daughter, not in her room, but down in the kitchen flying around with unnecessary haste in preparation for an elaborate meal to make up for her absence from the work in the morning. She seemed cheery, though her mother could see it was a forced emotion, but the wise mother judged it best to accept the cheeriness and not let her daughter know just at present that she was aware of her having remained at home all the morning.

They talked about the dinner and the mother ignored the fact that the dishes were out of the usual order of every-day planning. She entered into the work with as much seeming eagerness as Allison was manifesting and between them they managed to keep up a semblance of sunshine.

"Maurice said he would have the surrey ready right after dinner. He thinks it would be pleasant for you to take Miss Rutherford up the hill drive. The coloring of the woods will be in perfection of beauty now. You would better plan to start right after dinner so that you will have plenty of time. I will see to the dishes."

"O mother!" said Allison in dismay, appearing in the kitchen door with the butter plate in her hand, "aren't you going too?"

"I can't, dear. You know it is the missionary society day. I have one of the papers to read and it would not do to be absent. Besides, Miss Rutherford has sent some messages to them by me about the box we are packing. I really could not stay away."

Allison turned back to the table upon which she was putting the finishing touches before calling the family to dinner. She could see her brother sitting in the parlor by the window, his fine profile outlined against the window, and she could hear the soft strains of the piano touched by a cultivated hand. Allison could play herself, and had a tender touch all her own which reached hearts. But she knew she could not play like that. She could see the appreciation in her brother's attitude. Her heart rose in rebellion again. Was it jealousy also that was seizing her as its prey? She walked to the dining-room window where she had thought out so many disagreeable problems during the past three days, and leaned her head against the cool pane. As she studied the fretwork of vines and tendrils on the wall outside her chin grew firm with resolve. When she turned away from that window and went silently about her interrupted work she knew in her heart that she did not intend to take that drive in the afternoon, and she also thought she knew a way out of it. Nevertheless she sat at the table and listened to the plans, acquiescing quietly in all they said about the road to take and the hour of starting. It was arranged to give her time for helping with the dinner dishes before she went. She had hoped they would let her off to help her mother, but it became evident that something would have to be planned.

Promptly at the time agreed upon the carriage drove up to the door and Miss Rutherford was handed in. Allison appeared a moment afterward carrying two books in her hand.

"Well, sister, do you propose to pursue the study of literature this afternoon while the rest of us feast on nature?" asker her brother, as he took the books while she got in. "Library books!" he said, frowning slightly. "Now, Allison, you are not planning to go around there first, are you? It will delay us awfully, for you are morally certain to be longer than you expect, and besides, it is out of the way. Can't you let these go another week?"

"No, the time is up," said Allison with satisfaction.

"Well, what of that? A fine? I'll pay it gladly if you'll give it up."

Allison looked troubled. She had not thought of this. Maurice was apt to carry his point when he was anxious.

"Maurice, really they ought to go back today. Mrs. Lynch has been waiting for that blue book and I told her we should be done with it today and she promised to be there and get it before anyone else snatched it up."

Maurice whistled and reluctantly got into the carriage the while Allison's brow cleared. Having set her will not to go she really wished not to do so.

Arrived at the library she promptly arranged the rest. She had been gone but two or three minutes when Miss Burton, one of the ladies interested in the library, came out to the carriage.

"Dr. Grey, good-afternoon," she said. "Your sister has been so kind as to take my place as librarian this afternoon, as I have quite a severe headache, and she asked me to tell you not to wait for her. She is very good indeed."

As there was nothing to be said to this the carriage started on. Wily Allison knew there could be no contention over the matter if she sent Miss Burton to speak for her, and she set herself to straighten out a muddle in the books with the firm intention of forgetting her troubles if she could. However that was not so easily managed, as she found herself from time to time following the carriage as it wound its way among the hills, and about midway in the afternoon it suddenly occurred to her that if her object had been real love and fear for her brother she would have gone along, for surely the stranger could less easily exercise her wiles upon his unsuspecting heart with a third person present than if they were entirely alone. Poor Allison! She vexed herself with the thought that she had been selfish in staying at home, and made several mistakes in setting down the number of books returned. When the hour for closing came she was weary and glad to walk quietly home.

Meantime, the two who were riding into the glory of the afternoon could not be said to have really missed her. Her brother felt now and then a twinge of pity that she was shut up from the beauties they were enjoying all this long afternoon, but it never once came to his comprehension that his sister was really suffering because she was having so little of his own precious society. He was not an egotistical young man. Besides, his present occupation was pleasant.

They talked of many things. Now and then the young man would speak of his Christian work, or of the God who made the beauties they were looking upon. Once they stopped the carriage on the brow of a lofty hill where two other hills gave way and left an unexpected view of valley, river, and more purple hills in the distance. The clear October sky was perfect, as blue and bright as skies are made, with more of decision in it than comes in June, and with a few tiny, sharp, white scurrying clouds here and there like messengers hurrying about intent upon weighty matters in connection with the coming of the winter season.

They were silent as they looked. Such a view takes words away. Presently the young man said:

"I always think when I come to this spot how much I should like to be just here when Jesus Christ comes back to earth again. I like to wonder how the clouds will look, whether it will be sunset or early in the morning, or will the sky be like this. It seems sometimes, when there is a glorious sunset, as if he must be coming, and the gates of heaven have begun to open for the throng of angels. And the dead in Christ! How wonderful it will all be, with Jesus in their midst!"

The girl by his side looked up into his face. She had come into the front seat that she might better see the view. She could also the more easily watch the changing expressions on her companion's speaking face. His look was rapt now, and as he went on to speak in a few words more of the Jesus whom he loved, Evelyn Rutherford for the first time in her life felt that there really was such a person living now as Jesus Christ. Also for the first time, strange as it may seem, she saw a man who seemed to realize this presence as much as he did that of any fellow-creature. She could see that this was a reality with him, and she wondered and was awed.

They were both silent as the horse turned to wind down the hill again and around by another way home. Evelyn could not think of anything to say that would not seem frivolous, and she was conscious of a distinct wish not to seem frivolous before this man.

"Miss Rutherford, may I be so bold as to make a request of you?" asked the young man, turning his bright, earnest eyes upon her as they neared the foot of the hill. "I have prayed for you so long, will you let me feel that you are praying for yourself? It will be a true joy to me."

It was a long time before there was any answer. She had looked at him at first with a quick, startled gaze and dropped her eyes again. Her fingers twined among the red and gray fringe of the heavy golf cape she wore, and the color crept slowly up over her smooth cheek till it almost reached the shadow of the dark, drooping lashes. Afterward when he was far away, a vision of that fair face outlined against the dark green cloth of the golf-hood lingered in his mind, though he was not conscious of noting details as he watched for her answer. At last she said huskily: "How could I? I would not know what to say."

The answer was ready. "Will you ask him to make you willing to be his? Are you willing to be made willing? Can you ask him that?"

"Do you mean, will I just say those words, 'Make me willing to belong to — Christ'?" she said with a slow hesitation, like a child uncertainly learning its lesson. It was all so new to her.

"Yes," he said eagerly, "ask Jesus Christ that every day. Will you? And try with all your heart to realize as much as you can that you are talking to a real, living being, and try to want what you are asking?"

The silence was a long one this time, broken occasionally by a little explanatory word from the young man, who fairly held his breath for her answer. He knew she was considering it by the drooped eyelashes and the nervous fingers in the fringe. He prayed in his heart with longing that would not be denied.

They were nearing the village when at last she raised her eyes in answer to his low, "Won't you do it?" spoken for the fifth time with wistful beseeching.

"I will try," she said, in a tone that none of her New York friends would have recognized.

"Thank God!" was the immediate, joyous response.

They neither of them said any more, but the glow on his face told, as from time to time she stole a glance at him, but that he was deeply and truly glad. Just why she could not understand. Her promise seemed to her to mean so little, and yet she hesitated about making it because it had seemed to mean so much to him that it troubled and embarrassed her.

They drove up to the door with a quiet gravity in their demeanor. The glow of the setting sun illumined their faces and a glow of something even more beautiful uplifted their hearts.

Allison, as she watched them, decided that it had been very wrong for her to stay at home that afternoon. They had only had more chance to draw closer together.

Chapter 9
An Unexpected Summons

As Maurice Grey unharnessed the horse and closed the stable door he was planning how he might help this soul into a knowledge of Jesus Christ. He thanked God for giving him the opportunity, and man-like planned what he would say and do in the days that were to follow. He hoped it would be possible for him to prolong his visit into ten days or two weeks. He had written the busy physician, whose partner and assistant he was about to become, saying that he would like to do so if he was not immediately needed. He smiled to think how well things were happening, and what a wonderful plan was God's to allow his children to do such great work for him. There were one or two little books he would like to read aloud to Miss Rutherford if she was willing. Perhaps to-morrow would afford opportunity. Allison would enjoy hearing them too, though if he were alone with Miss Rutherford he might be able to help out with explanations which would fit her case, which perhaps might be embarrassing to her if another person were present. By the way, he must ask his sister to pray for their guest. Allison could be a great help. She was a grand sister for a man to have. She understood and had sympathy.

Poor Allison, at that moment cutting the bread with firmly closed lips and eyes that held the burning tears back by main force! If she could but have known what her brother was thinking in his heart.

Then the young man went in to find on the hall table a telegram just arrived. He tore it open in haste, and with that slight premonition of evil which always comes with those yellow missives. No matter how used we may be to them, or how much we may expect them, there is always that dread possibility of what they may contain.

"I am called abroad on urgent business. Sail to-morrow. Can you come at once? Wire answer."

Thus the telegram read, and the name signed below was that of the great doctor whose partner he was about to become. There was no getting away from that call. It was Duty, stern and plain and spelled with a capital letter. And yet he had thought but a moment before that a higher call had bidden him here to a work for which he was all eagerness. He felt a rebellious stirring in his heart, and then began to wonder if there was not some selfishness

51

in his desire to stay as well as eagerness to do God's will. Supposing he should answer, "I cannot come." What would happen? The world would go on just the same. Doctor Atlee would do something. Ah, but what would become of the cases that none but he and Doctor Atlee understood? What foolishness was he thinking? Of course he must go.

Then he went to the supper table with a grave face to match Allison's. He tried to be cheery and keep the news of his departure to himself until the meal was over, but he soon saw that his mother and the guest had noticed his abstraction. He must explain.

Disappointment and dismay fell upon the little group; the father, because he had planned a good talk with long discussions on various topics with this dear son, who was almost a stranger now; the mother, forgetting her own heart in sorrow for Allison, who she knew would keenly feel her brother's hasty departure; and Allison herself, because she was suddenly overwhelmed with grief at her own conduct, and saw before her her punishment: her brother gone, and the few short hours she might have enjoyed in his society lost because she would not share them with another.

As for the guest, blank desolation settled upon the town of Hillcroft, and she was again in a waste and barren land. Besides, how was she to know how to carry out that remarkable promise which she had but just made?

The fact being accepted, supper was no longer considered to be of importance. The time-table took a prominent position on the table, and a discussion about trains arose and was settled. In the midst of this the traveler discovered that it was growing late and rushed upstairs to make his few hasty preparations. Downstairs they sat about and waited, no one seeming to know what to do. Allison tried to clear off the table, but the hot tears blinded her, and she finally gave up the attempt and went to see if she could not help her brother.

Maurice was just snapping his gripsack together as she tapped on his door and entered. He turned to her with a loving smile.

"Allison dear, I am sorry you did not have the lovely drive this afternoon. It was too bad for you to miss it," he said.

She hastened to offer her assistance, and so kept away from the subject of the drive. She would not now have him guess her true reason for staying at home for anything. To have her dear brother know the foolishness, wickedness, and pride of her heart would be too great a humiliation, so she said:

"Isn't there something I can do to help you?"

"No, Allison, I have everything in, I think, unless — oh yes, I am glad I remembered that. Allison, I wish you would pray for Miss Rutherford — not in any ordinary way you know. Let us claim that promise, sister mine, as we have so many times before, 'If two of you shall agree on earth as touching anything that they shall ask, it shall be done for them.' Now it is time for me to go. Good-bye, dear."

There was a shadow by the door where Allison stood so that he could not see the expression that crossed her face as he stooped to kiss her. Miss Rutherford again! How strangely she had come into everything, even this good-bye to her brother! The tears blinded her so that she stumbled and almost fell as she followed the unsuspecting brother downstairs.

It was all over in such a very few minutes and the household were left standing where he had bade them good-bye, recalling his last words and looking at the place where he had sat and stood a moment before.

One word the young man had had with the guest alone before he left. She stood in the half-lighted parlor looking out upon the moonlit world and feeling a sudden homesickness. He stepped into the room and she turned. Taking her hand he said:

"Miss Rutherford, I cannot tell you how glad I am that I found you here. You will remember your promise? Perhaps you will also remember now and then that I am praying too? And, Miss Rutherford, my sister Allison lives very near to Jesus. Maybe she might be of help to you. And there are ways in which you can help her if you will."

The others coming in just then there was no chance for her to reply.

She went to her room almost immediately after he left. She felt that the family was depressed by his sudden going away. She was so herself and did not wish them to see it. She bade them good-night in a sweeter way than she had done before; they could not help but notice it. It was as if the winning way she had used with the young man had descended to them. Mrs. Grey pondered what it might mean. Allison, in a softened and reproachful mood, saw but one more reason for blaming herself for her impulsive prejudices.

Evelyn sat down in her room and let her whole acquaintance with the young man just gone sweep over her, culminating in the strange talk they had had that day and the ride and her promise. Why had she made such a promise? She began to see as the day drew towards its end that this promise was going to be a troublesome thing. Perhaps she would forget it. She half hoped she would. And yet — if she should meet him again? Oh, no. She would not like to tell him she had forgotten. She liked being faithful to what she had said to him even though he should never know. He was that kind of a man. One could not help admiring him and one must be true all the way through to him. And where was the fascination? Why should she, so differently brought up, with higher social standing, and believing herself to be worth the interest of any man living, feel in the presence of this man that she was humble as the dust at his feet and he almost a god?

He was like his family. It was a sort of fanaticism, this talk and this unnatural goodness. It was the kind of thing that she had always despised and sneered at. Was it possible that she had at last seen more than this in it? Yes, she admitted to herself, she could but see the effect that religion had on the lives of this one family, and that they seemed to be sweet and natural about their goodness and not overpoweringly egotistical and disagreeable with their oughts and ought-nots, like a few other religionists she had known. There was Allison. How sweetly she had seemed to give up that charming drive. And yet one could easily see that she loved her brother almost to idolizing him. She had seen the look that overspread her face on his arrival, and had been an unseen witness of his parting kiss to her and saw her turn away sobbing when he was gone. It must have been a great disappointment to give up the afternoon all for that fussy, little, dried-up old maid with a headache.

She herself never could have done it. She was sure she did not want to be made into a person who would always have to be thinking of others' comforts and forgetting herself in order to do disagreeable things for other people. What was that he had asked her?

"Are you willing to be made willing to be this?" Then he had known she was not willing, not ready, to give up her wishes and be this other thing that he and Christ — she thought the word reverently, for since the vision she had been given on the hilltop she would never think the name of Christ carelessly again — wished her to be. And he had asked her to pray against herself; to ask to be made willing, to be made to want something she did not want to want. She had promised to try to ask this. She had not realized how much that meant.

How could she ask it? She must ask to be made like — Allison perhaps, or like Mrs. Grey, who cared not for her world, and she did not want to be like them, though she looked at them with wonder and a certain amount of dawning appreciation. They were good and there was no pleasure in goodness. Why should she do this thing in response to a stranger whom she had met but three times, and who was dominated by fanatical views? She could not finish. The power of the stranger over her was so great that she admitted she would do what he had asked in spite of all her feelings.

And then her heart, accustomed always to questioning itself of these things, inquired why there was this power and this fascination, this desire to please a man who might never in this world even know of it? Was she in love with him? She had often asked herself that question about other young men whose friendship and attentions were hers if she chose to take them. Sometimes the answer had been, "I do not know," sometimes, "I like him," or perhaps, "I might care for him," but more often, "No, I do not love him," as these other men passed before her in review. Now as she asked this question of her heart it seemed a profanation. He had not offered her his love. Perhaps he had none left for earthly beings, except his own family of course, aside from the love of saving them, but she felt her heart throb with a strange new joy that he had cared for the saving of her soul. He was not in the least the kind of a man she had expected herself to love when the time came, and it was not a question of love now. It was something infinitely higher and greater, and she supposed better than any earthly love. It was a question of the love of this Christ which was offered her. She impatiently put that other question aside as improper even to think of now. She would not demean herself longer in her own eyes by classing this man with all the other men she knew. Her soul had recognized the true and the good, and for once she would shake off all prejudices and desires and do this one thing he had asked. She would not ask herself if she wished to appear well in his eyes again. Of course she did, but in what measure it did not matter. That she would stand very well with him if he knew her true self she had no hope. His ideal was his sister Allison. That was what he would like her to become. Had he not told her to go to her for an example? Well, there was no use in trying to be such a person, for she never could and did not want to if she could. Besides, her life would not admit of it. When she was back again in New York with Mr. Worthington and her other friends she would forget all about this uncomfortable conscience which seemed to be developing within her, or this strange fancy, but now she must do as she had promised, and the sooner the better, to have it over with. Then she would search her trunk for the very most exciting novel she could find, and read for an hour or two and forget all about the wearisome little town in which she was immured.

She turned the gas out and knelt down by the bay-window seat to pray for the first time in her life, for she had not been taught to pray as a child. It came to her as she knelt thus with a real intention to pray. Once a plain-faced woman who had come to be her nurse tried to make her pray, but she stamped her foot and declared she wouldn't, and the woman very soon afterward had been dismissed by the housekeeper because she threatened to tell of something the housekeeper was doing behind the master's back. She had actually been the only bit of religious life that had touched Evelyn's childhood intimately, and Evelyn had not liked her because she sat by the window and cried at night when her little charge was going to sleep. Weeping in a woman always irritated Evelyn. She rarely wept herself unless she was very angry, and then only when every other way of expressing emotion failed.

Two others knelt at the throne of grace in that same house and at that moment, the mother, with tender petitions for the one for whom her boy had requested prayer, but with a drawing away from the girl in spite of herself lest she had come between her boy and his family; Allison, with bitter tears of repentance and reluctant request for the salvation of her sometime enemy. The feeling against Miss Rutherford had been so deeply grounded that it was with the greatest difficulty Allison could overcome it and ask what she was bound to do with any degree of honesty. Even then the supplication was but half-hearted.

The moon, high in the heavens, looked into the bay window and shone upon the bowed head waiting there till she felt that she had performed the ceremony of a prayer to her satisfaction. And out under the moon-lighted sky miles away rushed the train, and one young man on that train was lifting up her soul in entreaty that would not be denied.

It was a hard thing, that first prayer. Evelyn Rutherford, Naaman-like in her pride, could not bring her haughty lips to utter those simple words she had been told. She knelt long, trying to compose a more formal petition, but they, unaccustomed, would not come at her bidding, and at last she said humbly, "O Christ, make me willing to be good." Even then, as she hastily arose, it came to her that he had asked her to try to say these words "with all her heart," and she feared that was not possible. However, she had tried, and her conscience was satisfied with the duty discharged. She hastened to relight her gas and search for the novel. Having found it, she settled herself for an hour of relief from the tension under which she had been; but the baron and the lady who were introduced in the first page seemed trifling and frivolous, and their ambitions so worthless beside the view of life she had been gazing upon recently, that she closed the book and went to bed.

Unconsciously her point of view in life had changed with even this short stay in such a household. Had she been put back into her old life at once this would doubtless have faded away like some half-forgotten dream, to be remembered only when life seemed vain and empty. But God had not so appointed.

From one stage of our being to the next
We pass unconscious o'er a slender bridge,
The momentary work of unseen hands,
Which crumbles down behind us; looking back,
We see the other shore, the gulf between,
And marveling how we won to where we stand,
Content ourselves to call the builder Chance.

. . . .

We call our sorrows Destiny, but ought
Rather to name our high successes so.

Chapter 10
New Reading for Miss Rutherford

The next morning they awoke to find the brilliant weather gone and a gray drizzle settled upon the face of the earth. The day seemed exactly fitted to their moods, for each of the three women in the house had spent a wakeful night. Mrs. Grey, however, had been able to leave her burdens at the foot of the cross in the early morning, and when Evelyn opened her room door to go downstairs, and then went back for something she had forgotten, she heard her moving about across the hall opening windows, throwing back bedding to air where the dampness could not reach it, and singing in the sweet, crooning voice she used so much about her work:

> "Ye fearful saints, fresh courage take!
>> The clouds ye so much dread
> Are big with mercy and will break
>> With blessings on your head.

> "His purposes will ripen fast,
>> Unfolding every hour;
> The bud may have a bitter taste,
> But sweet will be the flower."

Evelyn walked slowly through the hall to catch every clearly spoken word, and as she went down the stairs she heard the closing words:

> "God is his own interpreter,
>> And he will make it plain."

The listener wondered how it would seem to believe those things and live like that. Would she have been different with a mother like this one? No wonder Doctor Grey was such a man as he was. How could he help it living in such an atmosphere?

On Allison's face was a look of fixed purpose. The task her brother had imposed upon her should be performed, as much as in her lay, though she steadily believed that it was useless and she could be of no help to such a girl. Others might, but not she. Her nature had nothing in common with one from the world of fashion. Allison rather prided herself on that fact, though she was unaware of it. Well, three, her mother and elderly friend and brother, all thought she was the one selected of the Lord to convert this girl. She would show them that it could not be done, at least not through her. It may be that it was because of this feeling in Allison's heart that she was not given the highest honor in the leading of this soul to Christ.

The guest herself made the way easier for a change of bearing toward her. In the midst of her night watches had come a remembrance of the words: "There are ways in which you can help her if you will." It soothed her pride, and made it easier for her to accept the thought of being helped by Allison, not that she felt in any immediate need of Allison's help. Her ideas of things were too new and crude to feel any of her own shortcomings. If she were going to do anything in this line she would prefer to study it out by herself, and not be dependent upon one who was younger and not near so worldy-wise. But she was disposed to study Allison with more interest and kindliness than before, if for no other reason than because she was the sister of the man whom she could not but admire. It would be pleasant to know what sort of women were beloved by him. Therefore she set herself to study her young hostess. At least she would discover if there were any way in which she might help. She would have liked a chance to ask Doctor Grey what he meant by that. How did he imagine his good little sister could ever be helped by her? It must be in the way of the world.

It was in her favor that she came down to breakfast that morning after the young man left. They had supposed in their hearts that she got up early to be there with him, or to show him she was not indolent. But when she appeared that dreary morning in a crimson frock of exquisite fit, with touches here and there that showed no novice had been its designer, they could but admire her, and congratulated themselves that they could think a little better of her. Neither mother nor daughter questioned herself as to whether this willingness to see more good in the visitor was greater than it had been on account of the absence of the young man.

Evelyn talked politics with Mr. Grey during breakfast. Her father was connected quite intimately with some things in New York which interested Mr. Grey deeply, and Evelyn could talk well when she was on her native ground. The views she advanced were doubtless not her own, but those she had heard tossed back and forth across the table at the dinners in her father's house where she had presided. She had paid little heed to them, and if they had not been so oft-repeated week after week, year after year, she would doubtless never have remembered one, but now the well-worn phrases came back to her, and she surprised herself by being able to tell what this and that politician thought about such and such subjects. She had not realized that she knew their views before. Mr. Grey listened and nodded, putting in a keen question now and then, and his wife saw that what the girl said was of no little moment to him. Allison listened also as she came in now and again with plates of buckwheat cakes the like of which the New York girl had never tasted before, though she had eaten in many a place which boasted a famous cook. But somehow famous cooks know not the sweet, old, simple ways of quiet home grandmothers. Allison was trained to be interested in all the questions of the day. She had many a discussion with her father. She often read the papers to him in the evening when his eyes were weary with poring over his books in the office, and she was well-informed on both sides of many questions. She saw that what the guest was saying had a bearing on one of their much-discussed points, and once or twice she stopped and put in an animated word to her father, and he smiled and nodded and said:

"Perhaps you are right, Allison, after all, if these men think so."

Evelyn stopped then to watch this other girl and wonder. There was such a perfect feeling of camaraderie between her and her father. When the meal was over, instead of going into the parlor to lounge and read, as she had done the first morning, Evelyn asked quite pleasantly, "May I stay here and watch you?" and Allison had consented willingly enough, but she thought it would have been in better taste for her to have offered help, though she would not have accepted it. She did not yet realize how very far apart their two spheres had always been. Evelyn would no more have known how to go about helping than she would have known how to build a house or set a diamond.

That she did not know anything about housework, Allison began to understand as she listened to the simple questions such as a child of six brought up in a plain home might possibly ask about the commonest every-day tasks.

She grew weary after time and went into the other room. Allison watched her through the open door and saw her go over to the low bookcase. With an impulse to do what she could she followed her, and as the guest idly read the titles of the books she touched the upper shelf.

"These are all wonderful, if you have not read them. My brother and I have kept that shelf for books that we both unqualifiedly like, books that we feel are above the ordinary." She passed her hand lovingly over the backs of the volumes and went back to finish the pudding she was stirring up for dinner. She doubted in her heart whether the guest would care for any of the books on that shelf, and why she had opened her heart thus far she did not know, except for the memory of her brother's last words. It was a little thing, so little that it did not seem worth while for her to lift her heart in a petition that it might be blest, as she often did when trying to help others, her Sunday-school boys for instance. She never gave them a book to read without that earnest heart petition. But little as it was, it was one of the links in the chain of influence that God was preparing for Evelyn Rutherford's soul.

"A Singular Life," read Evelyn, and from some strange attraction took the book down from the shelf. These books, then, were what he considered fine; "above the ordinary," his sister had said. She would read one and see.

Ordinarily the opening pages, being a conversation between a lot of young theologues, would not have been interesting to her, but it struck her now as quite unique, utterly out of the line in which she had ever read, and she went on out of mere curiosity, becoming after a little interested in the story and the central character, the man of the singular life who, by the way, to her fancy seemed in some respects much like young Doctor Grey.

She laid the book down a little before dinner and looked wearily out of the window. The life portrayed there was so different from her own. It was not that it attracted her so much as it made her discontented with everything. There was a vague longing to get back into her former self-content. If she were only in New York. If she did but know whether Jane Bashford had gone back to the city yet. Jane would be glad to have her, and the Bashfords were such very old friends that her father could not object. Besides, Jane would be likely to invite Mr. Worthington sometimes if she suggested it. Jane liked dashing people as well as she did.

With the thought of Mr. Worthington, however, came a vivid flash of contrast between him and the man in whose company she had spent a part of the last two days. She tried to imagine him talking as Doctor Grey had done. She knew that his conversation would have been entirely of the smart set, their doings and sayings, and as much of a report of what occurred at the club as he dared to tell her. It was like spice to a sated appetite. It was something new and she enjoyed it. Here was a man who was not afraid to tell things as they were. Of course, he would not go too far; he knew just where to stop. Or stay! Did he? In her heart she wavered a little. There had been times when she had felt it necessary to exercise a little of her ready hauteur because she instinctively feared what he might say next; that is, he was not a man one could trust — not like this other one. But then — and she sighed a weary sigh.

This other lived a "singular life" like the man in the book. There might be one such in a thousand, but they were not for her. Why should she be unsettled and unhappy in the place that belonged to her, because somewhere in the world there lived a man like that? He would never look at her, would never likely come within her radius again. He had told her himself that when he went back to New York it was to hard work. This he had said when she invited him to call. He had thanked her, and after a pause, looking at her earnestly had said, "Perhaps I may," and then, "sometime." It was then he had explained that his practice in partnership with the great doctor would be very confining, and that he must not entangle himself with pleasures that would take his mind from his work. She thought of it humbly now. She did not believe he meant to come. She was not altogether sure that when she went back to New York she would care to have him come, but she wished that this day and these thoughts were over, and that this ridiculous compulsory visit was over, and she could get into her normal state again. Why had she made that absurd promise? She began to have a superstitious feeling that it was at the bottom of all her unrest. Then she was called to dinner.

The pudding was delicious, and so were all the viands which preceded it, but the guest did not feel hungry. Allison asked her how she liked the book she had been reading, and she answered listlessly, "Well enough." This answer, to Allison, meant a depraved taste in reading. To brand her favorite book which she had read and reread and then read again aloud to father and mother and brother, with a "well enough" was more than her spirit could bear. She relapsed at once into her critical state of mind, which did not even pass off when she discovered that Miss Rutherford had gone to her room and taken with her not only "A Singular Life," but also another favorite, "Heather and Snow." She could not care for either of them, Allison felt sure, and she sat down to enjoy herself for a while, and feel that she had performed her duty and it had done no good, as she had prophesied.

Several days of gloomy weather succeeded, during which time Miss Rutherford read not only two but several others of the sacred choice upper row of books. She made no comments upon them, and it cannot be denied that some of them actually bored her and she skimmed them.

Nevertheless, she had determined to find out this young man's idea of life and this was one of the ways open to her. Besides, there was nothing else in the world to do. There came daily messages of affection from the plague-stricken house she was supposed to be visiting, and there came no letters of encouragement to return to New York.

A week went by and a distant cousin, to whom she had written in her desperation, answered that she was sorry, but it seemed absolutely necessary for her to go to Boston for a little while, and she was not sure how long it would be before she would return; while another friend, still in her summer home in Tuxedo, apologized for not being able to invite her as she was having a terrible time with her servants and the house had been full of company and the baby was sick into the bargain. Evelyn curled her lip over the excuses through which she felt sure she could see, and settled herself to stay where she was with as good a grace as possible.

Then one morning a caller came to see Allison. After a few minutes in the parlor that young woman went to her mother with very red cheeks and the expression on her face that her mother knew always meant that she hoped she would say "No," to whatever request she made.

"Mother," she said, speaking in a low, nervous tone, "Ethel Haines has come to ask me to change places with her for to-morrow night — the club meeting, you know. She was to have it there and had arranged the whole programme and everything, but her invalid aunt arrived unexpectedly last night and is so ill to-day that they had to send for a trained nurse. She says they can't have the least bit of noise about the house, and her programme has a good deal of music, and you know the girls could never be still. It is quite impossible for her to have it. She wants to bring everything over here and just borrow our house, and she says she will fix everything for me when my turn comes and I can go over there. I told her I thought it was impossible, it would be too hard for you when Mary is gone. You don't think we could do it, do you?"

There was a note of almost distress in the daughter's voice as she asked this last question that made her mother look at her curiously:

"Why, daughter, I don't see why you cannot do it. It will be very little trouble. Mrs. Munson is coming to sweep the whole house the next morning, and if she brings her things over we shall only have a few cups and plates to wash. Certainly I would accommodate her if I could. It is very hard for Mrs. Haines to have her poor aunt ill so much. Tell her yes. It will help to relieve the monotony for our guest also. She is having a very dull time, I fear, with you busy so much of the time and no one even to talk to but me."

"O mother!" exclaimed Allison in real dismay now, "don't you understand? We can't have it here when she is here. She would criticise and laugh everything to scorn. You have not heard her talk and I have. I undertook to tell her about this club once and mother, what do you think she said? 'Do you dance or are you devoted to cards?' Can't you see how out of place she would be among us and how she would be a wet blanket on the whole thing?"

The mother looked grave. "Allison, I think you are really very wrong. In the first place, it matters very little what she may think of it at all or whether she laughs or scoffs. I should think this was clearly your duty. In the second place I give Miss Rutherford credit for being more of a lady than to manifest any feeling she may happen to have before a gathering of respectable young people. They may not be such as she is accustomed to be with and their habits may be different, but they live in the same world and speak the same language and have been educated in much the same courtesies. I am sure our guest will be a lady, whatever she may feel in her heart. As for being a wet blanket to the rest of you, if your club has no more spirit than to be quelled by the sight of one poor, lonely stranger from a different class in society I am ashamed of you. For one evening try to amuse her, even though it may be at the expense of a laugh or two. Laughs cannot hurt you when you are in the way of right."

"Mother, I do not like to be laughed at," said Allison, her eyes very bright.

"No, most people don't," said her mother; "but there are occasions when one might even have to pass through the fiery furnace of a laugh and trust the Form of the Fourth to keep the flames from consuming you."

Allison swallowed hard and looked down at the table. Her cheeks had grown redder, if possible. Her eyes looked as if she would like to cry if only she did not have to go back to that girl in the parlor. Mother certainly had a very blunt way of putting things sometimes. There was no getting around the truth when mother chose to speak it.

The daughter turned slowly and walked back to the parlor, to give an invitation most reluctant and ungracious for the usually hospitable Allison Grey.

The arrangements which the caller talked over with her in detail failed to interest her as much as usual and she feared that Ethel thought her not responsive enough, but her mind would wander to her own part in spite of herself and questions kept crowding into her thoughts thick and fast. What would Miss Rutherford think of it all? Would she condescend to come downstairs? Perhaps she would choose to remain in her room. Oh the relief that would be to this poor, tired soul! But if she did come down would she array herself in the low-necked dress or perhaps another one still worse? Oh, the horror of the thought! And how could it be prevented? She could not tell her it would likely be resented if she did. She had a right, of course, to wear what she chose.

On the whole, poor Allison's mind was in a tumult that night as she lay and tossed, trying to forget it all and go to sleep.

Chapter 11
Rebecca Bascomb on Evening Dress

It remained for Rebecca Bascomb to settle the question of full dress in Hillcroft and to set Evelyn Rutherford's mind in a tumult.

It was just after breakfast the next morning and the mother and daughter were hurrying to get the dishes out of the way that they might have all the preparations for the evening complete early in the day. The sun had come out bright and clear. The air was cold and a glowing fire was burning in the corner fireplace in the parlor. At one side of this Evelyn was sitting with a book in her hand. She was not reading, but looking into the fire with a dreamy expression. Something she read recalled to mind the expression of Dr. Grey's face during that view they had together on the hilltop. She was not always thinking of him. There had been two days when she banished every thought of the new influence which had come into her life, and though she performed her promise, she did it hastily and perfunctorily. She wrote many letters home and began to hope to get away soon. She had even written to her brother, as a last resort, though she was not quite sure where he was. His plans were not always confided to his family. Occasionally, however, the new and startling thought of a Christ — and for her — would come to her piercingly, and with it a clear vision of the face of the young man who had given it to her. She was wondering again about his life and if it was always as beautiful and spotless all through as it had seemed the few times she had seen him, when there came an interruption to her thoughts.

A wide shadow entered the hall doorway. If she had not been absorbed she would have noticed a strange voice in the kitchen and known that Mrs. Grey had asked some one to go into the parlor and sit down a minute while she went to look for a certain skirt pattern desired. Mrs. Grey was not a woman who entered people's kitchen doors uninvited and without knocking, and neither did she care to have prying eyes watching her every movement to report the same as soon as possible to the entire speaking acquaintance of the owner of those same prying eyes. However, there were people in Hillcroft who employed this method of making friendly calls, and Mrs. Grey used discretion in getting them into the parlor as the case demanded.

Rebecca Bascomb wore old, soft congress gaiters and a pair of decrepit "gum shoes," as she designated them, three sizes too large, therefore her step was not heralded.

Evelyn looked up, and she nodded a pleasant good-morning, with a motion half bow and half a ducking curtsy which suited her bulk. She approached Evelyn and eyed her with expectation and enjoyment as one approaches a particularly dainty morsel, rolling her tongue with anticipation.

Evelyn moved her chair back and would have risen to leave the room if she had realized that this stranger had come to stay, but Miss Bascomb said in a voice that Allison used to say was "all meal and oil": "Oh, don't you move. I'll set right here. Mis' Grey has gone to find a pattern for my sister. Are you Maurice Grey's wife?"

She fixed her bright, brown, little eyes on Evelyn's beautiful face and Evelyn, for some reason utterly unknown to her and thoroughly disturbing, was aware that the blood had leaped into her fce and mounted even to her brow. She was aware also that the twinkling eyes had observed this with satisfaction and laid it away to put with whatever facts might develop thereafter.

"I beg your pardon," stammered Evelyn, trying to summon her haughty manner and sitting up straight. She would have left the room without answering had it been any other man in the world whose wife she had been taken for, but for some strange reason she did not understand, she felt she must in justice to him set this matter right.

"Be you young Doctor Grey's wife?" came the direct question again, and the little eyes fixed her once more as a pin does a fluttering moth.

"I am Miss Rutherford, of New York," Evelyn answered in her most freezing manner.

"Oh, you don't say! Met him in New York, did you? Well, you're real handsome, anyway. I told my sister when I see you go by with that bright circus sack you wore the other day that I guessed Maurrie had picked up some actor woman, and I knew that would be hard on Mis' Grey, feelin' as she does about bare necks and short sleeves, an' I knew they mostly wore 'em. But, Rutherford, d' you say?" a new intelligence coming into the bright eyes. "Why, now you ain't any relation to Miss Joan Rutherford, be you? I wonder now? If you are, I was mistook. No member of Miss Rutherford's family ever wore anything indecent."

"Miss Rutherford is my aunt. I will wish you good-morning," said Evelyn, with a grand sweep of her fine figure, as she left the room at last, to almost come into collision with Allison, who stood wide-eyed and red-cheeked at the hall door.

Allison grasped her hand convulsively and she returned the clasp with her own, as by common consent they fled from the spot swiftly and silently.

"What did she dare to say to you?" questioned Allison excitedly, when they came to a standstill in a safe place, which happened to be Allison's own room, whither she had, without realizing it, drawn Evelyn. "I heard only the last few words, but I know she is capable of saying a great deal. The idea of her daring to speak of that lovely coat of yours in that way. 'Circus sack,' indeed!" And then both girls sat down and burst into peals of laughter.

It was perhaps the best thing that could have happened to them. Evelyn felt almost hysterical from the experience through which she had just passed, and she was not a girl who often cried. Besides, the laughter created a bond of sympathy between them.

"She is a meddlesome busybody!" said Allison, when she could speak. "Mother does not like to have her here, but is fond of her poor old sister. We always treat her well and get her away as soon as possible when she comes over. But she is just dreadful. She would fairly cut your heart out to see your thoughts if she knew how, and there is nothing — absolutely nothing — she does not dare to say."

"But what did she mean about your mother's feeling about bare necks? Doesn't your mother approve of *décolleté* dresses?" Evelyn asked the question curiously, but there was enough of her old tinge of superior scorn in the tone to bring the bright blood into Allison's face and deeply embarrass her.

Evelyn was quick. She had noticed that the family did not array themselves in fine garments for dinner, and she had not done so again; but she had set this down to the quiet home customs of the family and had not dreamed that there was a principle concerned, neither did she suppose that they did not wear evening dress on some occasions.

"It is not the custom to wear evening dress here," began Allison in confusion, and then her bravery came to the front and she looked up with a fine smile of loyalty. "No, my mother does not approve of it, but it seems discourteous to say so to you when you think differently about it. I know that people in society universally dress in that way."

The other girl did not argue the question. It had appeared to her only as an idiosyncrasy of this town. Allison was relieved when she asked quietly:

"Then what are you going to wear to-night at this — what do you call it — club meeting? You must tell me what to wear. I don't want to be dressed out of keeping with the occasion, you know. It might come to the ears of our friend downstairs and shock her."

They both laughed again, and the returning stiffness that threatened passed away.

With the question, "What are you going to wear to-night?" there came a cloud over Allison's face.

"I don't know," she answered hesitating. "I hoped my new dress would be done in time, but the dressmaker sent word this morning that she had been sick and could not finish it till next week. It is very annoying, for the last time I wore my blue silk waist I spilled some cream down the front, and try as hard as I could I have not been able to get the spot out so but that it shows a little."

"Dear me! That's too bad. Can't you cover it up with lace in some way? Where is it? Let me see it. Perhaps I can suggest some way," said Evelyn, glad to find a little chance to help this other girl, and interested at once, as she always was, in a matter of clothes.

"What a lovely shade!" she exclaimed, as Allison reluctantly brought out a blue waist of good silk plainly made. She knew it would not shine beside Miss Rutherford's elegant and varied wardrobe, and she would rather have kept it to herself, but her real anxiety to cover the spot made her glad of the help.

"That is just the shade of your eyes," said Evelyn, holding the silk to match them. "Come in my room and let me see if I have not a lace collar that would exactly cover that spot, and I know I have a velvet ribbon just the same color that will make the sweetest knot for your hair, unless you have one."

Allison acknowledged that she had not, and looked with wistfulness at the scientific carelessness of the other girl's arrangement of hair. She longed to ask her how she accomplished such results, but did not feel close enough. However, Evelyn was more interested now than she had been since the son of the house departed. She had some pleasant work to do with which she was familiar.

"Oh, let me dress you up and fix your hair, and then we can tell just how it will look. May I?" She said it with so much eagerness that Allison was amazed. This was a new girl, not the Miss Rutherford that had been with them for several days. She felt as if she might sometime get acquainted with this girl. So she submitted.

It was marvelous what a difference the deft touches of the artist gave to Allison's already pretty head. The arrangement of the hair was simplicity itself, with the tiny knot of torquoise blue velvet tucked in among the golden masses, but there was something about it which gave a needed finish to Allison and set off her quiet beauty to perfection. Evelyn would have called this something "style," but the mother, when she looked, called it "artistic." Allison in her heart knew that it was stylish, and she felt a certain satisfaction in seeing it belong to herself. The collar that Evelyn produced from the depths of one of the big trunks was a delicate sheer muslin, embroidered in a fine new-old-fashioned way and edged with the finest of real lace, dainty and unobtrusive. It fitted about the shoulders and over the soiled front in a pretty way, as if it had been made for the purpose.

"But I must not wear your collar," said Allison, surveying the effect with a lingering pleasure.

"I will give it to you, and then it will be yours, not mine, you see," said the irresistible Evelyn. "I am tired of it, anyway. Now you shall tell me what to wear," and Allison had the pleasure of going through the marvelous contents of those trunks, handling pretty materials and gaining many new ideas of originality in dress. It was a pleasure, for Evelyn had money and taste and her clothes were generally a work of art. Allison reveled in the pretty things until she suddenly remembered that it was growing late and there were many things to be done. Raising her eyes from the trunk she saw the other girl looking at her intently.

"You look fine," said Evelyn sincerely, as if she were merely thinking aloud. "If you were in New York and dressed well you would make an impression."

Allison's cheek vied with the scarlet of the dying sage flowers bordering the garden path, and she might have turned and fled, so much was her sensitive nature stirred, had not her mother, coming in search of her just then, seen her through the half-open door and stepping softly in kissed her gently on the cheek.

"What has she done to you, my little girl?" she said, holding her lovingly at arm's length and looking with pleased eyes at the sweet, blushing face. "It is very lovely." Allison, looking into those loving eyes and hearing the gentle praise, was soothed and pleased.

Thus was the perplexing question of dress settled for the evening and the two girls were brought nearer together. Dress has much sin and sorrow to answer for in the world. It is well when now and then it can be used for good.

Pleased with her effort to help, Evelyn grew interested in the evening affair. What were they going to do? Have refreshments? Could she help in setting the table? She always set the tables for any special affairs at home, and was very fond of helping in the arrangement for charity fairs. Perhaps she might relieve them a little. And Allison, charmed with the idea of having things arranged in true New York style, surrendered the dining room into her hands. The result was a thing of beauty. Evelyn even went so far as to rifle her trunk of a bolt of narrow crimson ribbon, and several yards of wide satin ribbon to match. The satin ribbon she fastened in large bows to the four corners of the tablecloth while the four long ends met each other and were fastened in an ingenious way under a branch of red leaves on the gas fixture. Allison had picked the last of the scarlet sage and that was massed in a big glass bowl in the center of the table.

The narrow ribbon adorned the little bundles of white sandwiches which had come in a basket from Ethel Haines, and made cunning little rosettes in the handles of the glass dishes that held the delicate sponge cakes, and there were bright red apples polished till they shone like rubies in a pile at each end of the table, set about with bits of green from an evergreen tree. It was easy to improvise scarlet shades for the tiny lamp and candles Allison possessed, and when the dainty cups were clustered on a white-covered side-table, with the little brass tea-kettle beside them ready for lighting, the whole was charming.

Yet in spite of all this Allison, as she went from her hairdresser's hand late in the afternoon to finish dressing, thought with trembling of the evening before her and wished it were over. The matter of dress was settled. Evelyn was to wear a white cloth dress with a touch of crimson velvet here and there. Allison thought of the harmony of it with the other decorations with satisfaction, and then smiled to think how she was reckoning Miss Rutherford as one of the decorations.

At the last minute there came a message from Ethel Haines. Her aunt was so very ill that she would not be able to come after all. She enclosed the programme and begged Allison to take charge. She also mentioned that the chief performer of the evening had the mumps and would not be present, so Allison would have to play.

Poor Allison! Her nerves already under a strain gave way. She sat down and let the discouraged tears come.

"I simply cannot play at all, mamma. What shall I do? You know I never play in public, not really fine music, nothing except ballads and things, without practising, and I would not play before Miss Rutherford for the world. She is a very fine performer. Didn't you hear the other night when Maurice was here? She is wonderful."

Evelyn stood in the door in the soft white dress with crimson touches at her belt and throat, and with her most gracious manner. She felt secretly elated at her success in helping the sister of that young man. She began to think she understood what he had meant and wished he were here to witness how well she was doing it. Moreover, she could but hear what Allison had said, and being proud of her ability to play was naturally pleased. Therefore when Mrs. Grey looked up at her smiling, and said: "Why don't you ask her to play then, dear?" and Allison, her head still buried in her handkerchief, sobbed out: "I wouldn't dare, mother. I am sure she wouldn't do it," she smilingly offered her services to any extent.

Allison looked up ashamed and pleased and troubled all in one. Then she burst out: "But Bert Judkins was to play on his violin and he doesn't know much about it, and will murder things dreadfully, I presume. Some one will have to accompany him and I simply can't do it. He is in my Sunday-school class and I should get so nervous over him I should break down."

"Can't you suppress him?" said Evelyn frowning.

"No!" said Allison decidedly, a flash coming into her eyes in spite of her misery. "It was a great thing to get him to come. We had to coax him and we hope to get hold of him through his love of music. Some of the girls are going to try to make him feel at home to-night so he will come again, and perhaps begin to come to church."

Evelyn raised her eyebrows. This sort of thing was beyond her, but she was determined that as far as the evening was concerned she would do her best to help.

"Never mind, don't worry," she said kindly. "I'm sure I can blunder through some sort of an accompaniment with him. Come, let us get those candles ready to light and pick the red leaves for the mantel. Are you sure you can find any more?"

"Yes, I know a sheltered spot on the back veranda where they are still bright. I'll go out and get them," and Allison dried her eyes and went away, wondering what spell had befallen this strange girl. If things went on like this she would be really liking her soon.

Chapter 12
The Club and Bert Judkins

The evening was a strange experience in Evelyn Rutherford's history, because of her first effort to help some one else. She felt extremely virtuous, and wondered what her New York friends would think of her. Then she wondered if that young man who set himself up as her mentor would be satisfied.

Toward the girls, who arrived promptly at five in goodly company, Evelyn maintained a stately distance, like a queen who chooses to grace an occasion but who will not mingle with the throng. From time to time Allison glanced her way with a troubled expression. She had feared Evelyn would hold off in this way and she felt sure the Hillcroft girls would dislike her in consequence. Why Allison should care whether they disliked her or not she was sure she did not know, unless for the sake of her old friend, Evelyn's aunt, who would be grieved thereby. But having presented her she naturally wished to have her liked, and feared that the evening would be filled with embarrassment in consequence of the new element in the midst.

Evelyn sat quietly and watched the exercises. There were papers and brief discussions which were not very animated because a sudden shyness had fallen on the girls. Evelyn decided that they were largely of the class that Allison was trying to help, with a sprinkling of girls of culture like Allison. These for the most part were quiet, unobtrusive creatures, and not particularly attractive. They looked like girls from good homes, and they were tolerably well dressed. The rest were awkward and embarrassed, all but a few, who were bold and talked loud and giggled when they spoke. Evelyn decided that it was a nice thing in Allison to give up her time to elevating these other girls. Perhaps this was what the young doctor had meant, that she might help his sister in her good works, if she would. If that was it she was entirely willing to do what she could, provided the work was all as pleasant as it had been to-day. She should not care to be too familiar with all these girls. This discussion part, with the ten-minute papers on what a young girl should read and how she should read and why she should read, and a number of other heads under the general topic of reading, Evelyn privately voted a bore. She yawned behind her jeweled hand and wished this part was over. The plain-faced girl who was enumerating a list of books for busy readers saw the yawn and hurried so that she choked, and wished she had not promised to write a paper, vowing she never would do so again.

But when the evening came on Evelyn began to be more of a success. Among the first of the boys and young men to arrive was the aforesaid Bert Judkins. He wore a cheap new dark suit and looked well. He had heavy handsome features and large eyes full of fun. His black hair and red cheeks were set off by a very red tie with a large, prominent glass diamond, which he wore without any apparent effrontery. His hair was nicely plastered in places where its original curls would submit to be subdued, and his hands were clean with a smooth black rim under each finger nail. It was not a part of his upbringing to finish his toilet by cleaning his nails. He came in with a swagger, his violin in a green flannel bag in his hand. He saluted one or two of the commoner girls with a nonchalant, "Hello, Nan!" "Ev'nin', Nell!" and lounged over to the piano, where he took, as a matter of course, a place of honor for the evening.

Evelyn sat on the piano stool. She had just been introduced to several of the young men, but so far all of them seemed shy and gravitated naturally out of her orbit. In truth they were somewhat afraid of her. The few older young men who had not left the town to go to some city where there was more enterprise, were so busy that they were generally late in attending such gatherings if they came at all.

So Evelyn eyed curiously the lad — for he was but seventeen — who had taken the seat beside her. She imagined from what she had heard and the violin bag in his hand that this was the musician of the evening. She wondered what he was going to attempt and studied him idly. His face was not altogether unattractive. There was a great good-humored conceit and a tremendous love of fun mingled in his face, and the merry eyes were wandering about the room, winking at one and smiling at another, and once he stuck his tongue in his cheek with a comical expression at another. It was evident that nothing ever abashed him. It was only when Allison came his way that a different expression crossed his face. A kind of lighting of reverence and embarrassment changed him into a really handsome fellow. Evelyn saw him look at Allison's hair. Was it possible that a boy like that noticed a change of finery in his Sunday-school teacher? He smiled when Allison came nearer and shifted his eyes to the other side of the room. Evelyn saw that was a sort of diffidence and wondered at it. He had not seemed embarrassed, even by the presence of her, a stranger. There was a gentle kindliness of manner in Allison when she spoke to this boy that Evelyn had not seen in her before, and she perceived that there was a relationship between teacher and scholar that she knew not of.

A sudden interest in the new specimen before her took Evelyn. Maybe she could help here. What if she should try? At least it would be better than sitting and doing nothing. Allison looked doubtfully at Evelyn, wondering whether to risk the experiment of an introduction to the boy. She feared he might not take kindly to the haughtiness Miss Rutherford would be likely to offer him. The hour was drawing near when they would have to play together. She finally risked it and walked away; to her surprise Evelyn turned to the boy all smiles and graciousness. Allison, watching from the other side of the room, was amazed and wondered if this was a side of her nature that Miss Rutherford kept for all members of the male sex. It disgusted her a little and she began to fear that her guest might with her frivolous talk dispel any good seed that might have been sown in his heart.

The two by the piano were getting on well. "Are you to play?" asked Evelyn, "and you will let me see your accompaniments?"

"Why, ain't Miss Norton goin' to be here?" said the boy, looking around the room. "Some of these pieces are pretty hard. Do you think you can play 'em without practisin'?"

"I believe she is ill," said Evelyn, reaching for the sheets of music he held. "I might try them. I think I have seen some of them before."

She was amused at the idea he had of her ability, but she was astonished at the really good music he had chosen, rather disappointed too, because it grated on her to have good music murdered.

The boy leaned over and pointed out one or two places where she must be sure to "hang on" as he expressed it, and he gave her a few other instructions in musical phrases mispronounced which nearly broke down her gravity, but she managed to keep her face straight, as she was almost immediately called upon to open the programme with a piano selection.

She had chosen a brilliant *valse* and took them all by storm with her rendition. Especially did Allison notice the expression on the face of Bert Judkins. He was evidently impressed. He drank in the music and watched the white fingers that moved easily and with such mysterious swiftness among the twinkling harmonies. When the first selection was over it was met by a perfect burst of applause. Hillcroft was not used to such music and it wanted some more. Evelyn goodnaturedly complied and jingled off a little medley of nursery melodies, which kept them laughing till the end.

When Evelyn turned back to her companion he leaned toward her and said in a loud whisper: "Say, you've played before a few times, ain't you? I guess you'll do," and he nodded his encouragement and admiration frankly.

There followed a recitation by a young lady who appeared to have been taking elocution lessons very hard, and who ranted and tore about over a few imaginary wrongs she was reciting. Evelyn did not care to listen and she noticed that the boy's face expressed a kind of fascinated horror. When it was done he said to Evelyn, in a kind of low growl, "Aw, she's no good, never was! Too stuck on herself!" and he threw himself back in his chair with a superior air.

It was very strange what a difference a little desire to help had made in Evelyn. At any other time sitting near an ill-bred young fellow she would have curled her lip and wondered how he came to be allowed to breathe the same air with herself; and here she was hoping he would not play too badly, that she might be able to praise him a little. She was indeed pleased to find that he had some idea of the feeling in the music he had selected and that his execution, though crude, was not unpleasant to listen to. She grew interested in helping him by following his eccentric playing and covering any irregularities by her own accompaniment. They scored a great success as the audience testified, and the boy sat down mopping his perspiring brow and saying:

"Well, we did 'em fine that time, didn't we? I never played better in my life. I never had anybody play so good fer the accompaniments before. They always make me get throwed out, some way. I wish you could go along with me every time I play."

She bowed her acknowledgment of his praise and wondered what her friends in New York would say if they could hear that. She fancied her brother Dick would shout over it, and tease her most unmercifully for months. She wondered if Mr. Worthington's black pointed mustache would curl in disdain and he would say, "The impudent little cur," as he had once at a little newsboy who ran against her dress to sell a paper to a hurried gentleman. And then in contrast came the noble, high-bred face of Doctor Grey as he had asked her to help his sister. He would not think she was in poor business, and what harm would it do her for just one night to let this ignorant boy speak his rough compliments. It was not like Evelyn Rutherford to argue thus, but she was being touched by an influence which as yet she knew not. She was praying that she might be willing to belong to Christ, and he was answering her unawares by letting her see himself in the souls of others for whom he lived and died.

The programme, so far as the music was concerned, was a success.

Just before the last selection by Evelyn, Allison read a bit culled from Ralph Connor's "Black Rock." The room was very still when she had finished. Evelyn was astonished at the power Allison had over her audience, at her ability to turn them from laughter to tears, and to imitate perfectly the speech of all the characters. Bert Judkins sat entranced. The story struck home to a world where he lived every day, and the truths contained had made to vibrate a vital chord in his heart. During a tender passage he had dropped some of his music, and in stooping awkwardly to pick it up Evelyn noticed his big, rough hand drawn impatiently across his eyes. When Allison sat down he turned to Evelyn after a moment of quiet and said: "Ain't she a rare one, though? I tell you now, she's good."

Evelyn turned to the piano marveling at the power the teacher had over the scholar, and she played a soft, sweet, mysterious, tender poem of sound that served to deepen the impression made by the reading.

During the hour of pleasant sociability and refreshment that followed before the company broke up Miss Rutherford and Bert Judkins were side by side.

The company were given pencils and cards and asked to go into the hall, where were arranged upon the wall a number of cards, each one representing in picture the name of some book. It was an old device in Hillcroft to make people feel at their ease, but it had never happened to come Evelyn's way, and struck her as quite a new and bright idea. She was quick at guessing, and during the last week in this house happened to have read a good many of the books represented, so that she was able to find out a goodly number, and she made the boy by her side help her. Together they puzzled out the names. He knew only a few books but those he knew he could guess quicker than she, and when the list was called out they found they had a good many numbers correctly written. By this time Evelyn was interested in spite of herself, in this rough, unfinished boy-man, who was so thoroughly frank and so refreshingly blunt in what he had to say. She came from a world where people hid their true thoughts with pleasant words. This boy said what he thought regardless of others' opinions or the world's. She had always been an admirer of free speech. The boy was worth doing something for. What was it they were wanting to do with him, anyway? Get him to church, Allison had said. And what did they want to do with him when they got him to come to church? Educate him? Elevate him? Or perhaps make him into that mysterious something that Doctor Grey wanted her so much to be. It softened her much as these days went by to think that any one had cared enough for her in any way to think of her every day for a year, and pray for her.

She resolved she would help them with this boy if possible. She could not help to make him over, for that she did not understand, but she might perhaps help to bring him into the place where they thought he might be made over. She recognized that he had the making of a man in him. She had always been able to wheedle boys and young men into doing her bidding. They had often sent her to coax this or that one into some scheme, and she had almost never failed. What if she should try to coax him to go to church next Sunday? What would Allison say if she told her she had asked him and he had consented? She resolved again to try.

To this end she led him to the dining room and seated herself, as had been planned beforehand, at the little tea table to pour tea. She retained her vassal, however, and found he was not at all a bad hand to serve cups of tea to the company. But presently there came a lull in tea pouring. All were served and satisfied, and they could sit and chat. She had treated the boy much as she would have treated a young man in her own social set, had given him little compliments on the way he helped her, and made him feel she liked to have him by her side. Only when Allison came that way she felt she had a rival in his admiration.

But after all it was he who opened the way for her to carry out her purpose. It was while he was devouring sponge cakes, a whole one at a bite, a large plateful within reach, and he not troubled by any feeling of bashfulness about taking all he wished. Allison had just passed by them into the other room. She hardly knew whether she was glad or sorry of this sudden devotion of her scholar to her guest. It certainly kept Miss Rutherford from curbing the spirits of the other guests, and kept Bert away from several mill girls who had been invited to-night as an experiment, also to be helped, who would not be helpful to the young man in question. But what were they talking about? Horse races? Dancing? What possible theme could they have in common? Well, she would be likely to hear of it next Sunday some time during the lesson. Bert would be sure to say, "She told me so and so." Allison sighed and went back to her mill girls and a shy boy who could not be induced to talk with any one else, and tried not to worry.

At that moment Bert swallowed a huge bite and washed it down with the entire contents of the tiny teacup, passing it for more. Then he leaned over the little table and said:

"Say, she," nodding his head in the direction Allison had just gone, "has been tryin' this long time to get me to come to one of their young folks' meetin's at the church Sunday night. She's tried every way coaxin' pretty near, an' I won't give in because I used to go there and they put me out fer whisperin', and I said I'd never go in there again. That was five years ago, and I ain't went since. But now she's got a new dodge. She wants me to take my violin next Sunday night and play for them. She's got the pieces picked out she wants me to play an' all. She's goin' to lead the meetin' herself. She's been at me again to-night, but I aint give in yet. But

I'll tell you what I'll do. I do hate to disappoint her, she seems to want it so much, an' if you'll go along an' play my accompaniments I'll do it. I will now."

With which magnanimous offer he leaned proudly back in his chair and swallowed the new cupful at one gulp and began on another cake.

Evelyn was too much taken aback to answer at first. The conceit, the impudence, of the young rascal was swallowed up in her amusement. What would her friends think to her submitting to such talk? But how strange that he should open the way to what she had decided to try to get him to do. If it were not for the absurd condition she would bind the bargain at once, but of course she could not do that. Go and play for this untutored boy at a public meeting and in a church! She never did such a thing in her life. It would not be dignified. And yet, why should she not? There was no one here whom she knew or for whom she cared a whit. No one would tell the story. She might as well enjoy this adventure to the end; there was little enough in this town to enjoy, surely. And this was harmless, only a joke. She felt sure Allison would be pleased.

Just at that moment Mrs. Grey passed through the room and smiled as she saw the two together with a lighting up of her face that reminded one of her son. Evelyn's decision was taken. She turned to the boy and said:

"All right, I will go. But you must bring me your music beforehand to practice."

The company broke up soon after that, and the boy swaggered off between two of the mill girls who laughed and talked so loud you could hear them down the street, and yelled, "Oh, Bert, ain't you too funny!" again and again.

Then Allison, after watching them go down the walk, turned silently and bent her pretty head on her hands and sighed. She was tired and discouraged and did not know how to trust what she had done to her heavenly Father's keeping, and above all did not know how to trust this strange, unwelcome worker who had been forced upon her.

Evelyn on the contrary went to her room well satisfied with her day's work. It was not so stupid after all to be good, if this was being good. She prayed her prayer with more vim and less humility that night, and was perhaps not so near to the kingdom as when she had not expected to be noted for what she had done.

Chapter 13
Allison's Meeting

"Did you say that you were anxious to get that boy to go to church?" asked the guest, as the two girls sat together the next afternoon over a bit of fancy work. Miss Rutherford had offered to show Allison how to make such a sofa pillow as she was embroidering and Allison had been glad to accept. It was not every day she had a chance like that. The conversation, however, so far had been confined to the pillow and the stitch and the way to hold the needle. Now Allison was mastering the difficult operation and the teacher felt at liberty to talk of other things. She had been waiting all day to get the right chance to display her triumph.

"Do you mean Bert Judkins?" asked Allison with quick apprehension, she scarcely knew why. "Yes, I said so. Why, did he talk about it to you?" Her interest in fancy work was for the moment abated. She feared that her work and her prayers were to be of no avail. Bert had been very shy of doing anything he was asked lately. He had even stayed away from Sunday-school several times. Now, doubtless, he had been laughing over her anxiety with this stranger. There was a real pain in her eyes as she looked at Miss Rutherford for an answer.

"Won't you tell me why in the world you care?" asked Evelyn interestedly, not ready to answer Allison's other questions yet.

Allison shrank from replying to this. She felt keenly that the other girl could not understand her motives, and would know no better after she was told. But she had asked and there must be an answer. It was her duty to witness for her Lord before this one as well as before Bert Judkins, though she wished in her heart that it were the rude boy instead of the girl of the world.

"Because I want him to be a Christian."

It seemed to be the only thing to be said but Allison felt it would be like Greek to her questioner.

"Yes, he is a good deal of a heathen," laughed Evelyn; "but tell me why you care? Why don't you just let him alone as he is? What makes you take so much trouble for him, just a young, ignorant boy? I'll admit he is bright and funny sometimes, but he is awfully impudent and ill-bred. I know you can't enjoy him always. What is it that makes you take so much trouble?

In other words, why are you such a good girl?''

Allison's face grew rosy under this and she scarcely knew how to answer. Had she been heart and soul enlisted in helping this stranger who had come within her gates, as others wished and hoped she would be, she would have welcomed this talk with joy and hastened with eagerness to explain her love to her Saviour and through him to all for whom he died. But so thoroughly had she fixed it in her mind that Evelyn Rutherford was beyond the pale of her influence in any possible way that she merely felt now an impulse to guard all sacred things from her polluting gaze. As the blood receded she made answer in almost cold tones:

"My Saviour died for him. If he is worth that he is worth any effort of the Saviour's followers.''

Evelyn looked at her curiously. It was the same language her brother had used more feelingly. She saw that Allison was shy about talking the matter over.

"And what do you expect to do with him after you have got him to church?'' asked Evelyn, after a moment's silence.

"He will hear of Christ, and will little by little begin to realize his love, and will' — she hesitated for a word — "be willing to be Christlike, I hope. And he will learn — he knows already, that we are praying for him.'' Allison spoke softly with her eyes on her work. It was necessary to explain all this, though she had not the least hope it would be understood.

But to Evelyn the words came with memory's reflections. How strange that she should use those words, almost the same that her brother had used in speaking to her. There seemed to be a language spoken among these strange people that was different from that of the world. She had never heard of the shibboleth, but she recognized it now without the knowledge and her heart warmed to the thought in a way that surprised herself. Then there were others going about praying for people in the same way in which he had prayed for her. She was not the only one to have this unique experience. Were there many? Allison had said "we" are praying. Did that mean all those other girls? Their plain faces and commonplace attire suddenly took on a new interest in the mind of the girl who had ignored them.

To Allison's surprise she presently answered in a thoughtful tone: "Yes, I see.'' Then she added with a laugh, "Well, you have your wish. He is coming.''

"Coming?'' said Allison dropping her work. "How do you know? Did he say he would?''

"Yes," said Evelyn with a sudden resolve to say no more yet. Callers came just then and took Allison to the parlor and when she returned Evelyn had gone to her room.

Evelyn managed to be at the door when Bert arrived the next noon with the music as he had promised, and as it happened, Allison had gone to the store on an errand for her mother, so that there was no question of why he had come. The guest with a guilty feeling went to the piano and began to play. The music was all unfamiliar to her except now and then a strain that she seemed to have heard in church; but Allison wondered much on her return to hear the several familiar tunes played over and over again. Once she opened the parlor door and peeped in, but Evelyn seemed to be looking over the church hymn book; doubtless it was curiosity which led her to try them.

The sounds ceased altogether soon and Allison heard her going upstairs. Troubled thoughts were going on in her turbulent young heart. A new difficulty had arisen. They would always arise with a foreign element in the house. There was a question of what to do now, or rather Allison said there was no question, though she knew in her heart there was. She had deliberately determined not to put it before her mother at all. She was fearful of what her mother might say, and in this case her impetuous will was determined.

It was just this. She was appointed to lead the young people's prayer meeting the next evening. It was now Saturday afternoon and she had not yet been able to fix her mind on the theme and prepare. Why? Partly because she felt that her heart was not right before God, and partly because she was troubled by the presence of this stranger. Of course she would not ask Miss Rutherford to accompany her to the meeting; it would not be necessary, nor a thing to be desired in any way. Equally of course, Miss Rutherford would not accept were she to be asked. Miss Rutherford would curl her haughty lip at a prayer meeting wherein the young and unlearned and the *girls* took part. Allison could talk and pray and lead a meeting well before her own circle of acquaintances and she had done it so much that it had ceased to be the terrible cross to her that it was to some, but to do anything in public before this other girl in whose presence her spirit seemed to be a groveling creature, she could not and would not. She had reasoned this out many times till her brain was weary and that night she put the whole matter into a deliberate resolve that she would have no more to do with it, and turned her attention to her preparation. Nevertheless she could not get away from the feeling that she was sneaking off to her meeting and leaving behind a duty undone. She thought she felt a little as Jonah did when he was told to go to Nineveh, only she would not admit that she had been told.

Miss Rutherford attended church in the morning with the family, and enchanted the eyes of the feminine portion of the audience with the hat she wore, though her entire costume, according to New York custom for church-goers, was plain in the extreme. It was the very elegant plainness that turned many eyes in her direction, and marked her a distinguished stranger.

Rebecca Bascomb had done her work thoroughly, and very few present did not know that she was "Miss Joan Rutherford's niece, the daughter of her only brother," and a few added touches that Miss Bascomb affixed according to the gullibility of her audience. There were a few, a choice few, who were given as a delicate morsel an account of her visit at the Greys' the other day.

In the afternoon Allison went to Sunday-school. She had eased her conscience greatly by asking Evelyn if she would care to attend, promising to take her into the young ladies' Bible class if she would, and went away to her work with a lighter heart. If she would not go to Sunday-school naturally she would not expect to be invited to go again that day.

But the afternoon was not all brightness. Allison's boys seemed to have arranged to take a day off from good behavior and fall back into their old ways before she took the class. Especially was Bert Judkins trying. He whispered during prayer time and whistled during the singing, and smiled at Allison seraphically whenever she turned reproving or pleading eyes his way. He growled in low bass whispers something about one of the girls in a classroom across the main aisle, till the other giggled, right in the midst of the most solemn part of the lesson. Allison had put much work into the preparation of that lesson and had hoped it would reach the hearts of two or three of her class in particular. Behold, those were the very boys who seemed most possessed not to listen. When Bert Judkins, during the first hymn that followed the lesson, leaned forward and said he had to go, he had an engagement, with a twinkle that made the other boys nudge each other and giggle, Allison dropped her head on her hand in despair, and if she had been alone would have cried.

Bert, however, did not go. He sat back in his seat and looked at her furtively, noting the sad droop of her mouth, and the discouraged turn of her head, and reflected upon his own behavior. He had not meant to be so trying. He was half ashamed that he had decided to please his teacher that evening, and rather puffed about it on the whole. He was obliged to equalize matters somehow, and hence his spirits during the class. He had known that it would annoy her to have him leave the class before the closing exercises were concluded. It was a part of the code of honor of the school not to run out during prayer and singing and remarks. He had felt that he must do something of this sort in order to hold his own among the boys and in part atone for the part he intended taking in the evening meeting.

But now as he saw her greatly troubled look and knew that she was really anxious over him his face grew thoughtful and the influence that had made him yield and go to the meeting kept him quiet during the remainder of the session. He touched his hat respectfully as he passed her at the classroom door, and did not tumble out over the feet of the other boys as he often had done before, and his teacher, ever watchful, thought he had not altogether forgotten his promise to her that he "would think about" what she had said to him concerning Christ.

However, she sighed deeply as she went home, and wished that it was not her night to lead the meeting. She did not feel in the spirit of it. She had a lurking bitterness toward Miss Rutherford for having in her opinion been the cause of Bert Judkins' behavior in Sunday-school. Just how she did not attempt to tell herself, but her influence was probably to blame in some way.

Just what she would have thought had she known that Miss Rutherford had been faithfully practising hymns ever since she left the house for Sunday-school, and only ceased as she heard the gate click and knew that Allison had returned, it is hard to tell. She was glad when she came in to find the parlor and library deserted, and to hear footsteps above in the guest's room, which told her she would have a little time alone. She went to her own room presently and tried to absorb her mind in the topic for the evening. When that failed to cheer her she knelt beside her bed, but while she was praying for help and strength her mind kept recurring to the thought that perhaps she should invite Miss Rutherford to go with her. She arose by and by and deliberately put her mind to making out her programme for the meeting and selecting her hymns. It was drawing near to the hour and her work must be done. She reasoned with herself that she was growing morbid over the whole thing and that after this meeting was well out of the way she would try to make an opportunity to say something to Miss Rutherford about religion. She must do it, hard as it seemed to her, and useless as she was sure it was, or her conscience would drive her distracted. Why had all her friends so mistakenly selected her as the one to do this work? Why, but because they had failed themselves? The thought was almost bitterly spoken to herself as she went to the glass to smooth her hair. Glancing at her watch she saw to her relief that it really was time to be off. Now in a few minutes she would have to put all possibility of doing that disagreeable thing that conscience kept suggesting, behind her.

She hurried down, declining her mother's offer of some tea, saying she must be there early to find some one to play and arrange about the hymns.

"Perhaps Miss Rutherford would go if you asked her," suggested Mrs. Grey.

There it was again! Mother and conscience! Allison turned with an impatient frown.

"O mother! She would not go, and I could not lead, if she did. I really must hurry. Good-bye. Are you coming to church to-night? There goes the first bell," and Allison was off down the front path before her mother could say more.

It was perhaps five minutes after this that Mrs. Grey heard her guest's door open and the soft swish of descending skirts. The sounds halted several times, and at last Miss Rutherford peeped cautiously into the room, dressed to go out.

"Is she really gone?" she asked merrily, coming in and sitting down to button her dainty gloves.

"Who? Allison? Did you intend going with her? Why, that is too bad —" began Mrs. Grey, with a troubled expression.

"Oh, no, indeed, I was not going with her. I have been avoiding her all the afternoon lest she should ask me. You see I'm in league with that absurd boy of hers, and we were going to give her a little surprise. He and I are going to play for her to-night, and she doesn't know it yet. It is all right for me to do it, is it not, Mrs. Grey? I never did such a thing before in my life, but he said he would go to church and play as she had asked him if I would go with him and play the accompaniments. It's really very funny, and I don't know how I came to say 'yes,' but I did. And then I thought it would be rather interesting to surprise her. There he comes now. Is it surely all right for me to go? Is it very public? Will many be there?"

"It is all right, dear, and I am very glad you are trying to help that boy too. Allison will be so glad. She has put a good deal of work and prayer on him."

Mrs. Grey put out her hand with that inviting motion she had and Evelyn before she realized what she was going to do stooped gracefully and kissed her hostess on the forehead. Then she went to the door to meet her young escort, who was resplendent in a new necktie and well plastered hair.

But Evelyn, as she walked beside him in the twilight, was marveling why she had given that kiss. Whence had come that impulse? Were there depths in her nature which she knew not of, which had never been sounded at yet? And what was it that was stirring her so unexpectedly among these strange people?

They walked demurely into the chapel, those two who had planned the surprise. The room was fast filling up but no one had come yet who could play. Allison sat doubtfully regarding the piano stool at her left, and wondered if she must take up her cross and play too, as well as lead. There were none of her boys here. Bert must have been joking when he told Miss Rutherford he was coming. She had hoped one or two others would come, but she had not seen them hovering around the gate when she came in, as they would have been sure to, she thought, if they were coming. Her heart felt heavy and discouraged. She did not raise her eyes to see who was coming down the aisle toward the front seats; she was intent on finding a hymn that she could play for an opening without giving much thought to her music. She wanted to be able to think what to do next. It was very embarrassing to have to play and lead at the same time. If only some one would come! She bent her head over her Bible in a little desperate prayer that Mamie Atkins or some one who could play just a little even would be sent quickly. Then she raised her eyes to behold suddenly before her, sitting as composedly as if they were accustomed to that seat on every Sabbath evening, Miss Rutherford and Bert Judkins! And Miss Rutherford was taking off her gloves! Could it be possible? And the young lady was smiling, a really merry smile. Was this the Miss Rutherford who could be so cold and haughty?

Suddenly Allison's cheek grew crimson. She remembered her goading conscience and her undone duty, the invitation ungiven, and the intention ungracious. And here had been help and a degree of sympathy, and God had been trying to show it to her through her conscience, and she would not hear nor answer the call to duty. She looked at Bert, saw his expression of sheepish delight in pleasing her, flashed him a happy smile of thanks and then another at Miss Rutherford. Allison was one who forgave royally when she saw she ought to do so. She came at once to the young woman's side:

"How good of you to come," she said in a low tone. "And I never even asked you if you would like to. Will you forgive me?" Then to Bert: "O Bert, I am so glad!" and the boy looked down at his violin and felt fully repaid in his heart for all the embarrassment among his kind that his had occasioned, and resolved to do it again if it made her as glad as that.

Chapter 14
"Yours Dismally, Dick"

The evening was to Evelyn a remarkable experience. In the first place had come her surprise at Allison's "Will you forgive me?" When had any one ever asked her forgiveness before? She could see that Allison was really in earnest, and about so trivial a thing too, as a neglect to invite her to go to church. It gave her a little inkling of the place that meeting held in Allison's heart. It also showed her that Allison regarded her for some reason as outside the sacred, privileged circle who might enter here.

She and Bert did their part well. The piano and violin together sounded a grand keynote for the singing, and the many fresh, untrained voices took up the music and sang with a will. At first Evelyn felt almost inclined to stop playing and turn around to watch and listen. It seemed her playing was not needed. The music swept on in high, sweet melody, even though the voices were some of them harsh and most of them more or less crude. There was in the singing a quality of true praise that rose above all little discords as if the sound of angel voices mingled in the air above their heads. Evelyn almost fancied there was a wonderful hidden instrument above somewhere like an Æolian harp, and in spite of herself raised her head to look when the song was over. She had never played for a large company to sing before and was astonished at the result. And how suddenly they hushed as they took their seats again. Allison was standing by the little table up in front talking, with her head bowed. Why, she was praying! Actually, a girl — a woman — praying before others! Evelyn felt the blood tingle in her own veins at the very idea. How dreadful it must be to do that! How could she? But her voice was sweet and clear: "Father in heaven, forgive us for our mistakes and our foolish willfulness, and undo any harm we may have done, and help us to show others that we love thee."

There it was again - that same loyalty to the One, Christ Jesus. The brother had talked that way too. She began to perceive the possibility of the wideness and the sweetness of such a tie.

Of the reading, songs, and prayers which followed, and the part taken actively and eagerly by many of the young people, Evelyn had very indistinct ideas afterward. It was a series of surprises. It was as new to her, nay, more novel, than to the wide-awake, interested boy by her side. He had been there before, though five years ago. He knew well who took part. To Evelyn it was like being set down in another world.

She and Bert Judkins played, when Allison gave them a sign, and though they had not practiced together, the result was very sweet. Evelyn entered into the music; especially did she do so when, at the close of a series of exceedingly brief prayers, Allison motioned them to play "Just as I am, without one plea." They had known she would call for it soon and were seated, ready. Very softly the unexpected strains floated out, like far-away, heavenly music. Allison rejoiced in her heart that Evelyn knew when to play softly, and had in some way succeeded in toning down Bert and his violin, which loved to soar loudly. Perhaps Bert too, was softened by the hour and the spirit of the meeting. The tender music filled the room and every head remained bowed. Just when the last note lingered tremblingly, Allison's sweet voice, tremulous with suppressed feeling, took the key and started them softly singing:

> Just as I am, thy love unknown,
>   Hath broken every barrier down;
> Now to be thine, yea, thine alone,
> O Lamb of God, I come!

Evelyn was not familiar with the words of this hymn; it was not an old household, church-time, childhood memory. More quickly to her lips would rise the phrases of the latest opera. But she had practiced this tune over and over, for the melody had caught her as being very tender, and though she had not realized it, the words had been before her and fixed themselves in her mind. Now, as she listened to them, voiced in what seemed a sweet and earnest prayer, she realized that the words had become her own property. "Thy love unknown, thy love unknown," kept going over in her mind during the remainder of the evening. Yes, that was the love Doctor Grey had told her about. She began to feel that there was an unrecognized relation between herself and Christ. Would that love unknown some day break down every barrier and bring her to him? It was the first time the possibility of such a happening really had come to her and it startled her. She tried to put it aside to study this curious gathering, but it would keep recurring to her from time to time.

When the meeting was out and Allison stood a moment talking to the pastor, who had come in toward the close, Evelyn turned to Bert: "Now, I want you to stay to church," she told him with an air of command which evidently pleased that young gentleman. He smiled a knowing smile and twinkled his eyes in a mischievous way.

"All right. I'm in fer the whole business," he remarked jauntily. "Got the rest of the gang outside waiting fer me to come fer 'em. I made 'em all come and we're goin' to occupy a front seat. Guess she'll get enough of us fer once," and he looked toward his teacher with that mingling of reverence and impudence which can only be possible on the face of a boy of that age and class.

Sure enough! The opening hymn was just being read when in filed twelve boys led by Bert Judkins, who had disencumbered himself of his violin. Down the long side aisle they came, embarrassed and grinning and almost falling over one another's feet in the long transit, but into a side seat near the front they all finally got themselves noisily seated, drawing the attention of many an astonished pillar of the church.

Allison had quickly bowed her head when she first saw them, and when a moment later she raised it, there were tears in her eyes, mingled with the pleasure in her face she could not conceal. They each in turn stole furtive glances back to their teacher and received her answering welcome smile and thereafter sat like twelve statues, listening respectfully, save during the singing, in which they joined with fervor.

Evelyn looked and wondered and pondered. What did it all mean, this new world into which she had come? It was not without interest to her. She felt that she had some part in it. She even caught the spirit and exulted the least little bit when all those boys came in. Anyway, it was less dull than any church service she had ever attended before. One service a day was as much as she ever forced herself to attend, and even that was only merely a Sabbath evening "sacred" concert.

Later that evening Allison stole timidly to Miss Rutherford's door and knocked. Evelyn, in pretty negligee of soft pink cashmere, opened the door and invited her in with a look of surprise.

Allison's golden-hued hair was all down about her shoulders in a shining wealth of waves, and Evelyn sat watching the delicate face in its lovely setting that looked like the halo of some saint.

"I couldn't sleep," said Allison, "till I had come and told you how wicked I have been. I did not want to invite you to go to the meeting with me lest you would laugh at me. And now you have been so good as to come without asking and influenced my boys, at least one of them, to come, and I want to thank you."

"You absurd child," said Evelyn, laughing; "you needn't trouble your conscience about that. It was quite a lark. I was richly repaid when I saw your face as those great hulking boys stumbled into church. Now go to bed and don't worry any more."

"But there is something else," said Allison hesitating and twisting a long lock of bright hair around her finger. "I want to ask you if you are a Christian?" The ready crimson mantled her face as she said it, but she looked bravely up at Evelyn. That young lady laughed.

"No," she answered gayly; "I'm a heathen. Bert and I are about alike. You'll have to think of some way to get hold of me." Then another swift impulse seized her for which she could not account and she stooped and kissed the pure white forehead and said in a voice of smothered feeling: "You are a dear little girl, and I wish I were half as good as you, Allison."

Her duty done, the worn-out little Christian slipped back to her bed, marveling much at this strange girl who had so many different sides to her nature. And she had called her "Allison" with something tender in the accent and had said she wished she were good. There must be more in her after all than one would think. Perhaps there were in most people. There were her rough, uncouth boys. It was easy for her to see the good hid beneath their unpolished exterior; but when it came to a girl of the world like Miss Rutherford, Allison had felt there was little good there to look for. She had been mistaken surely. She was wrong. Her brother was right, as he always used to be when they were children and any question came up for discussion. He always took the mild, charitable side and his sister the impulsive, prejudiced, critical. Well, at least she had done her duty at last. The other girl had admitted that she was not a Christian, and now it became her duty to pray for her; yes, and to work for her too, if there was any way in which she could work. Why was it that it was not so easy to try to influence her as it was that class of boys? She must examine into this. Of course it was God's work just as much. And it was apparent from what Miss Rutherford — could she ever call her Evelyn? — had said that she had been wrong too, in supposing she had no influence with her.

She fell asleep at last, weary with turning the problem over in her mind. To-morrow she would try to do better.

" 'Tomorrow,' whispereth weakness, and to-morrow findeth him the weaker, 'To-morrow,' promiseth conscience; and behold, no to-day for a fulfillment."

Allison found those lines not long after and remembered and searched out some others she had known a long time and printed them together on a card which she placed on her wall for her reminder in the duties that should come to her in future:

> To-morrow, oh 'twill never be
>   If we should live a thousand years!
> Our time is all to-day, to-day,
>   The same, though changed; and while it flies,
> With still small voice the moments say,
>   "To-day, to-day, be wise, be wise."

The morning dawned bright and clear, and the early mail brought a letter for Evelyn. She took it up to her room to read. It bore a Philadelphia postmark, and was written in a cramped hand, as if the writer were in an uncomfortable position. It read as follows:

DEAR SISTER: Your letter with its plaint has just reached me. I had forgotten the outlandish name of the place where Aunt Joan resides or I would have sent for you a week ago. I am in a worse fix than you even. In short, I'm laid up in a dismal hotel room with a broken leg. I slipped on a miserable little piece of orange peel and fell down three small stone steps right here in the hotel. I never knew before that legs broke so easily, and I didn't believe them when they told me it was broken, except for the abominable pain that made me faint dead away several times. If I had had my sense about me I would have been sent straight to the hospital, but they had me up in my room and the bones set before I knew what I was about, and here I am with a man to look after me. I have sent for John, but I am not sure I can reach him, as he went off to some back country place to visit his mother. If you have a mind to come on and stay here at the hotel I'll do my level best at chaperoning you as well as I can from my bed. It would be a relief at least to me to see a familiar face once a day. I have not sent a word to any of our acquaintances here, for the simple reason that I feel too simple at my accident to have them know about it. If I had been thrown from a horse or hurt in rescuing a young lady from a burning building there would be a halo of glory about me, and I could afford to hold *soireés* for my friends and be admired and pitied; but a man who can't stand up on a level landing and avoid a single square inch of orange peel is too insignificant even for pity.

Of course, if your quarantine is raised and you have found someone to flirt with and don't want to come, do as you please. But I thought this might be a little better than smallpox. I shall doubtless get on my feet some day if I live long enough, or don't get desperate and shoot myself. In the meantime this is the best I can do for you, and I guess daddy will excuse you for coming to nurse your broken-up brother. If he doesn't, I'll shoulder all blame. Yours dismally,

DICK.

Evelyn read this letter with mingled emotions. Ordinarily this invitation would have been anything but attractive to her. She was not a born nurse; she did not like to be with sick people; there had never been any deep, tender feeling between her brother and herself; and she had not many friends in Philadelphia. Nevertheless, Hillcroft was destitute of occupation for her unless she undertook the reformation of Bert Judkins, or his like, for which she did not feel particularly qualified. The waiting here was likely to be long and tedious if she had to stay till her aunt was out of quarantine, and she felt nervous about going to her even after everything was pronounced safe. Undoubtedly her father would be satisfied if Dick chose to send for her, and the change would be a real relief. Meantime, underneath all these questions which she weighed deliberately, there was an undertone of desire, or perhaps it was only willingness, to do something for someone else which would be accounted good in herself. In other words, she had watched the unselfish lives of those around her long enough to wish to work out a little salvation for herself. And so, without much thought, and certainly not "with fear and trembling," but with a full degree of assurance of success, she set out to work salvation for herself. She would be good to Dick, poor fellow! It was hard for him to be shut up there when he had expected to go off hunting in a few days. There had always been a certain degree of fondness between them, but never the deep affection — at least not suspected by themselves — that there was between Allison Grey and her brother. Evelyn wondered now, as she hurried downstairs to make known her decision to her hostess, if there ever could be cultivated such a tie between herself and Dick as existed between Doctor Grey and his sister. She felt a faint yearning for something of the sort. It would be nice to have one's brother care as much as that.

To do her justice, she was not anxious to shine virtuously before any human beings. She wished only to feel satisfied in her own heart that she had been doing some good to some one else, and — yes, before that other One, Christ. She would like to feel less small when she knelt to make that daily petition. It occurred to her on the way downstairs that it would be much pleasanter if Dick had fallen down in New York instead of Philadelphia. Perhaps he might have sent for his friend Doctor Grey. She would like to meet him again, though perhaps it was just as well, after all, not to, for she desired above all things to get away from the unrest with which the strange new thoughts had filled her.

Mrs. Grey fully agreed with her guest that she ought to go to her brother, and a message was sent by the doctor over the telephone to the quarantined aunt, who also cheerfully acquiesced in the arrangement.

Evelyn packed her trunks hurriedly as she discovered that she could leave by the noon train and make connection with the Philadelphia sleeper. There was no time to talk; everything was confusion and hurry. Almost before they were aware, their guest was gone and Allison was unhitching the pony from the post across the road and driving away from the station. She drove slowly and sighed several times. She could not tell whether she was glad or sorry that Miss Rutherford was gone. She felt that her attitude during her stay had been a mistake, and that she had let many opportunities for witnessing for Christ go by unheeded. She would be glad to live that part of her life over and do better, but on the whole it was a relief to her to have the dear home nest to themselves once more. Miss Rutherford was a person from too different a world to ever be congenial. Life with her had been at too high tension to be comfortable. Allison was glad to come in sight of the loved home and know that her round of pleasant duties would be again uninterrupted. Miss Rutherford had said, "You must come to New York and see me some time. I should love to show you New York." It had been spoken very cordially, but Allison meant never to go. She shuddered at the thought. What questions of right and wrong she would have to meet, what constant challenging of her views! How little her tastes would blend with the probable Rutherford home life! What agonies of social etiquette all new to her would she have to face! Never! Never!

Does our heavenly Father sometimes smile at our fierce assertion of what we will and will not do, seeing in his loving kindness that this is the very thing we need most, and forthwith brings it to us, that we may bear and learn and then give him glory when we understand?

Chapter 15
On a Mission to Dick

Evelyn was seated in the parlor car with her belongings about her, the neat farms and pleasant homes once more whirling past her, and Hillcroft a thing of history. She could not help remembering the journey thither and comparing her anticipation with the actual facts. How different it had been from what she had planned! She had not even seen her Aunt Joan. She found to her surprise a lingering disappointment about that now. She had lived for nearly three weeks where Miss Joan Rutherford was a loved and honored member of society. She had learned to respect her from what she had heard of her, if she did not love her yet, and now that she was actually speeding away from Hillcroft, she began to think how disappointed her father would be when he learned she had been there without even seeing his dear sister. For she knew that his sister was dear to him, even though he was a man who seldom spoke of his personal feelings. He always answered her letters promptly and insisted upon his children doing the same, much to their dislike; she could remember that one of the few times when he had punished her most severely was because she had spoken disrespectfully of this aunt. For the first time in her life it occurred to her that her father led a lonely life. It had seemed his natural part and she had never thought he needed anything else. She loved him, of course, and supposed he loved her, but they never exhibited this love in any way. What a difference it would make in their home if there were such ways as they had at the Greys'. Would her father care to have her meet him when he came home at night and kiss him? Could she do it? What if she should try? She began to realize that it was not all her father's fault that their home life was cold and each one went his separate way. Could it be that her father was lonely and would like his daughter to be affectionate and companionable? It must have been hard to have his young wife die and leave him with two children to bring up. He had his business, true, and perhaps all his thought and feeling had been absorbed into that. Still, she could remember times when he would drop his paper across his knee and sit back in his chair with a sad expression and his eyes shaded. Was he recalling his early life and dreams then? How strange that she had never thought of her father in this way before! Perhaps she might be a little good, like Allison, if she attempted to make things a trifle pleasanter for her father and brother. Suppose she should sometime be changed into such a girl as Allison. It couldn't be done, of course, but suppose it could. What would they all think of her, her father and brother and the servants? What would Jane think? And what would Mr. Worthington think? Yes, and what would Doctor Grey think? Ah, but he would never know, and why should she take all this trouble, anyway? Oh, dear! Life was a dismal thing at best. She was anxious to get back once more into the whirl of things and forget all this fanaticism. It was actually getting into her brain. She wished she had something to read. True, there was in her bag a tiny volume Allison had given her when she left her at the train, but she could see at a glance that it was more of this uncomfortable religion which she hoped she was leaving behind in Hillcroft. She wanted something better. She rang for the porter and asked him to summon the news agent with some books from which she could select one. He came whistling in from the door behind her chair, slamming it after him, and at the porter's sign dumped his pile of books in the aisle by her chair, while he selected a few for her scrutiny.

"Did you want a love story, ma'am, or some real blood and thunder? This here book is —" He stopped with an exclamation. "Hello! Is this you? You ain't goin' home so soon, are you?"

She raised her eyes with freezing dignity to the saucy, handsome ones above her and beheld Bert Judkins.

"I'm taking this feller's route while he's sick. I could get it permanent if I was to try, 'cause he's tired of it, but she" — he paused and nodded back toward Hillcroft — "she's awful set against it. She says I'll have to run Sunday, and I s'pose I will. But a feller's got to live, though she won't allow that. She says you've only got to do right and starve if you ain't looked after. There ain't any 'got' about living. Course, if that's the way you look at it, she's 'bout right, an' if I decide to do what she wants, I sha'n't try fer this. Say, has she roped you into this thing too, or are you one of'em? I didn't think you was quite their kind, but you're a jolly player."

He piled his books at her feet and seated himself familiarly in the chair next to hers, which happened to be vacant.

It was a trifle amusing and also embarrassing. Bert Judkins in the parlor of her hostess as an amateur violinist, among people who knew him and for whom she did not care, and Bert Judkins as newsagent on a parlor car filled with elegant strangers was two different beings. However, they were all strangers to her, and she glanced about and decided it did not matter in the least. She could, of course, order him off or send for the porter, but she had tasted of the joy of helping on a good cause, and to her credit, be it said, it did not occur to her to go back upon her one-time *protege* in this way.

He did not stay long. His business called him away soon, but he managed to get in a good deal of talk and a few troublesome questions.

"Did you say she'd roped you in?" he asked again, without the least consciousness of being impudent. Evelyn colored and understood. Was this boy even going to keep it up? She turned him off again and again. But he was keen enough to understand that she knew from the way he changed his conversation. It was as if he felt a responsibility upon him to do or say something that his teacher would have done were she in his place. He was awkward at it, but he was never shy.

"I say," he said, when she had for the fifth time turned off his question by picking up a book and examining it, "mebbe you'd make another partnership affair of it. I don't know as I'm just ready to say I'd do what she wants yet myself, but mebbe bime-by I'd say yes, if you would. Something like we did Sunday night, you know."

"Well, you let me know when you are ready," said Evelyn quickly, glad to have a chance to get out of the thing and at the same time say nothing to hinder Allison's work.

"I will, that's a bargain," said he with a brisk business-like air, "and I guess I'm about made up not to go on the railroad 'count o' Sunday travel, anyway not till I'm sure about the whole shootin' match."

With which elegant and reverent expression he whirled himself and his books into the next car and left Evelyn in a state bordering on hysterics. It was silly, of course, to mind what the uncouth boy had said, but again and again his sharp questions came back, making her think of other questions as searching, but asked in quiet, cultured tones. How was it that this thing seemed to pursue her as she went? Well, that boy would leave at Pittsburgh and then she would deliberately settle herself to forget it all.

Bert was very busy during the remainder of the way to Pittsburgh. He did not have time for talk. He paid her little delicate attentions that any gentleman might have done, perhaps, and she knew it was for Allison's sake. He came in with a book he had found among the stock, "The Sky Pilot," which he told her was "a dandy" and "she" was "awful fond of," and another time he quietly laid a box of Huyler's best chocolates in her lap. She showed her appreciation of these attentions by a quiet smile and would not offend him by offering to pay for what she knew he gave for love of his teacher, though she resolved to make it up to him when she should be where she could select some good music for him, which she would send through Allison.

Just before the train rushed into Pittsburgh he halted by her seat, pencil and note-book in hand.

"Where did you say you lived in New York?" he demanded. "Sixty-fourth Street? What number? I might be there some day and then I'll call and see you. Good-bye. Hope you have a good journey. Sorry you can't play for me some more. Mebbe you'll come back again some day. Ta ta," and with a familiar wave of his hand he swung himself out the door much to her relief, as other passengers were gathering about preparatory to leaving the car and looking curiously at the ill-assorted couple.

He appeared to her again as she was trying to find a place where a decent supper could be obtained, and pushed into her hands another volume. "It's 'Black Rock,' " he explained, "The other one. I knew you'd want to read it too. I got it off the agent in the station. There goes my return whistle," and off he went this time without the parting sentence which she had been dreading.

What had she done? Given him her New York address! What if he should suddenly appear there some day with his familiar "ta ta" and his strange mixing of subjects and pointed personal questions? He certainly would create a sensation. Nevertheless, as she settled herself in the sleeper two hours later she had to admit to herself that Bert Judkins had enlivened her lonely journey for her that afternoon and that she had him to thank for the two fascinating books into which she had dipped enough to know that they contained food for future thought. Gwen's Canon was to be to her a study. She did not understand it now. The canon in her own life which would come some day, as yet seemed so impossible that she could but stand outside the story of this other girl and wonder.

Finally the experiences of the day and, to a certain extent, of the past three weeks, faded somewhat and she began to look forward to to-morrow and its possibilities. As she thought of her brother lying in a gloomy hotel room she felt a pity for him new to her. Her own position as nurse was strongly influenced by the atmosphere in which she had been moving lately. A month ago she would have been going to Philadelphia more for her own sake than her brother's. Now the feeling of help for him was strong upon her and grew as she sped nearer to him. Something like love glowed in her heart. Of course it was love. She had always loved her brother, in a way, but she did not remember to have ever realized it before, except the time they thought he was drowned, for a few hours, when he was a little fellow. And yet he was a lovable fellow, handsome and bright and scholarly. His tastes were much like hers, but they had been separated during late years. She had been away to school and he to college, and afterward they each had their friends and engagements and came and went without much reference to each other, a fashion the Rutherfords had. Evelyn began to see that this had been her fault largely, for it is the woman of a home who keeps the home the center of the life of the family. A man does not know how to do it. She resolved at least to make some little changes in the way she had been doing. There was no reason why she should not have more of her brother's society. It might be very convenient, and she certainly envied Allison the love of such a brother. It would at least give her something to do. Yes, she would try to be more sisterly to poor Dick and see how it worked. Of course she would not do anything outlandish, but this was the spirit of what Doctor Grey had wanted her to do, she recognized that, the spirit of Christianity. At least it was the spirit he and his family showed and she would try on a bit of it and see how it fitted. With this reflection and the hurried prayer which was fast becoming a habit, she fell asleep.

Philadelphia looked almost as dismal as Pittsburgh in the early morning light. The air was full of a fine cold mist and the streets were wet and sticky. She took a cab and drove to the hotel at which her brother was staying. She sent up to find out how he was and word came down from the nurse that he was awake and very restless. Then she went up at once. She had not sent word she was coming, nor sent up her name by the porter, so her entrance was an entire surprise.

Mr. Richard Rutherford had lain awake nearly all night. He was suffering somewhat, but his main trouble seemed to be nervousness, the nurse explained, as he met Evelyn at the door. He had declared he would not lie there any longer, and demanded to be allowed to turn over or move or do something forbidden, until the nurse was well-nigh out of patience. He stood at the door, heavy-eyed, telling the story in a half-complaining tone to Evelyn and the patient called him in no pleasant voice from within. Something in her brother's intonation roused all the womanliness and motherliness and loveliness in the girl. She saw in a flash how some woman was needed, their mother if she had lived, perhaps — if she had been such a woman as Mrs. Grey. What peace and comfort Mrs. Grey would bring into the forlorn room in a little while! She saw as in a vision how she might try it herself; that this was meant for her to do, that it would be a good and right thing to do; and she seemed to know at once that it would be difficult because of her unaccustomedness and because of her ease-loving nature. Then without more ado she resolved to do it, at least for a few minutes or hours, till this need should pass. She would be Mrs. Grey, or Allison, as far as she knew how. She put the nurse aside without ceremony and entered. Going softly to the bedside where her brother lay, white and suffering and

impatient, she stooped over and kissed him gently on the forehead. She
reflected afterward that she was getting into a great habit of kissing people,
and it was rather nice after all, much as she used to despise it. It touched
her to see her brother's look of pleased surprise as she kissed him and said:

"You poor dear! I am so sorry for you!" Her words were from her
heart too, which surprised her even more. She had never had much to draw
out her sympathy and knew not that her soul contained any.

"Oh, Evelyn, is that you?" he said, eagerly grasping her hand. "Nobody ever looked so good before. I've been in this wretched spot for ages it
seems to me. Last night was a purgatory. That nurse is a fool!"

Evelyn meantime was swiftly taking off wraps and hat and noting with
observing eye what was needed. How could she the most quickly make him
comfortable? His forehead was hot when she kissed him. His eager
response to her greeting touched her more than she cared to show. She laid
hands upon a clean towel and tipped it unceremoniously into the ice pitcher
and went over to him to bathe his face and hands.

"Oh, how good that feels!" he said, closing his eyes and submitting to
her gentle passes on face and hands. "Why didn't that fellow think of it
when I felt as if my head was on fire. He is as stupid as a boiled owl."

The nurse meanwhile had taken advantage of the presence of the lady to
slip into the hall to tell his grievances to a sympathetic chambermaid, who
was answering calls from early risers and hovering near a linen closet.

Evelyn wiped her brother's face and hands gently and straightened his
bedclothes. She found his hair brush and brushed his hair. Then after ringing for a maid and a bill of fare she ordered up a dainty breakfast, and
strange to say she did not select expensive dainties such as she had been
used to do, but chose rather some of the plain, homely things which she
remembered as tasting so good at Hillcroft. They would not be so good as
Allison's, of course, but perhaps their very homeliness might coax Dick to
taste them.

He watched her as she moved about, setting a chair at just the right
angle here, opening a blind and arranging a curtain there. The room
looked like a different place since she had come into it. He had always
known that his sister was beautiful; but he had never noticed that tender,
lovely expression of womanliness that she wore this gray morning. Had it
always been there and he too blind to see it, or had some new influence
come into her life? He felt his heart quicken with a new feeling toward her.

When the breakfast came up she sent the heavy-eyed nurse to get something to eat while she remained and fed her brother herself and ate her
breakfast there with him from the same tray. The Evelyn he thought he

knew would have taken her breakfast before she came up to see him at all and then have left things to the hired nurse. This Evelyn seemed to know beforehand what he wanted. When the breakfast was over she darkened the room and soothed him to sleep by gentle passes of her hand across his forehead, utterly refusing to talk until he should have had a good long rest. She had seen Allison put her father to sleep in this way more than once when he came home in the evening with a hard headache after an unusually trying day. It was marvelous how much her three weeks' visit had taught her. There was not a turn she had to take now but something Mrs. Grey or Allison had done guided her in her untried way. It was strange they should influence her so, she thought. She forgot that they were almost the only people she had ever watched about homely work-a-day life. She sat for a while in the darkened room while her brother slept and thought about it all, and wondered what she should do next, and if she would be able to carry out her new character till Dick was well. Then she shut her lips a good deal as Allison had done and resolved that she would; after that she set herself to see what she could do to make the room more homelike.

When Richard Rutherford awoke after a long, refreshing sleep he thought that he had been moved to another place. The sun had come out and the curtains were drawn back to let a flood of it across the room. This had been done as he showed signs of waking. There was a glowing fire in the hitherto cold, black grate, and his sister in a crimson dress sat in a little rocking-chair by it with her feet on the fender. A large bright screen kept the light from hurting his eyes and the delicate perfume of Jacqueminot roses floated through the air from a large bowlful on a little stand near the bed, which also contained several new books and the morning paper.

Chapter 16
Miss Rutherford Plays Nurse

The transforming of that stiff angular dreary hotel room into a homelike spot was not a difficult thing for Evelyn Rutherford to accomplish. She was a girl who generally achieved what she set about. The reason she did not often do nice things was that she did not rouse herself from her own pleasure or ease to take the trouble. Now, however, it pleased her whim to leave no stone unturned to make this first attempt at goodness a success. Perhaps the very energy she put into this and the strange vagaries into which her fancy led her were only the ways in which she eased the pains of a newly aroused conscience which she knew not how to soothe to sleep again, or at least she had at hand none of her other means of doing so.

It was not difficult to do nice things with plenty of money and taste at command. She had known at a glance what was needed, and sent a messenger boy out to one of the great stores nearby with a written order for a few articles to be delivered on approval. After the boy had started down the hall a new thought came to her and she recalled him and added an order for a few plainly framed good pictures, within a certain price, to be sent, from which she could make a selection. Perhaps it was these as much as anything else which gave the "at home" air to the room when Richard Rutherford awoke, though he did not at first notice them. His sister had selected them by fancy rather than knowledge, for she was not an art student and did not judge pictures by their worth, only by the way they spoke to her. She had chosen from the lot sent over to her some horses' heads and dogs by Rosa Bonheur, a pretty etching, and Hoffman's child head of Christ. It was a curious collection. She knew that her brother was fond of horses and dogs. The Hoffman she had seen at the Greys' and been struck by the wonderful expression of the face, and a fancied likeness in the eyes of Doctor Grey. That it was supposed to represent the boy Christ Jesus, strange to say, she did not know until after she had bought it. She had this hung on the wall opposite the foot of the bed, and when her brother began to notice the pictures this was the first one his eyes rested upon.

He lay quietly looking about him for a moment when he first awoke. There was a restful, homelike quiet prevading the room. His sister had her head turned away from him and seemed to be thinking. The nurse was nowhere to be seen. The door opened softly and the doctor stepped in. The patient looked up with a smile.

"Why, you look more cheerful to-day, and what's happened to the place? It bears the touches of a woman's hand." He glanced about, and then seeing Evelyn, who had arisen in surprise and was standing by the mantel, a half-suppressed "Ah!" escaped him.

Evelyn wondered if it was her imagination that detected a note of pride in her brother's voice as he said: "My sister, Doctor MacFarlan, come all the way from Ohio to coddle me." At least, whether it were fancy or truth, it went far toward strengthening Evelyn's purpose in her new way. Ways of carrying out her plan crowded into her mind thick and fast. She actually began to plan for self-sacrifice, a thing she had always detested. It made her feel more virtuous when she had done something to please her brother to know that it had cost her an effort, or the surrender of something which made life pleasanter.

When the doctor was gone and the nurse had made his patient as comfortable as was possible, Evelyn ordered dinner. This time the table was set by the bedside in regular order, the roses in the center and everything as dainty as if she were serving a luncheon at home. This became the established way of taking their meals. Evelyn did not attempt to go down to the dining room at all, but stayed with her brother after she found that it seemed pleasanter to him. It is true this did not require much sacrifice on her part, as she was alone and would not enjoy dining by herself, but she liked to think she was doing a good deal by this little act. Indeed, in the days that followed she began to feel that she could almost compete with Allison herself for deeds of valor and sanctity. She intended to make up for it by a gay season in New York when this siege was over, but in the meantime why not cover herself with glory and still her conscience? So she wrought diligently, even arising at night once or twice to bathe her brother's aching head and read aloud to him when she heard from her adjoining room his restless moans and knew he could not sleep.

She gained for all this devotion a tender acknowledgment once, "Oh, you are a good sister!" This went farther into her heart than all her self-praise had done and brought her nearer to her brother. Nevertheless there were days when he was cross and hard to manage and soothe. And in these days she would have found it easy to return to her former habitual haughtiness and let him entirely alone, were it not for her growing interest in her experiment.

All this time her little daily prayer was uttered with a growing complacency and a tendency to forget its import, to merely continue the habit as a sort of talisman to keep her right in the eyes of a man whom she respected and honored.

It was the afternoon of her arrival that they had their talk about the Greys.

"I don't remember to have seen that Hoffman before," said the young man, looking earnestly at a picture hanging on the wall in front of him. "Where did it come from? Nor in fact any of these other pictures," looking around curiously. "I have not been moved, have I? This surely is the same room, for I have counted the cracks in the ceiling enough times to have them indelibly impressed on my memory, and that surely is the same little imp glaring at me from the wallpaper. I cannot be mistaken. How did you manage it, Evelyn? Are you a magician, to wave a wand and bring forth beauties everywhere?"

Evelyn smiled. It was pleasant to have her efforts noticed.

"Oh, I sent over to W —'s for some pictures and chose a few I thought you would like. What did you call that head you were looking at? A Hoffman? Who is it supposed to be? They had it in Hillcroft, and Allison was very fond of it. It seems a remarkable face. I was glad they sent it over, for I always liked it."

"Why, Evelyn, don't you know that picture? It is from the famous painting of the child Christ in the temple, by Hoffman," said the brother, who was more of a devotee of art than his sister and knew pictures and their artists, by name at least.

Evelyn started and actually flushed, she knew not why. Was this then the Christ picture? Was that why it had appealed so to her? And the likeness of Doctor Grey. Had she not heard in that young people's meeting in Hillcroft something said about the followers of Christ growing into his image, or likeness? whether from the Bible or elsewhere she knew not. Was this, then, the explanation? Of course the picture was but a figment of the artist's imagination, anyway, for no one knew how the real Christ looked, but still she could not understand the ideal. And this ideal Christ-expression was the same she had noted in his follower on that hill-top as he looked off and saw in fancy the opening heavens and his coming Lord.

Evelyn turned away from the picture with a sigh almost of impatience. Was this thing then to pursue her everywhere? Could she get away from it in no way? Here she had deliberately chosen this picture and now she could no more look at it in comfort. How annoying that she should not have known! Of course she had supposed it was some religious character or some saint, but not the Christ himself.

"No, I did not know what it was supposed to represent," said Evelyn slowly. "Perhaps you would rather have some other picture hanging there where you have to look at it all the time. We can exchange any of these."

"No, leave it," he said, looking at it thoughtfully. "It is a fine face and I like to study it. There is such buoyancy of youth and entire hopefulness in the face. It rests one. Somehow I shall not dare complain so much with the cheerful countenance over there. Who is this Allison you speak of? This is a peculiar name. I don't remember ever to have heard it before. Does it belong to man, woman, or child?"

Evelyn laughed. "Allison Grey is a very beautiful girl, Dick. You would simply rave over her, and say she ought to be painted and 'sculped' and have poetry written to her, and all those things your artist friends do. She lives in Hillcroft, and it was in her home I was staying, much against my will. Oh, no, it was not uncomfortable. I assure you I was treated most delightfully, and now that it is past I look back upon the experience as something rich. I don't know but I was rather sorry to come away after all. I never was in a place where people seemed to think so much of one another and of their home, before. Allison is Dr. Maurice Grey's sister. You remember him, do you not?"

"Grey? Why, surely. You don't say! How peculiar! I remember now, he did live out West somewhere, but I never bothered my head to learn where. Odd to think he lived in the same town with our revered aunt and we never knew it. The world isn't so large after all, is it? Grey was a good fellow. We would have been close chums if he had not been so overwhelmingly busy all the time. When he was not buried in his books he was out slumming or off at a prayer meeting. He tried to get me into all those things, but somehow I didn't incline that way. I sometimes think it might have been a good thing for me if I had stuck to him and his schemes. He wasn't any of your molly-coddles, either. He was captain of the baseball team at one time and a first-rate runner and good at all outdoor sports. And he had a voice like a whole orchestra, from the bass drum up. Did you ever hear him sing? No, of course you didn't. My, but he can sing! He was head of the glee club, but gave it up because he had so little time. He was one of the men that make you think there is something in life worth while besides just the pleasure you can get out of it. You like to have him around. You feel safe when he is by. You know nothing very bad can happen to him. Though I don't know but he makes you feel uncomfortable too; he is doing so tremendously well with his own life that you feel mean to look at your own. I have often wondered what kind of a home the fellow had. He used to speak of his mother and sister, and father too, with real affection; but he was one who would feel affection for a cat that belonged to him, so you could not judge by that. Besides, he is so unusual that there can't be many like him. His family are doubtless quite commonplace. How did you find them?"

"Anything but commonplace," answered Evelyn quickly. "They are the most extraordinary people I ever met. They do absolutely nothing to please themselves, so far as I could find out, without first inquiring whether it will help or hinder some one else. I felt smaller and smaller the longer I stayed. Not that they obtruded their goodness, oh, dear me, no! They were sweetness itself, but I could not help seeing how differently they looked at everything. Still, they seemed very happy."

She stopped, musing, and looked at the picture.

"Tell me all about it," said her brother, looking interested. "Humanity is always interesting. I like to get hold of a new type. What kind of a house do they live in, and what do they do from morning to night? Begin at the beginning and tell what they did the first thing in the morning and what they had for breakfast. I'm sick of all the people I've met lately; perhaps these will be a change. I suppose you found a good many pretty funny things didn't you?"

Evelyn hesitated. She suddenly found that there were some things she did not care to tell; also it grated on her just the least little bit to seem to make fun of the people who had been so kind to her. Dick doubtless would think some things very queer and they had seemed so to her when they occurred, but now that she had come to tell them for someone else to laugh over she shrank from it, she knew not why. Moreover, the thing that had impressed Evelyn more than any other habit of the Grey household had been the family worship, held before breakfast every morning. At first she had not known about it, because she came down late; but afterward, when she began to get down earlier, she found that they came together to ask God's blessing upon the day. Whenever the family were all gathered at the evening hour for retiring they also knelt in prayer together. This had been so utterly new and embarrassing together to Evelyn that she did not like to speak of it. She felt afraid of betraying her own emotion in her voice if she should attempt to do so. How could she help remembering the strange, creepy sensation that came over her when she first heard Mr. Grey's kind voice as if he were talking to a friend, say:

"And bring to the stranger who has come into our home for a little while a rich blessing. May she be a help to us, and may we in no way hinder her."

But her brother was urging her impatiently: "Go on, Evelyn. What time did you get up at Hillcroft?"

Thus urged Evelyn began:

"We had what they called prayers the first thing in the morning, and at night before retiring they had them again."

She paused, expecting her brother to rail out against a perpetual prayer meeting. He was looking dreamily at the picture and he only answered:

"Ah! that accounts for it!" then he turned to his sister, suddenly remembering that she had been for a time a part of this strange household. "I suppose it was rather hard on you, wasn't it?"

Why she should resent this she did not know, but she did. Nevertheless she went on to describe the white house with green blinds, wide porches, and pretty lawns: the village, and what people she had met; and above all, the life of commonplace, everyday work and kindliness. She did not use many words or express any opinions herself, but she gave a very true picture of Hillcroft.

"It sounds pleasant," said the young man with his eyes closed. "I think I shall visit Aunt Joan myself someday. It would be interesting to walk about that quiet little town and meet Miss Rebecca Bascomb. Do you think the star-eyed goddess with the gold hair would condescend to flirt with a fellow for a few days?"

"Dick!" said Evelyn, almost sharply. "Don't! You don't know her. She would no more flirt than she would commit murder."

"Really! That sounds interesting! A young woman who will not flirt! I shall surely visit Aunt Joan someday. Such a curiosity as a young woman who will not flirt ought certainly to be brought to New York. If you are right, which I very much doubt, there is still some hope for the human race," and he laughed as he saw the color mounting swiftly into his sister's face.

"Dick!" she said in a vexed tone.

"I beg your pardon, my beloved sister, but isn't it true? Come, confess. By the way, what has become of Hal Worthington, upon whom I last saw you exercising that art? Have you dropped him for another victim, or only loaned him to Jane while you were away. I hear she has quite taken him up."

Evelyn's eyes grew dark with irritation, but it was not her way to break into angry exclamation.

"I know nothing about Mr. Worthington," she said freezingly, "and if you talk in this way I shall certainly leave you to the tender mercies of your nurse."

"A truce! A truce, sister! I beg your pardon humbly. I cannot afford to quarrel with you now. Tell me more about Hillcroft. But, indeed, you have relieved my mind. Let Hal Worthington alone, he isn't worth your notice."

"You men always are hard upon one another," said Evelyn coldly. "There's nothing the matter with Mr. Worthington."

"Just as you women are on one another," responded the brother laughing. "But there's everything the matter with Worthington, Evelyn, believe me. I hope you won't have anything more to do with him."

"Indeed!" said Evelyn politely. "I'm obliged to you for your advice, but it's wholly unnecessary. I assure you I choose my friends where I please, and consider myself fully able to tell a *man* when I see him."

Richard Rutherford frowned and was about to speak angrily again, and perhaps tell his sister some truths which she might as well have heard then as later, and the whole of Evelyn's scheme was well-nigh on the verge of shipwreck when the doctor, with his light tap on the door, entered and put a stop to the talk.

Evelyn retired to her room to smooth her ruffled feelings. She was more annoyed than she cared to have her brother know. Two natures were striving within her for the mastery. The one was typified by her association with Mr. Worthington, the other by her chance meeting with that other man, Doctor Grey. Each was antagonistic to the other. Since she had been at Hillcroft she had begun to feel out of harmony with Mr. Worthington. If her brother had said nothing about him she would not have felt inclined to renew her friendship with him, but she hated above all things to be managed and advised and treated as if she were a child. Therefore she resolved to show her brother when she got home that she could take care of herself. In her private heart, however, she laid aside the warning and concluded that it was as well for her not to go with that young man anymore.

During the days that followed she told her brother many things about the Grey family, and Allison was mentioned more than once. Bert also came up for a description and the young man laughed loud and long over his sister's discomfiture in the Pullman car. He also showed surprise and hearty approval as she told of her adventure — for so she accounted it — in playing at a prayer meeting. He declared he should like to meet Bert and forthwith demanded to have "The Sky Pilot" and "Black Rock" read aloud to him. After these were finished Evelyn bethought herself of the upper row in the library at Hillcroft and sailed forth to the book store, returning with a number of them.

The young man seemed interested in these books. They were in a new line for him. They were studies of human character and as such he recognized their worth and beauty and was not a little touched with their pathos. He laughed till he cried over Abe, the stage driver, and Bronco Bill, and he turned his head aside to wipe away the tears over little Gwen and the coming into port of the Pilot. When they came to "Snow and Heather" and read of Steenie's "Bonnie Man" he lay with thoughtful eyes on the picture of the boy Christ before him.

It was while they read "A Singular Life" one day that Richard broke in upon the reading:

"He joined the student volunteers when he was in college I remember. Did you ever hear about it? I wonder if he outgrew it or what was the matter that he gave it up. He was very enthusiastic."

"Of whom, pray, are you speaking? Emanuel Bayard in this story? And what may a student volunteer be, I should like to inquire?" said the reader pausing and closing the book with her finger in the place.

"Why, I was speaking of Maurice Grey. Someway Bayard reminds me of him. He was much such a fellow. And a student volunteer — why Evelyn, you are certainly very ignorant. It was a movement that swept through the colleges; I don't know but it's going on yet. A great many students joined it, promising to go to foreign fields as missionaries if possible. I know Grey was one, for he tried his best to get me interested."

"Really! How strange! What would he want to go as a missionary for? It would be bad enough to be a missionary at home. I can't imagine anyone getting to that point of sacrifice. Not one so well educated and cultured as Doctor Grey. I suppose he has given it up as one of the follies of his boyhood. Of course he did not expect to succeed in his profession as he has, at that time."

Then she went back to her reading, her mind keeping up an undertone of thought of which Doctor Grey was the center, typified by the hero of the story she read.

Chapter 17
Mr. Worthington's Repulse

In the meantime Dr. Maurice Grey had not been idle. His new practice took every atom of time the day contained and sometimes much of the night. To fill the absence of a man so great required unceasing labor and energy. His life carried him into many homes where there were distress and sorrow in one form or another. Constantly he was appealed to, to do the impossible. He sometimes longed for the power of some of the old disciples to work miracles, till he remembered that He who was managing all the affairs of the world knew and loved each one of these sufferers more than he possibly could, and was working his best in each life. But all that was in his power to do to help he certainly did. He was indefatigable day and night. Neither did he slight the poor and lowly. He kept up well the reputation Doctor Atlee had always had of being no respecter of persons in his work of healing. His coming brought many a ray of sunshine into darkened homes.

But with all this hurry and burden of other lives upon him he did not forget to pray. He kept up his college habit of praying for certain individuals; but among them all there was one name which he never forgot, which stood at the head of his list, and for which he prayed with all the earnestness his earnest soul could feel, and that name was Evelyn Rutherford. Just what his feeling toward her was he had not asked himself. It was enough that he wanted her to belong to Christ, wanted it with his whole soul. He would put his energy into that thought. He had no time for any other. What did it matter? God would work out any plan in his life he chose, if he but waited and did his duty, whether of sorrow or of joy. If either were meant for him he hoped he would be given the right spirit in which to meet it.

He heard from home that Miss Rutherford had left them suddenly to attend upon her brother in Philadelphia. He was disappointed that she should have gone from there so soon. He had hoped much from her contact with Allison, both for herself and for his sister. Allison was too quiet and shy, and needed contact with a girl who was used to mingling with the world. Allison was consecrated, and must make an impression upon one who knew not Jesus Christ. He wondered why it had been planned to separate these two who had been so wonderfully, almost miraculously, brought together. Then he wondered if we should have all our wonders explained when we got on the other side, and he left the matter there.

He called at the Rutherford house one day to inquire how his old friend was getting on, for he thought they would have word, but he found the house closed and not a servant about. His card was among many others which Evelyn found as soon as she returned. It was crumpled and dusty, and she knew it must have lain under the door some time.

It was well on into December before the Rutherfords finally returned to their home on Sixty-fourth Street. The broken bone had not behaved well, and Evelyn's work had been much more trying than she had anticipated. Nevertheless, it was with a certain satisfaction that she reviewed the weeks she had spent in Philadelphia. They had not been altogether unpleasant. She had discovered that reading aloud was a very pleasant way of enjoying a book and getting a great deal more out of it than one could possibly get alone. She had discovered that there were lots of books in the world that she had never read which were vastly more interesting to her than the class of society novels she had been accustomed to devour. Of course she had a mind above these other books or this would not have been the case. She had discovered — and this was a very important revelation — that her brother was good company. Each had developed an unsuspected affection for the other, and the time had passed much more rapidly than either had hoped. It was therefore with a loving solicitude that she saw him hobble into the house on his crutch, and hastened to prepare a couch for him and make him comfortable on their return to New York. He would come before he was at all strong enough.

The father, coming upon them unexpectedly the day before they had thought he could arrive, was pleased to see Evelyn bending over her brother to settle the pillows comfortably. Something in her attitude reminded him of her mother as a girl, and he stopped an instant on the threshold to look before he spoke. He was gratified beyond expression to have his daughter put her arms about his neck and kiss him as if she were really glad he was come home once more. He could not remember so spontaneous a greeting since the days when she was a tiny child. He was not a father whose way was to show affection, but he had a well of it hidden in his heart, and though his blunt, plain-spoken words were often against him, he loved these two children of his deeply.

He cherished that kiss in his heart, though his only outward response beyond a smile was:

"We made faster time over than we expected, and got in an hour ago. I came right up from the steamer."

Evelyn was so satisfied with her experiment in Philadelphia that she set about establishing a new order of things in New York. She took the management of the servants more into her own hands, and finally dismissed entirely the housekeeper, who had been with them for several years, and had grown fat and lazy in her position and lax in her duties. She wrote to Allison for the recipes of one or two things she had eaten at their house and knew her father would enjoy, and once she essayed to go into the kitchen and attempt some waffles herself. Sorry looking affairs they were, and worse tasting; and a much bedraggled young woman it was, with burned fingers and aching back, who finally, with the aid of a trusted maid — it was the cook's afternoon out — carefully removed all signs of her experiment, resolving the while mentally to conquer waffles someday if it took a year to learn.

But her attempts were not all in the culinary line. She turned her attention to the library, and made it as attractive as her skill could; and then she would coax her father in to sit with her sometimes when he came home weary with his business, and ask him questions about politics and things in which she knew he was interested and for which she had primed herself by reading the morning papers. He was surprised and pleased with this attention, and would sometimes come into the music room when she was playing and lie down on the couch to listen, staying an hour or two if she played so long.

She marveled to herself that little things that could be so easily done could have such an effect on the home life. They seemed to be more of a family now than they had ever been, though she felt that there was something lacking, and that something she knew from the Hillcroft picture she had looked upon, was a mother. However, she was doing the best she could, and she plumed herself mightily upon her success, insomuch that she felt she was now quite able to compete with Allison in goodness.

And then one day on coming home from a round of much-neglected calls, she found Doctor Grey's card again, and suddenly remembered her promise. Yes, she had kept it, but for some reason her conscience did not entirely approve of her. She had said the words over every night, but she had been so engaged in working out salvation that she had forgotten that she was to ask it with her whole heart and try to desire it. The words had become so familiar that for the moment she could not tell their import. That is the way we do with things most sacred when we are otherwise occupied. It is the devil's one weapon against vows and promises and mighty words of warning or invitation. We hear the Bible till we let its meaning slip by us on oiled wheels of familiarity. We forget the relationships we bear to one another and their sweet and wonderful meanings by the very intimacy that the tie brings with it. And so Evelyn Rutherford suddenly realized that she had forgotten that she was to ask to be made willing "to be good," as she phrased it, in the very act of trying to get to herself that righteousness another way. Not that she reasoned it out in this way. Oh, no; she was too little familiar with such thoughts to reason. She simply was ill at ease again, and when she knelt that night to say the prayer the words would not come so easily, and the angel had to stand quite near to listen that he might carry up the incense of that feeble little orison to the throne.

The next morning was Sunday and she arose very early and underwent not a little inconvenience that she might attend the church service. It seemed to her that this might ease her restless spirit. As she did not belong to any church in particular and the family went where they chose when it pleased them to go at all, she idly chose a church where the pastor had lately become noted for his unusual sermons and where she knew the music was fine. Not feeling in the mood for meeting acquaintances she took a seat in the gallery, where she could look down upon the audience and where she was comparatively hidden. The opening music over, she settled back in her seat half-repenting that she had come, and began to search out one and another whom she knew in the audience. She wondered what they came to church for, and why Miss Spalding wore such hideous hats and did her hair in such a wretched fashion, and forgot entirely to note the text or the opening words of the sermon, which were usually exceedingly fine. So the papers said, about the preaching of the eminent young divine. Then suddenly the whole scene was changed for her.

The vestibule door swung silently on its hinges and someone stepped noiselessly into a seat just below the curve of the gallery and took a seat where she could see him, and behold, it was Dr. Grey!

His reverent attitude at once brought it sharply to her mind that this church was a sacred place; the worshiper below felt it to be such. She saw from the instant rapt attention he gave to the minister that he intended to make the most of the service. And now, behold, she heard the sermon herself, and heard it as through the ears of the quiet listener seated below her. The thoughts of the preacher were reflected in unmistakable lines on the speaking face, and all the way through to the end Evelyn felt as if she were being preached at, and by one who cared for her salvation. By the droop of Dr. Grey's head in prayer she recognized that the sermon had passed into petition and then she felt herself prayed for. Suddenly she was seized with a longing to hear him pray for her. Had he kept it up yet? He had said he would, and she believed he was a man who always remembered such things.

What did he say when he called her name before the throne? What name did he speak? How ran the words?

The closing hymn was announced and she suddenly recollected in confusion that she had not bowed her head or even closed her eyes during prayer. She was glad that few could see her where she sat. Then she began to dread the close of service and to half fear, half long, to meet and talk with Dr. Grey. Would he ask her if she had kept her promise? Would he say anything about that dreadful sermon that seemed to have cut straight into her life and showed how barren it was? Then the question was settled in an unexpected way. The man downstairs seemed suddenly to become aware of the outside world once more. He took out his watch and with a hurried motion put on his overcoat and slipped out of the church. Ah yes, he was a busy man. He had work in the world to attend to, something worthwhile. In a gleam of revelation she saw how useless her life thus far had been and went home more miserable than she had been for a long time.

Mr. Worthington dropped in that afternoon. She had not been cordial to him of late, but she hailed him as a respite from herself and for an hour was as gay and reckless as she ever had been before she went to Hillcroft. She laughed and chatted and used her fine eyes to good effect. Then suddenly her father and brother entered from the street, and the glance that each cast into the room as they passed by without coming in, reminded Evelyn of what they thought of her visitor. A vision of a fine, serious face in reverent, attentive attitude in the tinted shadows of the dimly lighted sanctuary came between her and the reckless face of the man with whom she was talking. All her brilliancy left her, and she declined coldly an invitation to an unusually fine musical performance and took the violets he had brought her, from her belt where she had fastened them, throwing them carelessly on the table. She seemed out of harmony with him all at once and shuddered at a joke he ventured to perpetrate. What would Dr. Grey say could he see her in such company? She mentally reviewed the conversation of the afternoon. It did not bear even her own scrutiny. She was ashamed and began to plan how she might rid herself of him. It was not an easy task seeing she had so far lowered herself as to encourage his attention. Was it true, as her brother had said, that she was a flirt? She would not have liked him to see her this afternoon.

Mr. Worthington was too keen not to feel the depression of the atmosphere and soon took himself away wondering what had come over Miss Rutherford so suddenly. He was as near to being in love as he had ever been in his life, and he was in great need of some girl's money if he would save the reputation under which he had been masquerading. Perhaps he had better be a little more guarded in his speech, though she had seemed at one time to be dashing enough and not afraid of anything. Well, there was no accounting for women. But this one was worth cultivating a little further and going slow for, if that was what she wanted. She appeared to welcome him heartily enough till her father and brother arrived. Probably that was the matter; they had taken a dislike. He had always considered her brother entirely too nice about some things. However *he* could pose as a moral hero if need be. And he whistled an air from the opera as he went his way toward Jane Bashford's, where he was sure to find five o'clock tea and a welcome.

Chapter 18
A Hospital for China

Although the busy doctor found little time for social duties he nevertheless made two more attempts to call on the Rutherfords, but on both occasions found none of the family at home. It was doubtless due to his being obliged to choose his time whenever there came opportunity, and to his lack of knowledge concerning the social engagements that would be likely to take the members of the family from home. As a college student when he had been in town occasionally he had informed himself about these matters, but now all was different. He must go when he could. Duty was ever present to watch over his movements.

The second time he turned away from the door quite disappointed. He had seen Miss Rutherford passing a house where he was visiting a patient only the day before. She had been in a carriage and leaned out to smile and bow to a lady on the sidewalk. Of course she did not see him. He had just stepped to the window to examine the thermometer for the patient's temperature, as the room was so darkened he could not be sure he was right, and looking up had seen her. The sight of her face awakened his strong desire to meet and talk with her again.

When, at a late hour that evening, he was able to return to his own inner sanctum and commune with himself, he sat for a time thinking with his weary eyes closed, and then abruptly arose, and going to a closet, searched out a large, wooden box, among several that had not been unpacked since he came to New York. He sent his office boy for the hatchet and opened it, and there were revealed myriads of photographs. They were relics of his college days, and had not been unpacked since he took them down from his walls when he left. He searched among them for some time in vain. Now and again he would stop and look thoughtfully at a face as old memories were brought up, but for the most part he went rapidly over them as if hunting for some certain one. At last near the very bottom he found the object of his search. It was a handsome photograph, somewhat faded and soiled by dust, showing a beautiful girl, with fine, dark eyes, and masses of black hair about her shoulders, standing by a boy with eyes like her own. They were apparently about fourteen and sixteen years of age.

He unceremoniously bundled the rest of the pictures into the box and tumbled it back into the closet, to be set to rights at another time. Then he seated himself and proceeded to study that picture.

He could remember so well the day when it came into his possession. It was the day they were all packing to leave college. He had gone over to Dick Rutherford's room a moment, for Dick was leaving that day, and had all his boxes nailed up, and his room entirely dismantled. He had wandered about the room and sat down on the window ledge while he talked, and noticing this picture slipped down face to the wall behind the bedstead, he had reached down, pulled it out, and showed it to Dick. He could see Dick's face now as he waved it aside.

"Never mind that old thing. Throw it in the waste basket, leave it on the floor. I haven't another crack of room where I could get in even a microbe, and everything is locked. I'm mortally afraid they will burst before I get home now. There's plenty more pictures at home, and besides that's only my sister and myself when we were kids."

"But you don't want to leave your sister's picture about for any one to get hold of, Rutherford," he had reminded him.

"Oh, well, I'll trust it to your safe keeping, then," he had said with a laugh as he went out.

Maurice Grey had not been sure to-night that he had kept that picture, but a dim memory of putting it in his box which stood in his room ready to be nailed up, caused him to go in search of it. Now, after looking at it a long time he carefully cut out the girl's picture, and placed it in a little oval velvet frame that had been given him with some baby-patient's picture, and stood it on his bureau. There he surveyed it with a curious satisfaction. No one could possibly know who it was, he thought, and no one would ever notice it. The original of the picture would scarcely be likely to find it out. After that he went to call again with the same disappointing result.

As he came down the steps of the house on Sixty-fourth Street he recollected a missionary conference which was going on at that time, and decided to spend his leisure hour there. It was long since he had been able to indulge in one of these meetings, and he was deeply interested in them. He had never quite given up his desire to go to a foreign field, although his opportunities in his own land had seemed to open up in such a way as to indicate his duty at home. Missionaries were by no means so hard to find as they were at the time he had eagerly pledged himself to go if opportunity offered.

He smothered his disappointment about the call as best he could, told himself it was just as well, that he was getting to long for the things of this world too much, especially when they were things he never could have, and went to the meeting.

The meeting was more than usually moving. The Spirit of the Master who said, "Go ye into all the world and preach the gospel to every creature," seemed to be there in very truth. There were present several returned missionaries who knew how to speak to the friends at home and stir their hearts to the love of Jesus, as well as to those who had never heard of him. The climax was reached when a missionary from China told in simple language of his work and of the needs of the region where he was stationed. He spoke of cases that had come to them for treatment, begging to be taken in and cured, but they had no room in the mission for this; that they needed a hospital in that region fully equipped with a good man at the head, and that there was no money for that. The man made the story live, until his audience saw before them the poor, suffering creatures. The listeners were roused to a tremendous pitch of excitement. There were men gathered there who represented a large amount of money. Some of them had been brought by consecrated friends to hear this very man speak. A few of them gathered in a group at the close of the address and talked, and their talk was not without a firm foundation. They were willing, these men, to put their hands in their pockets and help along the work, if that hospital could be established and put in running order before another year.

"How are you, doctor?" said one, as Maurice Grey pressed forward to get a word with the speaker. "We've about decided to have that hospital. I wish we could put you at the head of it. You would be just the man."

"I wish you would," was the unexpected response, fully confirmed by the eager face and eyes full of deep feeling. "Oh, I should like it above all things."

"Do you really mean it?" said the man, wheeling about and looking him in the face. "You, with your prospects and your position, would you leave it all to go to China and nurse those poor old women? Why, man alive, you'll be able in a few years, if you keep on as you've started here to support two or three hospitals yourself."

"I would count it the highest possible honor to go," said Maurice Grey solemnly.

"Well, then, if that's so we certainly ought to furnish the funds for your work," said the old gentleman, wheeling back to the others who stood silently listening.

And it did not all end in talk.

Evelyn Rutherford, upon returning from a play which she considered extremely lacking in interest, and during which she had been annoyed more than once by the obtrusive attentions of Mr. Worthington, who took it upon himself to monopolize the seat next to her in the box, was conscious of deep disappointment to find by the cards left on her dressing table that she had again missed Doctor Grey.

She frowned at herself in the glass and wondered if it was ever to be so with them, always missing each other. Why did she care, anyway? He only called from politeness, of course. But still she would have liked to be at home, just to see if he still continued to seem to her so much of a man. She was growing cynical about men. She had decided that there were very few good ones, always excepting her father and brother, for they were growing nearer to her in these days.

It occurred to her just as she was about to retire that she might make a way to meet Doctor Grey again if she chose. She wondered it had not come to her before. What more natural than that he should be invited to dine with them when she had spent several weeks in his father's home? It must have even seemed strange to him that no attention had been paid him at all. A quick crimson dyed her cheeks, for now that the thought had occurred to her it seemed inexcusable that it had not been carried into effect before. It is true she had sent Mrs. Grey and Allison both exquisite presents at Christmas time, but kindness such as she recognized theirs to have been could not be repaid by a few paltry gifts. What did they think of her that she had extended no invitation to the son who lived so near to her? Perhaps, however, she was more troubled about what the son himself would think than about his family.

She hastily scanned the leaves of her engagement book to see what day was unoccupied, and then sat down at her desk and wrote a note of invitation. She would wait till she could consult her father and brother in the morning before sending it, for she wished to be sure they would be at home that night; but her conscience felt easier with the note already written.

As it happened, both her father and brother had engagements on the evening selected, and it became necessary to wait until the next week and write another note, so that it was nearly two weeks after his useless call that Maurice Grey stood once more upon the brownstone steps and waited for the butler to open the door.

Evelyn, mindful of Miss Rebecca Bascomb's warning, had selected a dinner dress that was cut rather high, and filled in the neck with something soft, transparent, and white. The dress was black and very becoming. She studied herself in her mirror more critically than she had done in many a day. On the whole she was dissatisfied. Neither face nor dress looked as she thought his ideal woman would look. But why should she care? she asked herself as she turned away with a sigh.

She had hoped to have a moment or two with him before the others came in, but he was late himself, instead of her father and brother, as she had planned. He apologized; he came from a very sick patient whom he dared not leave sooner. He had almost feared it was too late to come at all, but he had presumed to come in spite of the hour, as his social pleasures were so few.

They went out to dinner at once. Evelyn presided like a queen, so thought the guest. He watched her as if it were a pleasure. Long afterward he could close his eyes and see her white hands moving among the cups and mixing the salad dressing, and recall the stately bend of her head as she answered the servant in a low tone.

The young doctor was almost immediately engaged in conversation by Mr. Rutherford and his old friend Dick, but his eyes feasted themselves on the beautiful woman who presided at the table. She said little herself. She could but be conscious of his eyes, and her own drooped in consequence. She wondered for what he was searching her so. Did he expect to see her life written on her face? Was he studying her to see if she had kept her promise? Looking up at that instant she met his gaze and smiled. It was a simple little thing to do, but her color heightened after it. There had been no outward reason for that smile, but in her heart as she knew it had come to answer his question about the promise. Did he know it? For he smiled back, a glad, happy smile, like a boy just out of school and enjoying his freedom to the full. She cherished that smile for many a day thereafter. She had never seen him in this bright, gay mood before; he joked with Dick and they told many stories of their college days, in which all were interested. In fact, the guest proved himself so fascinating that Mr. Rutherford strolled into the drawing room with the young people, later in the evening, to enjoy the conversation. It is needless to say he never did that for the sake of joining the group which contained Mr. Worthington.

Evelyn sat a little apart from the three men, but deeply interested in what they were saying, and watching them intently, thinking how well they seemed to get on together, and wondering at it, seeing that they represented homes so different. She hardly knew why this pleased her so much.

She did not thrust herself into the conversation; but they included her often and Doctor Grey would turn his eyes to hers as if seeking a sympathy he felt sure of finding there. It was an evening such as Evelyn had never passed, a vision into the might-have-been which it had never even entered into her heart to conceive before. She felt happier than she had felt since she was a child, and she did not try to question why she felt so; she simply accepted it as one accepts things in blessed dreams.

Then into this pleasant room, where for the time being pure happiness reigned alone, there entered the serpent in the shape of Mr. Worthington.

It is needless to say that he had not one thing in common with the hour or the company. Mr. Rutherford and his son arose and stiffly bowed good-evening to the caller, Dick looking extremely annoyed at the interruption. Doctor Grey was introduced and a shadow crossed the brightness of his face as he quickly looked the stranger over, placed him, and then cast a questioning glance at Evelyn. She wondered if he had seen her with Mr. Worthington.

The caller essayed to draw Evelyn into a *tete-a-tete,* but she did not respond. She answered him in a tone calculated to make the conversation general, and remained where she had been sitting before he came in. He drew his black brows together in a frown as he took in the situation and reflected that he had come at an unfortunate time, though, perhaps, it was as well to make his favorable impression upon father and brother now as at any time. Then he set himself to listen and join in the conversation as soon as an opportunity should offer.

The doctor had been telling a story that seemed to interest them all when the caller had been announced, and he was now finishing it. Evelyn wished he would talk on all night so that there need be no opportunity for the other guest to speak, for she felt unhappy and humiliated by his presence. She resolved that she would have nothing more to do with him hereafter. How could she, when she saw these two together?

"O Maurice, that is too good," said young Mr. Rutherford laughing at the conclusion of the story. "I tell you, we must manage to see more of one another. Can't you plan your time next winter so that we can have at least one evening a week together somewhere? I tell you, you will kill yourself, if you go on at this rate. Come, say you will. You could have done a vast amount of good to me if you had held up on some of your slum work in college and put in a little time with me." Richard Rutherford looked at his friend with the winning smile that always had brought to him friends when he chose, and it was met by one full of response, but with a tinge of gravity.

"Dick, I should like it better than I can tell you, but —" here the smile faded entirely and his face grew grave and almost sad, "but I do not expect to be in New York next winter."

"Not in New York next winter, man! Why, what do you mean?" asked Dick astonished, and Evelyn gave the slightest perceptible start which she hoped was unobserved. She did not know that her father from looking moodily at the young man by her side, had turned sadly toward her, wondering if his pretty daughter was going to throw herself away on that worthless creature, and seeing her slight motion, had speculated behind the hand that partly shielded his face what it might mean.

"I expect to sail for China in September," said the young man quietly, a great reverence in tone and voice as if he were going under high commission.

"For China? Have you a foreign commission? Are you going as an ambassador? What! You have not joined the army?"

"Yes, I have a commission," he answered, smiling with that pleasant way he had of talking his religion to his friends that reminded Evelyn of the day upon the hilltop; "but it is from a higher tribunal than the government of the United States. My commission is an old, old one, and in a sense I joined the army long ago, but I suppose you have forgotten it. I am sent as an ambassador of Jesus Christ. I go out as a medical missionary this fall."

During the silence and almost consternation that followed this statement, young Worthington, with inexplicable bad taste, saw his opportunity.

"Are you going to take your wife with you or have her sent out by Adams Express Company, selected by the people at home who pay the bills? I hear that is quite a fad among missionaries now, to have their wives chosen and sent over to them when they get ready. It must be a great convenience to those who find it hard to choose for themselves. I heard of a fellow the other day who advertised for one, but when she came he found she had but one eye. You'd better keep a sharp watch on them if you intend to try that way. You might get left."

If the young man expected to raise a laugh he was mistaken. The faces of both the Rutherford gentlemen expressed the extreme dislike and superiority one might feel for an impudent little cur that has snapped at one's feet.

The eyes of the young doctor flashed with a righteous fire of indignation. Evelyn thought she had never seen him look so handsome. She did not know he could be so roused. She involuntarily drew her chair sharply away from Mr. Worthington.

Then spoke Maurice Grey: "The man who will so dishonor a woman as to marry her when he bears her no love is, to my mind, not only unworthy of being a missionary of Jesus Christ, but also hardly worthy the name of man, surely not gentleman."

"You are married, then, or about to be?" persisted the young man, determined to carry off the situation in spite of the atmosphere which he could not help but see was hostile in the extreme.

"No, Mr. Worthington; a man would require a brave heart, indeed, to ask any woman he loved to share the hardships and dangers of a missionary's life. One would need to be sure that she also felt the call to go before daring to ask a woman to share such a life with him."

"Oh, the hardships and dangers are things of the past," sneered the young man. "Missionaries nowadays live like princes, with all that they need paid for and companies of servants to do their bidding. They really have very little to do."

"Pray, when were you a missionary, Mr. Worthington?" inquired Evelyn, in her most cutting tone. "You must have been on the spot to be so well informed."

Doctor Grey looked up in surprise. He had never heard this Evelyn. The icy tones did not belong to his ideal, nevertheless they did him good in this juncture.

Mr. Rutherford, Sr., relieved the situation by ignoring Mr. Worthington entirely, and, leaning forward, asked in earnest tones: "But what does Doctor Atlee say to this? I understood that you and he were partners, and my son told me this morning that he heard Doctor Atlee call you his better half. Does he know of this most extraordinary and self-sacrificing move on your part?"

A strange, sweet light overspread the face of Maurice Grey: "Yes, he knows, and I am going with his blessing. It is hard to give up the association with him. He is a grand man. Did you know it was his early dream to go as a missionary himself? Yes, and he gave it up to take care of his invalid mother, who was suddenly thrown upon his care. She is still living and still an invalid, and he is devoted to her. He says he wants me to go in his place. He has been wonderful. He is giving a large sum to the new hospital I am to have in charge.

Then did Dick Rutherford begin a fire of questions about China and the work, and Maurice Grey answered with some of the stories the returned missionary had told which had roused his sleeping desire to go, until they all were stirred.

Finding that it was of no use to try to turn the conversation to his own level, or to secure Miss Rutherford's attention, Mr. Worthington again essayed to take part in the conversation.

"If all that is true, I should think you would not care to marry," he said in his lazy tone. "One could scarcely find any attractive woman who would care to relegate herself into barbarism." He desired to erase, if possible the impression he had created by his last blunder, but he was on entirely foreign ground himself.

Evelyn's great dark eyes fairly flashed at him as she said in a low tone: "The woman who will not go to the ends of the earth for the man she loves is not worthy to be called a woman."

Maurice Grey turned his fine eyes upon her with the pleasant light of sympathy in them. Dick Rutherford looked at his sister with complacency. He was glad to hear such a sentiment from her lips, but he scowled at the young man who had called it forth and resolved to find some way to keep his sister from him.

The evening closed abruptly by the sudden recollection of Doctor Grey that it was time he looked in at the hospital to see how a man was doing who had that afternoon undergone an operation.

"Now, Evelyn, *that* is a *man,*" said her father as he turned from bidding their guest good-bye, "and that other fellow is a — a contemptible puppy!"

Chapter 19
Farewell to Doctor Grey

The days that followed were full of a suppressed excitement for Evelyn. She marveled daily over the spirit of sacrifice that could make the rising young doctor with such life and prospects before him deliberately go to that far-off land to do what any common doctor might do. It was again that same old problem that she had puzzled over at Hillcroft, what strange power was the motive? She began to feel a certain desire, faint, but still perceptible even to herself, to feel that power in her own life. She put more real earnestness into her prayer by fits and starts now. Sometimes she fancied she really meant it.

She was glad she had thought of inviting Doctor Grey to dinner. She watched daily to see if he would call. She remained at home a great deal afternoons, and often in the evening pleaded some excuse for foregoing a social engagement. She longed to have a talk with him, just to ask him one or two questions, and — yes, just to have him tell her once more he was praying for her, if he was. It somehow had grown to be a comfort to her when she was unhappy to think of that good man praying for her. Good? Oh yes, she was doubly sure of that, now that he was giving up all for his Christ.

Her brother met him several times in these days, for he talked of it when he came home. Twice he had gone to his office and been taken out by him among his patients. He told of some of the homes. He described a few of the desolate places among the poor where they had gone after answering calls to names well known in the social circle. He told how he had taken his clean handkerchief and wet it in a cooling lotion to place on an old man's aching brow, and how he had helped to wash a dirty little suffering child because there was no one else by who knew how. Mr. Rutherford senior seemed interested and questioned, always finishing with:

"Well, he's a man. I wish there were more such among our friends."

To all this Evelyn listened, now and then asking a question, but for the most part silently.

And still the days went by and the doctor did not call as he had promised.

It was late in the spring when he came at last and warm enough to have the windows open. There were faint hints of spring in the odors of the air, even in New York.

When his card was brought up, Evelyn secretly rejoiced that neither her father nor brother was at home that evening and she could have the caller to herself. There were so many things she would like to ask him if only she could muster the courage.

Marie stood waiting orders.

"Tell John as you go down, Marie, not to admit any other callers this evening. I shall not be receiving," said Evelyn.

"Yes, Ma'am," said Marie, and tripped away.

But John was not in the kitchen when she had expected to find him and her lover was waiting in the moonlight at the back door, so she slipped out for just a few minutes till John should return. She could run in if she heard the bell ring. Alas, for Marie's good intentions. The moonlight and the lover were absorbing, and the bell would need to ring very loud indeed to reach the pretty ears filled with such sweet words as the lover knew how to say.

The two people in the parlor had scarcely said the few preliminary words of welcome, and each was just taking in the pleasure of the anticipated hour together, when Evelyn heard the front door open and then John's accustomed voice announced; "Mr. Worthington," and without waiting for further ceremony, and quite as if he were on intimate terms in that house, the visitor entered.

Evelyn arose, her face flushed with embarrassment. "Why John, I am not — didn't Marie tell you?" she began, and then she saw the young man and as there was nothing further to be said, she bit her lip and gave him a cold bow. It could not be said to be a welcome. Her heart grew cold within her. What should she do? What could she do? If she had but had the wit to say plainly when he first entered that she was engaged — but no, that would not do, and he would misunderstand. If only he had not seen Doctor Grey! But there was no remedy for it now. Her ready wit and easy grace almost deserted her.

Maurice Grey saw her discomfiture and pondered what it might mean. He confessed his own disappointment, but told himself it was no more than he should have expected and perhaps it was better so, and he sighed to himself.

There was a pause during which the three considered how to proceed, and then Evelyn recovered herself somewhat.

"I was just asking Doctor Grey about his sister and mother when you came in. I visited them in the fall, you know," and she turned to Maurice and went on with her questions.

"I have been wishing I had Allison here with me for a while," she went on. "I tried to make her promise to come when I left there. Is she still as busy as ever? I have heard from her but once."

Mr. Worthington gloomily chewed his mustache and pondered. He had not been calling frequently at the Rutherford house lately and the few times that he had ventured he had found Miss Rutherford out, or otherwise engaged. He did not care for this pious fellow, who seemed to be monopolizing the conversation, but his experience at their last meeting had been anything but successful so far as his participation in the conversation was concerned, so he refrained from another attempt.

There were a great many things she would have liked to talk about, but Evelyn shrank from touching on any of them before this listener. For instance, there was their foreign meeting. Doctor Grey did mention it, a few minutes later, with a rare smile, and Mr. Worthington looked on curiously and wondered who this fellow was, anyway, who seemed to have been abroad with the family.

General conversation did not succeed. At last Evelyn bethought herself of her brother's words and an inspiration came to her.

"Doctor Grey," she said, "my brother tells me you can sing. He has talked so much about it that I do want to hear you. Won't you come into the music room and sing for us?"

"If it will please you," said Maurice Grey quietly and as if it were a matter of little moment; "but then I may ask you to play?"

Now Mr. Worthington was a singer of popular songs, with a voice of no little worth in his own estimation, and he followed them to the music room in no very fine frame of mind, determined to show this conceited fellow how little he knew about music. But, instead, he sat and listened as the magnificent voice rolled forth. He knew he could not sing like that, and he knew that Miss Rutherford knew it. Therefore when in the second selection he was asked to take the tenor he refused to sing at all and so put his voice into such comparison, pleading huskiness, suddenly developed, as his reason for declining.

The two at the piano had it quite their own way now for a time, while he sat in the shadow of the great piano lamp and listened, inwardly fuming. They even sang one or two duets, making Mr. Worthington half regret that he had said he was hoarse, and Miss Rutherford called for another and another favorite, which the singer willingly and gladly sang. Every word was written clearly in her heart for the future, though she knew it not. The echoes of "Calvary," which he found among the pile of music, kept ringing on in her soul for days.

Rest, rest to the weary, peace, peace to the soul;
Though life may be dreary, earth is not thy goal.
Oh, lay down thy burden! Oh, come unto me!
I will not forsake thee, I will not forsake thee,
    though all else should flee!

"And now," said he, sitting down and throwing his head back in the easy-chair in a listening attitude, "you are to play. I want all those things you played at Hillcroft."

And Evelyn forgot completely that other one in the shadowed corner of the couch and played to one listener only. She played as Mr. Worthington had never heard her play before, and he had heard good music enough to be somewhat of a judge.

"Oh, that is rarely sweet!" said Maurice Grey, as though he had been drinking at some delicious fountain. "And now can you play *'Auf Wiedersehen'?*"

Without replying and without waiting for the notes her fingers sought among the chords of the keynote, and the soft sweet strains of the old loved tune stole through the room.

Doctor Grey was very still when it was over. Mr. Worthington was about to attempt some method of breaking up this musicale, but was not sure how to begin. He did not seem to be in things at all. He felt like knocking the lamp over, or kicking the other fellow downstairs, or something desperate. But he found there was no need. At last he had sat him out.

"And now," said Maurice Grey, with an apology for looking at his watch, "it is my duty to say good-bye. Or shall it be *'Auf Wiedersehen'?* I cannot tell you how I have enjoyed this evening. I shall carry the memory of it with me for many a long day. I leave to-night on the midnight train for home, and in a week I start for the Pacific Coast, where I am to embark for China. Matters have been hastened a good deal. It seemed best that I should be on the ground and oversee the new hospital building, and so I am going at once."

She followed him into the hall. Something in her manner kept Mr. Worthington in the parlor after having shaken hands with the man whose whole body he would well have enjoyed shaking. Evelyn felt as if she were stunned by this sudden announcement. She did not know what to say. He was going, and none of the things she meant to ask and none of the — something, was it comfort? — she had hoped to get from him spoken. He took her hand a moment as he lingered at the door and said in his low, appealing voice:

"Have you remembered the promise?"

And she answered as low, "Yes," with her eyes down.

She looked up in time to see the light of joy in his eyes and then down again as she felt the tightening of his clasp on her hand when he said in tones almost triumphant:

"I knew it. I knew you would. And, may I know, is it being answered yet? Do you feel — are you any more willing to be — His?" His voice was yearning, anxious, as if he could not bear to go away without this answer.

Almost immediately she felt that it was so and answered in a slow hesitation: "I think so." The confession meant much to her and revealed much of her own heart to herself. Then she looked up in spite of her embarrassment to see the light of joy in his face, for she seemed to know it was there and to realize that the sight of it would soon be but a memory which she must fasten now or lose perhaps forever.

Then he was gone, but not until she knew how glad he was.

She waited an instant before she went back to the drawing room. Mr. Worthington was studying a book of fine engravings. She stood in the doorway for an instant surveying him with a fine scorn until as he looked up she said in her most cold and haughty tones: "I must ask you to excuse me. I am not feeling well," and swept from the room and up the stairs.

She did not stop at her own room, but went on up the next flight of stairs and the next, still wearing her magnificent air of pride until she climbed up into the cold dark attic, where trunks and old furniture were stored, and where were dust and utter darkness and silence.

There, after closing the door behind her, she sank down upon the dusty, bare floor, regardless of her soft white robes, and burying her face in her lap as she might have done when a little girl, she sobbed and cried aloud. No one could possibly hear her up here. The servants' rooms were far removed, and besides they were all downstairs. She could scream, if she chose, and no one would know. Never in her life had she wept so bitterly. Her whole being was broken utterly. "Oh, I love him!" she said to herself, though not aloud, for it was a secret too dear and sacred to be trusted even to the darkness and dust.

"I love him better than my soul, and he has gone, gone, gone, forever probably! He does not love me. At least not in that way. But I am glad, glad that he cares for my soul. Oh, what shall I do?"

Over and over again her heart cried this pitiful wail. The proud girl had reached the depths of humiliation. She wished she could die; no, could be utterly exterminated, and yet, no, that was unworthy of one to whom it had been granted to love a man like that. She must not. But oh, what should she do? And then his own voice seemed to float out of the shadows in a whisper to her heart:

> Rest, rest to the weary, peace, peace to the soul;
> Though life may be dreary, earth is not thy goal.
> O, lay down thy burden! Oh, come unto me!
> I will not forsake thee, I will not forsake thee,
>   though all else should flee!

Gradually the words soothed her turbulent soul. She began to realize that it was late and Marie would soon be returning. She must get to her room and be in the shelter of the dark before she came. No one must know this secret of hers. And so she got herself down without being seen, and wished, as she slipped from the cover of the darkness above that she had a mother to whom she could go, who would put loving arms around her and comfort her. She felt sure that Allison's mother would do that, and that Allison would not be afraid to go to her mother with such a secret.

And so she lay down with her aching, lonely heart, while once more a train flew through the night bearing one from her who prayed for her every waking moment.

Chapter 20
Bert Judkins Makes a Call

It was late in the autumn before Mr. Worthington ventured to call upon Miss Rutherford. In the meantime he cultivated Miss Bashford. Evelyn had introduced him to Jane. Jane had approved of her friend's admiration of him during the first of their acquaintance. She managed to help it along by invitations and in one way and another. Evelyn had often met him at her friend's home. Jane rather enjoyed inviting any one who was tabooed by the exclusive people. She liked a little dash of spice in her life. The two girls had decided at the outset that there was no real harm in a young man just because he had been wild. Just what the term "wild" and "fast" conveyed to these two is somewhat uncertain. They had been quite young, and enjoyed the company of one who was master of the delicate art of flattery; and they had come to think him unusually brilliant and wealthy. As a matter of fact he scarcely owned the clothes on his back, and lived from day to day by gambling.

To Evelyn, who was two years the senior of Jane, this was all in the past. If she had been confronted at this juncture with the things she had said and thought about this young man less than a year ago, she would have said, "How could I?" But Jane was still living the same illusions, and now that Evelyn had somewhat withdrawn, she was having a great deal more of that young man's society than was good for her.

Evelyn Rutherford felt as though she had passed through years of experience during the last few months. She seemed to be another person. She had seen very little of Jane lately, and had almost forgotten their common interests in the absorption of her own sorrow. She had spent the summer months in travel with her brother, but had come home feeling like the preacher of old, that all was "vanity and vexation of spirit."

But Mr. Harold Worthington was not one to easily give up a prize he had come to consider his own. There was something the matter evidently. He did not understand it, therefore he went to Miss Rutherford's friend, with whom he had whiled away the time in a mild flirtation. She surely would understand. He told Jane that Miss Rutherford was offended about something, and asked her intercession and advice. Jane gladly understood the office of peacemaker.

There were some private theatricals for a charity in process of development. Miss Rutherford had been assigned a prominent part, and had declined to take it, or in fact to have anything to do with the affair. They would go and argue the matter out with her. Jane had heard some remarks about her ability which she felt sure would touch her friend's vanity. She thought she knew how to reach her and bring her to reason. They would go that very evening. It suited Jane very well to carry out any scheme of Mr. Worthington's. She was not so sure she cared to have Evelyn change her attitude altogether, but it was pleasant at least to be made a confidante. So they went.

Jane was wily enough to send only her own card to Evelyn, and to tell John she wished to see her but a few minutes. In case John or the maid mentioned the presence of her companion, Evelyn would suppose she had stopped on her way to some other place.

Evelyn sighed as she received the card. She felt almost like declining to see any one that night. If it had been any one but Jane she thought she would have done so, but Jane was so old a friend. However, she did not feel at all in the mood for Jane's light chatter, and wondered how she ever cared for it. How little would she care to confide to this girl all that was now in her heart!

Over and over again she had turned the last few words Doctor Grey had spoken to her, as one will turn the last sentence of the dear dead over and over until every word becomes a precious dagger with which to stab the heart that loves, and until every wish the words convey becomes a treasured command to be obeyed at all costs.

She knew that the man who had gone out from her life probably wanted for her above all things that she belong to Jesus Christ in some peculiar sense which she did not understand. That he wanted this for her was not enough. She wished it for herself. It was with her as it is with one who grows to love the Lord Jesus with all his heart, whatever the Christ would have him do, that is joy indeed. And so through this sad love of hers the answer to her prayer had come, and she was willing to be made Christ's.

The young missionary, starting out to foreign lands in the service of his Master, knew not that he was leaving behind one whom he might have helped to the light, who was almost as ignorant of the way to find Christ as if she had been born in China, and who would have to grope along in the darkness and stumble many times ere she at last reached the foot of the cross. But he did not dream of this. Such ignorance in our dear civilized land is hard to be understood by those who have grown accustomed to think that everybody who is civilized is not a heathen.

And so Evelyn braced herself for going down to her friend, expecting to be bored with gossip of their petty world which had come to seem to her so small and insignificant. Strange how one can change in less than a year and not know it!

She felt indignant at Jane as well as at Mr. Worthington for the intrusion. She knew that he understood his last dismissal, and he had no right to force himself into her privacy in this way. She barely greeted him civilly, and was not herself even to Jane. This action on her part was calculated to make Jane more of a partisan for Mr. Worthington than ever, and she warmed up to her subject and made a most winning little speech in behalf of the theatricals, telling how disappointed Mr. Worthington was that she would not act, as he was to have had a part near to her, and did not like the proposed substitute.

But to all of this eloquent appeal Evelyn merely answered, "I really cannot do it, Jane. I don't feel in the least like it, and I don't care for some of the participants. I have not been feeling well. You must excuse me."

"But," said Jane, nothing daunted, "it will do you good, and get you out of yourself. I heard you were moping. You'll have nervous prostration if you keep on. It's just the dull weather that ails you. Come, you simply must. This will probably be one of the best things of the season. It is early, I know, but we are counting on enough being in town to make it a success. The Bartleys are coming up from the country early, and so are the Lexingtons, just especially for this performance."

Then Evelyn heard the opening of the outer door, and a strident voice, that somehow was familiar and awakened memories which set her heart beating faster, she knew not why, inquired:

"Does Miss Rutherford live here?"

Perhaps even the loud voice would not have been heard so clearly had not Evelyn's ears been quickened by a desire to have some interruption to this conversation which merely wearied her. She could not place it instantly, but it somehow spoke to her of freedom and interest and things in her life which awakened the sense of pleasure. There seemed to be a quiet parley between the stately John and the caller, whose voice perhaps held a dash of impudence in the tone, and then the dignified butler, with a deprecating air, appeared at the door.

"Miss Rutherford," he began in a distressed tone, "there's a young — ah — person at the door who insists —"

"Just tell any one she's very much engaged, John. She can't possibly be spared now. I have come to see her on very important business!" broke in Jane impatiently, with an apologetic laugh.

"Perhaps your business is just as important as mine, but I'll bet a two-dollar dog you ain't come so far to transact it," broke in the strident voice, and the impudence strongly marked, from behind John's liveried shoulder. "How d'ye do, Miss Rutherford. I told this gentleman here you'd want to see me, but he didn't seem to recognize his friends," this with a wink at the much scandalized John. "A mighty hard time I've had to find your place, but I got here, I did. Didnt' I say I would?"

There had been no time for any one to speak, but Evelyn had arisen and come forward with her hand outstretched exclaiming: "Why, Bert, where did you come from?"

"Oh, I just dropped down," went on the irrepressible youth sliding into a small gilt chair covered in pale pink satin and tilting it back on its hind legs. Then he suddenly rose and clapped his hands to either overcoat pocket.

"Oh, here! Got somethin' for you," He threw down on a small flower-stand a large bunch of sweet English violets and tossed a box of bonbons beside them. " 'Sweets to the sweet,' as the saying is," he went on, "and here," handing her a crumpled envelope, "Here's *her* letter."

Evelyn took the envelope eagerly, but just at this point Mr. Worthington decided it was time for him to act.

"Miss Rutherford," he said, with his most superior and English manner, and abhorrence in his every feature, "would you like this — person removed?"

Then suddenly Evelyn remembered that what she had once dreaded had come to pass. Two at least of her New York friends had heard Bert Judkins talk to her. She realized at once that she did not care now, and wondered why it was. She felt an irresistible desire to laugh and another almost as sudden and astonishing desire to tell the whole thing to Doctor Grey. How was it she felt so sure that Doctor Grey would enjoy an account of the scene?

It took no time for all this to flash through her mind. She did not give way to any of her feelings, but was studying the address on her letter with a perfectly collected manner, while with much the same assurance the irre-pressible Bert was studying his opponent. He had not seemed to see him before, and he felt sure he could look him out of countenance, but he pre-ferred to take neutral ground till he saw how the land lay. His glance was somewhat disconcerting to the city young man, however. Evelyn did not seem to notice him at all. She looked at Jane with a pleasant smile, quite as if she were doing an accustomed thing, and said: "Jane dear, please excuse me a moment. I must see what message this letter has from Hillcroft. Bert, will you come up to the library with me? My brother is there and he wants very much to know you."

She led the way and Bert followed, having first turned on his heel toward Mr. Worthington with a smile accompanied by a very amusing grimace.

"By-bye," he said, blowing an imaginary kiss, and disappearing up the stairs, three steps at a time, and then had to wait for Evelyn to mount the last one.

It may be that Miss Rutherford would have severely deprecated this action on the part of Bert had she seen it — he took good care that she should not — but she was in a state of mind to sympathize with him in spite of his manners.

She was glad to find that her brother was in the library.

"Richard," she said, "this is Bert Judkins, of Hillcroft. You remember him, do you not? I want you to entertain him till I get rid of some callers."

She waited a moment to glance over the note from Allison, and then seeing that it was of a nature that made her heart throb with longing, she put it back in the envelope for further perusal when she should be alone. She came back to the drawing room as coolly as if nothing had happened, and said as she took her seat once more:

"He is an odd boy, a *protege* of a friend of mine in Hillcroft, where I visited last fall. He is quite a musical genius in his way."

"I think he is a rude, bad boy," said Jane crossly, for her companion was in a hopelessly bad humor. "I think he ought to be arrested."

"He really does not mean to be rude. It is just his way," laughed Evelyn; and then she was dignity itself and no one cared to say any more about the matter.

The callers did not stay long. They saw it was of no use. Evelyn would not take part in the theatricals and she would not talk about them. The topics she continually started were not in their line and so it came about that the hostess was soon free to go upstairs, giving strict command to John that she should not be called down to see any one else that evening.

As she entered the library her brother was laughing loud and long, with his head thrown back against the big leather chair.

Bert sat in another chair, which he occupied with every bit the air of ownership the other gentleman wore, topped off by a well-pleased smile at himself for the impression he was making. He had but that moment completed a detailed account of the encounter downstairs, with the anti-climax which Evelyn had not seen. It must be confessed that Mr. Richard Rutherford enjoyed it. If Bert Judkins' teacher had been present she would have been tried in her soul that he should show no better breeding than this. Allison was trying to elevate Bert in manners as well as morals, but she found it still harder to do.

It became necessary to almost send the guest home when a reasonable hour had arrived, as he was not yet proficient in the art of early leave-taking, but Evelyn could see that her brother had enjoyed hearing his talk. It was something new and fresh to him and Bert's ideas were sometimes quite original.

"Now look here," said Mr. Rutherford, as the guest at last got as far as the hall door toward departure, "you want to have a good time while you're in New York. I suppose you'll go sight-seeing all day."

"You bet!" said Bert. "Got a list as long as from here to China of things I must see and places I must go. *She* made it out."

Mr. Rutherford had been fumbling in his pocketbook. He brought out two tickets. "Here, take these theatre tickets," he said graciously. "You'll find some one else to go along, I dare say, and I shall not be using them, as I have another engagement. It's a good play."

Bert took the tickets and studied them carefully a moment and then handed them back. "Much obliged," he said in a matter-of-fact tone, "but I don't want 'em."

The donor was a little taken aback at this lack of gratitude and said stiffly: "You don't care for the theatre, then?"

"Who said I didn't?" was the belligerent response. "I used to go every night I got a chance when I was back in Chicago. No, but *she* don't like 'em, an' I promised her 'fore I come that I wouldn't go near one of'em. When I make a promise to a lady I generally like to keep it, you know."

"Indeed!" said the astonished young man. "And who is the lady to whom you have made such an extraordinary promise, may I ask?"

"Why, don't you know her? Miss Grey, Miss Allison Grey. She's my Sunday-school teacher."

"You don't say so!" ejaculated Richard Rutherford, still bewildered, and then he bethought himself of another ticket which he searched for and brought to light.

"Let me see, didn't I hear that you were fond of music and somewhat of a musician yourself?" he said.

"I rather guess you did," said the boy, with no apparent embarrassment.

"Well, here is a ticket to one of the Thomas concerts. It's the great Thomas Orchestra, you know, as fine music as you can find in the world."

With shining eyes Bert clutched the ticket. "Now you're shouting!" he said, tossing his hat into the air and catching it to express himself more fully. "Gee whizz! Won't I tell 'em about that when I get home, though?"

Bert came again just before he left New York. He had enjoyed his stay immensely. He gave a few characteristic descriptions to Evelyn of the things he had seen. Suddenly he turned to her and said: "Say, who was that sucker you had here the other night?"

"Sucker!" said Evelyn. "What in the world do you mean, Bert? You seem to have a great many new words in your vocabulary. I wonder Miss Grey doesn't put a stop to your slang."

"H'm!" said Bert, twirling his hat thoughtfully. "Well, she does try pretty often, but it ain't much use. It kind of comes natural, you see. Why, I mean that cad who undertook to run me out the other evening. He ain't a particular friend of yours, is he? 'Cause I saw him last night down on the Bowery drunk as a fish. He ain't your kind. You better keep him out o' here."

Evelyn's cheeks grew hot in spite of herself. She did not like to think of her past friendly relations with the man in question, but she assured Bert he was no friend of hers now.

"Well, I'm mighty glad," he said with a relieved sigh. "And say, I got something else to tell you before I go. 'Bout that partnership of ours. You said I was to tell you when I was ready to make it a go, and I've about made up my mind I'll try it if you'll say the word. I'd like mighty well to tell Miss Allison you was coming too. It would sort of make up for me being so long about it if I brung you along."

How strangely were the different influences of her life closing around her, even this one which she had not counted an influence at all, this boy whom she had essayed to help; and was he perhaps to help her instead?

She looked at him thoughtfully and then gave him a bright smile and said: "I'll do my best, Bert."

"It's a go then," said Bert solemnly, taking her hand in good-bye as if he were registering a vow, and perhaps he was.

Chapter 21
Allison's Invitation to New York

Evelyn dismissed her maid for the night and sat down in her room to read her letter. It was not a long one, but it contained many things that set her heart throbbing wildly. There was mention of Allison's brother and of how much the church and Sunday-school were interested in his work in China; even her Sunday-school class had pledged each a dollar a year from their meagre earnings to endow a bed in the new hospital, this last started by the indefatigable Bert. Allison spoke of taking the same drive with her brother when he was at home that he had taken with Evelyn the year before, and described the scenery vividly, so that Evelyn closed her eyes and could almost feel that she was there again with that man beside her who could tell her so much. Oh, if he were here but for a little minute, how she would question him! She would find out what it was he wanted her to do, and how to go about it. Why had she never done so? Why had she not made opportunity? The letter went on to say that they had spoken of Miss Rutherford during their drive, and that Allison's brother had told her how kind Miss Rutherford had been, making bright spots of friendship in his desert of hard work. The tears rushed to Evelyn's eyes as she read this. How little it had been; barely one invitation to dinner and a call or two.

Allison closed by saying she wrote this at Bert's request, as she felt he would be more welcome carrying a message from her, though she feared Evelyn might not be particularly overjoyed with the visit.

Evelyn leaned wearily back in her chair at last and let the tears course slowly down her cheeks. She was not used to crying, but she seemed to be unnerved and not like herself. She had tried to tell herself all summer that she must get over this strange infatuation for a man whom she would probably never see again and who did not care for her. But somehow she did not want to get over it; it comforted and strengthened her to feel that she cared for him. A new desire had been roused in her heart to find out just what it was he had wanted her to do and just how to do it. All summer she had prayed, though the words of her prayer had changed. They were no longer "make me willing," but "show me the way." The first had been answered. She had come to believe in the miracle of prayer. Nothing could have been farther from her mind when she first began to pray than that she would ever be willing to give up her life of gayety and "be good," as she phrased it, but now there was no attraction in the world for her. Everything she had formerly enjoyed was distasteful to her. She could even understand how Allison was happy in her home and her work. Oh, if there were but a home and work for her, perhaps she too could be happy, yes, even with that great longing in her heart for a love that was not hers.

What if she should try the Bible? Was it as great a talisman as prayer? If she but had some one to help her. And then a thought came that moved her to prompt action. Allison was just the one she needed. She would write and invite her at once.

She went to her desk and wrote:

> DEAR ALLISON: Your letter reached me to-night and showed me exactly what I want and need. It is you. Will you come to me? I want you for two or three months, if your mother can spare you. Now, please don't plead that your work will keep you. One heathen is as good as another, and I think perhaps there is room for your work here in New York.
>
> Don't wait to fix up a lot of clothes. I am being very quiet this winter. Somehow I don't care to go out as much as I used to do. And I have hosts of things that we can fix up beautifully for you, should any occasion offer when you need more than you have to have in Hillcroft. Marie, my maid, is skillful at sewing and fitting, and time hangs heavy on her hands just now, so if there is anything you need, get it here and let her make it. I really cannot wait for you to come, now that I have set my heart upon it.
>
> We had a most unique visit from Bert. I am glad he came. I will tell you about it when you get here. Now, please don't say there is anything to hinder your coming, and do write by return mail to tell us when to meet you.
>
> Your sincere friend,
> EVELYN M. RUTHERFORD.

The letter written, Evelyn felt happier. She sealed it and then went into the library, where she was surprised to find a light still burning and her brother with a newspaper across his knees but his eyes shaded by his hand. He did not stir as she came in, and she thought he might be asleep. She searched silently in the bookcase for some minutes, and then mounted a chair to reach to the top shelf. In doing so she caught her foot in her skirt and almost lost her balance. A slight exclamation of dismay and the fall of a book she had been reaching for just above her head brought her brother to her rescue.

"What are you doing up there, Evelyn?" he asked, helping her down and putting the book back in its place.

She hesitated a minute, half annoyed, and then spoke the truth:

"I was looking to see if there wasn't a little old Bible up there that I used to have when I was in school. I want to see one a minute, and there doesn't seem to be one in the house. It is odd, when you come to think of it, but I can't remember that we ever had one."

"I have one. I'll get it for you," he said, not seeming to notice her look of surprise, and presently he returned from his room with a handsomely bound Bible, apparently new.

"Thank you," said Evelyn as calmly as her brother had spoken, but she went to her room with not a little curiosity.

Evelyn sat down with the book in her hand and turned to the fly-leaf. Written in a clear, bold hand were these words: "A parting gift to my dear friend, Richard L. Rutherford, with the hope that he will sometimes read it, and that it may grow as dear to him as to his friend, Maurice Hamilton Grey."

The date was in the last week before Doctor Grey left for the West.

Evelyn's heart stood still. It was almost like having another view of him to read these words. This, then, was how Richard came to have a Bible; and he too had been thought of and probably prayed for. She drew a long breath and wondered if her brother felt any longing for the things that had been growing more and more interesting to her. The Bible did not look as if it had had hard usage, but neither did it look as if it had never been opened before. As Evelyn sat back and turned the leaves it opened of itself to a place that had been marked, and she read:

"Then Jesus beholding him loved him, and said unto him, One thing thou lackest."

She read back a little way and thought how well that described her brother. Did the one who marked it think so too? Oh, that she could find a verse marked for herself! She put her face down into the cool pages and closed her eyes and tried to pray, but no words would come, and the prayer went up to the throne a great longing unphrased, and the Father who knoweth all knew the interpretation and the answer thereof.

When the invitation reached Allison she was laying out an elaborate plan of work for the winter. There were plans for her class, for the mill girls, for the young people's meeting, and for their club. She was the center of a great many things in the little village, and truly it seemed to herself that she could not well be spared. In fact, when she first read the letter she did not entertain the thought of going to New York for a moment. But gradually during her walk home from the post office her brother's words came to her: "Allison, Miss Rutherford told me that she was going to ask you to visit her some time. If she ever does, I hope you will go. It will do you and her both good. Go to please me, sister mine, if for nothing else."

Now, going to China was not quite like going to heaven, but Allison regarded her brother's request much as if he had left this world forever, and when the memory of his request came to her she stopped suddenly in her walk and looked down at the letter in her hand in dismay. When Maurice had said that she had hoped in her heart that Miss Rutherford only said it in kindness and had forgotten it by this time. Indeed, she had never expected to be invited.

She opened the letter again, and walking slowly read it through once more, almost stumbling over a root in the walk and causing Miss Rebecca Bascomb to wonder if she had a lover somewhere who wrote letters to her that she couldn't wait to get home to read.

It was a troubled face that she presented to her mother a few minutes thereafter as she threw the letter into Mrs. Grey's lap. The spirit of the writer had entered into her soul. She had read the real desire to have her in her second perusal, and stern duty was beginning to plead on both sides. It was not in Allison to want to go. New York meant to her the world of fashion. Her life had been sweet and guarded and hitherto somewhat narrowing in its tendency, in spite of the efforts at broadening that father, mother, and brother had tried to give. It was for this reason that Maurice Grey had long ago told Evelyn Rutherford she could help Allison if she would. He longed to have his sister see the ways of doing, view the world from another standpoint, and draw her own conclusions.

The mother recognized this side of the question — which Allison would not admit in the matter at all — even before she noticed the real appeal in the letter.

Allison retired to the sofa in gloom. She did not want to go. She did not believe she ought to do so. She did not care to go among other people and see new sights. It was enough to stay in her dear home with father and mother and work for those all about her. Were not these many young people who recognized her leadership of more value than the one girl in the city who probably would tire of her in a few days?

She said something like this to her mother, who reminded her what the Lord said about leaving ninety and nine and going after one lost sheep. It may be that her son had given her some hint of the state of Evelyn's heart, or it may be she only guessed it from the letter and from her boy's very tender way of asking mother still to pray for her.

Poor Allison saw nothing but giants in the way whenever she thought of the proposed visit. There, for instance, was the inevitable question of clothes, which has troubled every woman since Eve made her apron. It was all well enough for Evelyn to talk about going off without getting ready. Perhaps she, who had quantities of clothes made by the best skilled tailors, could do that, but Allison well knew that her own new dark blue broadcloth made in Hillcroft would look quite out of style put down in New York. Did she not remember her first sight of the gray broadcloth lined with turquoise silk? She had an eye for fit and finish even though she were not the possessor of it. It was not that her clothes were not plenty good enough for anything in Hillcroft. Indeed, Miss Bascomb had sometimes remarked that the Greys dressed their daughter entirely too well. It would foster vanity in her, she declared. She was dressed as well as any of the girls in Hillcroft, better than many; but, for instance, take that same blue broadcloth. It was made by the family dressmaker, the best the town afforded, and she had cut the left side gore of the skirt upside down. Now everybody knows how quickly the nap of broadcloth will turn itself back if made up the wrong way of the cloth, and to Allison her dress was marred. The goods had all been used, and they had tried in vain to get more of the same. It had been bought some months before and it could not be matched. Miss Betts said she cut "in the ev'nin'," and she didn't believe that it would "ever be noticed in the world." Allison knew that Evelyn would see it at once. Moreover, the skirt was not the shape she told Miss Betts to make it. Oh, it would be a great trial to go on a mission to New York. She would much, much rather go to China. And there would be theatres and dancing and cards, and, perhaps, — who knew? — wine offered her to drink, and she would have to decline or seem rude, and to tell all her sacred reasons why, and then be laughed at. Why had Evelyn Rutherford ever come to Hillcroft, and why had Maurice ever said that about her going to New York?

They were all against her, even Miss Joan Rutherford, to whom Evelyn had bethought herself to write. She came over the next morning with shining eyes to say how glad she was that her dear Allison was going to visit in her brother's home, taking it for granted that of course she was going. She stayed only a few minutes and she slipped a tiny chamois bag into Allison's hand as she went out saying:

"There, dear, you'll be needing some spending money while you are away and I'd love to have you spend that for me on yourself. You're part my girl, you know."

When Allison opened the bag she found five ten-dollar gold pieces gleaming there. After that the going seemed inevitable. Not that Miss Rutherford alone could have turned the scale, but father and mother urged her strongly also.

"It will do her good," said the mother while she yet shrank from having her daughter leave her. "She needs to get out of herself and to have wider views of life. There is no telling for what God is preparing her and she must be ready to fill any place. She needs to see a little of cultured society."

The question of dress did not worry the mother. A breadth or two up-side down was not such a serious thing at her time of life as it was to Allison.

"There is that black silk that has been lying in the trunk for two years waiting for a time when it was needed to be made up. You can take it as it is, and here is grandmother's real lace shawl. Take Miss Rutherford at her word and let her maid fix it up for you. She will only enjoy it. Don't you remember how she entered into fixing your old blue silk waist? You must have a new cloth dress of some sort, and that you can get in New York, ready-made, perhaps. Your father and I will attend to that. Keep your gold pieces for something you see when you get there."

And so Allison in fear and trembling bade good-bye to her class and her home and the dear protecting arms of mother, and started on her first trip into the world alone. Although she was twenty-one years old she had been so sheltered that in some things she was little more than a child.

When she had been on the train about half an hour the thought came to her that Evelyn would probably want to make her dress low-necked, at which she became so indignant and altogether frightened that if it had been possible she would have turned back home and declared that the visit was impossible. But trains do not stop on fancy, and she sped on her way.

Her letter accepting the invitation had reached Evelyn one evening when the family was at dinner. A smile of real pleasure lit up her face as she read it.

"Dick," she said, laying down the letter beside her plate, "Allison Grey is coming to make me a visit. I invited her last week and her answer has just come. She will be here Thursday evening."

"You don't say!" said her brother, looking up with interest from a legal document that had come in the mail. "I shall be glad to make her acquaintance. I have been quite curious to see her ever since your friend Bert was here. A girl that can influence a fellow of his make-up to keep away from a New York theatre when he has free tickets is quite a curiosity."

"Of whom are you speaking?" asked the father, laying down his paper and giving his attention once more to his soup.

"Allison Grey. She is Doctor Grey's sister, father, from Hillcroft. She is Aunt Joan's idol. You will like her, I am sure."

"Well, now, that will be quite a novelty. Anybody belonging to Doctor Grey and your Aunt Joan will certainly be welcome. I have often wished we could see some sensible young people around. When does she come?"

"Thursday evening," said Evelyn, again referring to the letter; "and, Dick, you'll certainly have to go with me to meet her. She will be lost in New York, for she never traveled alone before, and it is Marie's day out, so I can't take her."

"With pleasure," said the young man, smiling.

Evelyn took a childish pleasure in preparing for Allison's visit. She had not thought she could ever be so glad about anything as she was over the coming of this girl, who, after all, was but a mere stranger. She put the room next her own in dainty array for her reception. It might be that the true, homey look would be lacking, but Allison should have everything that money could buy to make that room beautiful for her.

The soft velvet carpet in blue and white gave back no sound. The heavy brass bed, with its draperies of costly lace over pale blue, and its blue silk eider-down quilt thrown across the foot; the elegant little dressing table, with its appointment of silver brushes, all spoke of a life of ease and elegance. Above the mantel she hung Hoffman's child picture of the Christ.

When at last Allison stepped bewildered from the train and looked about her at the crowds of people and the myriads of twinkling lights she wished she were at home. Then almost instantly her bag was taken from her by some one and a young man said in a pleasant voice:

"Miss Grey, I am Dick Rutherford. Welcome to New York! My sister is over here out of the crowd. Will you step this way?" and she followed him through what seemed to her a dense mass of humanity to where Evelyn stood.

It was all so different from the way they had met in Hillcroft. Evelyn had learned to be gentle and kind. Allison thought she had grown more beautiful, only paler, and wondered at the way she treated her. She took her in her arms and kissed her, actually, right in New York! No, not in New York yet, for there was that dreadful ferry to cross. She had been thinking of it with fear ever since it began to grow dark. How good it was of them to meet her on this side.

Then they led her to the ferryboat and Mr. Rutherford made a way for them to pass to the front that they might watch the lights of the great city coming nearer and nearer. It was like a fairy dream to Allison. Never having seen anything like it before, she could not help thinking her thoughts aloud, and she said almost under her breath:

"Oh, it doesn't look like a wicked place. It seems as if it were heaven we were coming to!"

Some one had crowded between Allison and Evelyn so that she did not hear, but her brother caught the low-spoken words, and his face grew grave at once as he watched the delicate profile against the darkness of the night. He realized that here was a pure, sweet soul.

"It is by no means heaven," he said, with almost a sigh, and Allison, becoming conscious of what she had said, blushed and looked up at him shyly. She was not much used to young men, not men like this one, excepting her brother.

It was all like a beautiful dream after that. They found the carriage waiting at the end of the ferry, and at the house Evelyn led her to that lovely room and helped her to take off her things herself. There was not even a sign of the dreaded maid. Somehow Evelyn seemed to have developed a way of making one feel at ease, or was it because the reality was so much less to be dreaded than the anticipation? Allison found she could laugh and talk quite naturally even when she was made to sit down in Evelyn's room with a substantial and inviting repast before her on a little table drawn before the fire, and afterward Evelyn made her tell all about her beloved Sunday-school class. Perhaps this more than anything else helped to still the homesick feeling. All the time they were talking Evelyn was studying the outlines of the other girl's face, drinking in every line and expression, and noting everything that could remind her of one who was to her as though he had been dead.

Chapter 22
Allison Finds a Mission

When Evelyn said good-night, before she closed the communicating door between the rooms, she kissed Allison on each cheek. "That is one for your father and one for your mother," she said smiling. "I know you will miss those kisses. I wish I had such a mother as yours, Allison."

Allison was just ready to turn out her light when Evelyn knocked at the door once more and said gently: "May I come in a minute?"

She was in her white night dress, with her soft cloud of blue-black hair behind her. Allison, looking at her, wondered how she had ever thought her haughty and cold.

"Allison, will you pray for me?" she said half shyly. It was not like Evelyn to be shy, but it suited her well. "I know you can pray," she added, "because you did in that meeting. I want you to pray with me now."

There was a sweet wistfulness in her eyes as she looked up at her guest, and Allison, trembling, awed at the new duty which had been so unexpectedly thrust upon her, yet knelt down hand in hand with the girl she had dreaded — and sometimes feared — and prayed in tender, trembling tones for her. It was harder, this prayer, than any she had ever offered before.

And when she finally lay down to rest, she stayed awake to marvel. She was beginning to know already that it was right that she should have come. She thought over all the happenings since she came into the house; she remembered the young man's earnest face and his tone as he answered her, and liked it and wondered what the elder Mr. Rutherford was like. Then the face of her father and mother drifted before her, and of her brother, so far away. She resolved to write him soon of her visit; he would be pleased. And her thoughts were lost in dreams. The next thing she knew she heard the busy rumble of the hard-at-work, wide-awake city, and awoke to find it broad daylight. She was surprised, indeed, to find it nearly nine o'clock when she looked at her watch under her pillow, and hastened to dress.

Evelyn came to her presently and told her not to hurry, that breakfast would be sent up to them presently.

Allison smiled to herself to think she had done the very same thing on her first morning that she had so despised Evelyn for doing a year ago,

144

slept beyond the breakfast hour. Was she beginning to learn already the lessons that had been set for her on this visit?

It was all so pleasant and dreamlike, this life that Evelyn lived. Allison began to half wish it belonged to her. The deft, white-capped waitress, slipping in and out with the dishes, the grace and ease and daintiness of everything — how much her mother would enjoy it!

After breakfast, Evelyn said: "Now, what about clothes? I am responsible for bringing you off in such a hurry, you know. What is to be made, and what is to be altered, and what is to be bought? I shall just enjoy helping you. Let us get anything of that sort off our minds and then we can be free to do what we please. You will not need to dress much, however, Allison. Is there anything to be done?"

Then Allison, in her own frank way, moved by the genial manner of her hostess, confided the story of the blue broadcloth and its left gore, and went on to tell of the black silk and the lace shawl and a few other details of her toilet, asking timidly if Evelyn thought the lace shawl could be used in any way. Somehow, in the light of New York, grandmother's real lace shawl did not appear so very splendid after all.

They went to unpack the trunk, and Allison's courage rose when Evelyn unqualifiedly admired the lace shawl and declared it would drape beautifully. Marie was called upon the scene and Allison stood meekly watching her quick fingers as she took measurements like one who understood her business. Her pretty face dimpled into smiles at Evelyn's playful charge to make the dress as pretty as if it were for a princess, and she promised to do her best.

They whiled away the morning and most of the afternoon in this and other talk, Allison luxuriating now and then between times in the latest magazines that lay about in profusion; and then the time came to dress for dinner — that dreaded hour! Allison had not yet seen Mr. Rutherford. At luncheon she and Evelyn had been alone. She dreaded the ceremony of the evening meal, with the butler and the handsome young man looking at her. She dreaded the question of dress again, and began to wish once more she were at home. Why was it that a Christian could feel so miserable and out of harmony with life just because her environments had changed? It was all wrong. There must be something the matter with herself. Meanwhile what should she put on? She stood helplessly before her trunk when Evelyn came in. Now, there was among her clothes a certain little cream-colored China silk, a relic of the summer, plainly made, and little thought of by Allison. She had not thought of wearing it.

"Put that on," said Evelyn; "I know you will look sweet in it, and where is that lovely old yellow lace scarf of your mother's you showed me? It will be charming. Here, let me fix you, dear — and a knot of black velvet in your hair."

Allison was amazed at the effect of the arrangement and the few touches. The white China silk no longer asserted itself for what it was, but served as a background for the long, rich scarf knotted fichu-style about her shoulders and hanging far down in front. The band of black velvet about her neck and touch of it in her gold hair completed the picture. She did not know half how lovely she was herself.

But some one else saw it as she shyly came into the dining room a little later. Richard Rutherford drew his breath in quickly, as he was wont to do before an exquisite painting or a lovely bit of statuary, when he came forward to greet her. He held in his hand a bunch of magnificent roses.

"These look as if they belonged to you, Miss Grey," he said, as he separated a half-dozen heavy-headed white buds from those he held and handed them to her, their rich, dark green leaves showing off their lovely petals to perfection.

"Here, Evelyn, these are for you," and he gave the pink ones to his sister.

Allison buried her face in the flowers in delight and then fastened them in the knot of the lace at her breast, where they gave the last touch of art needed. She sat down to the table feeling that she was at a grand party. Yes, she was unsophisticated or she could never have enjoyed it so intensely nor dreaded it so deeply. For after all it was quite easy. She looked up to find Mr. Rutherford's kind, keen eyes upon her inquiringly. They were eyes like her dear Miss Joan's, only with a sadness in them and a lack of that light of peace. But they were pleasant, and she could see by his expression that he was pleased by what he saw.

Strange to say, during that first dinner, which had been regarded by her with so much apprehension, it was Allison who did most of the talking, and she directed her conversation to Mr. Rutherford, senior. Afterward she blushed to herself to remember it, and wondered if she had seemed very forward saying so much; but at the time it had all been so natural. Mr. Rutherford had asked a question about Hillcroft, and Allison had been led on by a word from him now and then until she had described vividly the old stone house where Miss Joan Rutherford lived, the garden where she worked and which she loved, the country round about, and, above all, the dear lady herself. Mr. Rutherford's heart warmed as she went on and his eyes lit with pleasure. Here, at last, was a girl who knew how to appreciate real worth, even if it was in an old woman.

Evelyn watched her with surprise. Here was another Allison. She had seen her in her quiet home; she had seen her doing kind acts; she had seen her among the young girls and with the wild, rough boys of her Sunday-school class; yes, and she had seen her leading a public meeting: but she had never heard her talk at length before, and did not know how well she could appear when she forgot herself and let the color come into her cheeks and enthusiasm light up her dark blue eyes that shone and scintillated with her various expressions. And her language was most poetic. How well her father liked it! Why had she never thought to describe Hillcroft and what she knew of Aunt Joan's house to him. He was listening as eagerly as if he were hungry for the tale.

The young man watched her with a growing interest which changed little by little from the mere curiosity he would give to a new species of the human kind, to a look of genuine admiration. It was true, as Evelyn had said, that she was beautiful, and yet with the quiet beauty of the Puritan maiden. There was a shy droop to the dark eyelashes that made one long to see the flitting light in the clear eyes. And how well the simple white gown suited her! Richard did not know if it were costly or not, he merely knew it suited her.

On the whole, Evelyn Rutherford was pleased with the impression her guest was making. She had not known that she cared about this, but now she saw that she did. She was particularly pleased that Dick should like her, for then he would not be bored by going about with them. She knew her fastidious brother would not have liked a dowdy-looking girl, nor enjoyed an awkward, stupid one. Allison was neither of these, for while she fancied herself awkward in the extreme and dreaded each new course lest she should commit some error of form with fork or spoon, she was, in fact, quite generally free from self-consciousness, which is the source of all embarrassment and awkwardness.

"What have you young ladies on hand for to-morrow?" asked the young man as they arose from the table. "There is a fine collection of paintings on exhibition and to-morrow is the private view. I have secured tickets in case you care to go. You won't see many pictures because of the crowd, as it is the private view, but Miss Grey may enjoy seeing the people who think themselves worth looking at. Then we can go another time for a good look at the pictures when every one is free to come and very few are there. I wonder why it is that everything in this world that is to be had for the asking is discounted by the majority."

Allison took her delight at hearing of the pictures but felt dubious about the fashionable people. She was not sure she had anything that would do to wear to such an assemblage.

The evening passed very pleasantly in talk and music, Allison urging her hostess to play, and declining to do so herself, saying she was no musician and only played a little for her own pleasure.

Time passed without count. Allison was astonished to remember on waking the third morning of her stay that it was Sunday. A homesick feeling stole over her. They would all be going to the dear home church soon, and then would come the afternoon school. How would her boys get on with the man she had secured to teach them? She felt slightly troubled about it, but he had been the only available person and they had promised to keep things up during her absence for her sake. With a sigh she knelt to pray; giving them into the care of the Father who knew better than did she how to plan for their good.

The family breakfast was very late, but Evelyn had come down fully dressed for church, as had Allison, so that they had but to get wraps and gloves and start. And when they appeared with these on they found the two gentlemen waiting below to accompany them. To Allison this seemed perfectly natural, but to Evelyn it was an intense surprise. She could not remember that her father had attended church since she was a little girl. As for Richard he never went, at least not to his sister's knowledge. She had been going herself regularly but a very short time.

The great church, with its quiet, restful colors, and rich tones in costly stained windows, in woodwork, walls, and carpet, its deep-toned solemn organ that rolled through the hushed air like the earnest of the judgment day, all impressed Allison deeply. It was wonderful! grand! holy! It touched her sense of the poetic and traditional. All pictures, in her imagination, of the temples of old, were like this. It was different, so different from the bright little crowded church at Hillcroft with but two precious stained-glass windows and the rest clear white, through which the full boisterous sunlight could come at will, and with almost a buzz of kindly greeting from neighbors coming in before the service began. Nevertheless she missed something that made her feel lonely. What was it? Only homesickness? She felt it more when the first hymn began. How very few people were joining in the morning praise! It startled her, so that she almost stopped singing for a moment, frightened at hearing her own voice so plainly, and then Richard Rutherford with whom she was sharing her book took up the strain in his fine tenor voice and she took heart to sing softly once more. But why was it? Did the people not know the tune? At Hillcroft that music would ring out with deep volume, and even old Mrs. Banks, who had no voice above a quaver, would open her mouth wide, and one could tell by her eyes that she was truly praising in her heart if not in strict musical accord.

When the sermon began the "dim religious light" of the sanctuary in such harmonious accord with her ideas of all things holy, proved its restful power by putting her almost to sleep. The sweet, well-modulated tones of the preacher rather lulled her spirit to repose. She found to her distress that little by little the pulpit seemed to be moving slowly away from her and a delicious sense of losing consciousness was stealing through her being. She roused herself as best she could but still that droning kept going in her ears, and the desire to droop came over her eyelids, and she was glad indeed when the organ sounded forth again in the closing hymn.

As they walked home together along Fifth Avenue Richard Rutherford, who was by Allison's side asked:

"How did you like the sermon?"

Allison was slightly embarrassed. "It was sweet and — and all that he said was true," she began, then looking up into his laughing eyes she colored slightly: "I'm afraid I did not hear it closely, Mr. Rutherford. The truth was, the quiet place made me intolerably sleepy. I am ashamed, and I am afraid I did not get much help for the week out of it."

"Is that the way you judge of a sermon, Miss Grey, by its helpfulness to you?"

"Why, yes, don't you?" she asked innocently, looking at him.

"Indeed, I fear I never have thought of a sermon in that light with regard to myself at all," he said gravely.

Allison could not quite make up her mind what he meant by that, so she asked a question: "Why don't the people sing? I thought the first must be a new tune, but the second and third were no better. Half of them were not trying, some not even looking at their books."

"Why should they?" he asked in an amused tone. "They pay a good salary to the four individuals up in the choir loft to do it for them. Most of them feel that the exertion would be too much, and many that the professional singers can make better music, in which latter fact I suppose they are correct. The majority of people are very poor singers, when you come down to it."

Allison opened her great blue eyes wide in surprise.

"But praising is a part of worship," she said. "I thought a choir was to lead the people. To hire one's praise would be doing as the heathen do when they pay the priest for saying prayers for them."

"Indeed! It hadn't appeared to me in that light before, but now you speak of it there is a sort of similarity between them. By the way, Miss Grey, you have a way of bringing out startling contrasts, just as your brother does. He has made me feel anything but comfortable a number of times. However, as I am not a member of that congregation I cannot be supposed to be hit this time; but, upon my word, it seems to me that it would be much better to have the praising business done up by someone who knew how than to have the church filled with discord.''

"Do you know Browning's 'The Boy and the Angel?' " answered Allison thoughtfully. "Do you remember how when Theocrite left off singing 'Praise God' at evening, morning, noon, and night, and went to be the pope in Rome, while the angel Gabriel came and took his place, working at his trade and singing as Theocrite had done:

> God said, 'A praise is in mine ear;
> There is no doubt in it, no fear:
>
> 'So sing old worlds, and so
> New worlds that from my footstool go.
>
> 'Clearer loves sound other ways;
> I miss my little *human* praise.'

And when Gabriel came and sent Theocrite back to his cell, he told him that when his weak voice of praise stopped in that cell, 'Creation's chorus stopped.' "

He watched her understandingly, his eyes showing his appreciation as she spoke.

"Yes, I remember," he said, "and your point is well taken; but after all that is merely a fancy of Mr. Robert Browning's. You don't really suppose that God prefers to have Mr. Brown and Mrs. Jones and Mrs. Schuyler and Miss Morrison, who can't sing a note except out of tune, praise him in church in preference to those four wonderfully trained voices, do you?''

"Certainly I do," said Allison earnestly. "Of course I did not mean that Mr. Browning was an authority on the subject. I merely used that as an illustration. I think there are plenty of examples in the highest authority of all, the Bible, to prove the theory is true. For instance take this: 'It came even to pass, as the trumpeters and singers were as one, to make sound to be heard in praising and thanking the Lord; and when they lifted up their voice with the trumpets and cymbals and instruments of music, and praised the Lord, saying, For he is good; for his mercy endureth forever: that then the house was filled with a cloud, even the house of the Lord; so that the priests could not stand to minister by reason of the cloud: for the glory of the Lord had filled the house of God.' "

The young man looked at his companion in astonishment.

"Look here," he said half laughing, "do you manufacture verses to fit the occasion? I'm sure I never heard any such verse in the Bible, though that might easily be. But you must be very familiar with that book to quote so readily. That certainly sounds as if it was made to order. If that is to be found in the Bible I'll have to give up my point. Do you mean to say that the sermon would have been better if the people had all sung?"

"Possibly," said Allison gravely, "at least we might have felt the presence of the glory of the Lord. But the verse is certainly in the Bible," she added, half-laughingly, "though I cannot claim to be always so ready with a quotation. It just happens that we had this subject for one of our young people's meetings not long ago, and I have studied it quite recently. That verse seemed so unusual that I put it away in my memory."

The others came up then and they all passed into the house.

"She is a bright little thing and knows what she is about," commented the young man to himself afterward, "and she seems to have a wide range of knowledge. It isn't all confined to the Bible either. How beautifully she recited 'The Boy and the Angel,' and how quick she was to bring in that Bible verse. It was a unique application! I shall enjoy her."

Chapter 23
A Gleam of Light

Evelyn lay down in the afternoon and supposed that her guest was doing the same. Each would have been surprised could she have known that the other was studying the Bible. Evelyn had not yet returned the Bible her brother had loaned her and had it half concealed under her pillow ready to put it out of sight in case any one knocked at the door. She wanted to see if she could anywhere find rest for her poor, weary soul. The service that morning had only reminded her of the service she had attended some months before, and she had been unable to fix her thoughts on the sermon if perchance there had been some crumb of comfort for her in it. She lay there on her bed turning the leaves in bewilderment, catching a word here and there, now and then lingering over a phrase that sounded promising, but yet not knowing how to go about the reading of so great a book. To begin at the beginning and read it through was a task she could not wait for. She tried it for a few minutes, but just now she seemed too heartsick to care how the world was formed and light and man and sin came. She did not know where to turn to find the great Physician to heal the sin-sick soul. She had gotten a little more than half through the book in a desultory way when her brother knocked on the door.

"Evelyn," he said, in what he endeavored to make an indifferent tone of voice, "if you are through with that Bible of mine I will take it; I want to look up a point."

After the book was gone she lay back on the pillow, letting the sad tears trickle down her cheeks, and felt miserable, she knew not why. Her life seemed all black before her, and yet it was not changed in outward appearance one whit from what it had been a year ago when she had thought herself as happy as any mortal living.

In the next room sat Allison with her Bible. She did not attempt to conceal from herself that she was homesick at this hour. She was not used to Sunday afternoon naps. Her boys were gathering now. She brought each chair and its occupant before her as her classroom filled, and she went over the lesson she had begun to study when Evelyn's invitation had arrived. There were things in that lesson that seemed just fitted for Bert and Fred and a few others. How she would enjoy being there to teach it! Why was it that when one loved a work so much she must be torn away from it and sent to another place which was not congenial? True, she was having a good time in many ways, but of what use was it going to be to her? Would it not rather tend to make her own life less near to God, all this excitement and sightseeing and worldliness about her? Well, it was strange, but she must not question God's way for her. A little printed slip fell out from the leaves of her Bible. Her mother had placed it there last Sunday night as she took her Bible upstairs and had written on one corner "Dear child," and it read:

> God's plans for thee are graciously unfolding,
>   And leaf by leaf they blossom perfectly,
> As yon fair rose, from its soft unfolding,
>   In marvelous beauty open fragrantly.

Allison studied the lines a few minutes with a gentle longing in her face which in her heart meant she would try to be what she knew her mother yearned to have her be. Then she resolutely put aside all thoughts of her class. It would not do. She must turn them to God and try to do what he would have her do here. She turned to the topic for the young people's meeting and began studying that, and then growing restless as one or two hymns occurred to her that would certainly be sung at the home meeting that evening because they fitted so perfectly with the central thought of the subject, she stole softly into the hall and down to the music room.

There was no one there as she had supposed. It was growing dusky in the room. The heavy draperies of the hall door made deep shadows and the open fire played fantastically with the gathering twilight over the keys of the piano.

Allison sat down at the piano and her fingers touched the keys lovingly. She did not need the light to show her the chords, — her hands knew where to find them. She was no skilled musician, and she knew it; but there were dear old tunes by the hundred stored up in her memory and her fingers could unlock and bring them forth in sweet melody from the instrument at will. Neither did she need the music usually to guide her. Softly she played, lest any one should hear her and be disturbed, songs she loved, touching the tender melodies, or triumphant strains. One after another they followed, flowing into their key over the soft chords, and as she grew more used to being there alone she let her voice join in softly and the words came distinctly in the quiet room.

"My God, is any hour so sweet,
  From blush of morn to evening star,
As that which calls me to thy feet —
  The hour of prayer?

"Then is my strength by thee renewed;
  Then are my sins by thee forgiven;
Then dost thou cheer my solitude,
  With hopes of heaven.

"No words can tell what sweet relief
  Here for my every want I find:
What strength for warfare, balm for grief,
  What peace of mind!

"Hushed is each doubt, gone every fear;
  My spirit seems in heaven to stay;
And even the penitential tear
  Is wiped away.

"Lord, till I reach yon blissful shore,
  No privilege so dear shall be,
And thus my inmost soul to pour
  In prayer to thee."

Before Allison had half finished this hymn she became aware of the presence of some one else near-by, she could not tell if in the room or only in the hall. She had seen the faint light from the hall gas flicker out some minutes before. It could be only the butler or Marie. It might be that her little song would drop a seed of good into a listening heart. It could do no harm; she would not stop. But as she came to the last verse she felt that some one stood in the doorway by the heavy curtains. It startled her and made her voice quiver slightly, for she had been feeling the words as she spoke them, and it had been in reality, as in form, a prayer. It was not quite pleasant to be thus made self-conscious again, but she turned on the stool with the last sound and saw Richard Rutherford standing with bowed head listening.

"May I come in?" he said gravely. "I could not resist the sound; it was very sweet. Go on, won't you, and let me sit here and listen."

"Oh, no, I couldn't!" said Allison quickly. "I am not a singer, and I was only taking myself back to our meeting for a little while."

"Do they all sing like that there? Then it must be a wonderful meeting and I do not wonder you spoke as you did this morning. Please go on. Take me to your meeting too, a little while, won't you? I have never been and I should enjoy it. My sister told me of one she attended at Hillcroft once. Now you certainly must go on or you will drive me back again to my room and I do want to hear another song. You will not refuse, will you?"

Allison had been brought up to accede to requests if possible without making a fuss, and so, though she would rather have done almost anything than sing her poor little songs before this city gentleman, she turned back to the piano. After a few gentle chords, she gathered courage from the sound and went on, her voice low and sweet and tender, but every word clearcut and distinct, in Whittier's matchless hymn:

> "We may not climb the heavenly steeps
>   To bring the Lord Christ down;
> In vain we search the lowest deeps,
>   For him no depths can drown.
>
> "But warm, sweet, tender, even yet
>   A present help is he;
> And faith has still its Olivet,
>   And love its Galilee.
>
> "The healing of the seamless dress
>   Is by our beds of pain;
> We touch him in life's throng and press,
>   And we are whole again.
>
> "O Lord and Master of us all,
>   Whate'er our name or sign,
> We own thy sway, we hear thy call,
>   We test our lives by thine."

She touched more soft chords trying to think of another song. The music had somehow reached her soul and made her willing to go on, since he seemed to wish it. Perhaps he needed a song as well as the butler. Might she be the humble instrument through which it should come?

Suddenly he interrupted her. "You sing those words as if you meant every one from the bottom of your soul," he said curiously.

"Why, I do!" she answered, facing about toward the couch where he sat gazing into the fire. "Of course I do. I could not live if I did not believe and mean it all."

"It must be a wonderful thing to be able to believe all that. I have thought so for a long time. I would give a great deal if I did."

He spoke with so much earnestness that Allison was almost startled. She recognized at once that here was no trifler. The instinct for souls was keen in her. It was as if one of her rough boys sat before her, and she forgot her fear and awe of the city young man.

"There is a way," she said softly.

He looked up quickly. "What do you mean?"

"There is a way to test it, to make yourself sure. God has given a way. But it is so very simple that there are many like Naaman who will not even put it to the test."

"What is it?" he said half-wistfully. "I'm afraid I don't know enough about Naaman to know what kind of a fool you are comparing me to."

"Why, Naaman was a leper who was told to wash seven times in the Jordan and he would be made whole, and he was so angry that there had not been some hard thing given him to do that he started back home again without even trying it until one of his servants urged that it would do no harm to make the test."

"I see. He was a fool, of course. He got well, I remember now. But what is it you would have me do?"

" 'If any man will do his will, he shall know of the doctrine, whether it be of God, or whether I speak of myself,' " quoted Allison solemnly, and then after a moment's pause: " 'And ye shall seek me, and find me, when ye shall *search* for me with *all your heart.*' "

"And you mean that I am to go about doing the will of God just as if I were sure of it all?"

"Yes," Allison breathed softly, "and the promise will not fail."

He looked at her earnestly and steadily and said not a word. No more words came to her. She turned back to the piano and began softly playing again, and presently sang:

> "Father! in thy mysterious presence kneeling,
>   Fain would our hearts feel all thy kindling love;
> For we are weak, and need some deep revealing
>   Of trust and strength and calmness from above."

Evelyn was heard coming down the stairs, then, and in a moment more she spoke by the door of the drawing room which opened from the music room:

"Why, papa! Is this you sitting here in the dark? Don't you want me to ring for John to light the gas?"

The occupants of the music room wondered how long he had been sitting there in the dark.

"No, daughter. Sit down here. I have been listening to some sweet singing. Listen."

But Allison in sudden panic stopped playing and left the piano stool altogether.

"Oh, I am afraid I have broken the spell!" said Evelyn coming in. "But let us all sing something now. Father will like that, I am sure."

They sang a little while, but Richard suddenly stopped them by looking at his watch.

"Evelyn, isn't it about time we had some lunch? I have a mind to ask you and Miss Grey to go with me to hear another kind of preaching tonight, if you both care to do so. I'll warrant you one thing, you will not go to sleep, for I have heard him," and he named a preacher whose fame had reached Hillcroft long ago and whom Allison had often longed to hear.

It was something new for that family to attend church twice on Sunday. Mr. Rutherford joined them once more. It seemed to him pleasant, this little family life that had been springing up in his lonely household lately. Evelyn was growing more like her mother, or was it like his own mother, whom he could dimly remember, whose life had left its impress upon him, even though she left the earth when he was but a lad? He sat listening critically and with interest to the preacher.

Allison's face was full of eagerness. Her eyes shone with enthusiasm and her cheeks glowed. The young man by her side could not help watching her as well as he could by an occasional sidelong glance. It was something new to have some one about who took everything in this fresh, fervent way. He could see that this preacher did not put her to sleep, and that she would have a very different adjective from the morning ones with which to express her approval.

In glancing at Allison he caught a glimpse of his sister's profile beyond. He was suddenly struck by the grave sadness that it expressed and wondered what it meant. Was she too stirred by the same Jesus who was speaking to his heart? And if so, what had been the moving influence? This girl by his side? Very likely. What straightforward trust seemed to be hers! How quickly she had been able to give a plain direction, and it was simple enough too, he supposed, if one could but make up the mind to try it. Then he gave his attention to the sermon which was aglow with eloquence and earnestness.

Evelyn's sad eyes had been fixed on the preacher and she had been listening in a half-hearted way, thinking much of the time of her own unhappiness. All at once the speaker caught her attention. His voice had changed to a tender pathos. He was reciting a poem, she discovered, and these were the words that came to her ear, though she could not have told their connection with the rest of the discourse:

"The cross shines fair, and the church bell rings,
And the air is peopled with holy things;
Yet the world is not happy as the world might be —
Why is it? why is it?   Oh, answer me!

"What lackest thou, world? for God made thee of old;
Why thy faith gone out, and thy love grown cold?
Thou art not happy as thou mightest be,
For the want of Christ's simplicity.

"It is blood thou lackest, thou poor old world!
Who shall make thy love hot for thee, frozen old world?
Thou art not happy as thou mightest be,
For the love of dear Jesus is little in thee.

"Poor world! if thou cravest a better day,
Remember that Christ must have his own way;
I mourn thou art not as thou mightest be,
But the love of God would do all for thee."

The words were exquisitely recited and the house still in that hush that comes over even a quiet audience when the speaker has his hearers more than usually within his power. The few words that followed before the close of the sermon impressed the thought embodied in the last verse. Evelyn was deeply affected by it and as a drowning person will catch at anything that seems to be able to give support so she had caught at this poem; while the preacher repeated solemnly the last four lines she fastened them in her memory:

> "If thou cravest a better day,
> Remember that Christ must have his own way;"

and

> "But the love of God would do all for thee."

Would it? How? And how could Christ have his own way? Was she hindering? She resolved to do all within her power to discover.

Chapter 24
A Visit to Jerry McAuley's

Those were happy days for Allison and sped on wings of sunshine. Not one of the troubles she had expected to meet came her way. Not a theatre was mentioned. That puzzled her, for she knew Evelyn had been fond of going. Not a card was suggested nor a dance, and as for wine, they did not even have it in the jellies and custards. She found out afterward that it was a whim of Mr. Rutherford's, not a little scoffed at by the servants, but still adhered to, because, when Mr. Rutherford said anything, it had to be so. Even her dress was a satisfaction. Marie had found a way to cut the objectionable broadcloth skirt over and turn that breadth right side up. Allison never quite understood how it was done.

They seemed to study her fancies and try to do what would please her most. There were wonderful concerts, beyond anything she had ever dreamed of, in music, and lectures and entertainments; there were picture galleries which filled her with delight; there were rides in the park and shopping expeditions, and trips to this and that point of interest. And Allison never knew until she reached home again and learned it from his own blunt questions that she probably had Bert to thank for the omission of the theatre. They knew from Bert that she did not approve of the theatre, and they showed their perfection of courtesy by not bringing it up at all.

She, on her part, was responsible for initiating Evelyn into what gave her an occupation later and much helpful thought and sad pleasure.

"There are wonderful missionary meetings in New York," said Allison wistfully. "Do you ever go? They are women's meetings, you know. They meet in their own rooms and have the returned missionaries speak to them. I should like so much to go. It may be that my brother's work in China will be mentioned."

"By all means," said Evelyn with alacrity. "Let us go. Do you know when they meet? What evenings?"

"Oh, I think they meet in the mornings, and I am not sure, but I think it is every Monday, or every other Monday. I have my magazine in my trunk and there is an article there about the monthly meeting. I can find out."

To Allison's surprise, this seemed to interest her hostess more than anything they had attempted yet. She sent to ascertain the exact hour and place of the meetings, and she attended and listened with wide, surprised eyes as she heard the stories of hardships and suffering, of pain and loss and privation, joyfully undergone for the love of Him whose they were and whom they served. Was it possible, then, that Doctor Grey had wished to stay in this country and live his life as he had the opportunity to live it, as others in his place would have done, to enjoy his own pleasure and prosperity and comfort, but that he gave it up so that Christ might "have his own way" with him, and because the love of that Christ was great in his heart and not "little" as that poem had said? Her eyes filled with tears over the thought and her heart swelled with admiration and reverence for the soul that had so cheerfully gone out away from its luxurious life that others might be helped and saved by this same Jesus.

Some returned missionaries have an idea that the people here are weary of the tales and incidents of their work abroad; indeed, one said not long ago that he was told by his Board when he came back to talk: "Now, don't tell your little stories. We have got beyond them in this country. What we want now is facts" — facts in this case meaning statistics. Let our people take heed how they stop the mouths of the missionaries in this way. The "little stories" reach the heart. Humanity is the same the world over, and the story of some heathen's conversion and willingness to take up his cross and follow Jesus may lead another brother, even though he may be white and civilized, to see the worth of the Saviour.

It was just a little simple story of a poor old Indian woman and her childlike love for Jesus that led Evelyn Rutherford at last to the light. It suddenly dawned upon her, in one of these meetings which she and Allison attended quite regularly, that this love which had been carried so far at so great expense to these heathen had also been brought to her. It had been preached to her as she walked a sunny street paved with autumn leaves one day, and on a lofty hilltop, by a missionary sent to her all her own, and was now being preached daily by the sweet, gentle girl, his sister. It was like a revelation that she could just accept Jesus so freely offered her. There was nothing at all to do but tell him so and then "let him have his own way." She smiled to herself to think how strangely the way had been paved for that by the prayer her "missionary" had taught her to pray, "Make me willing to belong to Christ." She was entirely willing — nay, eager and glad. What it involved of sacrifice or trial she did not care to ask. It was enough that she longed to have him do his will in her that she might some day be made into the completeness he had planned.

"We seem to have nothing on hand for to-morrow night," said Richard Rutherford one evening at dinner. "Miss Grey, is there anything else in New York that you have not seen that you think you would like to see?"

Allison's eyes shone with wistfulness as she owned there was just one more place which she had been longing for several years to see, and that was the Water Street Mission. She hesitated as she said it, lest they would laugh at her, but Jerry McAuley's Mission had gained by this time so much respect from New York business men that Mr. Rutherford nodded his head emphatically.

"Yes," he said, "it's a very interesting place to go."

"Have you ever been there, father?" asked the young man, looking up at his father in surprise. "Is it a suitable place for a lady? Is it perfectly safe for one to visit?"

"Oh, yes, I think so, perfectly," answered the father. "I understand a great many women go. You need not wear any jewelry and I would dress plainly; but it is perfectly safe. Yes, I went myself several years ago, when Jerry was living, and I must say there is nothing like it any where in the city. More religion down there than in many of the churches, to my way of thinking."

Evelyn also seemed much interested, and so it was arranged to go the next evening.

"I wish I could go with you," said the father as they left the table. "I would like to see how the work is getting on and if it has changed any, but I have a Board meeting that I must not miss."

When the next evening came, Evelyn had developed a severe cold, which made her feel so wholly miserable that she was forced to give up the expedition. Allison was disappointed, but she tried not to show it, for she knew that Evelyn was feeling quite ill. But when Richard found out the state of the case, he proposed that he should take Miss Grey anyway, as there was to be an unusual meeting going on that night and one which he felt sure she would enjoy. He had taken pains to find out about it.

Allison looked at Evelyn eagerly. She was not altogether sure it would be the proper thing for her to do this, at least not in her hostess' estimation; but Evelyn was glad to have Allison enjoy the meeting and assured her it would be all right to go. They would be going on the cars nearly all the way. It was not like society functions where chaperones were necessary. Evelyn said she was going to bed to see if she could not sleep off her headache and cold and did not want Allison to stay and take care of her; she would much rather have her tell about the mission in the morning.

The father hearing the discussion said: "Why, yes, certainly, go. Two such steady people as you are don't need a chaperone. If we get through at the board in time, I'll step around myself about nine o'clock, but it's not likely, so don't wait."

So they started.

It was almost the first time in her life that Allison had gone out alone in company with a young man who was her equal socially and intellectually. The young men of that sort who belonged to Hillcroft had nearly all gone to some city. There was little or nothing to call people out in Hillcroft unless to church and Allison had always gone there with her father or brother. Besides, she was particular about her friends and had not chosen to be very intimate with any but those much younger than herself, and these only in a helpful way. This was partly the result of her training, for her father had not cared to have her running about at night with boys, as some girls are allowed to do, before she was fully out of short dresses, so she had grown into the habit of having an escort from home whenever there was occasion for her to go out at night.

But she had dreamed of a time somewhere in the misty future when she would be taken about and have attention from some one, perhaps from more than one; but always there was a some one who was a very special one in her pretty visions of the future. And now she was realizing her dreams, in part at least. She was a young woman going out for the evening with a young man. And the young man was not the foolish, vapid fellow that she had often read about, but a truly delightful companion in which she was deeply interested. Ever since that first Sunday evening when they had their brief talk she had been praying earnestly for him. They had never had another opportunity to speak together on the subject, but she did not forget and she hoped that sometime he would tell her that he had found that it was all true as she had said. Would the meeting at the mission to-night have any effect upon him, she wondered? She had read about those meetings, that they often reached the rich and refined as well as the low and degraded.

Allison had dressed herself quite plainly, but her escort thought her pure beauty just as great. It was not a beauty of adornments anyway, he told himself, but a loveliness of the soul.

They did not talk much on the way downtown, except about what they saw. It was all interesting to Allison. Heretofore her trips about New York in the evening had nearly all been taken in state in a carriage. Now she saw the every-day New York out having a good time. The Bowery presented a spectacle which to her wondering, unused eyes was worthy of long years of study. She would fain have lingered among the strange sights and sounds and she asked many clear-pointed questions which showed Richard that though she had never seen the Bowery before she had read and heard a great deal about it. She looked with sad, fascinated eyes upon the group of hard-faced little children who danced wildly about a hurdy-gurdy, and sighed for them, till the young man could almost read her desire to save them in her eyes.

The mission was all that Allison had pictured it in her mind. Her soul thrilled with the stories of those who testified to the saving power of Jesus. She looked at the young man by her side and saw that he was also deeply impressed. He looked at the poor drunkards as though they were his fellow-brethren and not a species of animals of a lower order. She gave a thankful sigh for that. She had believed he was great-souled like that and she was glad. Then all her attention was riveted to the face of a strangely handsome woman who in spite of her pallor and a certain sharpness, evidently had come of patrician ancestors. In her arms she carried a white-faced child fast asleep, whom she grasped convulsively while great tears were following one another down her hollow cheeks. She sat across the aisle from them near the end of the seat and presently a man who was at the end got up and went forward to speak to one of the leaders. Allison, seeing that other workers were doing the same thing, and forgetful of her escort, slipped quietly into the place beside the poor woman and began talking to her in a gentle way.

Richard looked up astonished when he felt that her place was vacant beside him and thereafter the meeting for him narrowed down to the two across the aisle. He could just see the sweet, earnest profile of the bent, golden head and the hardened look that came over the worn features of the woman as she grasped her child a little closer. But though she was repelled, still the gentle talk went on, and by and by he could see the fierce look grow less intense and soften and the bitter tears flow. The woman was shaking her head as if in despair, but still he could see that Allison was urging, urging, and the head-shaking ceased; the woman was considering. Allison had turned a little so he could see the yearning in her face. He wondered how any one could resist that look. He wished she would ask him in that way. He thought he would do anything for her. And now the woman was giving up. She looked Allison in the face with an expression of wonder and dawning acceptance, and a faint smile played where smiles are meant to be. A little more talk, and then the two heads bowed and Richard knew that Allison was praying in a low tone for the woman. There were other life-dramas being acted out all about him, but he had eyes for this one only. He was wishing he could hear the words of that prayer when a heavy hand was laid upon his arm on the other side, and a trembling, aged voice said low in his ear:

"Say, do you reckon he could save me?"

He started and turned to find a face bloated and wrinkled, with blood-shot eyes and features that told of long years of vice and crime. All at once his doubts seemed to leave him, he caught the spirit of helpfulness in the room, and said in clear, firm tones, "I know he could!" and then he motioned to one of the workers who was passing to give the man some help and made room for him to come in.

It was not long before the meeting broke into singing then. He saw that Allison had put her dainty white handkerchief over the sleeping baby's head to shade his eyes from the glare of light, and he saw that the mother was looking at her through her tears with eyes almost of adoration. Then he noticed that Allison's face was white, as if she had been through a long, hard struggle and he knew that the nervous strain upon her had been intense. He motioned to her that perhaps it was time they went home and she seemed glad to follow him away.

The power of the meeting was still upon them. They did not feel that they could talk just here, not till they were where it was quieter, but presently Allison drew a deep, quick breath almost as if it hurt her, and said:

"Did you see that woman? She tried to jump off Brooklyn Bridge to-day, but was kept from it by hearing her baby cry. She came here to-night to get him a warm place to sleep in for a little while — and — I think she has found Jesus."

"I saw," said Richard. "It is wonderful. An old wretch beside me gripped my arm as if he thought I was going to get away from him before I answered, and asked, 'Say, do you reckon he could save me?' "

"Did he!" said Allison, catching her breath with a little glad gasp, and then, "Oh, what did you say?"

"I told him I knew he could," was the decided answer. "And I was surprised to find that it was true."

"Oh, I am so glad!" said Allison, and then before either could say a word or know what was coming, around the corner straight over them almost, swept a crowd of frantic people hurrying to a fire with the engine clanging and clattering in their midst.

It must have been that they had been too much engrossed with their own conversation to listen to what was going on, or their ears were expecting hubbub and confusion in this quarter of the city, for they had no warning until it was upon them. It was a wild unmanageable mob of street gamins and men of the lower class, who care not for any one but themselves, and they were excited by the cry of fire and the sound of the engine gong. Everything that was before them must go down or go with them. There was no resisting their force.

With a quick exclamation that sounded almost like a prayer Richard caught Allison in his arms and held her within a doorway, himself bearing the brunt of the hurrying throng that surged and pressed against him.

Chapter 25
Enchantments

It was but for two or three minutes that they stood there, perhaps, with the wild, yelling multitude of men, women, and children, disheveled and dirty, tearing madly by, and the red glare of the engines lighting the scene weirdly, yet in that short time Allison, in her safe retreat, seemed to have changed into a new being. She hardly understood the sudden throb of joy and delight in her protector's strength that rushed over her. It was beautiful to be so taken care of. It was all a tumult below her, but she shut her eyes to the scene outside. In that doorway it was safe and peaceful.

When the uproar had passed, he drew her hand firmly within his arm and led her rapidly away.

She did not say a word. She walked as in a dream. She scarcely noticed what he did when he hailed a passing cab and put her in it.

"You poor child! Were you terribly frightened?" he asked tenderly.

"No, only at first," said Allison, with a ring of joy in her voice; "I knew you would take care of me."

He reached over and took one of her little gloved hands and held it in his own with a firm pressure. It was delightful to be cared for so tenderly. It was joy to have him hold her hand. What did it mean? She must not allow herself to love him. He was not for her. He was rich and in the great world — worldly. He was not a Christian; yes, and then the memory of the words he had spoken just before the crowd came upon them surged over her with another wave of joy and her hand trembled slightly in his. He placed his other hand over hers then as if she needed protection. It was as if their hearts could speak to one another through their hands and she felt in entire harmony with him. For a moment she gave herself up to the delight of it. Then conscience awoke and clamored loudly; but was this Allison? What was the matter with her? She who had been brought up to hold her eyes modestly from the world, who had always felt that no improprieties should be allowed, that flirting was dreadful, and had labored most earnestly with her mill girls to prevent them from dancing, on the ground that dancing permitted too much familiarity. She to do this? This was an undercurrent of thought. But she would not reason now. Several times conscience spoke loudly enough to be heard above the tumult of her happy heart and she almost tried to withdraw her hand. Once she quite succeeded in doing so and found her heart leaping in gladness that he had reached out and taken it again.

And so in this half-ecstatic state and talking both of them about the meeting and the fire and their escape, anything but the thought that was uppermost in their minds, they reached the house and were surprised to find that the cab had halted.

Allison's feet were scarcely on the pavement before her full senses returned. She turned and fled up the steps while Richard was paying the cabman, and had succeeded in bringing John to the door before the fare was amicably settled. She paused only a moment to discover that Evelyn's light was out and all was still before she went into her own room and locked the door. There she flung her wraps from her and sat down in the dark, with her burning face in her hands.

What had she done? Been just like any unprincipled girl! Allowed a man, who had not told her he loved her, to hold her hand for probably half an hour, perhaps more, she had no idea of the flight of time! It did not matter. What was time in an affair like this? Five minutes was enough to condemn her — one minute! Probably he was used to holding girls' hands. Probably the girls he knew allowed such liberties often. Her brother had told her once of a college classmate who made a practice of going around getting girls' handkerchiefs to make a collection. He had a hundred and thirty at that time. Who would want to be one of a hundred and thirty girls to share a man's — what? Not affections, in such infinitesimal parts. But he had not seemed like that. He had seemed good and noble. But then she must remember that he probably did not think anything of such familiarities, that he was just trying to be kind to her in what he supposed had been a time of fear. Oh, how she had disgraced herself and all her family! What would mother think of her? And father — father who objected to her going to a children's surprise party when she was quite young because he told her that they would be sure to play kissing games and he did not want his little girl kissed by any boys, and when she had insisted and he had yielded to her promise that she would have nothing to do with such games, lo, she had been caught by a foolish bet of one boy to kiss her just because she had declared she would not play in that way. She could remember now and feel again the remorse and anguish with which she went home with her father when he called for her at the appointed hour and confessed her shame and defeat. He had talked so kindly and gently to her about it and had explained the beauty of the purity of womanhood, and that familiarities should be saved for the time when one should come to claim her love and life companionship. She had believed it and rejoiced in the ideal her father had set before her, and now she had gone against all his teachings. How was it she had so fallen? He would think her a simple little country ignoramus, or worse, a flirt, whose talk of Christ had all been for show and whose real, inner life was against her profession. It would, maybe, lead him away from Christ, now, just now, when he was coming into the light. Something must be done. But what? Could it be explained? Could she do it? Oh, how could she speak of it, put it into cold words that she had let him hold her hand for so long and had done nothing to stop it? Her cheeks burned and burned till it seemed as if they would scorch the pillow against which she leaned her aching head. And then, as if trying to excuse herself, there would come over her again the joy she had felt. But she must not give that as an excuse. She knelt to pray, but she could only sob softly into her pillow.

Weary at last with the long excitement of the evening, and fully resolved, in some way, to make reparation for what she had done, she finally fell asleep and slept until the sun was quite high in the heavens.

It was a relief to her to find that the gentlemen had gone down-town nearly an hour since and that she and Evelyn were to be alone at breakfast. She did not want to meet Mr. Rutherford again until she could make her confession of wrong, and then how, how could she ever look him in the face again?

An hour later an escape seemed open for her. Her mother wrote that she was not very well and an invalid cousin had written that she was coming to spend a month. Mrs. Grey did not wish to hasten Allison's return, if she thought she was needed any longer in New York, nor did she want her to come if she was having a pleasant time and wished to stay a little longer, but if she felt that her visit was nearly over, they would all be glad to see her once more.

With a cry of joy Allison bent over and kissed the dear, familiar writing, and then her face crimsoned again as she remembered what a tale of disgrace she would have to tell that fond mother! Yes, she would go. She would go at once. She would take the evening train. There would be plenty of time to pack, and then she would get away from herself and forget this fearful surge of joy at the dreadful thing she had done last night, and forget this young man before she should have his image too clearly fixed in her heart, for that his companionship had been pleasant to her, she could not deny. He had but been kind to her, of course, as his sister's guest. She must never forget that again for one little instant. In some way she must plan to speak to him about last night. It was an awful, an almost impossible thing to do, but she must do it, for the honor of her religion and her family and herself.

Richard Rutherford had not been surprised that Allison did not appear at the breakfast table.

"How shy and sweet she is," he smiled to himself as he started downtown. All day long he was in a transport of ecstasy. It had been a delight to shield her from that howling mob. The ride home had been all too short. How soon could he dare to tell her of his great, deep love for her? Must he wait until he had proved to her that his belief in her Saviour was strong and true? He must be very careful, for she was a shy little soul, — he might frighten her before he had taught her to love him. What joy was this that had been given him right at the outset of the new life he had determined to live! It seemed to him like a pledge of God's faithful loving-kindness. What bliss to find another creature in the world whom he felt to be a part of his own soul! He had been used to think this would never be, and had in his heart admitted the charges of his friends that he was over-fastidious. But now here was one whom he could fully trust, whom he could love and care for with his whole soul. Would she consent to belong to him? Would she ever drop that shy reserve and give her life into his keeping, be his wife? His heart leaped with a new thrill of understanding as he pronounced that word over to himself. It had never seemed to him a particularly beautiful word before; but now what word so sweet in the whole English language as "wife"?

It was therefore with intense dismay that he learned, on coming home that afternoon, somewhat earlier than usual, that she was preparing to leave that evening and was at that moment engaged in packing.

It was Evelyn who told him and sent him out to telegraph and engage a berth for the evening train, as John had gone in another direction and there was need of haste, if Allison was not to sit up all night.

He went, of course; there was nothing else to do, but his face was clouded over and his heart was heavy as lead. The sunshine seemed suddenly to have left the day. Had the sun set so early? Why, oh, why had he not told her of his love before, that he might have the right to make a protest now against such a hasty departure? No, that would never have done. He might only have frightened her away the sooner. What was he that he should suppose any girl was ready and willing to fall in love with him at once? It is true there had been a time in his career when many girls had seemed to be at his beck and call and he had prided himself on being popular among them and able to have any one he wished; but he was older now. Or had the light of love shown him his true self, with all its shortcomings, in a truer sense? He sighed heavily and wished the car would not crawl so slowly, but at last he was back at the house again. He must plan in some way to see Allison at once, though he knew he ought not to venture to tell her of his feelings now in such a hurry; but at least he could see her alone and tell her how sorry he was that she was going, and perhaps, but it was not likely, it would be safe to risk it yet. Still, he would see her. How? Should he ask Evelyn to send her down to the library on some trivial excuse, or should he send the maid? Ah, it would be awkward business any way he could fix it. Then he turned the key in the latch and let himself in, coming face to face with Allison herself, in the front hall, poised with one foot on the lower stair, her cheeks flaming and her eyes bright with a fixed determination.

"Mr. Rutherford, may I see you just a minute?" she said, and he knew that there was something unusual the matter. He followed her to the music room without saying a word, anxiety written on his face.

She sat down in the fire-lit room. It was growing dark now and reminded them both of the first Sunday evening she had spent there.

"What is it?" he asked in a strained voice.

"I have a confession to make to you before I go away." There was intense excitement in her voice, and her fingers worked nervously together in her lap while the firelight played over her and showed her as a pretty picture of distress.

"I hardly know how to tell you," she went on rapidly, looking down at the locked fingers "but I must before I go. I cannot have you misjudge my — my religion, or my up-bringing — or myself — though I did wrong. I do not know how to begin lest you will think I am condemning you also, and I am not. I know that you must think very differently about these things, and — and it would not be the same for you anyway," she gasped, choking a little at the remembrance of the miserable day and night she had spent.

"I beg that you will tell me what I have done, Miss Grey. I cannot imagine what it can be that you are accusing yourself of. I assure you I am utterly unaware of anything," he said with white face, and voice that fairly trembled with intensity.

"Oh, it is not you. It is I. I knew better. I have always despised girls who allowed such familiarities. I want you to know that I think that I did wrong. It seems dreadful to have to speak of it at all." She paused, wishing he would help her, but she saw he did not yet comprehend what she was talking about.

"It is that I let you hold my hand last night," she said desperately, her face fairly blazing and her eyes filling with tears. "I am so — so ashamed, and I have spent such a miserable night and day. I did not know that I could deliberately go on and do a thing that I knew was so wrong, but I did. And I could not go without telling you how sorry and ashamed I am."

"Did you think that was so very wrong?" asked the young man with intense voice, gripping his hat which he still held in his hand as if it were trying to get away from him.

"Oh, yes, I think such things ought to be kept for just *one* — that is — I mean that a girl should not allow — mere friends — to take such liberties." Her embarrassment was intense. In every word she spoke she seemed to herself to blunder worse. She did not see the white, stricken look on her companion's face. She was occupied with her own distress.

"I see," he said, still in that repressed tone. "But you must not blame yourself. It was entirely my fault. I remember now you did take your hand away. I should have taken the hint. It was rude and inexcusable in me. But I do not think any of those terrible things of you that you have suggested. It was not that I did not respect you. You are as pure as a lily. I beg you will forgive yourself. As for myself I shall always regret that I have caused you this pain."

"Oh don't!" she said, and he seemed to know that the tears had come again to her eyes, and then Evelyn was heard calling:

"Allison, where are you? The man has come for your trunk. Is it ready to lock?" and Allison hastily wiped her red eyes and rushed back to her room.

The conversation at dinner was mainly between Mr. Rutherford, senior, and Allison. He openly expressed his grief at her withdrawal from the family group. He brought the bright blushes to her face by telling her that he was coming to regard her as another daughter, and neither Allison nor Richard dared look up, but each was smitten to the heart by the thought his words suggested.

Both Allison and Richard had been counting on Evelyn's cold to keep her at home. They hoped to have opportunity to finish that uncomfortable talk in some way that would not leave them with such torn hearts and minds, just how, neither knew; but each was looking forward to the ride to the ferry. Allison felt sure he would accompany her. But neither had counted on Mr. Rutherford, senior. Just as Evelyn had kissed Allison good-bye and was wrapping her own fur cloak about her for the ride across the city he appeared in his overcoat with hat in hand.

"I think I'll just go over along with you, my son. We want this little girl to understand that we are both very loth to part with her and shall expect her back again as often and as soon as she can come."

It was a long speech for her father to make and Evelyn marveled at it and felt that she had done well to bring Allison into their home. Her father had shown his tenderness for her so much of late. It was growing very sweet to Evelyn. With a sudden impulse she said, "Wait," and flew up the stairs, returning in a moment with a large fur-lined opera cloak and hood enveloping her.

"I am going myself," she said, "I shall not catch cold in this and I cannot have you all go off without me."

It was an outwardly pleasant party that rode along through the lighted streets, though two of them bore heavy hearts. There would be no chance to say anything, thought Allison, and she would have to go away remembering that grave, hurt look on his face. It almost broke her heart.

"There *shall* be an opportunity *made* for me to ask her *one* question," said the young man to himself as he ground his teeth with resolution in the dark. "Yes, even if I have to travel on to the next station for the purpose."

Quite across the ferry they went with her, and even into the train and sat chatting with her for a few minutes. Richard slipped away from them a moment to find the porter and make some little arrangement for the traveler, and then coming back grew suddenly anxious lest Evelyn would have to get off the train when it was moving. He thought he never would get them to take leave. He was so anxious about it that he almost forgot to shake hands with Allison at all himself and then did it in a very hasty manner.

Once they were finally outside and walking along by the train looking up to find her window, he suddenly remembered that he wished to speak to the porter again and rushed back in spite of Evelyn's warning that the last whistle was sounding. He cared not. He did not even pretend to look for that unnecessary porter. He strode up the aisle to the surprised Allison, who had begun to settle into the dreary retrospect that she knew would be hers during the journey. He cared not that his father and sister were looking through the window outside. He bent over her and said in low tones which only she could hear:

"Did you mean that there was some one else? Are you engaged, Allison?"

She met him with a relieved smile of astonishment. "Oh, no!" she said, in such a free glad tone, "what made you think of such a thing? Please forgive me for making you feel so uncomfortable. I cannot tell you what a happy time you have given me. And, oh, please, won't you get off quick? I am afraid you will be hurt!" This last with that feminine anguish of face and voice in which even the strongest-minded women indulge when those they love are lingering beyond the warning, "All aboard!"

He caught her hand, his face lighting up once more, and wrung it with a last good-bye, and then ran, while she watched anxiously till she saw him as the train, moving rapidly now, passed him on the platform where the Rutherfords waved her farewell.

Richard Rutherford was not very talkative during the ride home. His father and sister monopolized the conversation. He was trying to justify his heart in feeling so much lighter than it had done during the drive down. Could it be possible that he had mistaken her meaning? It had looked as though she were trying to tell him gently that she belonged to another, or at least that she did not and could not care for him. But she had disclaimed that with such a clear, true look that he knew it could not be. Also, there had been something else in her face, taken unaware, when he had returned to the car, a lighting of joy. It might or it might not mean good to him. Why had he been such a fool? Why had he not explained to her that it had been honest deep love for her that had prompted him to take her hand. Instead, he had allowed her to leave his home thinking he was a dishonorable man, a man who would toy with a girl's affections for an hour and think no more of it. He never had been that kind of a man and he could not understand now why he had allowed himself to be silent. Still he had feared to tell his love when she seemed to be trying to show him that it was not for her.

But something must be done. He would justify himself now at all hazards. She must know his love even if it frightened her and did seem premature.

When he reached home he wandered up toward his own room and in so doing passed the open door of her deserted room. It was dark there, but he could see the outline of the furniture from the light in the hallway. He stepped in and sat down in a low rocking-chair and tried to think. This room had but a few hours before sheltered her. It seemed a hallowed place. He would stay here a little while and think what he would do. It might be that some sweet influence from its former occupant would show him the way. He must write and tell her, but he wanted guidance. What would *she* do? Ah! she would pray!

A few minutes afterward a light step entered the room and Evelyn stood beside her brother, her hand resting gently on his head.

"Dick, dear," she said tenderly, "what is the matter? I couldn't help seeing. Can't you tell me about it?"

He raised his head and kissed her hand. There was an uplifted look upon his face.

"Evelyn," he said, "I am going to visit Aunt Joan, and I am going tomorrow!"

Chapter 26
Trouble in China

Allison had scarcely settled herself to the thought of the journey and was preparing to puzzle her brain over what those last words of Richard Rutherford had meant, when a surprisingly deferential porter stood beside her with a large box and two smaller packages. He with difficulty made her understand that they were for her, and she opened them with much delight, unmindful of the watchful eyes of her fellow passengers. The large box contained flowers, she was sure. Yes, great, dark, rich crimson jacqueminots with long, strong stems and crisp, green leaves. She buried her face in them to hide the tears that had rushed to her eyes in spite of herself.

The other packages contained two new books that were being much discussed and a box of fine confectionery. Suddenly the fact that he had called her "Allison," in parting came forth and stood out from all other facts and confronted her. She turned rosy red, and the gentleman across the aisle who had been watching her curiously decided there was no use hoping to get a glance from those eyes. She was too much absorbed, and besides she seemed to be already secured. The dreary retrospect that had been summoned to attend her journey got off at the next station, and Allison went home in a confused state of mind, now smiling to herself as she looked from the dark window and now keeping back the tears that would come as she thought of some of the things she had obliged herself to say. They seemed rude and almost cruel now. What did he think of such a strange girl?

It was the second day. Allison had tried hard to settle into the old routine of little daily duties at home. She had unpacked her trunk and told her mother a great many things that happened in New York; not all — she was not ready for that yet — and the wise mother saw and understood and waited.

She had gone out for a few minutes to a neighbor's now on an errand and Allison was left alone in the house. It was not quite time for her father to come home for supper. She hovered about from room to room feeling a strange unrest, and chiding herself for it. She lighted the gas and went over to the table where stood a tall vase filled with roses and bent and laid her cheek upon their cool, sweet petals.

It was just at that moment that some one was coming up the walk and saw the pretty vision through the half-drawn lace curtains. He paused a moment to take in the beauty and the meaning of it for him. His roses! His heart quickened and he went up the steps with a bound and rang the bell.

Out on the street a boy stood watching him up the path. He was a handsome boy with heavy features and large, saucy eyes. He stood a moment and then took a step or two back out of the way of a tree that hindered his vision. He watched until the hall door opened and let in the stranger and then said aloud:

"Well, I'll be whacked! It's him. It is, sure. Well, I s'pose it's got to come sometime, and he's a mighty nice feller." Then he drew a long sigh and turned up the street whistling a tune he had learned in the Sunday-school.

Allison had not lighted the gas in the hall yet, but the open door from the parlor gave light enough to tell who the stranger was when he came into the hall. She stood, looking at him almost as if she saw a vision, and unbidden by her will her lips spoke one word:

"Richard!"

"Allison!" he answered, depositing his dress-suit case on the floor and taking her in his arms. She did not draw away nor even try to take away the hand he held in one of his.

"Allison," he said, "I had to come and explain to you that it was because I loved you that I took your hand. I could not bear to have you think another day that I had been dishonorable, or playing with you. My darling, will you forgive me now?"

For answer she raised her sweet face to his, all smiles and tears, trustingly as a flower would turn toward the sun, and he stooped and laid his lips upon hers.

Suddenly, out of what seemed a clear sky to the unthinking, pleasure-loving part of the civilized world, there burst the trouble in China.

Evelyn Rutherford had not been one who cared to read the daily papers much. She would glance them over occasionally, but she had not been taught to read the news when a child and did not care for it when she grew older.

Her father and brother were talking about the Chinese trouble when she came down to breakfast one morning. She paid little attention, supposing it to be some political trouble. There were so many wars and rumors of wars that came not near her.

That afternoon she was on her way to the elevated train and the pinched face of a newsboy who was madly crying, "Here's all about your Boxers!" attracted her attention. She supposed it was some sporting news and did not care for a paper, but bought one for the sake of the little pleading face of the boy who offered it. Once in the train she leaned back and thought no more of the paper till looking down her eye caught the words **"TROUBLE IN CHINA"** in large letters. She drew a quick breath and grasped the paper tightly as she read. What horrible story was this? She read every word. There was little known as yet, except terrible surmise. She bought every paper the next newsboy carried when she got off the train and read with fevered haste. So many contradictory reports, so many theories and ghastly conjectures! They were all clamoring about the legations. What was the danger of the American minister, a man who had gone to China purely from business motives, or from ambition, to be compared to the dangers of the missionaries, of one true man in particular who carried the message of love and peace and who had really given up his life that he might help those brutal people? She searched hungrily for word of the missionaries. She had been to the women's foreign meetings enough now to understand a little about it. There was very little said about the missionaries in particular. They were mentioned as in great danger. In some places there was report of a general massacre of the missionaries planned, and one paper had the audacity to state that it was more than likely that the Christian missionaries were the underlying cause of all this hatred toward foreigners by the Boxers.

She reached home in a state of excitement. She plied father and brother for information and they gave it plentifully, but in language far too technical for her to gain much help. Their talk presently branched off into a discussion of the political situation of the whole world with regard to China, and Evelyn ceased to try to follow them. Her heart seemed to be settling down in dull thuds and throbs to stand the strain that was put upon it. Only one more sentence did she catch from her brother as she started upstairs. It was spoken in a low anxious tone to her father.

"I am afraid it will go hard with Grey. He is right in the midst of the trouble, and he's not one to run away from danger if he thinks his duty calls him there."

She stopped on the stairs, her hand to her heart, but heard no more. She remembered that Maurice Grey would presently stand in the position of brother to Dick. He had a right to be anxious and to speak of him. How she envied Dick! She must keep her anxiety to herself. She had no right to even feel it, and how could she help it?

She turned out the gas in her room and sat down in the dark. The slow tears trickled sadly down her cheeks and she let them stay wet on her face. She thought of the night when she had gone up to the dark attic and poured out her trouble in long sobs. She would like to cry like that again, only she could not. She was too tired. She was tired a great deal in these days. Presently she went and knelt down beside her bed and tried to pray, — to pray for the one she loved and for herself. Her cheeks had grown hot many a time as she thought of that confession she had made to herself in the attic the year before, but to-night with such grave calamities imminent she forgot that it was any shame to her to love a man who loved not her and had never even shown her any but the simplest of attentions. She forgot everything but himself and herself and the God who could care for them both. She knew so little about prayer yet; she did not know how to ask; but she prayed that she might be enabled to pray as she had prayed for her conversion.

The days that followed were harrowing ones; they were such for all the country, but so very hard for her since she must not show her feelings to any one. No, for that would be disgrace and shame to him and her both, to think that she should give her love unasked.

But she could go to the missionary meetings and she did, and found there mothers and wives and sisters who were mourning and praying and anxious for their dear ones, and sometimes she could put her arms about some distressed mother or sister and weep with her; often her tears of genuine sympathy did much to soothe and comfort. People wondered at this elegant young woman who spent so much time and money in the missionary work, and who seemed so anxious for China, and so sympathetic. Evelyn never said much nor did her deeds openly. She did not stop to question now what people would think of her changed ways, that she, a queen of society, should eschew all social haunts and instead spend her time in missionary meetings and studying about China. What mattered it to her what they thought?

"Evelyn does not look well," said Mr. Rutherford to his son one day. "She is white and thin."

"Oh, she'll be all right when the weather gets settled. It's spring fever. You know she didn't look well last spring," Richard said cheerily. He had a letter from Allison in his pocket and he was anxious to get upstairs to read it over again.

Into the midst of the days of anxiety and disquietude came Jane Bashford. She was Jane Worthington now. Her father had been strongly opposed to the match and so the young people had taken matters in their own hands and been secretly married. It had been just the kind of thing Jane delighted in, so romantic. But it was not nearly so romantic when the brief honeymoon was over and she discovered that her dashing young husband had not the wherewithal to pay their hotel bills. Jane had to be very humble and go back to her father, begging forgiveness, and the father had granted it within certain limitations. They were living quietly, Jane said, all too quietly for the young son-in-law's ideas. He made his wife miserable by calling her father all kinds of names. He intimated that he had been given to expect plenty of money, and he plainly told his wife that he cared more for several other girls but had chosen her because he supposed that she was able to command the money and had sense enough not to bawl all the time like a baby. He hated sniveling women, he declared. "And he says," wept Jane, her pretty face sad and swollen with much weeping, "that he always loved you, and that he only took me to spite you."

Evelyn's own pale face flushed deep with angry scorn. This was the man with whom she had been glad to make merry only two short years ago! From what had she been saved! "The scoundrel!" she said under her breath, while Jane unmindful save of herself and her own sorrowful little tale, poured out the story of her wrongs.

"He often comes home dead drunk," she said with a strange hardness in her child-eyes that would have reminded Allison of the woman in the mission. She said it as if that were the smallest of her sorrows. Poor thing! She actually seemed to love him yet in spite of it all. "He talks dreadfully to me, then, and he struck me the other night," she said, showing the black and blue mark of his brutal fist.

Could she show this poor child-wife the way to Jesus, Evelyn wondered? Might it be possible to reach her through her love for that poor wretch of a husband, and show a higher, dearer love that would not fail her?

Evelyn's heart was filled with compassion, while she looked down upon her old-time friend from a height to which she had climbed in these two years. How could they ever have been friends? she wondered. What possible tastes could they now have in common? How incredulous Jane would be if she should tell her of her interest in China. China was a far-away land to Jane for which she cared not one whit.

Evelyn, with a prayer in her heart that came with the wish to help her former friend, set herself to remember all that had been said to help her to Jesus. All the steps by which she had come she would try to lead her friend. But when she attempted a little word she found she would have to begin down the ladder much, much lower than she had started.

"I don't know what you mean, Evelyn," said the weeping wife, looking up through her selfish tears. "How strangely you talk," half-petulantly. "What have you been doing to yourself? You look quite shabby and your dress is entirely out of style. Doesn't it make you feel awfully gloomy to think of such things? My! I couldn't bear it! Life is hard enough without being so poky. I go out all I can to forget my trouble. I went to the theatre every night last week. Harry likes the theatre better than anything else, only he will go back behind the scenes and talk to those horrid actresses. But then he says he always did that, that all men do, so I suppose I must put up with it. Pray? Dear me, no! I couldn't do that. It would put me in the blues worse than I am. You need a good dance to stir you up. Evelyn, you are growing morbid. Come over to our house to-morrow afternoon and I'll introduce you to some of Harry's friends. They are awfully interesting men. A little wild, perhaps, but after all, very interesting. You don't want them too slow, you know."

And so she met all Evelyn's efforts to bring her any true help, and Evelyn with a sigh concluded she would not do for even a home missionary. She determined to pray for her at least. She tried to tell her so as she was taking her leave.

"Thanks, awfully, Evelyn," she said with a stare, "but what good do you think that will do? Harry's my husband, and I don't suppose praying will make my life any brighter. Good-bye. You better not waste your time so; it will make you gloomy."

Chapter 27
The Coming of the Boxers

June and July dragged their horror-laden lengths along and Evelyn grew thinner and whiter. She forced herself to read the papers from beginning to end. She read the names of all the missionaries printed. Once she saw Doctor Grey's name among those who were missing, with a hint of hope that he might have been saved; but the next report of those saved did not mention him. From Allison there came anxious letters, telling of their sorrowful hearts, but showing withal a high hope in Him who had power to save. Evelyn thought as she read her prospective sister-in-law's sweet words of trust that she herself was not worthy to be named among those who had faith. She could only lie in God's hand and "let him have his own way" with her and all things that concerned her. But nevertheless she envied the other girl her freedom to show her anxiety. How sweet it would be to have a right to ask and wait to be told, even though there was little hope of any joyful message on this side of heaven.

She grew still thinner and whiter in these days and her father took her away to the shore out of the city's heat, and then to the mountains, but she seemed to care as little for the one as for the other. She was sweet and gentle to him and seemed pleased with any proposition he had to make, but he could see there was something the matter with her which was deeper than he knew. He grew worried and proposed a trip abroad, but she laughed away his fears and begged to be taken home again, saying she was only homesick.

She went down to one of the missionary meetings as soon as possible after getting settled once more. Her heart was aching to know what the workers thought or knew, but she listened in vain for any word. They spoke of the service just past in memory of the dear dead missionaries, her heart crying out against it. His memorial services and only a little while before he had been with them talking and smiling! Oh, it was terrible! She went home feeling too ill to endure it longer, and there she found lying on her dressing table a letter. It was a foreign letter with a queer unfamiliar stamp and on strange, thin paper, but the writing on the outside, though she had seen it but once before, she seemed to know at once as she had known its owner's voice and face long ago.

She calmly took off her wraps, praying the while. She knew not why she went about the little things she had to do with so much attention to detail before reading it. It was as if she were trying to steady her heart for an ordeal through which she had to pass. She did not let herself think. No question of whether he was alive or dead, or why he had written to her, was allowed to form itself in her brain. She held everything in abeyance for the reading, well knowing it might hold much of good or ill. Her door locked she sat down and opened the letter with cold, trembling fingers.

Her full name and address were at the top of the sheet and the letter began abruptly:

I am sitting to-night in the small whitewashed room that serves for a temporary hospital. Near me on an iron cot lies a China-man on whom I yesterday performed a severe operation. I am sole nurse, missionary, and doctor. The others were all ordered off to-day. They have gone to Peking for safety from the Box-ers, who it is rumored will be here in a few hours. The man on the bed beside me is not a Christian. He will not be in danger from the Boxers. His family think that I have cut his heart out to offer to my God and then to make strange medicine of. I also was ordered to Peking, but if I go away and leave this pa-tient with no one to attend him now in his critical condition the man will die. It is a choice of deaths. I may be able to save him by serving him a few hours longer. Perhaps his people may come to believe in the living God if he recovers. Undoubtedly my life is in danger. In all probability I shall be cut off from any communication with the rest of the missionaries in an hour, if I am not already. There is scarcely any hope that I can be saved. It is for this reason that I am writing this letter. If I thought I should live I would not trouble you with my story. I have arranged with one of the mail couriers whom I know well and who has great respect for anything bearing the government stamp, to take any letters that he may find in a certain crack in the wall near by, known to myself and him, and he will, I feel sure, mail this. If I live I shall not put the letter where he can find it, but destroy it and so no harm will be done. If I stay quietly in this room it may be two or three days before I am discovered and by that time the sick man will, I hope, be able to get on with the nursing of the old Chinese cook whom I am instructing.

Therefore, though I feel that death is not far off I am content to-night, and I have decided to let my heart have this much indulgence.

Do you know, Evelyn Rutherford, that I have carried your image in my heart since I left you? That I hear often above all other sounds the music of your piano as you played *"Auf Wiedersehen."* I did not look the fact quite in the face that night though I felt it dimly, but I think it will be "till we meet again" in heaven. I may tell you just this once that I love you, may I not? It has been my joy and my delight when, weary with hard work and lonely, I could sit down a moment, to let the strange foreign city melt away and the Chinese jargon cease to ring in my ears while I walked the autumn-leaf-strewn street with you once more and saw the sun-light shining on your hair, or watched the shadows glancing from your long lashes when you raised your eyes to mine to answer a question. Sometimes I let myself dwell on the ride we took together that wonderful afternoon. You can never know the joy of the moment when you promised me you would pray for yourself. I think I would like to stand hand in hand with you on the brow of that hill where we stopped to look, and await with you my Lord's coming. There are times also when I go back to our first meeting in New York and to the afternoon we spent in the old castle while the storm roared outside, but they are not so dear, because of those times we had not spoken of what was nearest to my heart, the love of Jesus, and I had not yet begun to pray for you, that sweet, that blessed privilege which has been my one daily pleasure. I have come to feel sure, my Evelyn, my darling — you will let me call you that for just to-night, will you not? — that you have drawn close to Jesus. Sometimes when I am kneeling at the throne of Mercy I can almost hear the echo of your whispered prayer and feel the wafting of your breath, and I think — I have dared to think — you are praying for me and my work. I have not been so wild as to fancy you could love me. I know you have no such thought. I might have dared to try to win you had I stayed in New York and attained the success which seemed to be mine for the trying. But I could not ask you to love me and leave all the life that to you would be almost necessity to come out here and suffer — nay, what I may have to suffer to-morrow or the next day. I could not be so calm about the coming of those fiends if you were here beside me. And yet, oh, Evelyn, if you were here! I tremble to think of all it would mean for me if I were to go on living and you, *you* here beside me. The wild thought has just rushed through my mind that I might have dared after all. I might have asked you. Men have done as selfish things before. Women have loved and dared, and, yes, have set their love upon just as unworthy men as I, perhaps. Thank God that I did not, Evelyn, with the Boxers coming to-morrow!

I have a confession to make. Close to my heart I carry a picture of you as a little girl, with sweet wondering eyes and a cloud of hair about your face. It was left by your brother in his college room after packing and he asked me to take care of it. Since I have known you I cut your face from the card and placed it in a small case which I always carry with me; this is since I knew you in New York, the last winter of my stay there. I do not think you will grudge me the small comfort of carrying it with me to my grave. No one will ever know who it is.

And of my love for you which has grown during the years and with the few bright glimpses I have had of you, how can I write? It is a thing to be told, not put upon paper. It is something intangible, which only eyes and lips may fully interpret. But I want you to know that your image is in my heart where no woman was ever enshrined before, and that to me you are at once the most beautiful, the most lovable, and the sweetest of all womankind. Of your queenly bearing and your many graces it would take the years of a lifetime to speak. It may be that in heaven I may tell you the meaning of it all for me, and that there our souls may welcome one another and understand.

And now, dear one, whatever your life is to be, whether long or short, joyous or sorrowful, I have told you with my last word of my great, great love for you, and I commend you to "Him that is able to keep you from falling, and to present you faultless before the presence of his glory with exceeding joy."

I shall take every precaution that this may be sent you in case I am killed, as I can hardly escape being. Do not let that part of it trouble you. I do not fear to go to my Saviour, and I shall count it all joy if I may suffer a little for his sake. It may be that through it the soul of this poor heathen on the bed beside me may be brought to Jesus in some way. I have learned to love

Christ's way for me, even though it means separation from you whom I love.

Now I shall fold and address this, sealing and stamping it carefully that it may be sure to reach you if it is sent. Then I shall place it in the pocket of my coat next to your picture. If the Boxers come, as they most surely will, it is but the work of a moment to conceal this in the place appointed between two heavy stones, where even fire will not be likely to reach it. I think my courier is trusty. And be assured that I love you too much to allow this ever to reach or disturb your happiness as long as I live. Evelyn, my darling, I love you. And now "Auf Wiedersehen."

> Go thou thy way, and I go mine;
>   Apart, yet not afar;
> Only a thin veil hangs between
>   The pathways where we are.
>
> And "God keep watch 'tween thee and me"
>   This is my prayer.
> He looks thy way, he looketh mine,
>   And keeps us near.
>
> Yet God keeps watch 'tween thee and me,
>   Both be his care.
> One arm round thee and one round me
>   Will "keep us near."

The smarting tears dimmed her eyes so that she could not read the name signed clear and bold below as it danced in dazzling characters before her. Her pain and her joy struggled together which might first and hardest strike her. She had read slowly, dazed, and unable at first to comprehend all the love and the horror and the pity of it. Gradually, as she sat and stared at the closely written pages she seemed to see the Chinese hospital room with its whitewashed walls, the sick man lying near, the quiet figure writing, the whole surrounded by those demoniacal creatures lurking in dark shadows ready to spring when the moment came and the letter was finished.

Gradually the one who was writing became the center of the vision and everything else faded away. Then she began dimly to understand three things: that he loved her — ah, that was wonderful, beyond her understanding how it could have come about; that he was a hero — that she seemed to have known forever; and that he was dead. Slowly, slowly this dreadful fact was forced upon her. It was like having the anxiety of the summer all over again with the gradual growing certainty that there was no hope, only now it fell upon a heart fresh from his words of love and she could not tell whether there was more of joy or sorrow in being allowed to mourn for him.

There was a sound at the door now. It was repeated several times before she understood that she must answer it. She came back to the present world with a start. She had promised to go with her father to a missionary meeting in a large church that evening. She had been very anxious to go and had coaxed him. He had been somewhat surprised, but had yielded, putting aside a very important business engagement to please her. He was standing in the hall below waiting for her now. Marie called to know if she needed any help.

She folded the dear letter into its envelope and hastily put it inside her dress. The force of months of habit made her feel that she must not disappoint her father now. Her mind was not fully working, or she would have known that she could not bear that meeting in her present state, but she felt that she must go and get it done that she might earn the right to be alone in her room and think. She must understand it all before she told any one a word of the wonderful, awful news, if indeed she could ever trust the precious secret out of her own heart. She called to Marie that she would come in a moment and did not need her. Then she moved about gathering the wraps she had but a little while before placed so carefully away. She wondered now at the uselessness of the action. It did not occur to her that she had eaten no dinner and that no one had questioned it. The circumstances that had made this fact possible were unusual. Her father had taken a hasty meal at the club in order to meet some gentlemen and dispatch his business so as to be free for this evening meeting. Marie had been out for the afternoon, not having returned until a few minutes before Mr. Rutherford. Richard was away on a business trip, and none of the servants had seen Evelyn come in, as she had a key with her. When no one came down to dinner they supposed that she was invited out, and Marie had forgotten to mention it, and they did not trouble themselves further.

Evelyn's white face attracted her father's attention during the trip to the meeting. They were in a crowded car and were separated, but her large eyes had a restless, unsteady fire in them that made him uneasy. They had a few steps to walk after getting out of the car and he asked her if she was quite well and still felt equal to a meeting. She answered that she was quite well, scarcely knowing what she said. Indeed, she seemed to herself to be walking through a strange, unknown land, always with that whitewashed room before her and the Chinaman stretched on the bed beside the man who was writing. Her eyes felt hot and dry, and seemed as if they were burning the lids when she let them close a moment as they came into the bright church.

They were late. The meeting had already begun. The church was crowded. The heat was intense, though outside it had been clear and cool. A place was made for the new-comers back by the door. Evelyn did not seem to see the throng of people before her; she was looking straight through them, miles and miles over land and sea, watching every moment for the creeping diabolical fiends to rush about that white room. She could see the man stop his writing and bend over to attend to the patient. She knew the very tenderness of his touch and the gentleness of his voice. She could see the earnest gaze of the sick man and knew he was judging the Saviour by his physician. Then quick to her watch again. She could see them now, those devils, stealing through the dark. There was singing all about her. Her hand held one side of her father's book, but she did not know it. Her eyes were fixed upon the dark objects. There were so many of them and they were coming now so much faster since it was all still. Some one was praying, thanking God for his martyrs; ah, that word, he was martyr as well as hero, sitting there so quietly with death standing at the door. They were a great mass outside now, and were yelling, and what was that? A shot! She saw him fall, and the ball seemed to go through her own heart. She fell back in her father's arms.

It was all confusion of kindness in a moment. They bore her out to the air and offered various assistance. Some one called a carriage and they took her gently home. A doctor who had been in the meeting went with them. She had come to herself just a moment. The young man kept his finger on the pulse. He talked to Mr. Rutherford about the meeting and the mission work, and confided his own desire to go out on the field. The father scarcely heard. He had sent for Doctor Atlee. He did not trust these young, inexperienced graduates. He was glad when the ride was ended and they had placed the still, white girl on her own bed.

Then began the reign of white-capped skillful nurses while Evelyn lay in the grip of fever and knew naught of what went on about her. Always there was that same tragedy to be acted over and over again. He loved her — and he was there — ahead of her — in danger — and she could not save him — and then that shot!

"I want to bring a former colleague of mine in to look at her," said Doctor Atlee, as he drew on his gloves one morning preparatory to leaving. "It is almost time for the crisis and with your permission I will let him watch her through. He is exceedingly skillful in such cases. I would trust him as myself. I cannot be here so constantly as I would like, and some one should be within call to-night."

"Certainly," said the grave father. "Anything you think best, doctor. We trust you, you know." There was something almost pitifully wistful in the father's appeal to the doctor's skill.

"I count it a Providence that he is here at this time," went on the doctor. "He is just arrived by a roundabout way from China this morning. He was for going to his people in the West at once, but I have persuaded him to wait over and help me for a few days. He has had a marvelous experience among the Boxers; was saved as by a miracle after they thought him dead. He was nursed by an old Chinese whose child he had saved from blindness and smuggled out of the country by an unusual route and he has just landed in New York. You will be interested in talking to him. Good-morning."

"Ah, indeed," said Mr. Rutherford dryly. He did not wish to be impolite to the great doctor, but he did not wish to hear any more of Boxers or missionaries. Was it not a missionary meeting that was the cause of Evelyn's sickness? This he firmly believed.

Chapter 28
A Battle with the Fever

"What! Here?" said the younger doctor as the carriage stopped. "Not Evelyn Rutherford?" and there was something startling in his voice which made Doctor Atlee look at him curiously.

"Why, yes. Do you know her? Didn't I mention the name before?"

"Yes, I know her," answered Doctor Grey, his voice under perfect control but his face white and anxious as he tried to recall everything the doctor had said about the case. There was very little hope. He remembered that. And it was an "obscure case."

It was with his own quiet manner that he entered the sick-room and looked with grave eyes at the wasted face of the beautiful girl. Her eyes were bright and restless and she seemed not to see what was going on about her.

He laid his practiced finger on her wrist. For one instant her eye seemed to be caught by his, and then the restless tossing went on and a low, inarticulate moaning.

Doctor Grey studied the nurse's chart carefully.

"Her pulse is very irregular," he said in a low voice to Doctor Atlee, and then bent his head to listen to her heart. The soft rattle of thin paper caught his ear as he bent down to listen. He stepped back and called the nurse. "What is this paper, nurse? I cannot hear well because of the rattle."

"It is a letter, doctor, which she put there when she was first taken. She will not let us touch it. It makes her so much worse that we have left it there."

"It must come out for a little," he said. "Let me try."

"Miss Rutherford." He spoke in a quiet tone which usually commanded attention. She fixed her bright eyes on his face.

"I want to move this letter for a moment," he said, still in the same firm voice. "I will put it back."

Whether she comprehended anything or not she did not stir her eyes from his face as he gently took the little parcel which the nurse had wrapped in a soft white handkerchief when she found that the letter must be left in its hiding-place. He laid it beside the pillow where it could be easily given back and went on with his examination of the heart. At last he raised his head.

"I will stay," he said to Doctor Atlee, his professional unreadable mask on; but Doctor Atlee thought he detected a strange tremble to the usually firm voice.

He did not leave her side. The night came on. The father and brother came in and wrung the hand of the watching doctor with grave welcome, but daring not to ask a question. They had heard of his wonderful rescue by this time, but it was no time to speak of rescues. Death as grim, if not so horrible, stood waiting to snatch another dear one from them. They went out and each strong man sobbed in the silence of his room. They knew as if by instinct that the crisis was at hand.

There settled upon the household the hush of expectancy which always comes when the last hope has been tried and the dear one seems to be slipping, slipping into the beyond.

The new doctor was very particular, the day nurse told the night nurse. He did everything himself and seemed to think no one else knew how.

As the evening drew toward midnight he did not leave the bedside nor take his eyes from Evelyn's face. She was sleeping now and had been for several hours. They would soon know whether it was a sleep unto life or death. He had given orders that the father and brother be near at hand that they might be instantly called if there was any change. As the hands of his watch neared the hour when he expected to see a change of some sort he signed to the nurse to go and prepare some nourishment which had been previously ordered. She had scarcely slipped from the room when the great eyes opened and fixed themselves upon the doctor with what looked to him like recognition. They seemed to light with a sudden joy:

"Is this heaven?" she asked in the thin, high-keyed voice of those who are almost over the border land. There was wonder and delight in her tone.

"No, dear, this is your own room," he answered gently, his heart sinking.

A shadow of disappointment seemed to cross her face. She made a quick motion to her breast as if she had remembered something and found it gone. He divined her intention and put in her hand the letter still wrapped in the handkerchief as the nurse had laid it by, but she did not seem to recognize it. Her hand kept fumbling for the letter where she had placed it, an agonized expression coming into the great hollow eyes.

"My letter! Was it all a dream? You wrote me a letter sitting by the sick man in the little whitewashed room, and the Boxers were coming!" she said.

He was unfolding the handkerchief to show her the letter, but he started suddenly and almost lost his professional control of himself until he remembered the great necessity for care. With a superhuman effort he steadied his voice to reply as he spread his own letter before her eyes and his own astonished ones.

"Yes, darling! It is all true. The letter is here and I wrote it." His voice steadied as he spoke with the great love for her that was in his heart.

He was calling her that dear name at last as naturally as if he had always been allowed the precious privilege and had not been longing for it for months, yes, and years. But in this supreme moment no thought of it came to him. She was dying, perhaps, but she loved him. He loved her and he would save her if he could. She must be quiet.

The nurse came in with the nourishment and he gave her some.

"You must not talk," he said. "You must sleep. You have been ill."

"But you were dead," said Evelyn, her eyes still upon his face.

"No, I did not die. I am well and here, and now you must sleep and get well. Then I will tell you all about it."

She half smiled and said, "Kiss me," as a child would say it to its mother.

He stooped and kissed the white forehead, much to the amazement of the nurse, who could not understand this strange doctor and disapproved entirely of so much conversation.

Evelyn smiled and closed her eyes obediently, then opened them again and made a little groping motion with her hand.

He sat down beside her and held the wasted hand in his own. She smiled again and fell asleep as gently and naturally as a little child.

But the watcher, when he had dismissed the nurse by a sign to the other end of the room, sat immovable, scarcely daring to breathe. Gradually the truth was dawning upon him. It was his letter. He had known it at once. But how did it get here, since he had never placed it in the crack between the two stones as it said? The shot had taken him unaware. He had fallen near the sick man's cot, and the old faithful servant hurrying in had dragged him beneath the Chinaman's bed and hastily spread the bedclothes so that they would hide him as he lay. Then the faithful Chinese friend had gone out and told how all the foreign devils and the secondary foreign devils had fled to Peking and left only the poor old Chinaman who was lying very ill with his heart cut out, and begged that they would keep that quarter as quiet for his sake as possible. When they learned who it was that was sick and had sent a representative to look inside, who found it was true, they went away most marvelously and left them, so that after a few hours the faithful old cook dared to bring out his beloved doctor and friend and hide him in a little loft over the kitchen, where under careful directions he had dressed the wound and nursed him back to some degree of strength, and then smuggled him by night in strange ways until he found assistance to reach home. But the letter! How did it get to America? It must have fallen on the floor when he was shot. He had questioned the cook, but he said he knew nothing of it and supposed it must have been destroyed. A wave of thanksgiving went up from the heart of the young doctor that God had taken the matter out of his hands and sent the letter in spite of him, since it had come to a welcome here.

But his face remained the same, as the nurse from her post of observation from time to time glanced that way. He did not change his position. He held close the small white hand, though the breathing continued steadily on and the sleeper did not move. He shook his head when the nurse, with the importance of her office which seemed to be ignored, rustled up, by and by, and offered to take his place and let him rest. From time to time his watch came out and he studied the fluttering pulse. Little by little the strain of anxiety relaxed, and he watched her face hungrily as Evelyn slept on. Toward dawning she opened her eyes, took medicine and nourishment, smiled, and slept again.

He watched her for a while, then drew a long sigh, and turning to the nurse, who had come to take the medicine glass, he said:

"You may tell her father that I think she will live."

She crept slowly out from under the shadow of danger like some ship that has almost foundered and is scarcely yet sure of her way. But close beside her day and night stayed her faithful physician.

"If anybody could save her I knew Grey could," said Doctor Atlee the next morning, and the nurse heard him and bit her lip in vexation. It was her opinion that Doctor Grey was entirely too officious.

Evelyn, when she came to herself, lay smiling and obedient, content to lie and rest and be at peace. Her Saviour had "had his own way" with her, and though it had led her through sorrow, it had come out into a blossoming way of peace and joy. She did not question at all during those first days. It was enough to see Maurice Grey and to have his ministry. The vision of the whitewashed room was not with her now. It had vanished at his voice. One morning she put her white hand shyly on his as he gave her some medicine, and said:

"Maurice, I love you."

It was to them both an answer to his letter.

"Dear heart," he murmured low, and touched her closed eyelids with his lips, getting back to his dignified position just in time for the nurse to appear in the room.

The days of convalescence were sweet. He would not let her talk much of the time that had gone between this and their last meeting. He feared the excitement of recalling those sad days, but together they went back over their brief meetings and told each other all that was in their hearts.

"Do you think that I shall be too stupid to ever be able to help you just a little in your work when we get back to China?" she asked him suddenly one day almost timidly. "I would rather have died than feel that I should be a hindrance to you."

She never seemed to doubt for an instant that he would go back as soon as the way opened and it was safe to go, and she seemed to take delight in making little plans for the voyage and their home when they should reach there.

"Well, young man," said Mr. Rutherford one evening, when he had been spending a little time in his daughter's room, the first night that she was allowed to lie on the sofa after the evening meal, "it seems that you have saved this girl for us, and now the only thing in decency that I can do to reward you is to give her to you. She tells me she can only be happy hereafter converting Boxers in China. It's a good deal you ask, sir, but I guess you deserve it," and the father went out hastily, wiping his eyes.

After that Evelyn's strength came rapidly. She began to walk a few steps about the room.

After a triumphal procession one evening across the length of her room and back in the presence of her father and brother, she lay down on her bank of soft pillows smiling.

Doctor Grey turned to Mr. Rutherford, Sr., a curiously grave look upon his face. "Now, with your permission, father," he said, "I will marry her and take her down to the shore. I think the sea air would be just the thing at this time of year."

The father looked up a little surprised, but he was too practical a man to be long astonished at anything that appealed to his good sense.

"When?" he asked laconically, after the two had looked one another calmly in the eye for a moment.

"To-morrow," answered Maurice Grey promptly.

"Well, I suppose that'll be a very sensible thing to do," answered the father, after a moment's thought. "What do you say, Evelyn? Can you get ready for your wedding in one day?"

"I'm ready now, father," said Evelyn smiling, and closing her eyes lest any one should see the too-much joy shining there, that was meant only for one.

"Well, upon my word, you are rushing things," said Richard Rutherford in amazement. "Why, here Allison thinks she can't get together enough flounces and feathers in six months to be married, and you, Evelyn, are willing to go wrapped in a blanket. I declare I never saw two such people in my life." There was jealousy in his tone and the rest only laughed, and they all separated quietly as if nothing unusual had taken place.

In the middle of the morning, with only Doctor Atlee and her father and brother for witness — with Marie and the nurse in the background — Evelyn was married by the same minister who had once preached a sermon to the bride and bridegroom some two years before. They had dressed her in a soft white chinasilk wrapper, "Because I am going to China, you know," she laughingly explained, and when the ceremony was over they wrapped her in a great white fleecy shawl and laid her on the sofa with the windows open, so that she might get a breath of outside air while she rested. She ate her wedding breakfast of beef tea obediently and went to sleep a little while before the carriage came to take them to the train.

And so the elegant Miss Rutherford, without sound of music or profusion of presents and flowers, or heralding of cards and weary rush of dressmakers and tailors, passed out of New York society and became the unknown missionary's wife, just Mrs. Grey.

Oh, those days by the sea, where in spite of the time of year the sky was blue and the wind as soft as summer sighings, with a deep spice of life-giving power. Oh, those rides in the wheeled chair, with her dear husband to push her and to halt by her side and read aloud in the sun-parlor or Casino when she was ready to listen. It was like heaven on earth. She grew strong and well like her former self, only with a depth of sweetness unknown to the Evelyn of old.

There were cards of announcement sent out. Richard attended to that. He was enough a part of the world yet to think of those things. Evelyn never even knew about them till she received one at the shore addressed "Doctor and Mrs. Maurice Grey," and below the regulation announcement was written in Richard's hand, "Lest you may have forgotten that there really was a wedding." They laughed over it, and were glad together that they had escaped it all. And Evelyn never even wondered at herself.

They were going home soon, not to New York, which was very dear, of course, and was home and always would be, but to Maurice's mother and father and sister. They would be there when Allison was married, and for a time afterward, perhaps, until it should be decided when they could go to China. "Back to China," Evelyn would continue to say, for since that awful night when she had watched the vivid picture of her Boxers coming and heard the shot, she said it was just as if she had been there. Whether China would look as the vision had done remained for the future.

It was down beside the sea that they told the story of the trials and sorrows and love that had grown during their separation. It was to that one tender listener who sympathized with her every heart-throb that Evelyn told the story of her visit to the attic on the night of his departure, and he in turn recounted every thought of his heart toward her in those lonely days when he had only a memory without hope to cheer him.

They went back together to New York when Evelyn was quite strong, for a few weeks before going to Hillcroft.

Jane Worthington came over in her old-time fashion to call. She looked older and worn and hard. She talked of her gayeties in so reckless a fashion that it almost broke Evelyn's heart to hear.

"Oh, yes, Harry is going on worse than ever," she said in answer to a gentle question. "He drinks and gambles away every cent he can get from me or father or Cousin Ned. Besides that, he disgraces me by running around with actresses. But I don't care any more. I have found a few friends of my own. There is one man who just worships me. Harry fairly hates him, but I like him very much myself, and I find I can have a little fun of my own. In fact, Evelyn, I'm more than half in love, to tell you the truth." She laughed in a wild, unnatural way while Evelyn shuddered.

"Oh, Jane," she said in a pained voice, "don't! I cannot bear to hear you talk so. You are a married woman."

"Married!" and Jane laughed again that empty, hard laugh. "Yes, what have I married?"

Evelyn was relieved that her husband came in just then for a moment. He had a question to ask, and here called her "Dear." There was no ostentation, but the visitor could not help but see the affection in voice and look and the perfect confidence between the two.

"My, but he is fine looking!" commented Jane before he was fully out of hearing, "and he really thinks a lot of you, doesn't he? How nice. I hope it will last. You deserve it. You had a very romantic marriage, after all, didn't you? But do you really mean that you are going to bury yourself in China? What makes you? Won't he give it up? I've heard he has fine chances here if he will only stay."

"We are going for the love of Christ, Jane," said Evelyn in a sweet, low voice. Her testimony was shy, for she was not used to speaking as Allison had been brought up to do.

"Haven't you got over those notions yet?" said the caller, getting up to go. "Well, I wish I was half as good as you. Good-bye."

And Evelyn sighed as she thought of the days when she had great influence over this girl, and might perhaps have led her into better paths where she would have been saved from all the sorrows and sins with which she was now surrounded.

Chapter 29
Rebecca Bascomb on the Wedding

It was the day of Allison Grey's wedding, and Miss Rebecca Bascomb was sitting by her window nearly worn out with her labors. She had watched the people as they came from the train; she had watched the expressmen as they went toward the Greys'; she had watched any member of the family that went to the post office or store, and announced to her sister at work in the next room just what shaped parcel was carried and what it was supposed to contain. She had spent so many years at the occupation of guessing other people's private affairs that she hardly ever made a mistake nowadays in matters like these.

"There goes another cut glass bowl, I'll bet a hen!" she soliloquized in her loud tone that had grown a habit with her, for her sister was nearly always in the next room when she was not running to the window to see something Rebecca pointed out.

"That's a shame, and the ceremony over and they gone! There was thirteen last night, a mighty unlucky number, for one of 'em 'd be sure to get broke 'fore the year was out. But this one was a good-sized one. It was a square wooden box. O' course it might a been another clock, but what would they want with any more o' them? They've already got five, and it's likely there are a few in the house at New York, seein' the family have scraped along for years afore Allison came for *her* fixings out. There's another carriage comin' back from the *dee*-po. No it ain't, either, it's Grey's phayton, and if I ain't beat! It's Maurice and his new wife in it, and she's got a red sack on. I should think she'd have a little sense about dressin' decent, now she's a missionary's wife. If she should go out to China with that thing on she'd draw the whole pack on her at once. Them Boxers probably don't like red any better 'n bulls."

"They'll think she's one of 'em," suggested the sister, hurrying in to peep before the curtains of the other window. "Boxers wear real bright costumes. When I was over to the Corners last summer there was a boxing match there between some college men, and they wore red and black stripes and great big gloves, and looked as much like heathens as any Chinese you ever see."

"Well, I think somebody ought to give her a little advice," said Miss Rebecca, setting her chin blandly, as if she would enjoy the task. "I wonder where Maurrie is goin'? He's turned up the road instead of down. It don't seem decent fer folks to rush around in public after a weddin' any more than they would after a funeral; seems kind of as if they was glad it was over and they was rid of the bride. I must run over in the morning and see if that really was another cut glass bowl."

Out upon the hill drive the pony flew, with Evelyn, close wrapped in warm crimson robes and furs, sitting beside her husband. When they reached the spot where they had stopped that day and paused to look down as before, Evelyn laid her face against her husband's shoulder, and he put his arm around her and held her close.

"This is what I would have liked to do before, darling, if I had dared," he said, looking down into the sweet eyes upturned to his. "Do you know those lines of Mrs. Browning's:

> "Nevermore
> Alone upon the threshold of my door
> Of individual life, I shall command
> The uses of my soul . . . What I do
> And what I dream include thee, as the wine
> Must taste of its own grapes. And when I sue
> God for myself, he hears that name of thine,
> And sees within my eyes the tears of two."

She looked up to meet his smile, her own eyes dimmed with tears of joy.

"Maurice," she said, "I have been thinking; suppose I had not come to Hillcroft that time. You know I did not want to do so. Suppose I had had my own way. Then I would never have met you again, perhaps, and you would never have told me about Jesus."

"His way is best always, isn't it, dear? Shall we try to always let him have it with us? Now we must turn back, for it is growing cold, and mother will be wondering what has become of us."

THE CHRISTIAN LIBRARY

Classics of the Christian faith in deluxe, hardcover, gold stamped, gift editions. These beautifully crafted volumes are in matching burgundy leatherette bindings so you can purchase a complete set or pick and choose. All books are complete and unabridged and are printed in good readable print. **Only $7.95 each!**

ABIDE IN CHRIST, Andrew Murray
BEN-HUR: A TALE OF THE CHRIST, Lew Wallace
CHRISTIAN'S SECRET OF A HAPPY LIFE,
Hannah Whitall Smith
CONFESSIONS OF ST. AUGUSTINE
DAILY LIGHT, Samuel Bagster
EACH NEW DAY, Corrie ten Boom
FOXE'S CHRISTIAN MARTYRS OF THE WORLD,
John Foxe
GOD AT EVENTIDE, A.J. Russell
GOD CALLING, A.J. Russell
GOD OF ALL COMFORT, Hannah Whitall Smith
GOD'S SMUGGLER, Brother Andrew
HIDING PLACE, THE, Corrie ten Boom
HIND'S FEET ON HIGH PLACES, Hannah Hurnard
IMITATION OF CHRIST, THE, Thomas A. Kempis
IN HIS STEPS, Charles M. Sheldon
MERE CHRISTIANITY, C.S. Lewis
MY UTMOST FOR HIS HIGHEST, Oswald Chambers
PILGRIM'S PROGRESS, John Bunyan
POWER THROUGH PRAYER / PURPOSE IN PRAYER,
E.M. Bounds
QUIET TALKS ON PRAYER, S.D. Gordon
SCREWTAPE LETTERS, C.S. Lewis
WHO'S WHO IN THE BIBLE, Frank S. Mead

Available wherever books are sold.

or order from:

Barbour and Company, Inc.
164 Mill Street   Box 1219
Westwood, New Jersey   07675

If you order by mail add $2.00 to your order for shipping.
Prices subject to change without notice.